Elisabeth's writing career began w
Harlequin's *So You Think You Can W*
hasn't looked back. She teaches F
rather write full time because, unlike five-year-olds, her
characters generally do what she tells them. She spends most
of her spare time reading and is a pro at cooking one-handed
while holding a book.

She lives in Cheshire because the car broke down there in 1999
and she never left.

elisabethhobbes.co.uk

 twitter.com/ElisabethHobbes
 facebook.com/ElisabethHobbes

Also by Elisabeth J. Hobbes

Daughter of the Sea

Writing as Elisabeth Hobbes

The Secret Agent

Daughters of Paris

THE PROMISE TREE

ELISABETH J. HOBBES

One More Chapter
a division of HarperCollins*Publishers* Ltd
1 London Bridge Street
London SE1 9GF
www.harpercollins.co.uk
HarperCollins*Publishers*
Macken House, 39/40 Mayor Street Upper,
Dublin 1, D01 C9W8, Ireland

This paperback edition 2023
1
First published in Great Britain in ebook format
by HarperCollins*Publishers* 2023
Copyright © Elisabeth J. Hobbes 2023

Elisabeth J. Hobbes asserts the moral right to
be identified as the author of this work

A catalogue record of this book
is available from the British Library

ISBN: 978-0-00-849817-7

Printed and bound in the UK using 100% Renewable Electricity
by CPI Group (UK) Ltd

To my sister Jenni, who helped me debate trees. XX

Prologue

When does a story begin?

With a boy – a child – running up the hill towards the spreading sycamore? He pauses as he reaches the top of the mound, breathing heavily, and looks up in contemplation.

He glances round to see the older boys – jeering smiles on their faces, taunts in their voices.

"Go on. Do it if you dare. See if the witch who was hanged comes to get you."

Coldness descends on him despite the hot August afternoon.

Climb the Witch Tree. Bring back a leaf. Prove that at seven he's not a baby.

He drops to his knees, newly breached so no longer bare, spotting a child-sized crack in the hedge surrounding the sycamore; crawls through the barrier of hawthorn and dog roses; breaches the barricade.

The Coronation Day of a new king a fitting date for the first time in seventy years that anyone has set foot inside the grove.

He stands alone in the grove beneath the sycamore. The light is dimmer, the air cooler, the sounds of voices from the picnickers by the stream muffled. A new world, where he is the only occupant.

He places his hands on the bark, feeling the mottled flaky roughness against his palms. Using his knees and the insteps of his boots, he manages to push himself higher until the lowest branch is within his reach. He tugs with outstretched fingers, almost freeing a leaf.

A high-pitched cry from above makes him almost let go out of sheer surprise. An unknown instinct for self-preservation makes him cling on.

He raises his head, the tale of the witch fresh in his mind.

A child stares down at him.

A girl.

He flushes as he dangles. Beaten to climb the tree by a girl.

"What are you doing in my tree?"

"I want a leaf."

She sneers, scorn in her voice. "You can't even climb it properly, Sapling."

He reaches along to a stem and begins to twist off one of the jagged, red-stalked leaves.

"Stop that! You can't just take something!" She glares at him. "Men always want to just take things."

He jerks, fingers slipping, grabbing at nothing but catching his wrist against a spur of branch. He cries out and hears another cry of alarm.

Soft fingers brush against his wrist and trail down across the palm of his hand, almost linking with his fingers but not strong enough to hold him.

He lands on the ground, crumples and hears breaking twigs. Searing pain shoots through his arm. Not twigs, but his own arm snapping, pinned beneath the weight of his body.

He lies on his side, his head twisted upwards. The girl is still there, though it seems she is growing larger – as large as the tree. She *is* the tree; her bare limbs the branches themselves, her dress the leaves. Her hair the sycamore seeds that twist down in autumn gales.

He closes his eyes as pain and fear drag him away from the world and into darkness.

A woman screams; his nursemaid, he thinks.

Time stretches.

Men's voices. Arms lifting him.

And as he is borne away, a voice drifts to his ears.

Come back soon, Sapling.

Yes.

Let the story begin here.

Chapter One

SEPTEMBER 1902

I t took a little over three weeks of pain and bed rest before Edwin Clarence Hope was deemed fit enough to be summoned to his grandfather's study in the house they shared.

When Edwin entered, Stephen Brice motioned for the boy to stop on the rug at the other side of the vast oak table upon which sat ledgers and designs for printed silks. He stood with his hands behind his back staring at Edwin.

"I am extremely displeased with you, Edwin. You behaved in a very reckless manner. Robert Carfax and your cousin, Harold, have been admonished for their part in daring you. They are older than you by some years and should have known better. Your punishment is the pain you have suffered when your arm broke so I will not whip you this time. Perhaps I will have that tree cut down as I should have done years ago."

Edwin rarely cried. As Annie, his nursemaid, told him,

boys of seven did not cry, but now his eyes filled with tears. The tree had stood for years and Edwin would be responsible for its death.

"Please, sir, don't do that. I promise I won't go anywhere near it again. You have my word."

His words came out in a rush, strangled in his throat by his panic. His grandfather watched him throughout with a dispassionate look.

He rarely looked at Edwin with any other sort of emotion.

"See that you don't. Mr Sykes had to go to considerable trouble cutting through the hedgerow to reach you. On the day of His Majesty's coronation too! You are no longer a baby and I expect you to conduct yourself like a young gentleman."

Edwin nodded in agreement with his grandfather's assessment. Stephen Brice smiled fleetingly, skin stretching over his thin jaw.

"Now, it is time you learned what your future responsibilities will be. Come with me."

Edwin walked at his grandfather's side, stretching his legs to keep pace as the old man strode through the house, out of the front gate, and on to the path. They were going to the factory. They walked a hundred yards along the pavement from the front of Greete Mill House to the arched brick gateway set into the wall. Over the gateway was an iron sign.

Greete Mill
est. 1877

"It isn't a mill, though, is it," Edwin said. "And Greete was my grandmother's maiden name."

"That's right on both accounts. My late, dear Cornelia." His grandfather nodded approvingly at the insight then as quickly as the smile had appeared it was replaced with a frown. "It's a shame you are a Hope not a Greete, but that's how it is. The name won't change, even when you inherit the business, as it didn't when I married your grandmother. I had no sons so your father joined me in the business when he married your mother, God rest their souls. You will join me in turn. We are a factory because we do not spin our own silk but purchase silk that is spun and woven elsewhere. We print it here and turn it into the cravats and ties that we then sell to the shops."

"Morning, Mr Brice, sir. Morning, young Edwin."

Stephen and Edwin turned and greeted William Wills, the foreman. He was a friendly, stocky man with dark-brown skin the shade of horse chestnuts, and tightly curled black hair. The first time Edwin had met him, when little more than a babe in arms, he had squealed and hid behind his mother's skirts in fear, much to the mortification of his father.

His mother, far from being angry, had picked him up and introduced him to Mr Wills and explained that people all over the world came in skins of different hues. It was one of the few memories from before she died that Edwin possessed. Fortunately, Mr Wills had not been offended, but Edwin could never greet Mr Wills without feeling a little ashamed of how fearful he had been.

He stuck out his hand. "Good morning, Mr Wills. I'm very pleased to see you. Grandfather is bringing me to show me the factory."

Mr Wills shook his hand and gestured towards the door. "How excellent. Mr Brice, we've had a letter from Crofts in

Manchester. They are asking for samples of anything we have in blue at your earliest convenience."

Stephen tutted. "Of course. I'll come now and we can discuss what to send them. Edwin, return to the house. I can trust you to go straight to your nursery, I assume."

Edwin agreed readily because he really did intend to go straight back to the house. He probably would have if the front door had been open but it was closed and he didn't want to bother the servants so he walked round the side, planning to go in through the servants' entrance or the garden doors.

As he rounded the corner behind the house, he glanced up and the sycamore caught his eye. He hesitated, hand outstretched in readiness to knock.

Autumn's colours had not yet affected the leaves and the tree was still lush and green, the domed shape full. It stood alone on the hill, and though there was only a small breeze, the branches appeared to sway. They looked like arms waving to beckon him. Unbidden, a face flashed into his mind. Tangled hair, gleaming eyes. The girl who had watched him fall. He hesitated.

It occurred to Edwin that he had never taken a leaf and, more than anything, he wanted one. He could be at the tree in under ten minutes and back in the house before he was missed by his nursemaid. His grandfather would not return from the mill until lunchtime.

With September had come rain, as if the sky had waited until the new month before bursting forth, and the air was damp and chilly. The gutta-percha cast on his arm felt twice as heavy as usual and his new trousers were uncomfortably damp around the ankles by the time he reached the tree. The sensation was so uncomfortable he wished he was still in short trousers. Mr Sykes, the gardener, had done a thorough job in cutting his way through the hawthorn hedgerow and the discarded branches and twigs had been cast to one side, leaving a clear entrance to the circle. The gap was wide enough that Edwin estimated he could walk through it with both arms outstretched and the tips of his fingers would only just brush against the spiky twigs. For the first time he stopped to consider that the hedgerow had been planted intentionally and had not grown in the regular formation naturally. Why anyone would want to stop someone getting inside and close to the tree was beyond him.

It started raining again so Edwin cast aside his pondering and dashed through the gap to the shelter of the overhanging branches.

The air as he had walked up had smelled fresh and sweet and had sounded alive with the buzzing of insects and song of birds. Beneath the tree it was quiet and still, too dark for what should still be a mild day. With the thick branches above him, the temperature had dropped and he shivered. It occurred to him then that perhaps the hedges had been planted not to keep people out, but to keep something inside.

Under the tree, the ground looked merely damp, unlike the meadow grass outside which was slick against Edwin's legs, and the muddy sludge he'd walked through. He sat back against the trunk. Ivy tickled his neck and he scowled. He turned round and pulled a vine off.

"Horrible."

It felt satisfying to tug it free so he stood and pulled more off. It took a while using only one hand but by the time he had finished there was a satisfyingly large pile. He would carry it out and leave it with the remains of the hedgerow.

The rain was a calming rhythm as it pattered onto the leaves. Edwin closed his eyes and listened to it. Large drops, small drips. His eyes began to feel heavy and he struggled to keep them open. He didn't think he had fallen asleep but at some point he became conscious that he was not alone. He opened his eyes slightly and looked to his left then right. Finally, upwards. The girl was sitting astride a branch, peering down at him.

"What are you doing up there?" Edwin demanded, aggrieved at being spied on.

"I'm watching you," she said in a wispy voice.

She swung her legs, pointing and flexing her toes. Her feet were bare and filthy.

"You are the boy from weeks ago. You fell. You're not very good at climbing, are you? How old are you, four or five?"

"I'm seven," Edwin said indignantly.

"Well you climb like a five-year-old," the girl said. She giggled again. "You're just a little Sapling."

Edwin flushed red. Robert Carfax had teased him about being a baby before goading him into climbing the tree.

"I'm not a Sapling."

The girl leaned down, pushing her face further through the leaves. She was facing him now, lying on her front with her elbows crossed and her legs dangling down as if she were riding a horse properly like a boy, not sideways as ladies did. She reminded him slightly of the picture of the Cheshire Cat reclining in the branches from *Alice's Adventures in Wonderland*. Brown hair framed a face with a pointed chin and browny-greenish eyes. Her arms and legs were a nice light-brown colour, though he had a feeling that was on account of her being used to living outdoors because he didn't think her features looked like any of the few people from India who lived in the town.

He wasn't quite sure what she was wearing, but it looked to be made of something floaty in green with brown swirls that almost matched the colour of the leaves and bark. It all added to his belief that she must be a gypsy child rather than one from the town.

He stood up. "Why don't you come down and talk to me properly rather than sitting in the tree. You shouldn't even be here. You're tripsassing."

"Trespassing," the girl replied giving him a condescending look. "You can't even say it properly, and anyway, I'm not. This tree isn't yours. You're only a little boy."

"My grandfather owns it. He owns this field and the one behind it. And the one down to the stream, and the house at the bottom with the croquet lawn and walled garden, and the factory beyond that," Edwin said. He stuck his tongue out at her. "So I will own it one day and then it will be mine and you will never own it."

The girl tilted her head on one side and looked at him. "I don't need to own it. It's still my tree."

"Are you the witch that was hanged?" Edwin asked.

"That's a lie. It never happened like that." She pouted then smiled again and lifted her chin proudly. "I'm the goddess of the tree."

Edwin laughed scornfully. "That's blasphemy. There aren't such things as goddesses, only God."

The girl glared at him then her expression changed to disdain. "You're wrong, but you're only a Sapling so don't know any better."

"You could be a goddess. I suppose the ancient Greeks and Egyptians had both," he said quickly.

"In that case I forgive you."

She smiled and Edwin felt like the sun had come out from behind a cloud. He thrust out his hand.

"I'm Edwin Clarence Hope, by the way."

"Hello Edwin Clarence Hope-By-The-Way."

Edwin burst out laughing then covered his mouth with a hand, worried he might have offended her. "No. Just the first bit. Edwin Clarence Hope."

"I know that. I'm teasing you. I know how names work. They don't change so much. Why are you here again?"

"I came back to get a leaf," Edwin said. "I don't know how I'm going to climb up with only one arm though."

The girl folded her arms and appeared to be thinking hard. She wriggled around to face him again. "I'll get you one, but I want something in return. To make the taking fair and equal."

Edwin stuck his hands in his pockets but there was nothing there that a girl might value. Only a glass marble with a swirl of green inside it. He drew it out and held it up.

"Yes! I want that," she exclaimed. "You can take your leaf. Let me pick one for you."

She plucked one then jumped down to land beside Edwin with a grace and confidence he envied. Her green dress fell to just beneath her knees and was sleeveless. Her legs and feet were bare.

"Aren't you cold?" Edwin asked.

She twirled on the spot, throwing her head back so the tangles of her hair spun out.

"I'm never cold."

She snatched the marble from his open palm then twirled the leaf by the stalk before pressing it between both her hands, holding them as if she were praying in church. Each of the five points peeked out over the top of her fingers. She brought her fingers to her lips and blew gently then held it out.

"It will bring you luck if you keep it safe."

He took it and was about to thank her, but before he could speak he heard a sharp voice.

"Master Edwin, come out of there now!"

He looked over his shoulder and saw Sykes striding towards him across the meadow, waving an arm in the air.

He'd stayed too long. His stomach twisted with foreboding at the inevitable consequences.

"Quickly, lad!"

Edwin held out his hand. "I'm going now. I'm sorry. It was nice to meet you. I'll come again soon."

The girl grasped his fingers. Her eyes were wide and her mouth twisted.

"Don't let them plant the hedgerow, again. Please."

Edwin nodded, not quite understanding her fear. He walked through the gap and into the meadow. Rain began to pour again as Sykes reached him. For an old man he had crossed the meadow very quickly. He looked out of breath but his voice brimmed with anger.

"You were forbidden to come here!"

"I was just talking with the little girl."

He pointed back. The girl was standing in the entrance to the circle, her hands loosely by her sides. Her head was on one side and her hair tumbled over her shoulders and half her face. As Sykes turned round to look, she slipped behind the hedge out of sight.

"There's no little girl," he said firmly, angrily even.

Edwin pushed his bottom lip out. "Yes there is. She wants me to make you promise you won't put the hedge back."

Sykes took hold of Edwin's shoulders. His fingers were tight and it felt like there was no flesh on his old bones. "I should have put an iron fence around it, never mind dog daisies and hawthorn. Now come away before your grandfather decides to burn the tree to the ground."

He took Edwin by his good arm and led him back across the meadow. Edwin dragged his feet. In his hand he clutched the leaf.

By the time they reached the house, Edwin was drenched to the skin and certain he would not be able to hide the fact that he had been out. His grandfather was waiting in the hallway. Annie was standing beside him, her cape and bonnet in her hands. Her face was red and she was crying. Edwin's heart tore into little pieces seeing her distress. He went to give her a hug but Stephen grasped him by the shoulder and pulled him firmly away.

"I have had enough of your disobedience. I cannot raise a child by myself and also tend to my business. Come with me."

He walked into his study. Edwin followed, slipping the leaf into his pocket, suspecting that his grandfather would destroy it if he found it. Stephen sat down at the desk and picked up a sheet of writing paper.

"I am writing to your aunt, Madeline, and asking her to take you in as a favour to her late brother's memory. You need a mother."

"Will Annie come too?" Edwin asked.

"Annie has proven herself incapable of caring for you adequately. I have no further need of her services. I will pay for your schooling and board wherever your uncle chooses to send you."

School? How long would he be gone for?

Edwin gave a sob as remorse flooded over him. Annie would lose her position and home and it was all his fault.

"That's not fair. It isn't her fault. I'm sorry."

His grandfather's face gave the first sign of becoming calm.

"Good. You can think of others, I see. I am not vindictive. Annie may stay with you until you leave. I imagine it will take a fortnight to arrange. I shall write her a good reference and suggest her next charge be a girl who might be more biddable. Now, return to the nursery. You are confined there until you leave for Yorkshire."

Back in his room, Edwin picked up a diary bound in green leather with his initials, ECH, embossed in copperplate. It had been a Christmas gift from his grandfather. He was supposed to write in it nightly but often forgot so he was not even halfway through.

He took the leaf from his pocket and put it in the centre pages then closed the diary and slipped it into the drawer of his beside cabinet along with his Bible.

As Stephen Brice predicted, it was a little over a fortnight before Edwin left for Yorkshire. His clothes, favourite toys, and sundry other belongings were packed into a trunk and his name stencilled on the side ready for the train. The rest of his belongings were packed into boxes, ready to be moved to the attic after he had left.

It was only when Edwin was unpacking to settle into the cosy blue and yellow painted room in Aunt Madeline's house in Malton that he realised his diary had been mis-packed and had been left behind, but by then it was too late.

The Old One returned a fortnight after he had taken the Sapling away; strode into her grove as if he owned it.

He stopped beneath the branches, sharp eyes searching.

"Where are you?"

The Sapling's attention had nourished her more than she realised she had needed. His words had been so pretty and innocent and she was ravenous for more. She sighed contentedly at the memory; a susurration in the silence. After years alone, the hedgerow had been breached; noise and confusion, life and activity intruding into her isolation after so long constricted in the solitude of the grove. She straightened her limbs in preparation of the descent.

"Show yourself. I demand it."

Her limbs flexed in indignation at his tone. Sooner or later, they always believed they owned everything. No reverence or wonder, only dismissal and contempt. And anger in this one's case.

The Old One searched high in the branches but she still did

not reveal herself to him. Why should she, when he'd given nothing in exchange? Not even a kind word.

She tightened her fist around the glass marble that the Sapling had given in exchange for a sliver of the luck she was able to bestow.

"I want my Sapling," she murmured and the wind caused the leaves to rustle almost imperceptibly.

The feeling surprised her. She wasn't given to wanting, knowing that wishes were rarely – if ever – granted, but he'd been a strange, determined little Sapling and had piqued her curiosity.

The Old One jerked his head upwards at the movement in the branches.

"Young Edwin said he talked to a little girl." The old man stuck his hands into his trouser pockets and narrowed his eyes. "Now, I don't know what he saw, but I do know that according to my father, my grandfather planted this hedgerow when my grandmother's tears at his straying up here to visit a woman became too much to bear."

He gestured around with an arm, taking in the circle of thorns and thistles that enclosed her grove. She followed the arm with her eyes but her mind was on his face. A memory stirred of a younger man who shared this Old One's features. Handsome and tall, with hair so fair it was almost silver and hands that loved the soil. It was unsettling. A grandson? How long had she been sleeping while the thorns grew around her?

The Old One put his hands in his trouser pockets and walked back and forth, his eyes on the ground. He cleared his throat and looked up again.

"I'm not certain what your kind is, but if anything the old

stories say is true, I know you'll tempt and beguile just to be loved."

She laughed then.

Loved? Foolish Old One. It wasn't love she desired, but veneration; that's what she deserved.

He pulled his hand out of his pocket. There was something in it. Interest caught, she peered closer, trying to see what the gnarled hand contained. A gift or an exchange? She watched closely, tempted to reveal herself.

"Young Edwin is not yours."

He put the object in both hands and fiddled with it. She heard a scraping sound and then there was a flare of heat and light; an explosion in her head.

Her core felt the sharpness of fear.

"Do you know what this is?" the Old One asked.

She shuddered and the branches rippled.

Fire.

"I promised the Sapling not to replace the hedge because that clearly matters to him and I am a man of my word."

He looked up and for a moment she would have sworn on her heart that he saw her. She stared boldly into his eyes.

"My word is this: you leave him alone or you will burn."

He sighed and shook his head sadly, as if his threat pained him.

"You're too green now, but in another month those leaves of yours will change and before the winter sets in there will be a time when you're good for kindling."

He lifted the fire to his mouth and blew gently, extinguishing the small dancing flame.

She sighed with relief as the flicker died away, leaving only the wisp of smoke rising upwards and the scent of soot in the air. She slipped down from branch to branch.

"He's leaving and he won't be back for many years, but when he does come, you'll remember my words."

She closed her eyes. She would remember them as clearly as if they were carved onto her trunk.

The Old One nodded his head towards her and backed out of the grove. It was the most meagre deference but the acknowledgement that she deserved courtesy gave her a sliver of the reverence that sustained her. She directed a burst of hatred towards the Old One, with his aggression and accusations and threats, but she knew it was futile. She, who should be able to cause branches to strike, could do nothing more than raise a slight undulation of twigs. An immeasurable fatigue descended upon her, lethargy weakening her limbs. She slid down from branch to branch and landed at the foot of the tree. The soil was moist and cold beneath her feet and she wriggled her toes, grounding herself. She inhaled, savouring the musky, damp scents that surrounded her.

She leaned back against the trunk, drawing comfort from the reassuring roughness of the bark and closed her eyes. The beat of her heart and the pulse in her limbs fused with the slow, steady rhythm of the tree – too slow and low for the Old One to have heard or felt but it was there all the same.

Autumn was newly here but winter would follow with dizzying rapidity. It was a time to rest and draw what strength she could from the soil. For the first time in longer than she could recall, the natural sustenance from the earth was augmented by the vestiges of veneration the Sapling had given her. She would be stronger at this barren time than she had been for decades.

She would sleep and when the season cycled again, the Sapling would return. The Old One could not stop him returning if he chose.

She would not have to wait too long.

Chapter Two

AUGUST 1913

A t eighteen years old, Edwin Clarence Hope was as much a gentleman as a Yorkshire upbringing would allow. His early growth spurt had ended at seventeen and he had filled out more generously than proportionately, but he had a thick mop of sandy brown hair that slipped fashionably over his hazel eyes. Combined with a ready smile that not only invited but practically compelled his companions to laugh along with him, he had already caught the eye of any number of giggling schoolgirls who came to visit his aunt with their mothers.

He turned that laughing smile on his cousin, Harold, now.

"Surely you are joking with me, Har? You don't really intend to give your life to God?"

Harold's serious expression made him drop his smile slightly.

"I do. I have thought about it hard and prayed about it even longer." Harold looked at Edwin through wire-rimmed spectacles that made him already resemble a caricature of a village parson from a *Punch* cartoon. "My bachelor's degree in theology was only the start and I am applying for acceptance to the Community of the Resurrection in Mirfield. It's a seminary."

Edwin whistled.

"What will Aunt Madeline say?"

Harold settled on the sofa in the sunny corner of the library and crossed his legs.

"I told Mother last night. She took it rather better than I anticipated. She knows what comfort I took in the church when Father died."

A shadow crossed Harold's face. Jonty Verne had lost his life to a tumour five years previously, throwing his only son into a deep depression. Edwin had felt fortunate that his own parental bereavement had been when he had been in short trousers, so before he fully understood his loss. He had only dim memories of a life with a mother or father in it.

"Perhaps Aunt Madeline hopes you will be a bishop one day and she can bring out the best Wedgwood," he said. He sauntered to the drinks cabinet and poured them both a whiskey, the news still making his head spin slightly.

"Soda or neat?" he asked, turning back with the glasses in his hand. He grinned.

"Perhaps you should just have the soda and you can transform it into wine as your Lord did. It would save you a fortune."

Edwin flung himself onto the other end of the sofa and sprawled out. Harold accepted the glass from him and raised it to clink against Edwin's.

"When I am ordained, I shall make a special project of you and save your soul," Harold said. "You are in dire need of a spiritual advisor, heathen that you are."

Edwin laughed. "I'm not a heathen. That suggests some sort of pagan influence. I have as much doubt concerning the existence of Zeus and Odin as the next sensible man." He took a small sip of his whiskey. He didn't have much of a taste for alcohol but he'd learned to hide it. "The scientific method is the way forward. I believe that is where the answers will lie."

"It depends on the questions you want answering I suppose," Harold said.

Edwin rubbed the side of his chin where he could feel the annoying prickle of an impending spot.

"I'll start with how I am best to live with a grandfather I have barely seen in eleven years and how I am to take over a business I have no interest in. He didn't even ask whether I have any plans of my own, just sent a letter informing me that as I have finished school I should return."

His belly churned with indignation. He took a larger glug of whiskey and let the warming sting of peat trickle down the back of his throat.

"To nineteen-fifteen."

"Odd toast. Why?" Harold asked.

"That's the year I reach my majority and his guardianship ends. He can have me for that long and then I'll make my own choice whether to continue, or whether the business can go hang."

Harold smiled at Edwin with the calm, knowing expression that should have made him insufferable but instead endeared him to everyone.

"Score one to me, I think. Even Our Lord struggled when he had to endure His Father's plans."

Edwin guffawed. "Well I don't intend to follow *His* path and get nailed to a tree. Shall we go join the ladies? This old habit of segregated after-dinner drinking feels very strange when there are only six of us and we are so outnumbered. It's a jolly shame Panos had to go down to London."

Together the cousins walked into the sitting room, which was a hive of female activity. Aunt Madeline had caused a brief flurry of gossip recently by entering into an engagement with Panos Hatzis, a widower of Greek origin who came with three daughters. The girls, aged between twelve and twenty-three, were lively young things. The middle and eldest were dancing to a gramophone recording of Edward Lloyd's 'Come into the Garden, Maud'. The youngest, Joanna, threw down her novel and greeted her stepbrother and Edwin with loud pleas that they immediately join a late evening game of croquet on the lawn.

"How much of your religious fervour is to do with not having to share a house with those glorious maenads?" Edwin laughed as they followed the girls out into the garden where the croquet pitch had been set up.

"I'm not renouncing women, you realise," Harold said. "I am strictly Anglican. Defecting to Catholicism would have ended Mother. No, I'll do my time and then find myself a nice sensible woman who can be a model vicar's wife."

"Edwin, are you coming to play?" called Eleni. She was a black-haired fifteen-year-old with a deep olive complexion which nevertheless showed her blushes quite distractingly –

which she did whenever she spoke to Edwin. "Be my partner. We'll be red and yellow with Demetria."

"Then Joanna, Mother, and I will be black and blue," Harold called to her. He prodded Edwin in the ribs, causing Edwin to scowl. "Watch out you don't get caught in her siren's call. She'll have you proposing if you aren't careful."

Edwin felt himself blushing to the roots of his hair. Eleni was clever, frank, and funny and when she was older she'd be a real devil with the men, no doubt.

"I'm not in any rush for that," he said. "Besides, I'll be leaving for Cheshire at the end of the week so there's no point becoming too attached to anyone."

Harold wrinkled his nose. "I was hoping we could have a few more tennis matches. I promised Poppy and Anthony Seaforth that we'd visit and go riding as soon as the Glorious Twelfth was past and their father won't object to horses galloping about the grouse moor, but I suppose you can't do that now. It's a jolly shame your grandfather wants you back now."

Edwin grimaced, tasting a sudden sourness in the back of his throat as if the whiskey were planning to make a reappearance. Stephen Brice required him back, but whether he *wanted* him was an entirely different matter.

Harold patted his shoulder. "You still resent him, don't you. I can tell. Your expression changes whenever you think of him."

"Do you blame me?" Edwin picked up a croquet mallet and gave it an experimental swing, gripping the handle tightly in both fists. He'd had occasional outbursts of all-consuming anger during adolescence but since those difficult years were finally ending, he was usually placid. Thinking of Stephen Brice waiting for him back in Cheshire made his temper rise.

"He was happy to leave my upbringing to your mother, even when she was widowed herself. I am fortunate she did such an excellent job. I owe her everything for the man I might become. I owe him nothing but the money he paid her for my upkeep."

"It's a jolly shame you won't get to finish your education," Harold said.

Edwin strolled out onto the croquet lawn, wishing Harold would let the matter drop. His commiserations were ruining what could be a fun evening and Edwin suspected there would be precious few of those when he returned to Cheshire.

"I have no vocation in mind, other than a passing interest in botany. If I had the urge to be a doctor – or a priest for that matter – or was desperate to be called to the bar I might have had grounds to argue my case for a place at a university, but I've always known that my future is in the factory. I have adequate education to suffice me there."

"You *were* going to be an explorer, I believe, or a naturalist." Harold took aim at his ball but sent it wide into a bed of roses, much to Eleni's delight. "Do you remember the day you broke your arm? It was the old king's coronation and that awful boy laughed at you for looking at snails."

Edwin struck his own ball and sent it smoothly through the hoop. He grinned triumphantly at Harold who huffed good-naturedly.

"Yes. How could I forget? Then he dared me to climb the tree and I fell out of it."

Edwin tipped his head on one side, half closing his eyes. The memories were vague and confused. He'd been in a lot of pain for the weeks after the bone was set and somehow that had resulted in him being sent away.

"Edwin, are you going to play or just talk?" Eleni called. She put her hands on her hips and looked grumpy.

"Better play," he muttered to Harold.

He bounded over and joined Eleni and Demetria.

"So will you write to me when you're gone back to Cheshire?" Eleni asked.

Edwin smiled at her. He didn't know many girls and was quite shy around them, but it felt good to be admired.

"Occasionally, if I remember," he said. "You do know I'm terribly lazy, so don't hate me if I forget. It won't be because I mean to."

"Of course I won't. Eleni sent Aunt Madeline's ball careening into the bushes and gave him a smile. "I can't imagine there being a woman capable of holding a grudge against you."

Greete Mill had prospered in the decade Edwin had been absent. The wrought-iron gates over the entrance had been freshly painted and a second story built above the stable to act as an office for William Wills. Stanley, the dappled grey drayhorse no longer occupied the stable and had been replaced by a bay-coloured mare. To Edwin's surprise, he learned from William Wills that Stanley now lived in retirement in the meadow behind the lawn and summer house at Greete Mill House.

"The old chap served his time faithfully and your grandfather did not have the heart to send him to the knacker's yard," William explained. "That meadow never gets used. Your grandfather... well, he doesn't really venture into the estate beyond walking round your mother's walled garden, from what he tells me. He's an indoor man, like myself. Give me a comfortable chair and a pint of beer and I'm content."

William took off his cap and scratched his head. His tight black curls were now shot through with grey. Edwin wondered what his grandfather now looked like and how age had changed him. He was nearer seventy than sixty, Edwin calculated.

"I'm happy with either," Edwin said. "My school believed that the seven mile walk to the church on a Sunday was good for our souls, though in winter I'd happily have risked mine to stay in the common room and eat toast."

The two men laughed.

"It's good to see you again Edwin," William said. "I imagine your grandfather will be pleased to see you when he gets back from Manchester. It's unfortunate he was called away at such short notice."

"Yes." Edwin tried to keep his voice neutral. He'd arrived on the twelve twenty-three train from Manchester only to discover Stephen had left from the opposite platform only fifteen minutes earlier, heading to the city. If they had glanced up at the right time, they might have seen each other from their respective carriages. It was hard not to imagine the slight had been intentional.

"Now my grandfather has asked me back, I should become acquainted with the workings of the factory," Edwin said. "Might you be free to show me around and take me through things? It would be good to show him I'm keen and have taken the initiative."

William's brow furrowed slightly. "I'm afraid I can't. I have a large order to itemise before your grandfather's return, but if you wish to come and look around the factory now I would be more than happy to find someone to show you. I'm sure one of the girls wouldn't mind spending her tea break with you."

Presumably releasing one of the workers from her duties wouldn't meet with Stephen's approval.

"Thank you but I wouldn't dream of putting any of your women out during their breaks," Edwin said hastily.

William smiled with relief and Edwin knew he'd made the right choice. "In that case, I can recommend Bennett's Coffee House on Church Hill, or if you are more inclined, the George Arms on Crompton Way serves a good pint and will do you a pie with it."

"I think I shall visit my parents' graves," Edwin said. "It has been far too long. Is there still a gate at the end of the old road between the pastures?"

William nodded. "Yes, there is. No one really uses it. But I dare say with the weather having been dry your shoes won't get ruined. I will look forward to seeing you on Monday."

William held his hand out and Edwin shook it. He felt a buzz of pleasure at being treated as an equal instead of a child by someone who had once carried him on his shoulders.

The two men bade each other farewell and Edwin walked back along the short distance to Greete Mill House and through the gate. A creeping sense of unease made the skin across his back crawl as if tickled by beetles. If the factory had prospered, the house had done the opposite. The window frames at the front were painted a glossy black, but when he knocked, and his travelling case was taken inside by the maid who answered the door, there was a definite smell of mustiness from within.

He walked around the side and looked up at the rear wing, jutting out into the L-shape. Here, there was evidence of neglect hidden from the eyes of passers-by. Paint flaked off in patches from the window of his parents' room and the dining room beneath it. Edwin frowned. He knew his grandfather was a wealthy man – whatever else his faults, his neglect of Edwin had been only emotional. Financially he has been very generous so Edwin doubted money was the reason for it.

Weeds grew between the Yorkstone flags on the terrace, and the rectangular fishponds at either side of the steps down to the croquet lawn were filled with stagnant green water. The grass on the croquet lawn itself was cut short but the summer house at the end looked in equally poor shape.

Edwin walked along the road by the stream, heading towards the churchyard. He had forgotten that there was an incline and soon found himself growing warm. Presumably as a small child with boundless energy he had thought nothing of climbing it. Now as an eighteen-year-old with more inclination to play cards and billiards than rugby or tennis, he was slightly less fit than he should be.

He stopped at the top of the hill and looked around him,

catching his breath. The hills rolled away in the distance but there were more rows of houses covering the lower ones, as well as a new factory standing where he reckoned the railway line to be and two beside the canal. The old cottages still stood beyond the hedge that bordered the Greete land, each with its own garden, but they now had other homes filling the spaces between them. The old church and the graveyard where his mother and father were laid to rest still stood aloof inside the stone-walled grounds, but the rectory that had once sprawled alongside it had been torn down and replaced with two pairs of modern three-storey houses.

Edwin's belly twisted and the unease that had floated around his shoulders now settled like a bolt of sackcloth. The changes were a stark reminder of how long he had been exiled. This was not his home any longer. He felt a pulling in his heart for the loving surrounds of Danby Croft and the familiar heather-covered moors, combined with rage that his grandfather had summoned him back and could not even spare himself to be present. The obligations ahead of him weighed heavy and he swore aloud.

"Damn Stephen Brice and damn Greete Mill!"

A crow cawed in the sky, as if dismayed at Edwin's language. He looked around guiltily to see if anyone human had overheard him, but he was alone. With a sigh he trudged on, thinking that if he were braver or richer, he'd get on the next train back to Yorkshire and damn the consequences.

He chewed his thumbnail – a bad habit that no number of whippings and no amount of foul-tasting lacquer had broken. He stomped the short distance to the churchyard and found the pair of graves. He'd expected them to be as neglected as the rest of his grandfather's life but it was far from the case. At least, in one case.

His mother's headstone was spotlessly clean, and fresh stems of purple-flowered lilyturf stood in a vase that was held in place by an iron band. Edwin stopped before it in surprise. Lilyturf grew well in autumn and the flowers were fresh. They hadn't even had time to wilt. Edwin had to assume that his grandfather was responsible as there was no one else he could think of who would care enough.

His father's headstone was clean of moss but had no flowers; it looked unloved beside his wife's. It made Edwin's stomach twist to see the difference and he felt a stab of anger towards his grandfather's spite. A single stem from the bunch would have sufficed to show Archibald Hope wasn't forgotten. Edwin wished he'd thought to bring some flowers and resolved to return soon and lay them beside the others.

He put his hands on his waist and leaned back, flexing his back muscles and staring towards the house and mill that stood in the dip beyond the gentle hill.

There was the sycamore tree that stood alone on the top of the mound. This was the tree he had climbed and from which he had fallen. He remembered now how fascinated he had been by it and his pulse fluttered briefly.

He was barely conscious of the decision to detour and walk via the tree before returning to the house through the meadow, but he found himself taking that route. Stanley, the old horse, was standing in the centre of the field, head down and grazing. He lifted his head and regarded Edwin solemnly before turning away and walking down to his stable.

Edwin continued on his way to the mound. The hedgerow

he had pushed his way through had never been replanted. The sycamore was now only enclosed in three quarters of a circle, leaving a wide gap to walk through. He felt a deep trembling of satisfaction at seeing it, though couldn't explain why the sight affected him so.

The ground at the edge of the circle was partially covered in thick grass and dappled with small white flowers. The ground under the tree was soil, where the top of roots pushed up. Edwin stopped in front of the trunk and stared up into the branches, trying to spot the route he had taken upwards. Climbing the branches would have been a real challenge. Now he reckoned he could scale the heights with no effort at all.

He had only climbed it on that one occasion, but he could clearly remember the cool shade offered by the branches and the scent of dry soil amid rain. He closed his eyes and inhaled deeply. The smell was the same even though the last time he had seen it had been late summer. Now it was autumn and the leaves had almost finished turning from green to yellow. The branches were heavily laden with bunches of seeds, waiting to be caught by the wind and sent spinning on their way.

He had a vague memory of being egged on, as Harold had reminded him, and of one of Robert's sisters laughing at him and teasing him for being useless at climbing. He was seized by the sudden urge to try and climb it now until the thought was overtaken by speculating what Robert's sisters would make of Harold's new sisters. Demetria would be about the same age as the eldest of the Carfax girls.

A cold sensation ran down Edwin's back, as if someone had lightly run a finger down it. The canopy of the branches cut out almost all the sunlight and he was growing chill, even though the air outside was mild. For old times' sake he reached out and patted the trunk.

"Nice to see you're still here, old girl."

The leaves swished fiercely overhead as if a sudden gust of wind had stirred them but there had only been a soft breeze all day. Perhaps a bird had taken flight. Edwin had a feeling there were birds in this tree because he definitely remembered birdsong from the day he had climbed it. He wondered why he had thought of the tree as female. Presumably because he'd been thinking of the various sisters.

Edwin yawned. His journey had started well before dawn and he felt an urge to sit back against the tree and take a nap. He might have done if his trousers weren't light grey. Meeting his grandfather with mud stains on his rear wouldn't be the best plan. As Stephen popped unwelcomely into his head, Edwin decided it was time to go. If his grandfather was not back, Edwin thought he might walk into town and take advantage of the coffee shop.

He walked out into the sunshine. It definitely felt warmer outside the grove but as he walked down the meadow, heading for the summer house, another shiver ran down the length of his spine.

Someone stepping on your grave, Aunt Madeline had always said (until Uncle Jonty's death after which she presumably found it too near to the bone).

At the bottom of the hill he stopped and turned back, feeling eyes on him and expecting someone to be watching him from the road beyond the tree, but there was no one there. He gazed back at the tree. It was unusual to find a lone sycamore. Usually the seeds spread and at least one or two children grew from their parent. The ancient stump of the previous sycamore marked the boundary of the grove but there was not another tree anywhere.

"No saplings," he murmured, then frowned, wondering why he had spoken aloud.

Chapter Three

Edwin's feeling of displacement continued into the evening. His grandfather returned home and greeted Edwin stiffly. They shook hands in a very formal manner and settled across the dining table to eat. The vichyssoise was excellent, but they ate in silence until the soup plates had been taken away then Stephen cleared his throat.

"William tells me he offered to find an employee to take you on a tour of the factory and you refused."

Stephen had naturally changed in the past decade. He was still handsome for an elderly man, but his chin was weak and his skin had thinned to show the veins beneath. His hair was ash grey but receded in a way that boded ill for Edwin's future unless he took after his father. The expression of displeasure that settled on Stephen's face was as familiar as if Edwin had only seen him the day before.

A flicker of betrayal brushed over Edwin that William had informed on him, though he didn't entirely blame William for doing so when confronted by his employer.

"That's not entirely what happened. I asked if he could show me round but he was busy. He offered to find me someone else but I declined," he clarified. "It was only a spur of the moment idea and I didn't want to cause anyone bother."

"I wonder if William did not make himself clear enough, in that case," Stephen said, tapping his fingers on the table.

Edwin leaned back in his chair and gave his grandfather what he hoped looked like a sincere smile.

"A misunderstanding. No blame should be attached to William at all."

A ghost of a smile crossed his grandfather's face. "I'm glad to hear you say that. A man should take responsibility for his own mistakes and not pass them off onto others."

The maid brought in a serving tureen and a rich fragrance filled the room.

Edwin inhaled. The scent was no herb he could name.

"I assume you have had curry before?" Stephen asked. The maid ladled the thick, meaty stew onto two plates along with fluffy mounds of rice.

"Never," Edwin answered, as he looked at the plate of reddish-brown stew. As well as what he thought might be mutton, there were large cubes of a vegetable and a scattering of raisins. He picked up his fork and speared a piece of vegetable. It turned out to be swede and the sauce was delicious, though a moment after Edwin swallowed, his tongue began to feel intensely hot. He reached for the water jug and Stephen laughed, showing the first indication of humanity since Edwin had arrived.

"Wait until you finish before you drink or it will seem hotter. It's delicious, isn't it. I ask Maria, the cook, to make it for me once a week. I am a man of habits and I see no reason to break them now you are here."

Of course not. Edwin got the sense he was being shown his place, and it was lower than the cravings of Stephen's stomach.

"I'm sure I'll get used to the heat if we eat it that frequently." The silence resumed but it felt tangibly less awkward.

"Why did you think it was appropriate to go traipsing around the factory in any case?" Stephen asked, laying his fork down on the empty plate.

Edwin raised his brows. "To get a head start on what I'll be doing."

Stephen frowned. "What you will be doing? You know nothing about business or silk or printing. Why do you assume I need you here for work?"

"Because the business will one day be mine, won't it?" Edwin shrugged his shoulders, affecting a nonchalance he didn't feel. He leaned forward. "If you don't want me for that, why did you summon me back?"

Stephen stared straight at him. "Because your education is finished as far as I have the wherewithal or inclination to pay for it. Your aunt has remarried The Greek and there is no reason why he, a man with whom I have no connection, should pay for your upkeep. Therefore, to here you must return."

"Well now I'm here I would like to put myself to use," Edwin said. A heaviness descended on his stomach that was nothing to do with the curry. He'd hoped briefly that his summoning had meant he might be wanted, but it had been a financial decision.

"I have no particular desire to work in the silk industry, it's true, but as you said before, this is my inheritance and therefore I should learn." He picked up his wineglass and twisted the stem between his fingers, swirling the burgundy liquid, and tried to look nonchalant.

"Of course, if you have no need for me, I suppose I could look for another employer in town. There have been other mills built, I see."

As he had suspected, this would not satisfy Stephen who laid down his fork and gave a tight smile.

"Absolutely not. No, if you must work then you will work for me. It is, after all, what your late mother would have wanted, I suppose. But I will work you hard and you will receive no preference."

"Of course not," Edwin agreed, hiding a smile.

Pudding was chocolate ice cream served with bottled cherries.

"From Angelli's?" Edwin asked.

He scooped up a spoonful, finding it odd that he could remember the name after so long. A memory stirred of Annie who'd had a soft spot for the handsome young Italian who sold it.

"What happened to Annie after you sent me away?"

Stephen laid his spoon down. "She stayed here until her full month of notice was ended then she found work as nursemaid for the headmaster of the preparatory school and his wife who had an infant and a babe-in-arms. Within two years she had married one of the masters. She has twin girls of her own. It is likely you will encounter her but I doubt she bears you any ill will."

"Ill will?" Edwin frowned in confusion.

"For her employment being prematurely ended."

Edwin dropped his spoon into the empty bowl where it clattered against the crystal. "It was hardly my fault you decided to send me away."

Stephen sat forward, glaring. "You were undisciplined and had already broken one limb, thanks to your insistence on climbing a tree. Not only that, but you proved yourself ungovernable by returning to the scene of the transgression when you had been expressly forbidden from doing so. You were fortunate that your aunt and uncle agreed to take you in or you would have been boarding from the tender age of seven!"

Edwin's pulse began to race in anger. "I consider myself very lucky indeed that they gave me such a loving home. I wish you had never ordered me back here and as soon as you tire of me I shall gladly return to Yorkshire!"

He pushed his chair back and stood. "Permit me to leave the table. I wish to retire to bed early after my journey."

Stephen raised his eyes theatrically.

"Yes, you may go and sulk in your nursery. Breakfast is at eight and will be cleared by half past the hour. I will expect you at nine-fifteen in my study so we can begin discussing your role and duties."

"Tomorrow? But it is Saturday." Edwin curled his lip, his plan to storm off momentarily put aside. Back home in Yorkshire, the weekend was for relaxation; walks or bicycle rides in the countryside, leisurely reading of newspapers, tennis matches.

"And on Monday you will be expected to start work. You

will not embarrass me by showing ignorance of what we do. I hope your education, and your aunt and uncle's influence, have given you the makings of becoming a gentleman, though the evidence presented so far does not fill me with optimism."

Edwin flinched. He gripped the back of the dining chair tightly, feeling tremors of anger coursing through his arm. He looked at his grandfather, curling his lip to demonstrate his contempt.

"I didn't want to be sent away but you chose that for me. I didn't want to be summoned back but, again, you made that choice for me. I am under your control until I am twenty-one but once I reach my majority I will no longer be beholden to you. Work out what you have paid for my upkeep and tell me what I owe to buy my freedom. When I have cleared my debt then you may consider yourself free of your embarrassing association. Goodnight, sir."

He stormed out of the room and upstairs to his bedroom.

His nursery!

Damn his grandfather for his mockery. Edwin walked into the room and stood in the centre, his breath coming hard and fast. At least his grandfather had installed a bed fit for an adult rather than the small one Edwin remembered. His travelling case had been taken there and left beside the chest of drawers for him to unpack. The large trunk would arrive the following week, having travelled second class, so for now the room was bare.

He looked at it moodily, wondering if he would ever summon the courage to take it and walk out of the house. Enjoying the fantasy of that rebellion settled his temper enough for him to know he'd never do it. Instead, resigning himself to his fate, he unpacked, hung his clothes in the wardrobe, and arranged his toiletries on the washstand. He stacked the three books he had brought with him on the shelf then sat on the edge of the bed, sinking into the slightly soft mattress.

His room has been emptied when he had left, but he hadn't taken all his belongings with him. Assuming Stephen hadn't been cruel enough to dispose of everything they would probably have been stored in the attic. He wasn't even sure what would be in the boxes. Some old toys of course, and books. When he had time, he would search for them. It might be fun to reminisce and it would give him something to look forward to.

Despite what he had said it was too early for him to go to bed but he would rather eat hot coals, as Portia had, than return to the company of his grandfather. He walked to the window and heaved up the sash to let air into the room. Harold's room had overlooked the conservatory and one hot summer night the boys had clambered out and down the ivy. Edwin's room provided no such possibility of escape as it was at the front of the house and overlooked the town. He stared at the twinkling lights that had almost doubled in number since he had been away. It was colder now and felt much more autumnal. The Yorkshire house had been on the edge of a village where the only smells were from animals and plants. Here, the air was heavy with smoke and fumes, almost obliterating the earthy smell of falling leaves and mulchy soil.

A cold wind that blew down from the hills took him by surprise with an earthy freshness and he was filled with the longing for freedom.

He put his coat on and old school scarf. He passed his grandfather on the way out.

"Where are you going?" Stephen asked.

"Just to get some air."

Stephen nodded curtly. "If you see Sykes say hello. He'll probably be putting Stanley away if he hasn't already."

"Sykes is still here?" Edwin lifted his brows. The old gardener had been about seventy when Edwin had left. It was Sykes who had carried him back when he had broken his arm. But it had also been Sykes who had forced him away from the tree when…

When what?

Had he been there again? He couldn't quite remember.

Stephen walked off in the direction of his study. Edwin wandered outside again. So that was how it was going to be: awkward conversations about very little. He strolled over to the summer house and the stable that now backed on to it. Stanley was inside his stable, head peeking out over the half-door and Edwin spent a few minutes giving him a scratch between the ears.

"At least you are happy to see me, old chap."

He leaned back against the stable door and sighed. "What am I doing? Talking to trees and horses? I suppose I'll have to reacquaint myself with Robert at some point. I hope he's a little less dreadful now."

He stared upwards. Heavy clouds blocked out the moon so that only a faint edge was visible. On the horizon the sycamore tree looked lonely. Some movement at the edge of it caught his eyes. He stood up a little straighter. Perhaps that was Sykes. He walked across the meadow in a straight line. He regretted it almost immediately because the long grass was wet with evening dew and before he had taken a dozen steps his trouser cuffs were sodden. He grimaced, an almost physical memory of revulsion springing up inside him.

"Hello?" he called as he drew close. "Is that Mr Sykes?"

The only answer was the sigh of the wind in the leaves and a rustling from close to the tree. He walked closer. In the darkness the shadows played across the branches and the trunk. The tangle of thorns in the hedgerow now looked unwelcoming in the shadowy half-light.

Taking care to tread quietly, Edwin walked inside the circular mound. The hair on the back of his neck prickled and he had the distinct impression somebody was watching him. He couldn't see Sykes, but as he turned to go, he saw a flicker of movement from the corner of his eye. What would Sykes be doing hiding? His heart pulsated as he wondered if he had interrupted a poacher or a vagrant. He froze, then turned around quickly, hoping to catch whoever it was by surprise.

Standing in the shadows, half-concealed behind the trunk was a tall girl.

Not the image he had of a poacher.

Their eyes met and the breath caught in Edwin's throat. The young woman – he realised now that she was around the same age as him – looked startled, and then guilty. She darted behind the tree.

Edwin took a step towards her.

"I know you're there. There's no use pretending you aren't."

She didn't answer but he saw her hands creep around the trunk of the tree. Perhaps she had been caught trespassing before. One day about six years previously he had climbed into the rectory garden with Harold and a friend and they had scrimped apples. They had been caught and sent to bed with no dinner as a result, as well as being made to write a letter of apology to the vicar to be hand-delivered. Edwin could imagine that Stephen Brice was much less lenient than Dr James (who had contented himself with delivering to the boys a thirty-minute-long sermon on Eve's sin). What he could not imagine was why the girl would want to trespass at the sycamore tree which didn't even bear fruit.

"You're not supposed to be here, you know." He remembered the expression on her thin face and the way she had darted away and thought for a minute. "But I promise you won't be in any trouble."

He took a step back then spoke in a gentler voice. "Are you already in trouble? Do you need help? I'm not going to hurt you."

He raised his hands to show they were empty and took another step backwards, as if appeasing a scared animal. The girl peeked out from behind the tree. Her large eyes were fixed on Edwin, thick lashes edging them, and he lost a moment staring into them.

"Are you here to meet somebody? Are you hiding from someone?" She still didn't reply. Edwin turned away in irritation.

"Well, stay there if you insist."

He walked out of the circle but stopped when he was halfway through the hedgerow and then spun around quickly to look. She had moved silently and quickly because she was now standing in front of the tree trunk. Her face was pale and her hair was long and loose. It looked like a cloak, falling over her breasts, almost down to her waist.

She wasn't as pretty as some of the girls that Edwin knew. Demetria and Eleni were much more striking, but there was something about her angular jaw and cheekbones that drew Edwin's attention. His school had once collaborated with the girls' school in the neighbouring town to perform *Hamlet* and she reminded him of the girl from the fifth form who had played Ophelia in the last stages of her madness, with tangled hair and a bedraggled dress. Presumably she was a tinker or a vagrant to be dressed like this and hiding in a hedgerow. He shouldn't even be wasting time talking to someone of her class.

"You know this is private property," he said, gesturing around him. "It belongs to the house and the mill."

He sucked his teeth. Something in his brain told him this was all familiar. If only he could remember where he'd seen the girl before. Her eyes widened and she edged a couple of steps forwards. She was very thin, and very pale. She almost blended in against the tree. No wonder he had found it hard to see her at first. Edwin looked down and saw that she was barefoot.

"Good grief!" he exclaimed. "You must be frozen."

He stuck his hands in his pockets, wondering if he had any spare change, but they were empty and his money clip was back in his room.

"Do you need to eat?" he asked.

She still didn't answer, merely stared at him with a pensive expression. Edwin started to grow annoyed. He'd told her she was safe, and even that he would help her. She was just being rude. He blew out a breath and rearranged his scarf.

"I'm going to go back to the house at the bottom of the meadow. It's where I live. If you're in some sort of trouble, you can come to the door. My grandfather owns that factory." He pointed at it.

"He could probably find you employment if you needed it."

The girl was staring at him intently now, her eyes flickering up and down, side to side.

Edwin sighed. "Well, I said I'm going. If you do decide to come to the house or go to the factory, tell them that Edwin Hope told you to. That way there shouldn't be any trouble."

He turned and walked away.

Sapling?

He stopped, unsure at first that anyone had spoken. He glanced over his shoulder.

"Did you say something?"

The girl shook her head. He walked back towards her but she retreated into the shadows of a trunk.

"Don't come closer!"

She had a sweet voice, high and musical, but for a pretty girl's first words to be a warning would be crushing to any young man and Edwin was no exception. She had sounded genuinely scared, which made him hesitate. He stared at the ground between them, hoping his face didn't betray his dismay. He wasn't even the sort of lad who flirted with the waitresses in teashops.

"I won't," he said gently. "But really, there's nothing to fear. My intentions are entirely honourable."

"I don't think I'm supposed to be your friend."

Her brow furrowed but the faintest flicker of a smile

48

brushed over her lips and she tilted her head to one side. She reminded Edwin of someone. He could not tell who.

"Well, you don't have to be. I'll go now, but you had better go away before anyone else catches you."

A gust of wind blew down from the hills, bringing a flurry of rain. Edwin unwrapped his scarf.

"Look here, you're obviously cold. Take this. You can borrow it for tonight. When you're finished, hang it on the branch for me and I'll collect it."

He held it out, not expecting her to take it so wasn't offended when she didn't. He walked back into the grove and laid it at the base of the tree. He nodded at her, stuck his hands deep in his pockets, and walked past her. Resisting the temptation to turn back was hard but, telling himself that he was stronger willed than Orpheus, Edwin managed it. At least he would have something to tell Harold about when he wrote home.

The Sapling was back. He had grown so much that until he had spoken his name she had not recognised him. No longer too small to reach the branches of her tree, he could have scaled it in an instant. He was almost a man now. Indeed, in times past that she dimly recalled, he would have been a man. There was something green about him still. Something soft and unformed. It was… She struggled for the word.

Exciting?

Intriguing?

Something to anticipate.

She stretched her limbs, noticing they had lengthened, grown more supple and shapely. He'd noticed it, she knew. He might not even have been aware of the subtle flush of warmth to his throat and cheekbones but she had seen it. It gave her a feeling of power that had been absent for so long.

How long had he been gone? Too long. He'd said he would return but he had lied.

She had watched until the leaves fell, feeling indignation that he hadn't returned, then sorrow, then resignation and finally nothing but a sense of loneliness and the passing of time. There had been seasons, but she hadn't cared how many had passed; hadn't taken form but had been content to be only a thought deep within the tree.

But now the Sapling had sought her out once again it was like the arrival of spring. She sighed. No, he hadn't. There had been no recognition in him. He had come by accident, not intentionally. The kindness he had shown her, thinking she was a lost woman, was endearing. What a gentle man he had grown into. She stroked the scarf he had given her and wound it around her neck as she had seen him wear it.

Green and blue. Sky and leaves.

She smiled with lips unused to the movement. He'd offered it freely, asking nothing in return. Did he know what he had done, placing it at the base of her tree with the reverence of an offering to the gods?

Demanding nothing. A rare thing for a man.

She wanted him back. But the Old One had made her cautious. The threats he had made still cut her deeply.

Fire and insolence.

She shivered with anger and fear.

If the Sapling returned of his own accord, however; if he came back to her willingly that would be a sign that all was right. Then there would be no obligation on her to turn away from him, would there?

Winter was almost upon the world but it felt like she was waking again. Just a little veneration after so long would sustain her through the harsh, barren months of darkness that the falling leaves heralded.

Tentatively she stepped out of the grove and when nothing prevented her, she gave a laugh of delight. It had been such a long time since she'd been able to. It had been so many years since she had woken after a hard winter to discover that while she had slept the hawthorn hedge had been encasing her within its ring. A reasonably athletic man could have jumped over it but of course she couldn't. That was the charm. It had effectively made her a prisoner. Now that the Sapling had unintentionally caused the circle to be broken there was nothing to prohibit her walking through the gap.

Nothing beyond her own nervousness of course. She took four or five steps forwards before she felt the tug pulling her back. Years ago, when she'd been stronger, she could have run across the fields, bathed in the stream, danced through the streets of the village. Now she felt bound.

Stymied.

It was unenjoyable. What good was the promise of freedom when the prospect of limitation came along with it?

But if the Sapling returned, she would grow strong.

It would be worth risking the Old One's wrath for that.

Chapter Four

S unday arrived, grey and damp. Reluctantly, Edwin
dragged himself from bed and dressed for church. Aunt
Madeline had always insisted on empty stomachs before the
morning service, so Edwin was overjoyed to discover the smell
of bacon drifting from the kitchen. He mentioned it to his
grandfather, who was already seated in the dining room with
an empty plate in front of him, as he piled three rashers onto
his plate alongside two poached eggs.

Stephen took a mouthful of coffee before answering with a
frown.

"I don't know why Madeline insists on that. We always ate
well before we attended in our family. Adelaide used to cry
otherwise."

Edwin paused, midway to adding a spoonful of fried
mushrooms to his plate. He could not remember the last time
Stephen had spoken of his daughter. He took the plate to the
table and sat opposite Stephen.

"I didn't know that. I'd like to know more about her. I don't really remember her."

"I do. Every day." Stephen stared at him then pushed his chair out. "Be ready in twenty minutes."

Edwin finished eating in silence, his appetite vanishing. He'd hoped for an offer from his grandfather to tell him more, but it was possible that admitting he had almost no memory of his mother had been tactless.

There were three main churches in the town. The largest was the Anglican one that dominated the square next to the town hall and the public library at the top of Church Hill. The Catholic church was on the London Road that led out the town, and the square, red brick Methodist church was almost equidistant from both. Edwin was most inclined to attend that establishment but Stephen was insistent they attend the Anglican. When Edwin looked around the congregation, he realised that this was where the town's "society" worshipped. The mayor was in attendance in the first row of pews, as was the local member of Parliament. The next rows were filled by the owners of almost all the mills in the town along with their wives and children.

Edwin hid a smirk. Of course his grandfather would want to be in their company, even though Greete Mill was smaller and less profitable than the businesses that turned out the silk thread and cloth in their raw forms.

The left side was entirely filled with boys in blue coats and caps and Edwin was pleased he had attended when he spotted a familiar face in the crowd. After the service, as families were chatting in the churchyard, he left Stephen making small talk with Dr Graves and his wife, and wove his way through the bustling groups to the woman standing with the schoolboys.

"Annie!" he exclaimed in delight. "You haven't changed at all."

It was only slightly a fib. She didn't look much older but the hair that was curled into a large bun beneath her hat had one or two lighter blonde strands, and she had a few fine lines around her eyes and mouth. She looked slightly confused, then her expression changed to astonishment, then pleasure.

"Why, Edwin!" she exclaimed. She pulled him into a hug then released him. "Look at you, such a handsome young man you've become! I did not know you had returned. I wasn't sure if you were ever coming back, to be honest. It's Mrs McAvoy now, by the by. These are my girls, Morag and Mairibeth."

She presented Edwin with two girls aged six or seven who were identical in all aspects except one had her plait over her left shoulder with a blue ribbon and the other had her plait over the right shoulder with a green ribbon. Their hair was carroty-red, presumably from their Scottish father.

"My husband is over there, marshalling the junior boys back to the school. I suppose I must call you Master Hope now."

"No, I'm Edwin to you, always," Edwin said with a smile. "It's so lovely to see you again, Mrs McAvoy. I believe yours is the first, no, the second welcoming conversation I've had since I returned. Mr Wills seemed pleased to see me yesterday."

"Well that's very nice to hear," Annie said. Her brow creased slightly. "I'm sure your grandfather is pleased you are back."

Edwin smiled, though he felt it was forced. "Yes, I'm sure

he is looking forward to instructing me in the workings of the factory. I only arrived back yesterday of course. I went to see my parents' graves. Oh, and I went back to that old sycamore tree. The one at the top of the meadow."

Annie laughed. "Oh my goodness, the trouble you had with that tree. My blood still runs cold at the thought of your poor arm and Dr Graves setting it. The way the bones creaked!" She shuddered. "And then of course you insisted on sneaking away back to it. I do believe that was the straw that broke the camel's back."

This was news to Edwin. Surely it had been climbing the tree that had resulted in him being sent away and Annie being dismissed from her job as his nursemaid.

"I went back after I broke my arm?"

"Yes, while it was my afternoon off and your grandfather was at the factory. You kept insisting you had been playing with someone but you may have been making up an imaginary friend. Children do, of course. Morag used to have an elephant in her dollhouse."

"Mammy don't tell him that," Morag whined.

"I don't remember going back another time," Edwin said slowly. "Are you sure?"

Annie smiled. "Well, little children's minds get muddled with memories but I distinctly remember Sykes bringing you back and you were arguing, so you must have been somewhere."

Annie's little girls began to grow restless and tug on her skirts.

"I need to go," she said, detaching their hands gently.

"Please come and take tea with us at our house one afternoon. You are staying now that you're back, aren't you?"

"I am," Edwin answered. Doubt crept into his mind, if not into his voice. "It would be nice to come and see you. I feel like I need a reason to stay, rather than just the obligation to."

Annie touched his cheek affectionately. "You look so much like the portrait of your mother when you smile. It's quite astonishing."

She and the girls walked away to join the crocodile of young boys waiting with Mr McAvoy. Annie hugged the girls and Edwin felt an almost physical emptiness in his stomach as he remembered the way she had hugged him as a child. He wrapped his arms around himself – not much consolation for the lack of a mother's love.

Stephen Hope spent the afternoon ensconced in his study, reading his way through the newspapers. He offered them to Edwin who picked out one or two, more out of politeness than interest. He read through them then wrote letters to Aunt Madeline, Harold, and Eleni. They were all variations on the same news but tailored for different audiences, though in the end he left out his strange encounter with the girl at the tree.

An encouraging smell of steak and kidney pie wafted from the kitchen but there was a whole afternoon ahead of Edwin before dinner. The weather had turned from drizzly to lashing rain so a walk was out of the question. His trunk would not arrive until Monday and he had little to keep him occupied so he decided to visit the attic. Searching for some of his old childhood belongings would give him something to do. At the bottom of the stairs to the top floor he paused. The door to the room that had belonged to his parents was still shut and he wondered if anyone had been in it since he had left. He had never been allowed to cross the threshold as a child, though he had apparently spent the first years of his life sleeping with his parents.

Really it was quite a gruesome thought that it was a relic to the dead couple. His grandfather's admission that he thought of his late daughter daily now seemed slightly concerning. Aunt Madeline had presumably grieved for her brother, and again for her husband, but she was about to remarry. Perhaps Edwin should encourage Stephen to do likewise. It might make him slightly more agreeable.

The top floor of the house was divided into three rooms for servants and one large space for storage. Amongst old mirrors, a wicker basket chair and various large vases, Edwin found two boxes with his name on them. Back in his room he opened them, keen to see what was inside. One contained toys, the other books, which accounted for the weight. He spent a happy twenty minutes flipping through old story books, history books, and an atlas with crinkled pages before one book at the bottom of the box caught his attention: a leather-bound journal.

"My diary!" he exclaimed aloud. He opened it excitedly. The childish handwriting proclaimed it had been given as a gift in the Christmas of 1901, and that Edwin intended to write in it daily from the 1st of January, 1902. Clearly, given that the first half of the book was dog-eared while the last looked pristine, he had failed.

He flicked through the pages, reading mundane details of the weather, walks he had taken with Annie or his grandfather, puddings he had consumed, and sketches of interesting insects. When he reached the final page of his recordings, something fell out. Curious, he picked it up. It was a fold of blotting paper and he opened it to reveal a sycamore leaf. He held it in the palm of his hand and slowly his belly began to tighten.

Memories flooded back.

A little girl.

There *had* been a little girl in the tree when he had climbed it.

He walked to the window and held the leaf to the dull light. It had been well preserved and a deep green. If the season had still been summer, he would swear it had only been picked the day before. He ran his fingers over the paper-thin surface and closed his eyes.

The memories were clearer now. The girl had taunted him. Had she pushed him from the tree? No, he was sure that his fall had been a genuine accident. But what then? Why did she seem so significant? He'd gone back and she had traded the leaf for something. He sat back on his heels and tried to remember until it came to him. He had swapped a marble.

Now he knew why the brief encounter with the young lady in the tree the previous day had seemed so familiar. It must have been the same girl. That was why she had looked familiar.

He was right to think he had known her, and of course she would have grown. Now he knew why he was desperate to see her again.

More memories started to drift back: Sykes carrying him home from the tree; Sykes pulling him away insistently; Sykes telling him there was no little girl. She must have been a child of one of the factory workers or a farm worker from the local village, and Stephen in all his glorious social-climbing snobbery would not have seen her as a suitable friend because he could not bear to be embarrassed. That, Edwin was certain, had been the reason he had been sent away.

Now it was understandable why the girl had been so wary when he had spoken to her, and why she had been insistent that he stay back when he told her his name.

Edwin folded the leaf back into the blotting paper and put it inside the diary. One evening in the week when he had finished his work at the factory he would walk up and see if the girl was still there. Stephen may have stopped his friendship with her when he was seven but now Edwin was eighteen and the thought of defying his grandfather with an illicit friendship lifted his spirits like nothing else since his return.

Edwin started work at the factory promptly at eight o'clock on Monday morning. He hadn't been sure what to expect but his first day was spent reading through ledgers and order books dating back to the previous five years. It was worse than being at school and being forced to learn the names of innumerable kings and queens and dates of battles.

"What good is this doing me?" he asked.

Stephen looked up from the letter he was writing and gave a slight cough that sounded disapproving. "It gives you an understanding of how much we sell, when we sell it, and how much profit we make."

"When will I get to do anything useful?"

"When you can demonstrate an understanding of the financial side of the business. The only side there is to understand, really. Now"—he peered at Edwin over the top of his glasses—"tell me which of the lines was the most profitable last spring, and why you think that might be."

It was tedious work and felt very similar to being at school. Fortunately, William Wills noticed Edwin's apathy. On the Thursday afternoon of Edwin's second week, when Stephen had gone to inspect a display of the merchandise in a Stockport department store, William suggested they visit the printing floor.

"Now this is fascinating," Edwin commented enthusiastically, as he peered at the silk frames. Watching the bolts of white cloth being printed with layer upon layer of different colours and patterns until the completed design emerged, it was like watching a magician doing sleight of hand tricks. One minute there was an outline, next a jewel of olive green, a bud of dark plum, and finally a swirl of teal and the teardrop flowers were finished.

"This is incredible."

William laughed at Edwin's pleasure.

"Is it the first time you've seen this? I suppose it is. I remember bringing my daughters and they loved it too. So much so that Eliza took it upon herself to try painting my Sunday shirt. Mrs Wills was very vexed."

He laughed and Edwin joined in.

"I can imagine the whipping she got for that!" Edwin said.

The humour faded from William's eyes.

"She didn't get a whipping. She didn't do it out of naughtiness but inspiration."

"Oh."

Edwin turned away so that William didn't see the emotion that flared inside him. If only Stephen had been as generous with his assessment of childish behaviour when Edwin had been younger. He coughed and moved on to the end of the room, smiling at the women as they worked.

"Who creates the design?" he asked.

"We employ artists," William said, joining him. "Three different ones, actually, depending on whether the theme is based on plants, animals or something else."

Edwin stared out of the long row of windows, designed to flood the workspace with as much light as possible. They looked out over the hills, cleverly avoiding a view into the private formal garden behind Greete Mill House. The rain had been solid for nearly a fortnight but today there was a brief lapse and the heavy charcoal clouds were parted enough to let sunlight penetrate. The lone sycamore stood proud, elevated on the mound above the oak and horse chestnuts further in the distance. It was caught in the sun's feeble glare and the now copperish-coloured leaves glowed against the grey surroundings as if lit from within.

The sycamore seeds and leaves would make an interesting pattern for a winter scarf. Edwin could almost visualise the design and the assortment of browns and yellows that he'd need.

"I wonder if I might try designing something," he suggested.

William looked doubtful. "It's worth a try, I suppose,

though don't expect your grandfather necessarily to agree to it. He has very fixed ideas about what designs will sell well."

Edwin tore his gaze away. "Of course."

He walked back towards the office, muttering under his breath. "I expect nothing from my grandfather that he does not desire to give."

That evening he excused himself and went to his room where he took out the sycamore leaf from his diary. He sketched out a repeating design on the next clean page of the book. His drawing was rough and the leaves misshapen, and he realised with regret that he would never produce a design good enough to share, but the idea was there. He took it downstairs and found Stephen sitting by the fire in the sitting room.

"I went to look at the silk printing this afternoon," he said. "It gave me an idea for a design."

He held it out to Stephen who slowly replaced his whiskey tumbler on the side table and took it. He brought the book to his face, held it further away, then turned it by ninety degrees.

"What is this supposed to represent?"

"Sycamore leaves," Edwin said.

Stephen's brows knotted. "Sycamore. Indeed. Your inspiration came from the tree on the mound, no doubt?"

"I suppose it did." Edwin shuffled his feet. "I know it's a bit rough and we'd have to get someone else to properly draw it but—"

Stephen closed the diary with a snap. "Are you proposing I waste time and money having this scrawl turned into a design? I thought it must have been a relic from childhood you had unearthed."

He held the book out to Edwin who snatched it back.

"Did your school not teach you how to write with the correct hand?"

Edwin reddened. He'd shown a marked inclination to write with his left hand as a child until that had been drilled out of him at school by judicious use of a ruler on the knuckles or a piece of string binding his wrist to the chair leg. It had worked and he could write passably neatly with his right hand, but he would never be an artist. He lifted his chin and stared down at his grandfather, feeling a burst of repugnance that bordered on outright loathing.

"Never mind. I won't waste any more of your time."

Stephen reached for his drink.

"It's your own time you're wasting. Time better spent making connections within local society than obsessing about that dreadful old tree. You haven't made any attempt to seek out your old friends."

"I'm not sure Robert Carfax counted as a friend even when we were children but I'll pay him a visit at some point."

Back in his room he looked at the design, wishing he had not shared it, but suspecting that even if it had been a sketch worthy of Michelangelo it would have been rejected. His grandfather didn't intend for him to be employed on the manufacturing side of the business. He closed the book with the leaf in it and put it in his bedside drawer. He hadn't managed to go out and see if the girl was at the tree because the rain had been too hard, but regardless of whether it was clear on Saturday, he'd go. The more his grandfather was determined to be disparaging about the tree, the more determined Edwin was to seek it out.

Chapter Five

Saturday was free of rain, but freezing mist hung in the air. The windows of Edwin's bedroom had been glazed with swirls of frost that were infinitely more delicate than any scarf design could be. He'd experienced it, as the temperature had plummeted rapidly and he had asked for his bedroom fire to be lit for the first time since his return. He dressed in a jumper and tweed trousers, before putting on his overcoat and walking out to the tree. The ground was solid underfoot but he hesitated before crossing the meadow. He walked instead along the bank of the stream and up to the gate before following the line of the wall until he reached the mound. He spotted the figure of Sykes bending at the edge of an herbaceous border near the house and raised a hand, but the old man didn't see him.

He whistled as he walked, deciding that he would give the girl notice of his arrival, assuming she was there. He paused and looked over to the houses beyond the wall, wondering which was hers. Movement from near the tree caught his eye and he turned his head sharply. The girl was standing at the edge of the circle, just where the branches overhead reached furthest.

"You came back."

She tilted her head, looking at him through eyes that were framed with dark lashes. She was dressed in something brown and loose-fitting with coppery pattens and an old-fashioned-looking cloak over the top in the same fabric. Her hand went to her throat and Edwin realised she was wearing his scarf looped around her neck beneath the cloak. His heart did a rapid dance that was slightly unexpected at the sight of her wearing it. When puberty had hit, he'd had the usual crushes on girls from Aunt Madeline's circle, and once or twice on the dewy-eyed boys in his boarding school (which had been perfectly normal, he'd been assured), so the sensation of attraction towards someone wasn't unfamiliar, but he hadn't expected such a strong reaction before now.

"Yes, I've come back," he said.

He dug his hands in his pockets and strolled closer. The ground was covered in fallen leaves, no longer mulchy from the rain but rigid from the frost. They crunched underfoot, the only sound that filled the silence. He walked cautiously, feeling as if a sudden movement would frighten her away, which was silly on reflection. She was a girl, not a deer or a rabbit. He let out a long breath that collected in mist before his face and hung before dispersing. The mound wasn't much higher than the house but there was a stiff wind that intensified the cold.

"I'm sorry I didn't come back sooner but I've been busy

and the weather has been awful. I remember you now, and I think you remember me too."

"It's been longer than that since you came. You've changed," she said. "You were a little boy when I saw you last."

She stepped backwards into the clearing beneath the tree. Her hair flopped in front of her face and she pushed it back behind her ears. Edwin wanted to touch it. It looked thick and lustrous despite being worn loose. He followed her. The sky was clear and sunlight filtered through the thinning foliage and bare twigs that crisscrossed above them.

She pointed at his arm. "You healed."

Edwin rubbed his forearm. There was a slight indentation just below his elbow that an X-ray photograph might show meant the bone had healed crooked. It only bothered him in very cold or wet weather.

"It's been eleven years since I broke it. You've changed too."

"Over a decade! So long?" Her eyes widened, the fine line of her brows arching. "Why didn't you come before now? Surely it must have healed sooner than that."

"I was sent away. My grandfather…"

Edwin leaned back against the tree and stretched his legs out, locking his knees. Everyone in his family already knew the circumstances of his departure and he was slightly relieved that it obviously hadn't been a source of gossip in the local area. Out of a sense of loyalty he hesitated before continuing. Family business was family business, after all.

"Well, my mother and father had both died and I think

trying to bring up a child alone was very difficult for him. Men aren't suited to that, of course. And I was a troublesome child by all accounts – like running off and breaking my arm."

"I remember you," she said.

Edwin smiled. "I'd like to be friends."

"I can't. I shouldn't." She retreated in on herself slightly, drawing her bare arms into the folds of the cloak. "I don't want anyone to get hurt."

He blinked in surprise. "No one will get hurt, I promise you. There's nothing to be afraid of by being friends with me. If your parents aren't happy about it, I can meet them."

"I have no parents; there's only me," she said.

"Ah." Edwin pursed his lips, sympathy blooming. She was an orphan too, and in a poorer state than he was from the looks of things. "I'm sorry to hear that. It's awful, isn't it."

She took a couple of steps towards him and tilted her head one way then the other. "You really want to spend time in my company? You must do, as you've come back. And the Old One will allow it?"

Her eyes radiated intelligence along with a healthy dose of scepticism. They looked as if she had seen the world pass by and decided it was beneath her. It sent a frisson of excitement coursing through Edwin. None of the girls he knew had ever seemed half as enticing.

"I'll be honest," Edwin said, "my grandfather won't approve, but that's part of the attraction. He's a miserable old snob and I would happily thwart him."

The girl's lip curled. "So you don't really want to be friends with me; you just want to annoy your grandfather. What a seductive offer. Forgive me if I decline to be used as a pawn in your familial skirmish."

She rolled her eyes and turned away, tossing her hair back over her shoulders as if she were an empress dismissing a servant. Edwin and Harold had once been privileged – or so Aunt Madeline had told them – to be presented to a dowager viscountess at an open day, and this girl's manner was distinctly reminiscent of that esteemed lady's. A horrible feeling began to creep up on Edwin that this girl might not be all she seemed. He'd assumed she was poor but what if she was actually affluent and eccentric? Eleni's wealthy godmother apparently kept seven rabbits in her boudoir, each with its own bed.

Whether or not the girl was rich, Edwin was conscious of having insulted her. He ran his hands through his hair in awkwardness. What an idiot he was making of himself.

"No, no. I-I don't mean it like that. I mean, he will disapprove but I am prepared to defy him because I think you're interesting and I would like a friend."

She half turned back, looking over one shoulder, her lips curled into a contemptuous sneer.

"I would like *you* as a friend," he said, holding out a hand. Feeling he needed something more, he rummaged in his other hand and produced his diary. "I found the leaf you gave me in an old diary. It reminded me of how I had enjoyed playing with you. I'm an idiot and that was rude of me. I beg your pardon."

She turned fully round and regarded him with a look that made him feel he was being turned inside out. Despite the cold weather, a flush of heat travelled the length of his spine, causing him to shiver. She laughed, obviously seeing his discomposure.

"Granted. How could any woman refuse such a petition? Now, what form do you suggest this friendship takes? What do we have to offer each other?"

Edwin shrugged. "Whatever form you want. We could walk and talk. I could read to you, or I could bring paint and paper and we can sketch. We could play cards." He thought for a minute. "Do you know how to play croquet?"

He pointed down to the lawn where the old pitch had been set up. The hoops and mallets were bound to be in the summer house. "We could definitely do that when spring comes, even though they're only two of us."

She came and stood at his side. He'd thought she was shorter than he was by some margin, but her eyes were level with his chin. She looked unconvinced.

"I don't know. I've never been that far from the tree. That's your land, not mine."

"Well, I invite you to join me. It's going to get colder before too long and we can't keep meeting here. We'll both freeze."

She smiled. "No we won't. It's never too cold here. Your breath isn't even showing."

He huffed a couple of times and discovered she was right. The branches must be giving some protection from the elements. She laughed and he grinned, happy to see her amused. She lifted her face and looked into his eyes.

"I do like the sound of everything you are suggesting, but there's always an exchange to be made, isn't there. You must want something from me."

"Only company and a friendly face." Edwin chewed his knuckle then frowned. "I remember you saying that before."

"Do you remember why?" She walked past him to the edge of the clearing and stood between the two edges of the hedgerow.

Edwin closed his eyes, digging deep into his memories. "Did you tell me you were a fairy or something? I think I remember that."

Her eyes narrowed and she looked outraged, but then her face broke into a smile.

"I told you I was the goddess of this tree; of this whole grove."

Edwin laughed and then stopped because she did look serious. She was an odd thing but her eccentricity was appealing. If she wanted to play at being a goddess then who was he to object?

"So is this your church?" he asked, spreading his arms around.

She inclined her head. "My *grove*. Churches are for Christians. Long before your gods came to this land, my kind was worshipped."

"Of course." Edwin grinned. He'd pored over passages from Caesar's *Gallic Wars* in Latin prep and had a memory of the druids with their sacred grove and sickles. Now he thought of it, the Romans and Greeks had had tree nymphs.

"So I suppose you're a dryad, really."

She gave a laugh that sounded slightly derisive.

"Dryads belong in oak trees. This"—she waved her hand around regally—"is a sycamore."

Edwin looked down his nose at her. "I thought they lived in olive trees, actually. Coming from ancient Greece, that is."

She put her hand on his arm. Through his tweed coat, woollen jumper, and cotton shirt it shouldn't have been possible for her touch to affect him so acutely, but it seemed as if her cool fingers were stroking his flesh itself.

"You have a lot to learn," she said. "I've been called nymph before now. That's good enough."

He suspected she was making it up as she went along; he was really too old for make-believe. Then again, one of the old boys who had returned to Edwin's school for a formal dining in had regaled the upper sixth with scurrilous stories of an American woman he had romanced. She apparently liked to pretend she was a duchess and he was a wicked highwayman. The boys had got a lot of mileage out of that tale once lights had been turned out.

"Well then, you can teach me how to behave," he murmured.

"Gladly, young Sapling."

He bit his lip at the nickname. "I don't know your name. You know I'm Edwin. What should a goddess be called?"

Her eyes widened.

"I think you are the first man ever to ask me that. What do you think you would like to call me?"

She reached out a hand and placed her fingertips on his cheekbone. His skin fluttered and he could feel an awkward stirring in his trousers that he did his best to ignore. When he had left the house he hadn't been planning on seducing anyone, even less on being seduced.

"I don't know. It doesn't seem my place to decide for you,"

Edwin said. He looked at her angular face, glossy hair, and gleaming green-brown eyes. He could easily imagine she was unearthly but summoning a name to encapsulate that was proving impossible. His mind was empty.

"Why don't you write me a list and I'll pick from that," the girl suggested.

"Let me give it some thought and I will tell you the next time I come. I have to go," he said. "I'll try and come again next Saturday. Can you be here at dusk?"

Her lips curved into a beguiling smile and Edwin wondered what it would be like to kiss her.

"I can be here whenever I choose. When you come next, call me by the name you choose and I'll come to you."

He nodded and held his hand out to shake it. She slipped hers into it and on impulse he lifted it to his lips.

"Farewell for now, goddess."

He left the clearing and walked down the road back to the house. As he neared the bottom, Sykes hailed him and he changed direction, walking across the meadow to join the old man at the edge of the croquet lawn.

"Mr Sykes, how good to see you. I'm surprised I haven't already."

"Master Hope."

The gardener nodded. He barely appeared to have changed; his face was as lined and suntanned as Edwin remembered and could not have got any balder. He had always looked about a hundred years old in Edwin's memory. Edwin supposed that at some point of aging the body became preserved.

Sykes cocked his head towards the hill. "Been up to the old tree?"

"It's a fine day. I thought I'd go and look at the view." Edwin smiled and glanced at his arm. "Revisit the site of my accident. Pay my respects, if you like."

"Pay your respects?"

"To the tree."

Sykes pursed his lips. He looked even more like a walnut than he had years ago. "Well, you're a grown man now so what you do is your business. Gone are the days when I could carry you home in my arms or drag you by the collar."

Edwin pressed his lips together. It sounded foolish. *He* sounded foolish. More than that, however, he had the impression that Sykes had an inkling of what he had meant. Sykes had been the one who had revealed that Edwin had gone back to the tree which had resulted in his banishment. He stood up a little straighter.

"Look, Sykes, I remember you disapproved of my being there. It's understandable because you're the groundsman here and if any trespassers cause problems it'll fall on you, but I'll answer for the conduct of anyone I choose to meet there."

"Trespassers. Aye." Sykes grinned but it wasn't pleasant. He bent and picked up his trowel and the bucket of mulch he had been spreading then stared towards the tree. He clicked his teeth.

"Probably about time I repaired the hawthorn hedge. It's good protection."

"The tree doesn't need protecting," Edwin said. "It's growing good and straight. In fact, I was thinking I might cut a bit more of the hedge down."

"I didn't say it was protecting the tree, did I." Sykes turned his face to Edwin and gave him a measured look. "But I'm sure you know all about that. Well, as you say, you'll answer to the conduct of anyone. It's good you know your own mind. Good morning to you, Master Hope."

Sykes ambled off towards the stables, leaving Edwin seething that he had failed to get the last word.

He walked into the town centre and bought a copy of *Punch* from the newsagent's then found a table in a café and ordered crumpets and a pot of tea.

What would he call a goddess? He took out his diary and began writing a list, based on what he could remember from myths he'd read at school.

Chloe
Eleni
Artemis
Daphne
Olivia
Phoebe
Titania
Hathor

He smiled at the last one. Appropriate but not exactly attractive and she needed something that was as pretty as she was.

A shadow fell across the table. Edwin looked up, expecting the waitress, but instead a stout young man with a pencil-thin moustache stood in front of him.

"Edwin Hope? Good grief, it is you. I'd heard you were back."

The man stuck his hand out. "Carfax."

"Robert, of course." Edwin shook his hand. "Please, join me. I've just ordered crumpets."

"Can't, I'm meeting Mother," Robert replied. "I'm taking her to buy a new hat. Not the most exciting thing to do on a half day. Pa got me a job at the office, did you know?"

"I didn't," Edwin replied, remembering that Mr Carfax was a solicitor. It seemed he wasn't the only one to be pulled into family business.

"Yes, I have a desk of my own and I'm working as a clerk for the time being. Dull stuff, copying out documents, but it'll do me for a year or two while I decide whether to commit to the old *legum baccalaureus*." Robert craned his head round to look at what Edwin was writing.

"Girls names, eh? Are they all the hearts you've broken? Are you some sort of lothario nowadays?"

"Hardly." Edwin gently closed the book. "Just something I'm working on."

Robert raised an eyebrow, obviously hoping for some further explanation. Edwin delighted in saying nothing, especially when Robert looked a little grumpy. Perhaps it was childish, but he could remember numerous occasions when he'd been the butt of Robert's jokes or hounding. It was odd how resentment flared up after so many years. The tea and crumpets arrived, sparing Edwin the need to talk for any longer. He thanked the waitress and reached for the butter, smiling at Robert.

"Well, it's good to see you. I'll give your regards to Harold when I write to him next."

Robert's smile froze. "We must go for a drink soon and catch up. Reminisce about the old days and all that. Come to dinner one day, in fact. I'll send a man over with an invitation."

Before Edwin could reply, Robert nodded curtly and turned away.

Edwin reopened the book and looked at his list of names. It was a start and he had a week before he needed to decide. Inspiration would come to him, he was sure.

He tucked into the crumpet enthusiastically. He'd wanted something to keep him here, and this intriguing friendship looked like it might be just the thing.

She reclined with her back against the broad trunk, her bare limbs spread out before her on the sturdy branch, halfway between the lowest branches and the slender twigs that reached above. It was her favourite position to sit as a sentinel.

She reached out a hand and let her fingers play lazily with the woollen scarf the Sapling had given her. She needed no clothing to be warm and was content in her nakedness, but the men that came to court her often found that unsettling, at least at first. Before long they all wanted the blessings she could give them and were obsessed with seeing and touching her. They had to earn that privilege through their devotion; a goddess did not grant her benediction too easily.

The attire she wore when she appeared to the Sapling had been conjured from her thoughts, as clothing always had been, based on what she saw the women in the houses wearing. This was the first real garment that had ever touched her flesh. The sensation of weight and softness was enthralling and she speculated what other fabrics might feel like: the heavy coat he wore; the thin shirt; the trousers of soft cloth. She closed her eyes and pictured her body clothed in such attire, trying to conjure what the sensations might be. Perhaps he could be persuaded to bring her more.

She looped the scarf around her neck from front to back, letting the ends trail down behind her and dipped her face to catch his scent on the wool. She closed her eyes. His own scent was there, salty and animal, but buried beneath layers of others that she found hard to identify, not native to this island.

'Drusilla?'

His voice. Gently cautious.

A word.

A name?

She felt warmth spreading through her limbs, sweet as the first rays of sun on the first day of spring. She rolled onto her belly and peered down through the branches. There was no cover thanks to the bare branches but he didn't see her. He was standing outside the grove, looking up. So young and comely, with barely the first down on his jaw. She watched him walk back and forth, enjoying the way he moved: graceful and alert, a slight tension in his shoulders. What a treasure she had found in this one.

"My acolyte," she purred, letting the words carry to him beyond the boundary of her grove.

He stopped walking and looked up. She allowed him to see her.

"Drusilla!" he called. "My goddess, come to me!"

She slipped from the branches and approached him, remembering at the last moment to clothe herself in a gown the colour of umber and sand.

"Is that the name you have chosen for me? It's pretty."

He turned to see her and his eyes lit up. It gave her a warm glow, taking root in her core and spreading through her limbs.

"Yes." He looked bashful. "Do you like it? I wrote a list like you asked but this was my favourite."

She walked closer and put a hand on his chest, spreading her fingers wide.

"Oh!" He drew a sharp breath and she could feel the blood stirring in his veins, rushing throughout his young body. The fine threads within him springing to life were too raw.

He was untouched. Virgin wood for her to shape.

Too soon for seduction, but what a prize when he was ready. She lowered her hand but stayed close, drawn to him.

"Can I see the other names? Read them to me."

He reached into his coat and drew out a book from a hidden pocket – a marvellous creation. Every garment she fashioned for herself from now on would have one. He opened the book and the long-preserved scent of her sap wafted towards her.

"The leaf…"

"Yes, I kept it. I'd forgotten all about it until I came across this old diary."

He thumbed through the book and opened it at the page where the leaf lay. Her head swam, looking at the preserved leaf. She stroked it with the tip of her forefinger. The threads of veins and the serrations of the edges were as familiar to her as caressing her own body. It made her shiver. She'd imbued it with protection but he'd left it ignored for a decade. It was as potent as ever.

"Do you remember what you gave me in exchange?" she asked.

"A marble, I think."

She scaled the trunk, her bare feet and fingers finding knotholes and ridges that anyone else would find impossible to take hold of. In eleven years, the cleft between branches had grown higher and deeper. She eased her hand inside and brought out the glass sphere. She jumped down, landing elegantly, and had a vision of the Sapling's childish body tumbling from the branches. An immense feeling of nausea made her nearly retch.

"Here. It's the nicest gift anyone has given me, I think. Except for the poet; he'd sit under my branches and compose odes to me."

She sighed. Dunstan would be bones in the ground by now. An obsessive man with pale skin and ash-blonde hair who had been devoted to her for one passionate summer, but ultimately blamed her when his works failed to catch the public eye.

"I'm not your first?" Edwin asked, and she knew men well enough to spot the jealousy that bloomed.

"I am not a muse and would not claim their role or gifts, but I can be a muse for people who want to be inspired by the land. I've had a poet as a lover. A gardener. A painter once. How would you wish me to inspire you?"

The Sapling's eyes filled with dreams. She tensed, waiting for the appeal to her gifts, wondering what she would ask in return this time. He glanced over his shoulder away towards the house and she saw the exact moment the dreams died.

"I don't know. I don't think I'll be any of those things, though I do love nature."

She smiled.

"Tell me my name again."

He tipped his head on one side and looked into her eyes. He licked his lips and smiled.

"Drusilla."

Chapter Six

"**D**rusilla."

Edwin liked the way it sounded on his lips, but even more he loved the way her eyes lit up. They were almost in total blackness with only a faint gleam of moonlight to give him anything to see by, but all the same, he was acutely aware of how brightly they shone. They almost glowed, as if the light was coming from within not elsewhere. It stirred a shivering longing in his belly and groin that brought him out in a cold sweat, even though the temperature was unseasonably bitter.

"I'm pleased you like it," he said. "I had a very long list but nothing on it seemed right, then it came to me as I was walking up the hill. Would you like to see the list?"

He pulled out the book and leaned against the tree.

"Sit down with me," Drusilla said. She lowered herself to the ground and curled her knees under her at one side. She looked up at Edwin, those fascinating eyes turned on him in appeal. His heart thumped ferociously.

ELISABETH J. HOBBES

"It's a little muddy even under the tree's shelter," he explained. "I'm happy standing."

It felt safer standing too. The way she had touched his chest had fired him up more than he was comfortable with. He had a sense that she'd realised that though, because she'd taken her hand away and much as he'd been relieved, it left him aching for another touch.

"At least you're dressed more warmly," he remarked.

She smoothed her skirts out. Her dress was old-fashioned, but not merely out of date as if it had been sewn ten or twenty years ago. More like something from a painting by one of the Pre-Raphaelite Brotherhood, or a diptych harking back to mediaeval times. There was almost no waistline and it was made from some sort of soft woollen cloth so it draped interestingly over her breasts and her hips. Over it she was wearing Edwin's scarf, but she had hung it from front to back so that the long ends trailed down her back as if it were an accessory to an evening gown. He wondered what she'd look like dressed in one of Eleni's dresses.

Edwin flicked to the page with a list of names and read them to Drusilla. He kept one eye on her expression, wondering if she would find a name that pleased her better. When he had finished, he closed the book.

"Well that's it. Would you like to change it?"

"No. I'm very happy with it, thank you. It's a lovely name. The nicest one I've had."

"What did your poet call you?"

Edwin asked the question honestly and without any ulterior motive, but as he spoke, he realised there was a slight

84

flicker of jealousy inside him. He didn't like the fact that she'd had another man.

Drusilla put her hands on the ground and leaned back. "Oh, he called me his brown-eyed lady. He didn't bother giving me an actual name."

Edwin squatted down beside her. "Your eyes aren't brown," he said slightly uncertainly. He had a vivid memory of them being greenish.

"They were for him," Drusilla said, giving a little laugh. She knelt higher. "So, you've given me your name and your presence here is paying homage to me. What do you want from me in return, Edwin?"

She leaned in towards him and the skin behind his ears fluttered as if someone were stroking fingers down his neck. It would be very easy to let her seduce him.

"You don't seem to want what my previous acolytes have wanted, yet you mentioned wanting my company."

"Yes, company," Edwin said. He straightened his legs and leaned back against the trunk beside her, considering his answer. "Friendship. Conversation, I suppose, with someone who doesn't view me as an annoyance or a child."

"Oh no, Edwin, you are very much not a child." She tilted her head slightly down but lifted her eyes so she was gazing at him through her lashes.

"Stop that," he said a little more sharply than he intended. "I mean to say, I barely know you and it makes me feel awkward." He could feel a blush spreading across his neck and up his throat. Soon his entire face would be flaming.

"I'm not very experienced," he admitted.

Drusilla leaned back and adjusted her sleeves. "Forgive me.

It's a habit I fall into. It's just what all men want in the end, in one form or another. At least until they tire of me."

She reached for his hand. He stiffened, fingers beginning to curl into a defensive fist. She looked into his eyes. "Don't pull away."

Feeling slight reservations, he let her take his hand and turn it palm upwards. "Hands untouched by hard labour. A rare thing. Once it would have signalled how highborn you were."

She held it in both her hands, letting her thumbs fold over on either side, and ran them gently in circles over the soft mounds. The pressure sent ripples of pleasure galloping up Edwin's arms. She was right; he did want her.

"Not so much these days. At least not for people like me. I'm definitely not highborn but the worst I am likely to get is a callus on my forefinger and a few unwanted ink stains on my sleeve."

She gave a little laugh. "You are funny, Sapling."

"Why do you still call me that?" he asked.

She smiled mischievously. "Because it's what you are. It's what you were when I first met you and you still are. You're green inside. Fresh and young. Unbent and unformed. My tree has stood for a century and more. It could live another hundred with care. You are like a newborn lamb to the old shepherd."

She folded her hands, closing his in the process. "If you want me to teach you – *when* you want me to teach you, because in the end all men do – just ask."

"Teach me what?" Edwin wrinkled his brow, though he had an inkling what the answer would be.

"Teach you the art of pleasing a wife. You do want a wife, don't you? Or would you prefer a man?"

"Oh I say!" Edwin blinked in embarrassment and pulled his hand away. At the same time he was shockingly excited by the way she referred to those sorts of desires in such a matter-of-fact manner.

Drusilla tossed her head back and laughed. "Love between men – and between women – was good enough for the ancient Greeks, those paragons of civilisation. Why should it be any different for your generation? I've known men who desired men. Men who desired *me* as they might a man."

Edwin's pulse began to race and his neck felt hot. Discussing such criminalities with anyone was disconcerting enough, but with a young woman … it was excruciating. She was scandalous and it was unnervingly exciting.

"I want a wife!" he croaked out. "Eventually, of course."

He tasted resentment in his throat and an aggravation greater than his awkwardness reared up in his breast. He sagged down against the tree trunk. "Actually, I think my grandfather already has plans that I'm going to marry into some great dynasty and our silk will become world-famous."

"Well there you go then." Drusilla smiled. "I can teach you how to charm any woman you choose."

Her eyes gleamed, the amber flecks standing out against the green and hazel. He had no doubt she could charm anyone, though he was considerably less confident about his own abilities.

"Well, thank you," he said, smiling awkwardly. "I'll bear that in mind when the time comes. Now I have to go, I'm afraid. I'm being taken to dinner by an old— Well, I suppose I should call him *friend* because *nemesis* feels overly dramatic. The boy whom I told I could climb the tree all those years ago."

"Definitely a nemesis," Drusilla said seriously. "Be careful to whom you assign the title of friend."

She unwound her legs from beneath her and stood on tiptoe to reach into the branches. She twisted off a small twig and held it out in the palm of her hand. It was about the length of her little finger but a third of the thickness.

"Take this. Keep it in your pocket and when you feel your nemesis is in danger of besting you, touch it and remember you have a goddess on your side. It's an amulet."

Edwin took it, touched it, and slipped it into his pocket.

"Thank you. I'll try and come back next Saturday, but earlier. I could come in the early afternoon. I could bring some cakes and the newspaper or a deck of cards. Do you know gin or rummy?"

Drusilla wrinkled her nose. "I don't drink."

Edwin grinned. "Very funny. I'll bring a deck and we can see how far we get."

At dinner that evening he was subjected to piano recitals from Robert's youngest sister, as well as assorted tales of Robert's triumphs in the world of banking, at cricket and at golf.

"We could do with a decent course in town," he said airily as he reached for the wine. "Perhaps I'll try to persuade Pa to donate a field or two from the estate. Do you play golf? I remember you had a dreadful aim with a football so a smaller target might be beyond you. No Hope we called you, didn't we? Or was it Hopeless Hope? I forget." He laughed uproariously. "Just joking of course."

Edwin forced a grin and did his best not to look at the clock he could see through the open dining room door. He slipped his hand into his trouser pocket and felt the sycamore twig. He wasn't superstitious but as he closed his fingers around it the tips of them tingled. He imagined Drusilla's tree toppling and crushing Robert beneath it.

"N-never played golf," he said with a smile. "A course would be an asset, however. Perhaps I'll talk to grandfather too. The fields behind the house would be an ideal location. So central and convenient with plenty of hills to carve out bunkers."

Robert grimaced and Edwin suppressed his glee. The Carfaxes might have acres of land but it was on the furthest outskirts of town in the opposite direction from the railway station and all the amenities. He didn't really imagine Stephen would surrender the land to build a golf course when he could expand the factory, but it was fun riling Robert.

The following Saturday Edwin duly arrived at the tree with a copy of the *Manchester Guardian*, a pencil, a picnic rug, and a Thermos flask of cocoa. Drusilla watched him as he took them out and placed them on top of the blanket. It was a musky November day; not actually raining but damp enough underfoot that he was glad of the blanket.

"It's quite dark under here, isn't it," he commented, looking up. The branches were practically bare. All the leaves seemed to have dropped in the space of a week but the sky was overcast and it was one of those days that barely seemed to get lighter than at dawn.

Edwin frowned. Drusilla looked tired. Her face seemed to have grown thinner and her usually glossy hair was dull and straggly.

"Why don't you come down to the house?" he suggested.

Drusilla drew her coat around herself. It had long, wide sleeves edged with russet and the fabric of the coat was a dull grey-brown with a nap that suggested it was old. "I can't do that."

Edwin poured out the cocoa into the flask lid and a bone china cup he had brought. Perhaps she was being sensible. His grandfather would certainly query Edwin presenting the slightly unorthodox guest.

"Of course you can," Edwin said. "I'm inviting you. If you're worried about my grandfather or even old Sykes, that needn't bother you. I've already told Sykes that I will answer for you."

"The Old One?" Drusilla shivered and drew further into her coat. "Can you protect me from him if need be?"

It was an odd request, or at least a strange way of putting it.

"Oh, his bark is worse than his bite," Edwin said airily. "He's worked here so long he has delusions of his own importance."

"You are wonderful," Drusilla said, smiling at him in a way that made his stomach flutter. "Perhaps I will come down to your summer house. I suppose that now the hawthorn circle has been broken there is nothing to keep me tied to the grove."

She dropped onto the picnic blanket beside him. "Perhaps I could travel the length of the country. The breadth of the world."

"We could do that together," Edwin said. "I could take you to Greece and you could find some dryads in the olive groves."

"Oh no." Drusilla gazed at him seriously. "I couldn't do that. It would be invasive. It would feel like wearing another woman's shoes. Or, I don't know, something far too personal in any case."

"Borrowing another man's hairbrush," Edwin suggested. "Or worse, a toothbrush."

"I expect so." Drusilla turned to the newspaper and looked at the front page. "So this is the news."

"No, they're the advertisements and notices. The news is inside." Edwin flipped through the pages to demonstrate. "Let's play a game of gin and drink the cocoa before it gets cold."

He offered Drusilla the china cup. She held it between both hands and inhaled the vapour that rose off it.

"Lovely and warm," she said.

"It is now but before too long it will cool down and I always find it does not taste half as good."

Edwin took a mouthful of his but Drusilla didn't drink.

"I don't know if I should. I don't know what effect it might have on me."

"Goodness, whyever not. It isn't laced with rum or whiskey. It won't make you drunk. Are you part of the temperance movement?"

"If I knew what that was, I would be able to answer," Drusilla said, shrugging.

Edwin gave her a suspicious look. The whole fantasy of being a dryad or goddess was slightly wearying when the weather was so cold and he'd rather be sitting by a comfortable fire.

"Well I dare say you will be fine," he said briskly. "The gods are well known for accepting offerings from their worshippers. I've never heard of Zeus coming to any harm, but if you don't want to drink it I will."

"No I'll try it," she said. She lifted the cup cautiously to her lips and tilted it slightly so that the cocoa just touched them, then sipped and swallowed. Her face changed and her eyes rolled back in her head. She tilted her head back and her lips parted.

"Oh Lord, are you alright?" Edwin exclaimed. He reached for the cup to relieve her of it, but her hands tightened about it and she drew it to her chest.

"Oh Edwin," she breathed looking up at him through heavily lidded eyes. "This is absurdly good. I feel as if I could begin to blossom in winter. So rich. So… so… decadent."

She took another sip and groaned ecstatically, running her tongue around her lips.

"Steady on! It's only cocoa." Edwin took another sip. It was good. Maria had laced it with cream the way Aunt Madeline used to make it after they'd been for a long winter walk, but she was acting as if it was the most pleasurable experience of her life.

"Is there more?" Drusilla asked, eying the Thermos.

Edwin poured her another cup and topped up his own. "You don't seem like you're going to pass away," he asked grinning.

"Oh, far from it," she said. She reached out a finger and stroked his cheek. "Edwin, you are now my absolute favourite acolyte."

"Well I'm very pleased to hear you say that," Edwin said. He had the impulse to put his hand to his cheek, which felt as if it were glowing red. He busied his hands reaching for the deck of cards. "Though you might not say that when I trounce you at gin."

He lost three games in a row.

"I thought you had never played," he grumbled good-naturedly as he tidied the pack away.

"I haven't, but I'm never going to lose a game sitting underneath my tree. Maybe next time you'll be luckier. If I let you be."

Edwin picked up the newspaper and Thermos flask and stood.

"May I borrow this until next week?" Drusilla asked, pointing to the newspaper. "I feel like there is so much of the world I don't know."

"Of course. I'll come again next week."

He shook hands with her, feeling that gesture at least was safe, and strolled along the ridge towards the path. Halfway to the gate, Drusilla called his name. He turned. Drusilla waved a hand regally.

"Edwin! Bring me more cocoa."

He walked off laughing to himself. She was amusing, if odd.

Chapter Seven

On Wednesday, Edwin visited Annie for afternoon tea. He ended up staying into the evening and had the nicest afternoon he could remember since arriving home. Annie's husband was warm and friendly and intelligent, the small house attached to the boarding house was welcoming, and the twins were lively. They danced around waving dishcloths and performing a sort of ballet with their hair freed from the tight plaits.

"They like to pretend to be Isadora Duncan, the dancer," Annie whispered. "They read about her in one of my magazines and now they are obsessed with her. They even begged for Grecian tunics when it was their birthday."

"Ah." As Edwin watched the girls, a chord was struck. Drusilla evoked the same elegance. Her affectations became suddenly clearer now. The rejection of formality and passion for Greek mythology was simply her embracing this vogue.

"I have a friend whom I think would like to see you dance," he said to the girls.

After a game of Ludo with the twins, Edwin regretfully announced his departure. As he did, his eye fell on a pile of women's periodicals stacked by the fire.

"Annie, may I take one of those?"

"Don't you have more masculine reading matter?" Annie asked with a laugh. "Or is this perhaps for ideas of new patterns for the scarves?"

"Neither. I have a friend who might enjoy looking at some – the one whom I think emulates Miss Duncan's style."

Annie smiled and raised her brows. She picked him out a few. "Then of course take as many as you like. I'm very pleased you've made friends already. Who is she?"

"Her name is Drusilla. She's quite unusual. Do you remember I told you years ago about a little girl I met in the sycamore tree? She's the same girl."

"Is she more than just a friend?" Annie asked. Her brow furrowed slightly. "What does your grandfather say about your friendship? Does he like her?"

Edwin rolled the magazines up, twisting them tighter than he intended. He gave Annie a slightly guilty look.

"He hasn't met her. I'm not sure he would approve though."

Annie put her hands on her hips, reminding Edwin of when she used to scold him as a child. "Perhaps you had better introduce them sooner rather than later so he doesn't have any reason to complain."

Edwin considered her words as he walked home. Annie was almost certainly correct that Stephen Brice would disapprove of his son's friendship, and that he should learn of it sooner rather than later. Edwin rather looked forward to dropping it into conversation, and then quite by chance the opportunity arose sooner than he expected.

Back at the house he found a letter from Harold waiting for him. Life in the seminary sounded fascinating and mind-numbingly dull at the same time, but the section which most caught Edwin's eye was the invitation to spend Christmas with the family in Yorkshire.

I'm sure you must be wonderfully busy with your new life, however Eleni and Joanna entreat me to invite you. They say charades won't be the same without your dreadful flailing and that no one sings Gilbert and Sullivan half as well as you. They would like to see your Major General in all its glory (I think they thought that was rude because they both laughed a lot more than they should have, silly things).

Best anyway, Har

Edwin laughed aloud, feeling a deep sense of homesickness. Yorkshire was home, not here. He broached the subject with his grandfather the following morning as they sat in the office at Greete Mill. William Wills had gone into the factory, leaving Edwin and Stephen to drink their morning coffee.

"I know we haven't spent Christmas together in over six years," he began. He stopped talking, wincing inwardly at the mention of the year Stephen had been persuaded to join the family in Yorkshire. His presence had been like a tombstone in the corner of every room he entered. He had refused to join in the games or the dancing, had scowled when asked to sing carols around the Victrola, and had declined the eggnog.

"He's Ebeneezer," Eleni had whispered once.

Edwin suspected everyone else was as glad as he was when his grandfather had left. Aunt Madeline had invited him the following year – mostly out of courtesy – but there was unspoken relief when he declined the offer.

"I've been invited back to Yorkshire for Christmas. I would like to spend a day or two there. The train timetables mean I'll be gone at least—"

Stephen cut him off.

"Go if you wish. In fact, why not see if your aunt will extend the invitation to New Year and the fortnight either side. It is of little consequence to me to be alone. I very rarely mark the day, beyond attending the morning and evening services. I am sure young people have their own ideas on how this season should be spent."

"Oh." Edwin sat down on the chair at the other side of Stephen's desk. He'd been anticipating needing to argue his case and to receive such a dismissal stung. He looked for evidence of disappointment in Stephen's face but his grandfather had turned back to the letter he was writing.

"Well, perhaps I should stay here and you and I can celebrate together. We could bring a little more jollity into the house."

Stephen replied without looking up. "I have no need of jollity. I shall visit your mother's grave, attend church, and pay my respects to various families in town. If you wish to join me in that plan, you may do so."

"Thank you," Edwin said. "In that case I think I shall accept

Aunt Madeline's invitation. If you'll excuse me, I'll go and reply now. I've finished writing the bills you asked me to prepare."

As he left, he muttered under his breath, "Perhaps we'll do a reading of *A Christmas Carol* this year."

"Edwin!"

Stephen's voice was sharp and Edwin cringed, thinking he'd been overheard. He turned back.

"You dined with the Carfaxes last Saturday, I believe."

The change of subject took Edwin by surprise. "Yes, I did."

"Good. Do you have any other social engagements planned?"

"Not really. Robert suggested we might go fishing when the weather is better but that will not be until spring, I imagine."

Stephen pulled a disapproving face. "I would have expected you to enter into society a little more by now. You've been here for almost nine weeks and haven't attended any of the clubs I suggested or made the acquaintance of any of the families I listed for you."

"As a matter of fact, I have made an acquaintance," Edwin said.

"Oh?"

Edwin walked to the window and looked out over the yard, unable to conceal his smile at the interest in Stephen's voice.

"Yes," he said, his back to the room, "I think she's someone from the town, or perhaps the village out past the meadows. She's quite eccentric. Models herself on Isadora Duncan, the dancer, I think. Embraces the natural world."

He walked back to the desk and picked up his coffee cup.

Stephen was smiling too, though there was a nasty curl to his lip that suggested a guard dog about to reveal its teeth.

"Ah, my dear boy, you're completely infatuated. Is she a prostitute?"

If Edwin had been drinking his coffee at the time, he would have choked on his mouthful. He gripped his cup tightly by the handle and flushed, feeling heat spreading across his face and up into his hairline.

"What? No, of course she isn't."

He heard a slight waver in his voice and tried to think back over the conversations he'd had with Drusilla. There had been a great deal of suggestive talk but she'd never tried to coerce him or suggest terms or money. No, he was certain that she was nothing of the sort. He coughed to clear his throat.

"What a dreadful allegation to make. Of both of us."

"You're a young man. It's natural to have those urges. Get it out of your system before you settle down and marry a respectable woman from a good family. I have a few in mind." Stephen pushed his glasses up his nose. "Good families, I mean, not ladies of ill repute."

"I told you she isn't!" Edwin snapped.

"Then I expect she's hoping for charity at best or a husband at worst. Neither of which she will procure through friendship with you. It's too late to arrange anything over the Christmas period with less than a month to go, but when you return I believe I will throw a party and invite some of the better families."

He fixed Edwin with a steely look.

"Your dubious friend is expressly *not* to be invited, in case you were wondering. Now, you were going to reply to your aunt, weren't you? Do give my regards to her new husband."

He turned his head away and picked up a fresh sheet of notepaper. His cold dismissal burned Edwin's breast. He'd liked the idea of his friendship with Drusilla being irksome to his grandfather, but now it made his stomach curdle to think of the accusations that had been levelled at her.

"Why did you want me here?" he asked. "You don't like me. You don't really have anything useful for me to do in the factory. If the best you can say is that I might one day marry into a rich family then it's a poor reason."

Stephen looked at him, unblinking. "You are my grandson. This is where you belong. One day this factory will be yours. When your father married your mother, he took over the responsibility for it. I govern it in her memory. I expect you to do likewise when the time comes for you to inherit."

Stephen stood and walked around the desk. He placed his hands on Edwin's shoulders. Edwin flinched at the unfamiliar interaction and Stephen's fingers tightened slightly.

"You will be the owner of this establishment one day. The third generation to do so. You'll be wealthy and responsible for the wealth and welfare of your employees. It's time you stopped behaving like a sulking child."

Stephen released his grip. His face twisted into a bitter smile.

"Even if you cannot bring yourself to do it for my sake, do it for your mother's memory."

Edwin hung his head as a lump filled his throat. He had so little memory of his mother that it was almost impossible to imagine doing anything in her name, but it was the first thing his grandfather had said that had genuinely moved him.

"I'll try."

He walked out of the office and returned to the house to write his acceptance letter. He felt no guilt about leaving for the season, but as he made the short journey back to Greete Mill House he realised there was someone he was going to miss.

The day of his return to Yorkshire came quickly. Edwin visited Annie, leaving gifts for the twins and a tin of shortbread for husband and wife. He did likewise with William Wills and his family. He even left a wrapped gift of a book for his grandfather in the centre of the dining table.

There was one more present he wanted to give. The day before he was due to leave, he visited the sycamore tree. Drusilla was dressed in her faded cloak. Her face was thin and there were light-grey smudges beneath her eyes. The green in her irises looked dull and rimmed with red. Her hair was parted in the centre and lacked the lustre with which Edwin was familiar. The only brightness came from Edwin's scarf which she wore. He froze, temporarily paralysed by shock at the change in her.

"Are you ill?" he asked, stepping towards her and reaching a hand to her shoulder.

"Just tired," she said, her voice little more than a whisper. "This time of year takes its toll. I feel better for seeing you though."

"I came to tell you that I'm going back to Yorkshire for the Christmas season. I'll be there for New Year and a couple of weeks afterwards. It doesn't feel right not going, especially as my cousin, Harold, will only be there for a short while this year." He shuffled his feet, scuffing up leaf mould. Drusilla had no parents and, as far as he was aware, no welcoming aunt or cousins. "I don't like to think of you being alone if you're unwell. Is there anyone I can ask to help you?"

"There's no one."

If she'd sounded plaintive or self-pitying Edwin would have been happier, but her tone was matter-of-fact. Her life was apparently solitary and she accepted that. A little of Edwin's excitement at leaving for Yorkshire ebbed.

"I could try to delay leaving for a few more days."

She smiled, but it was a ghost of what it usually was. "That's very sweet of you, but no, please don't do that. I shall spend my time resting and thinking. Usually I would have been asleep by now anyway. Winter always tires me out. There's not enough sunlight and everything is cold and lonely. Spending time in your company has been invigorating but I'm ready to rest for a while."

As if to illustrate her words, Drusilla yawned, covering her mouth with a pale hand. She took it away and waved it, reminding Edwin of snowflakes flurrying down or leaves swirling in the wind.

"Come and see me in the spring, when the days are starting to get longer again. Come back to me on the first new moon after the snowdrops appear and the land is not so hard and unwelcoming."

It was an odd way of setting a date but Edwin happily

agreed; the thought of tramping across the field in January or February blizzards to stand shivering beneath a tree didn't appeal. He resolved to persuade Drusilla to come and visit him in the house.

He remembered the reason for his visit and reached into his coat pocket.

"I brought you a gift."

He held out the small box wrapped in red and green paper with silver ribbons tying the lid.

"It's beautiful," Drusilla said. "Thank you. But what should I give you in return?"

"Nothing. That's the thing about gifts. They aren't in exchange for anything nor do they come with conditions."

"That doesn't sound right. Everything has a condition."

"No, it doesn't," Edwin said. He wrinkled his brow in thought. "But if it helps, you can think of it as thanks for making these last couple of months bearable. I think if I had been alone here with Grandfather as my only company I would have ended up in an asylum or prison. I couldn't say which for certain. I'm sure I would have returned to Yorkshire and planned to stay there, but knowing I have a friend makes returning bearable."

She smiled more warmly and gave a rippling laugh. "Then I thank you and I accept your gift."

"You can open it now," Edwin prompted. "You don't have to wait until Christmas Day."

"There's something inside it?" Drusilla asked, her eyes widening.

"Of course," Edwin said. "I mean, the paper is pretty and I

suppose you could put the ribbon in your hair but a box isn't much of a gift."

Drusilla tugged the end of the ribbon loose and unwound it. She opened the lid and rummaged in the tissue paper.

"Sugared almonds and chocolate-covered hazelnuts," Edwin said. "I guessed you have a sweet tooth from how much you liked the cocoa."

"Oh, I do." Drusilla beamed at him. "Thank you, Edwin, my darling. It's the nicest thing anyone has given me." She delved into the box and pulled out a pale-yellow sugared almond. She put it in her mouth and sighed with delight as she tasted it.

As she sucked, her lips became a rosebud and Edwin couldn't take his eyes off her mouth. If he kissed her, would she taste of sugared almonds too?

The wind began to blow and the branches stirred, giving a low whistling like a growling dog.

Drusilla stiffened. "It's going to snow soon. You should go."

"Can you smell it?" Edwin asked. Snow-laden air had an unmistakeable scent to it but he couldn't smell it.

"Can't you?" Drusilla inhaled again. "The air smells cold and sharp. It tastes grey."

Edwin sniffed.

"Not like that," Drusilla said. "From here and breathe slowly."

She put a hand to his sternum, pushing gently into the soft spot beneath his ribcage. She inhaled deeply and he did the same, closing his eyes and drawing in air to the bottom of his lungs. His heart was throbbing and her palm was a hot brand in his centre, but his mind filled with a hundred thousand swirling snowflakes and on his tongue was the unmistakable taste of snowfall.

He shuddered and put his hand up to where hers still rested on his chest and covered it. He had the strongest urge to slide his hands beneath her cloak and pull her to him in a kiss. He wanted her in his arms, her warm body held against him. He shifted uneasily, aware of blood rushing through him to parts of his body out of his control. He stepped back clumsily, appalled at the thought of her becoming aware of how aroused he was.

"I have to go. Merry Christmas for when the time comes, Drusilla, and Happy New Year also."

She nodded and looked into his eyes. He stared into the green pools, only half noticing that they seemed brighter than when he had arrived. "What year will it be when the change comes?"

"1914," he answered.

"Ah." Drusilla looked upwards then back at him. "May it be a good one. The blessings of the midwinter on you too, Edwin. May your days be filled with light and love and all things rich and warm."

He stepped away, then had a last-minute change of mind. He moved closer then stopped again, caught in indecision. Drusilla pursed her lips and licked them.

"I have a gift for you, Edwin."

She stepped forward and lifted onto her tiptoes and kissed him softly on the lips.

He was right; she did taste of sugared almonds. He wanted to kiss her properly, to swallow her whole and draw her into his very being.

"Not now, Sapling," she murmured, her lips still brushing against the corner of his mouth as she spoke. "Spring is a time for beginnings, not winter."

He wanted to argue but she stepped away and put both her hands against his chest, pushing him gently. Edwin inclined his head and stepped back.

"Of course."

He turned and walked out of the grove, the wind swiping at his legs and neck. It was bleak, and as he reached the garden he wasn't surprised to feel the first icy shards of sleet beginning to fall.

Drusilla lay back in the branches, soothed by the gusts of wind that caused them to rise and fall. The swaying was violent but she had no fear of falling. The days since the Sapling – Edwin – had left had all been cold, drenched in sleet that did not settle, but tonight was different.

She inhaled, tasting the sharp, sour scent of snow that was edging closer and which would settle. The darkest days of winter were approaching fast but her roots were deep and her branches well formed. Lesser plants and younger trees would be feeling the impending seasonal death more than she would. With the strength she gained from the Sapling's attention she would be even more resilient, and for the first time she looked forward to the months of famine with no trepidation.

Bells rang out from the churches all over town, the peals reverberating across the sky. Christmas Eve. On nights such as this the stars were visible in the clear blackness. No clouds provided shelter from the endless unforgiving universe that spun away and the moon was only a sliver of fingernail.

The stories that the world celebrated on this night meant nothing to her but she could taste the belief that filled the air. Some sweet and loving, some with a fiery certainty that was unnerving. Ah, to have that worship laid at her feet. What could she do if it was hers? How mighty would her tree become with such fidelity? Still, she had Edwin's devotion, even if he did not truly believe what she told him. No matter. His attention was sustaining enough.

She stretched out her limbs, feeling the icy breath of the world buffeting her. If he didn't return...

For a brief moment fear struck her.

She'd diminish again. A small thing, waiting for the next acolyte to discover her. How long could she wait now that she'd grown used to his regular visits, each one giving her a little more strength? She was becoming greedy.

Her centre pulsed. A throb slow enough that only the tree would be aware of it.

Edwin would return. A little older and a little readier for her. Of all the human lovers she'd had, he was the one she wanted most. He was sweet and untouched by cynicism. She reached her hand down into the box and put an almond in her mouth, letting the sugar melt and trickle down her throat. There were eight left, and three of the chocolate cobnuts.

A genuine gift, like the scarf. She'd always bargained her favours but the Sapling had asked nothing in return, and she found it frustrating and unsettling. She wanted – more than she expected –to make him happy, not only to settle the balance but to see his smile. There must be something she could give him but she was at a loss to discover it.

She sighed. Time to rest and let the confusing emotions surrounding Edwin remain dormant for the while.

She took a last look at the stars clustering above, closed her eyes, and let the warmth of her tree claim her as she sank back into its arms.

Chapter Eight

The festive season in Yorkshire was as loving and riotous as Edwin remembered. The house was open for anyone who happened to drop by unannounced and Edwin found himself occasionally longing for the more sedate surroundings of Greete Mill House. By New Year's Eve he was quite exhausted by the relentless company. The house appeared to contain every neighbour within a half hour walk for the final party of the year. When Edwin's head began to buzz from his third gin buck, he slipped off to the library and found a quiet corner.

Harold, Eleni, and Demetria discovered him within twenty minutes.

"You old man, what are you doing here?" Eleni exclaimed, flopping onto the sofa beside him. She smelled of marigold scent and vermouth and carried four Champagne flutes. "What are you reading?"

Edwin showed her the book. "Greek myths and legends. I knew Uncle Jonty had something lying around."

"Daphne and Apollo." Harold peered upside down at the volume. "He pursued her and she was turned into a tree, wasn't she?"

"It seems to me to be a high price to pay for not being raped, and a little unfair on the girl to be changed," Demetria remarked, frowning and slicking back her short bob. She sat on the arm of the sofa and lit a cigarette. "I hope she at least had the sense to trip him over with a root."

Edwin snorted.

"It's an allegory of the triumph of love over lust," Harold said, giving Demetria a look of mild reproof. "Her physical transformation led to his moral one, and it was love that spurred him to immortalise her. Now, it's nearly midnight so let's stay here and drink this. I lifted it from the table without Mama or Panos spotting me."

He brandished a bottle of Champagne. Eleni waved four glasses and giggled. Edwin closed the book, wishing he'd not been interrupted. He wondered what Drusilla would make of the story. The book had a photo plate of Bernini's statue of the couple, but in his head Daphne's face blurred with Drusilla's. He hoped she was feeling better than when he had last seen her.

"Demi is right. It seems rough on the woman that she has to be the one transformed. There was Myrra who suffered the same fate. Do you think other trees might have been women too?" he asked.

"I doubt it. None of them are true stories, in any case." Harold shrugged. "Now, Edwin, by August I'll have some time free from my studies. I intend to come and visit you and see how dreadfully grim your grandfather has become. We could even make a party of it and I'll see if the hoydens are free."

He nodded to his stepsisters who laughed gleefully and declared that yes, they must see Cheshire.

"Though I shall probably be married by then if Simon Dow actually gets round to asking me," Demetria said. She pouted. "I've dropped enough hints. Perhaps I'm destined to be an old maid."

"You? Never," Edwin said gallantly, slightly relieved that she appeared to have found someone.

"Well, I don't intend to marry at all," Eleni announced. "I intend to retain glorious spinsterhood and share a house with my friend Marianne. Her brother is the doctor in Dellvale and we intend to look after him and keep chickens and breed terriers. Or perhaps I shall run away to Ithaca and become an artist."

"I've seen your attempts at painting," Harold said, nudging her in the ribs.

"You don't have a young lady yet, do you?" Eleni asked, once she had finished laughing.

She stared at Edwin intensely and he felt his cheeks reddening, thinking of the times he had spent with Drusilla. He licked his lips and tasted the memory of sugared almonds.

"Be fair; he's only been in Cheshire for a few months," Harold laughed.

"Ah well, too bad for you, Edwin," Eleni said, leaning against him. He unobtrusively took the glasses from her hand and passed them to Demetria. She must be sixteen now but still shouldn't be drinking too much.

"Isn't there anyone that you have met?" Demetria asked.

Edwin shook his head and hoped it was enough to disguise a flutter in his belly. The flutter that came whenever he thought of Drusilla and their brief kiss on the lips.

"Actually, I do have a friend, but she's certainly not the sort of woman with whom my grandfather would like me to associate."

"And I bet that's half the appeal," Harold guffawed, waggling his eyebrows.

"Well…" Edwin stood and walked to the bookshelf, using the act of reshelving the book to buy him a bit of thinking time. "I'd be lying if I said no, but she's rather intriguing. She's eccentric to say the least."

"But pretty?" Eleni asked.

Edwin couldn't help but smile. "Yes. She's pretty."

"And is Robert still in town and as awful as he always was?" Harold asked.

"Yes and no. I dined with him once and it was a passable way to spend the evening. He's still boorish but I suppose he has grown up too. It was good to get out of the house, if I'm being honest. Grandfather can be…" Edwin sighed, struggling for a word that was tactful enough. Being away from the house and the mill was quite illuminating. "I'll go with 'taciturn'. I don't know. I spend my days doing enough work to keep me busy but I feel like a junior clerk and it isn't exactly taxing. I think the factory is doing well. We certainly employ plenty of staff and Grandfather can obviously afford to keep William to work in the office as well as employing me, but I feel we could be doing more. New designs – more interesting ones; less traditional, I could say. New items even."

He began to pace around the room as his enthusiasm began to grow.

"We buy in the silk cloth and print it ourselves, so what's to stop us making new things and exploring the latest fashions? Eventually, every stately banker or lawyer in the northwest must have sufficient neckties and cravats to last. What about people our age?"

"Well, it's good to see you have ambitions anyway," Harold said.

The clock in the hallway started to chime.

"It's New Year!" Eleni exclaimed.

From the direction of the village the church bells rang out; from closer by came a series of gunshots, followed by the frenzied barking of hounds.

"Old Colonel Davison isn't breaking with his traditional salute, I see," Edwin grinned.

"No, some things never change."

Harold popped the cork from the bottle of Champagne. The four filled and raised their glasses to toast.

"Happy New Year!"

Edwin wrinkled his brow trying to remember what Drusilla had wished him. It sounded quite old-fashioned. Something out of an Arthurian story. He tipped his glass back and let the sharp fizz of Champagne slide down his throat.

"I feel quite renewed," he said, holding out his glass for a refill. "I've been a bit of a resentful ass, I imagine. When I go back I'll have to speak seriously to Grandfather. If he wants me to work for him, he'll have to let me work with him."

"Cheers to that," Harold cried. "Let's see what changes 1914 brings. May the new year be good to us all!"

March 1914

The new year brought heavier snowfall than usual, with drifts a good foot or two deep. It was two weeks into March before relentless rains washed them away. It was the last Thursday of the month before there was a new moon and Edwin had seen the first glimpse of snowdrops tentatively edging their way into the light.

It was time to visit Drusilla.

He estimated he had an hour between leaving the factory and dinner being served so rather than wait until afterwards when dusk would have snatched away what little heat there was, he set out. The ground was boggy after three days of rain but this time Edwin was prepared and wore gumboots and a raincoat. He whistled as he picked his way through the mud. Over his shoulder he carried a canvas bag.

He saw her waiting before he reached the grove. She left the shelter of the tree and began to run towards him. He increased his pace and they met where the gentle hill began to level. Drusilla flung herself into his arms then pulled back, took him by both hands, and looked at him from a distance.

"Edwin! You came back!" She spun around, drawing him into a wide circle.

"You look well, Drusilla," Edwin said. The last time he'd seen her she had been so pale and lifeless-looking. Now she was rosy-cheeked and her hair was glossy, and when she tossed her head the locks that tumbled down her back appeared to defy gravity, drifting for longer than was natural before settling.

"I am well. It's spring. The world is waking up. Are you happy to see me?"

"Of course I am. I missed you while I was away."

"Ah, that feels good to hear."

She let go of his hands and danced away down the hill and back up again. She was wearing an odd garment resembling an artist's smock in light-green silk that fell to mid-calf. Visible beneath that was a cream skirt dotted with pale yellow clusters of blossoms. It rippled as she moved. Edwin couldn't tear his eyes away from her. She ran back to him and took him by the arms.

"I knew you would come today! The snowdrops have appeared and you remembered the new moon. Oh, I feel alive!"

She gave a squeal of delight and tossed her head back, laughing into the sky. Her humour was infectious and Edwin tipped his head back too. They both gazed upwards. The sky was cloudy but patchy blue streaks appeared between the grey. The sunlight was thin and the air was cold, but in another hour or so it would set and the sliver of moon would appear.

They looked back at each other, eyes meeting. Both stopped grinning at the same time. Something shifted. Edwin stepped a little closer and put his hand to Drusilla's cheek. It was warm and soft. She leaned into his palm, a dreamy expression on her face.

"My Sapling," she murmured.

"I did miss you," Edwin repeated. He leaned in and kissed her cheek. He caught the scent she was wearing – fresh and floral, reminding him of freshly cut grass and blossoms. He might have kissed her again but before he had the chance Drusilla danced out of his reach.

"What is in your bag? Did you bring me more sugared almonds?" Drusilla asked. "Come and show me."

She raced to the tree but, seeing he hadn't followed, rushed back to Edwin.

"No, there aren't any sugared almonds. Wait a little and I'll show you."

She stood there, bobbing from foot to foot restlessly and twisting her torso around.

"Steady on! You're very giddy," Edwin said, laughing, as he stopped her trying to tug the bag from his shoulder.

"I'm sorry. It's the time of year. I always feel most playful when spring arrives," Drusilla said with a deep sigh. She tossed her head back. "Don't you feel it too?"

Edwin took her hand. He was starting to feel more playful with every passing minute in her presence. If he didn't know better, he would say her enthusiasm was as contagious as influenza.

"Let's sit down and we can tell each other what we've been doing. Do you think the picnic blanket is still in the hollow? The ground isn't dry enough yet."

He put the bag down and pulled out a game of Mikado and a greaseproof paper parcel containing two slices of buttered fruit cake. When he looked up, Drusilla was standing in front of him with the blue and green tartan blanket.

"You found it. Well done. It looks as good as new. I was worried the insects or some animal or other might have eaten it."

Drusilla waved her arms in the air to unfurl the blanket then laid it on the grass, half under the spreading boughs of the tree. She dropped gracefully onto it and reclined.

"Come sit by me and tell me what adventures you have had. Was the winter kind to you? What else do you have in your bag?"

Edwin dropped down beside her. He took his final item out of his bag and showed it to her.

"Cherry cordial. I mixed it with water so it's ready to drink."

Drusilla pulled the bottle from his hand and uncorked it. "Delicious!" she exclaimed after taking a swig. "Now, tell me everything. Where have you been? Who have you met? Have you discovered your purpose in life?"

"Sadly not," Edwin replied. "Well, where to begin? I think I told you that I had previously lived in Yorkshire with my cousins. Harold is in the process of training to be ordained so he only had a brief visit home. I'm almost envious of his vocation."

"A man of God? Well, you are a man of a goddess. That's much better."

Drusilla shrugged and stretched out her legs, flexing and curling her feet. They were bare once again, now the weather was becoming warmer. Her skirts had rucked up slightly when she sat down, revealing shapely calves. The pale hair that covered them was almost imperceptible, giving the impression of smoothness. He wanted to run his fingers over them, imagining the contrast with the thick hair on his own.

"Anyway," Edwin said, tearing his eyes from her legs. "Harold and his stepsisters were very interested when I told them about you. They'd like to meet you. They are hoping to come in the summer. Of course, I'll have to ask Grandfather's permission for them to stay at the house." He frowned and sat forward, resting his hands on his knees and staring down the hill at the house.

"It might be better to put them up at the Station Hotel but I'd like to plan a couple of croquet parties and picnics here at the very least. I'm not sure what he'll think of that but I dare say if he wants me to have friends, he will put up with it."

"You don't like him very much, do you," Drusilla murmured. She knelt up at his side and tilted her head, peering intently at his face. Again, he caught the scent of blossoms and something unidentifiable that he could only describe as freshness.

"I don't know him." Edwin twiddled his fingers. Her presence so close was a little unsettling, waking his senses in a manner he found too distracting. "He doesn't appear to like me, more to the point."

He took a sip of the cherry cordial and gave Drusilla a slight smile.

"That's what I really want, of course. I'd like to know what exactly he holds against me because I am at a loss to know. Can you do that for me?"

Drusilla dropped her head, letting her hair cover her expression. She had grown more still since they had been sitting together, he realised. She sat back and pushed her hair behind her ears, giving him a thoughtful look.

"If he came to me I might be able to discover it. He has no wife and I'm sure I could charm him into my confidence, but I don't think you would like that to happen."

Edwin coughed, halfway through a mouthful of drink. She couldn't really be suggesting seducing his grandfather? The man was ancient!

"No I damned well wouldn't! No man would."

Drusilla burst out laughing. "Don't worry – I'm not going to do it. I am very selective in those with whom I choose to associate. I'll be honoured to meet your friends though."

"Good. In that case I'll write to Harold and suggest they all come at the start of August. Now, do you know how to play Mikado?"

Drusilla looked at the bundle of thin wooden sticks Edwin held out. She looked at him, eyes gleaming.

"I don't, but if you think you can win a game involving wood while we're sitting this close to my tree then you'll be very sadly disappointed."

She was correct and beat him hands down. They ate the slices of cake and finished the cherry syrup.

"I'm very pleased you came back to me," Drusilla said as she gathered the sticks. She held them out to him. "We'll play again."

"Next time we meet I want you to come to the summer house," Edwin said.

"Not yet, but one day, I promise. The time needs to be right. It will be."

Chapter Nine

Edwin had returned home to discover that his grandfather seemed to have decided to make more of an effort to get to know his grandson. He invited Edwin to join him in the sitting room after dinner rather than retreating into his office. They would chat about what was in the newspaper or the weather – nothing personal or deep, but Edwin appreciated the effort.

"It's reasonable to say neither of us made much of an effort to reacquaint ourselves," Stephen said over dinner. "I'm going to introduce you properly to the families I know and we're going to work together on giving you a more prominent face in society."

He leaned over the table and poured Edwin a glass of Madeira, a wide smile on his face, and waited until Edwin picked it up.

"To that end, I've secured you an invitation to join the May Hunt a week next Saturday. It's the final one of the season, and by all accounts the Hunt Ball afterwards is magnificent. I'll join you there. I've never been on a horse in my life and don't intend to start at my age."

Edwin's stomach curdled as the distant memory of baying hounds and the scent of blood and innards assaulted him. He put the wine down. "That's very good of you, but no thank you."

Stephen frowned. His left eyelid twitched and there was a pained look on his face. "I think you have misunderstood me. You don't get to decline. It isn't a matter of choice. I have secured the invitation at some trouble, so you will attend. You learned to ride in Yorkshire I know."

He spoke officiously, with no notion that he might be opposed. He picked up his dessert fork and began to tackle his apricot fritters. Edwin's heart pounded as he anticipated the argument his words would no doubt provoke. He pressed his fingernails into the palms of his hands.

"I hate the hunt. I only went once and that was enough for me. It's barbaric. I'm not going to take part in it, whatever you say."

Stephen laid his dessert fork on the dish.

"Are you refusing?"

"Yes. I'm terrible at riding and I have n-no interest in watching a poor creature be torn apart, even if it does keep the chickens safe." He struggled to keep his voice steady.

Stephen stood. He raised both hands and then slapped them down on the table, leaning over it towards Edwin. His shoulders were hunched and his face growing red.

"Don't you understand, I'm trying to get you into decent society! It's an uphill struggle. I feel like Sisyphus pushing the stone constantly upwards and just when I get to the top it rolls back." He slapped his hand again. "You are that stone. We have a degree of respectability in this town, but not enough."

"What exactly do you want?" Edwin asked in frustration. He tempered his voice, remembering he had resolved to find common ground with the old man. "We're doing well; the factory is profitable; we're well spoken of. What could my joining a hunt do for us?"

Stephen looked at him pityingly, transporting him back to the schoolroom where a patient teacher had tried to hide his frustration at Edwin's lack of ability to memorise the monarchs of Britain.

"Mill owners can become mayors or aldermen. Can even become Members of Parliament. Could get knighted. Why can't I aim for that? Why shouldn't you? Don't you have any ambition? The factory is profitable but small. Wouldn't you like to see the fields behind the house developed into a second factory? A larger house? Wouldn't you like a wife with a title?"

Edwin blinked. Aside from the issue of a wife, the idea of covering the fields with buildings was horrendous. Blocking the view of the hills and casting shadows over the gardens was unthinkable. He covered his unease with a laugh.

"Good grief, Grandfather. Finding me a titled wife, for goodness' sake. You sound like something out of an Austen novel!"

Stephen didn't appear to find it amusing. "If I had a granddaughter, this would have been so much easier."

"Well I'm sorry you don't," Edwin snapped, rising from his chair.

Stephen lifted his head and Edwin took a step back

involuntarily. He'd never seen the bleak expression that filled his grandfather's eyes. It was like looking into an Egyptian death mask.

"I wish to God every day that I still had a daughter," he said.

Every word was enunciated clearly; spears of ice aimed directly at Edwin's heart. They struck home with terrible accuracy. Stephen walked to the door and looked back over his shoulder.

"You will attend the hunt. I don't care if you fall at the first fence or if you trot along at the back with the old biddies and the lame dogs. You will go, you will wear your red, and then you will attend the ball. Take your cue from Robert Carfax. He has half your brains, by all accounts, but he knows how to behave as a gentleman would."

Edwin slumped back in his chair. The idea of the hunt revolted him but the hurt inflicted on him by Stephen's bitter words refused to ebb.

He arranged to meet Robert in the Cairfax Arms pub the following evening. Though the name was slightly different, it was a reminder that the Carfax family had a lineage going back four or five hundred years. They sat in the corner, nursing pints of bitter.

"Grandfather is insisting I attend the May Hunt," Edwin explained.

Robert looked unimpressed. "Yes, I know. He called in a favour with Pa to get you invited. Don't tell me you're scared? What is it that bothers you, Hopeless? Being blooded?"

"Don't call me that. And I don't need to be blooded."

Edwin grimaced both at the nickname and at the memory of a warm smear of scarlet on his cheeks and the livery smell of fox blood making him retch. The taste of bile filled his throat. "That happened when I was fifteen."

"Well lucky you," Robert said.

"Lucky?"

Robert swigged his pint. "It was a stroke of luck your aunt taking you in. You got to go to a decent school, mingle with the landed gentry, learn how to fit in, and you're still an ungrateful whiny little child, aren't you. Look at this place." He waved an arm around.

"Carfaxes or Cairfaxes have lived in this patch of the world for centuries. We used to have proper money and land further than the eye could see, but some bloody ancestor or other backed the wrong horse or threw a bad die and now we must actually eke out a living."

"I'm not sure I understand your point," Edwin said.

Robert drained his glass and put it down. "My point is that I have the money to do what I want, but compared to the family ghosts it's a pittance. 'Oh, Old Carfax, yes, his ancestors used to be aristos, didn't they, but now they have to work in the law to make ends meet.'" Robert made his voice high and drawly. Edwin assumed the slight slurring was incidental. "So do you, but doors will still be shut to you because you had the audacity to earn it. What makes us any less worthy than someone else simply because they have a title?"

He drained the dregs of his pint, put the glass back on the table and looked at Edwin meaningfully. "Father is making me a partner in the firm. It'll be Carfax and Carfax Solicitors before

I'm thirty, I promise you. I plan to be a magistrate one day and I intend to marry a rich, ugly, sensible girl. No reason I can't aspire to be MP eventually. We owe it to our ancestors. We owe it to the children we'll have."

Edwin finished his pint. There had been some eloquence among the rant.

"You're right of course. I have to say that grudgingly, mind. But that doesn't mean I want to chase all over the countryside to do it. I'm hardly likely to meet the love of my life galloping across farmland."

Robert gave a leering grin. "Well, the ball afterwards will be worth it. Plenty of young blood. The women love it you know, the sweat and blood. They can smell it. It taps right into their primal need."

"Does it?"

Robert rolled his eyes. "Oh come on now, Edwin. Don't tell me you're one of those bloodless abominations? I don't mind if you are of course. I've known plenty in my time – all fine chaps. But you'll still have to marry someone. Keep your bloodline going and all that. If you weren't such a poor specimen, I might even officially introduce you to one of my sisters."

"I remember your sisters," Edwin said, "and I thank you for your generous offer, as much as it is. Look, I have plenty of women friends. And as far as I know none of them have ever been aroused by the scent of fox blood or sweat. But yes, I'll come on the bloody hunt and go to the damned ball, if only to shut Grandfather up."

He went to the bar and ordered two more pints. "This is

good beer, you know. Maybe this is the business to get into instead."

"Now that's a venture I could gladly back." Robert said.

They clinked glasses and drank.

❧

"Have you ever tried beer?"

Drusilla wrinkled her nose and looked at the bottle that Edwin held out. "No, I've never tried beer. I've never tried anything really, but if it's as nice as sugared almonds and cherry syrup then I am sure I will like it."

They were sitting on the picnic rug outside the grove at the spot where the mound began to flatten. Each time Edwin visited, Drusilla seemed happier to venture a little closer to the house. One day he hoped she would join him in the summer house or at the table on the terrace. Stanley, the old horse, had walked over to investigate them before turning his attention back to the grass and weeds that were becoming lush and succulent. Mr Sykes was working on something at the bottom of the field close to the wall of the formal garden. Occasionally he would stop and stare upwards. Edwin waved once or twice but received no acknowledgement.

Edwin opened the bottle then realised he'd neglected to bring any glasses. "We'll have to drink straight from the bottle," he said, holding it out to her.

Drusilla took a sip and immediately began coughing. She held the bottle out at arm's length. "Take it," she gasped. "It's horrible."

She was still coughing so Edwin patted her on the back. I'm sorry. It's fizzy."

"But I wasn't expecting that," Drusilla said as Edwin took a swig.

"Tasty though," he said. "One day I'll bring you some Champagne and then you can try something really fizzy."

Drusilla lay back on the grass. She flopped her arms out to the side.

"I feel quite light, as if I could float up to the sky. Let me try it again." She reached out her arm, waving it about until her fingers brushed Edwin's forearm. She took the bottle from his hand and sat up enough to tilt the bottle into her mouth. She sipped cautiously.

"That's better. This time I was expecting the bubbles so they didn't take me by surprise." She sat up again and passed the bottle back to Edwin. "It's a Thursday afternoon. You don't normally come to see me at this time. Something's troubling you, isn't it."

"A little, I suppose," Edwin answered. His stomach churned as it had every day since his grandfather had told him about the hunt. The day had almost arrived. His old riding boots, red jacket, and jodhpurs had arrived from Yorkshire in a box reeking of mothballs and were currently being aired to rid them of the smell.

"I wanted some company and a friendly face. To be honest I'm feeling a little glum. My grandfather has gone to a meeting with some of the guildsmen of the town so I'm free."

He huffed, remembering Stephen's scathing response when Edwin suggested he accompany him.

You know nothing about the business. I'd rather take William

Wills, only the darkness of his complexion will prevent him being taken seriously.

Stephen might be unjust to his grandson, but he was fair to all men, regardless of their race.

Drusilla patted his shoulder. "Why are you glum? Tell me about it."

Edwin took a drink of beer. It was cool and refreshing on what had turned out to be a hot day. The weather looked set to be fine for the weekend of the hunt; he'd rather hoped it would be called off because of unseasonable snow. He took another drink and wiped his hand across his brow before answering.

"My grandfather wants me to go on the last hunt of the season. It's two days away."

"You refused, of course," Drusilla said.

Edwin stared at the ground in front of him. "I hoped to. I tried to, but he was adamant. It's important to him."

"So you are going to attend?" Drusilla's eyes grew wide with shock. They glinted darkly. "But think about those poor animals who will get hounded in terror, not even considering the damage that will be done to the countryside. Edwin, you mustn't be part of such destruction and death."

"That's what nature is, isn't it," Edwin muttered uneasily. "I mean, the foxes have to eat but there is wild prey. The farmers have a right to protect their livestock from the foxes."

"Which is why they do it in such a dramatic fashion, I suppose," Drusilla sneered. "No, it's horrible. The earth feels the pain. I'd never let such barbarism happen here. Edwin, I can't believe you agreed to do it!"

She shifted on the blanket, scuffing the edge with her bare feet.

"Why not?" Edwin asked. "I have other commitments. My grandfather says it's important to develop friendships in the community. I am a big enough disappointment to him as it is. Don't you understand he expects me to play a part? I've already told you that."

Drusilla's eyes flashed, her brows arching before plunging together in a frown. "Yes, but you didn't tell me it involved torturing living creatures," she said. She drew her knees up to her chest and hugged them tightly. "I thought you were talking about tea parties and dinners. We were going to play croquet with your friends in the summer."

"We'll do those things too." Edwin faced her. He tried to reach for her hands but she slipped them behind her knees. "Look, you must understand, grandfather wants to sell or develop some of the land and these fields will be gone. How would you feel if all this became houses or more factories? Do you want your tree to be in a small square in the middle of some streets? Because that's what could happen."

"Are you threatening me?" Drusilla's face whitened.

"No!" Edwin reached for her hand but she pulled away. "I don't want it to happen. If I can find other ways to make money for the business then he might not be so keen to do it. The least I can do is try to build connections."

Drusilla stood and took hold of her skirts, shaking them out. "Go to your hunt then, but maybe I won't be here the next time you come calling for me. I might have better things to do. Better company to keep."

"Really?" Edwin snorted. "Which company is that? The old gardener?"

The question that had been on his mind for months spurted

from his lips. "And where will you be? Where do you go when you aren't here? Do you have a house or a job? How do you support yourself? Are you a kept woman? How many others pay court to you here?"

"None." Her mouth twisted down. "I knew you didn't believe." She raised her head and curled her lip. "Perhaps you shouldn't come anymore."

"Perhaps I shouldn't." Edwin folded his arms across his chest.

"Perhaps I should go now." Drusilla folded her arms too, mirroring him.

Edwin swept up the deck of cards and mashed them together.

"I'll go. Goodbye, Drusilla, or whatever your name really is."

He stomped away from the grove, head bent. When he reached the edge of the croquet lawn he turned, hoping she would be watching but unsurprised when she wasn't. He walked across the lawn and up the steps between the fishpond, trying not to stare back.

He rounded the corner of the house and almost collided with Sykes who was carrying a rake over his shoulders. They did an ungainly dance of avoidance.

"You look troubled, young Mister Hope," Sykes remarked.

Edwin's jaw tightened. He didn't feel inclined to share the details either of his argument with Drusilla or the circumstances that led up to it. "Just a slight headache," he said in as jolly a manner as he could summon. He held up the beer bottle in explanation.

Sykes pursed his lips and Edwin felt unpleasantly

scrutinised. "Ah, you don't want to get into the habit of drinking alone, especially not out in the fields. Could lead to all manner of talk."

"I'll bear that in mind." Edwin gave him a tight smile and walked off, feeling Sykes's gaze in between his shoulder blades. This time he did not turn back.

A deep sense of betrayal filled Drusilla. The fact that Edwin had turned back to look for her did little to reduce it.

She had concealed herself in any case so watched him looking fruitlessly.

She had believed he was gentle, one like her poet or gardener, but now he was preparing to witness the deliberate shedding of a blood sacrifice. For all that he swore he was not happy about it, he was still going on the hunt.

She didn't need this sort of acolyte.

She paused, standing a little straighter and cocked her head, as if listening to something out of her hearing.

Was it that odd drink they had shared that was making her feel so rebellious? It must be something, because she felt no panic at the thought of their affair being at an end.

Regret and sadness, because she had liked him, but no fear at the prospect of years alone once more.

The tree was strong and true, it would grow stronger much quicker with Edwin's devotion, but she would survive without it until another came to take his place. She gathered her belongings and stowed them safely within the tree. Her fingers caressed the bark. Strong and firm. This was herself as much as the form she took.

Perhaps it was the stories in the newspapers he had brought her, of women and what they did in this time. What they did without men. Could she do that? It was an entirely new idea to her that she might not need him. That she might not need any man. She clambered into the high branches and lay back, basking in the sunshine and pondering this new bud of confidence that had somehow taken hold of her.

Time passed and it was dark when a voice interrupted her peace.

"I know you're there. Come out and face me."

Not Edwin.

"I'm calling you."

The harsh voice pricked her meditation. She opened her eyes again.

The Old One.

Over a decade had passed since he had confronted her (and it still unnerved her to think that much time had passed without her consciousness marking it) and yet he was still alive. He'd had the air of ancientness about him even then. She lowered herself through the branches and dropped lightly to the floor. He stood in the entrance to the grove, hands at his sides, visible but close to the pockets that had contained the fire when he had threatened her before. Danger made her limbs shudder. What would he expect to see? What might placate him? She inhaled, trying to catch his scent for a hint.

She hesitated briefly, a dozen scenarios flitting through her mind. Lifting her head, she stepped forwards from the deep shadows into the silvery starlight and let him see her.

Naked.

He started as she approached. His old, rickety frame tensed. Without moving his head, his eyes travelled over her body. She could feel his gaze settling on her breasts, down to the flat belly and the thatch of hair over her pubis, the long limbs.

"So that's how it is to be, is it." His eyes came up to meet hers. "Is this how you appeared to the boy?"

She sneered. "A child wouldn't want to see this form."

"Oh, I know that. He raved about a little girl when I carried him from here." The Old One tilted his lips upwards and bared his teeth in something that wasn't at all a smile. "But recently, is this how you've shown yourself? I know you've seen him since he returned. I met him earlier, looking angry and addled."

"I can be whatever the observer wants me to be." She tilted her head on one side. "I don't think he has even imagined me naked."

She knew that was a lie. She had been almost able to see the blood rushing through Edwin's veins, his need had been so great.

She stepped closer to the old man, slowly and lithely. To his credit he neither backed away in awe nor advanced on her with lust. She'd known men to do both. He looked her up and down again and there was indifference in his eyes. Annoyance rippled over her skin, causing it to shiver.

"How should I appear to best charm you? Like this?" she breathed.

She concentrated her energy, forming her flesh with subtle

changes, breasts enlarging, thighs growing fuller, lips budding into fullness.

He blinked and she felt a ripple of triumph that he was not immune to her power. No desire though. She stepped closer again, hips swaying as she walked, searching inside her memory for the form that might jolt him into a reaction. She knew him now, this one. His grandfather had courted and flattered her, begged for a glance and prostrated himself before her.

"This, perhaps."

She stood straighter, subtly broadening her shoulders and reducing her breasts until her torso became mannish, thickening at the waist and widening her hips. Her jaw squared and her forehead grew broad, losing the femininity in her face. It had been many years since she had taken this shape and she had forgotten the feeling of strength that came along with the larger frame.

"I don't have to appear womanly, if that is your fancy. You wouldn't be the first to want me like a pretty youth," she purred, her voice deeper and creamy.

"Enough!" For an old man he moved speedily and his hand was about her wrist before she could react. "I am not here to play games, nor be seduced."

Every fibre of Drusilla's body recoiled in distaste. The fragile leaves that had so recently unfurled constricted and the buzzing insects ceased as a wave of revulsion emanated from the tree.

She concentrated on her form and released her breath, returning to the shapelier aspect that she preferred. She wondered if the old man knew, or suspected, that his grandfather had wanted her that way.

"You aren't scared of me," Drusilla murmured. Unlike the sensations she was feeling at his touch.

"No. You could look as tempting as Cleopatra but you're still a whoring succubus."

Drusilla laughed. "Is that what you think? A demon? You stupid old fool! I don't steal souls. I give men what they want in exchange for a little attention. Many of your kind do just that." She jerked her arm and he let go.

"I'm not interested in what you have to say. I am who I am and I'm not ashamed of it. How could I be?"

"What you are, not who. You look like a woman now but you aren't a human one. I know that."

"How do you know?" Despite her nervousness around this strange man, her interest was piqued. She walked slowly, cautiously around him. He was old and bent. If he'd possessed a tree it would have been gnarled and stunted but impossible to uproot. He turned as she walked, never letting his glance fall from her.

The old man's eyes narrowed. "Like I said, my grandfather was one of your devotees."

Drusilla's face softened as she fell back into her memories. Working hands that loved the plants, made rough by work but tender when he touched her. The plants he tended had blossomed thanks to her devotion to him.

"Jasper Sykes. I remember the man you mean. I loved him."

"Did you?" The Old One snapped his head up. "Is your kind capable of love, or is it just that he gave you what you craved?"

"The Sapling doesn't believe what I say I am. He thinks it's a game I like to play, or an affectation."

She tasted bitterness, recalling the angry words she and Edwin had exchanged. She felt a flicker of regret now.

"Does that change things for you?"

Drusilla hid a smile. The old man was interested, despite his hatred of her. She met his eyes and a flash of something in them cautioned her not to tell the truth. Why give him that power? Why tell him that even his hatred was nourishing attention? Instead, she forced her face into a haughty expression.

"The tree doesn't care if the cloud believes in it, as long as the rain falls. Tell me why you believe though."

"My grandam was from near Pendle and they say she had witches in her family long back. That or the Fair Folk. She knew what you were. He left you and was faithful to her until the day he died. That was her doing." He stuck his hands deep in his pockets. "He planted the hedgerow to keep you in, and that was also her doing. Now, if it was me, I'd have used iron to encase you."

His blood was touched, then. That explained his age and his sense of knowledge, even if he did not understand it himself. But the threat he had made … he knew enough to use that!

Drusilla realised she was trembling. She flexed her feet, planting them firmly and feeling the nourishing grass beneath her toes, the soil in her instep. She wriggled her hand free from his grip, conscious that he was permitting it. Iron would seal her into the boundary of the grove. Worse, if he banded the tree itself, she would be trapped within, or without, depending on when he timed it.

"Go away, old man, and leave me to my affairs. I've never hurt anyone. I never hurt your grandmother – no more than a mortal woman could have if Jasper had strayed with one."

She stepped towards him.

"You don't have to be my enemy. The Sapling is safe with me. I caused his anger today, but only because we crossed words. I wasn't the cause of his broken limb and I'm not taking him away from a grieving wife."

The old man smirked, yet his expression was less confident. "He doesn't have one yet, but he will. He'll leave you."

Drusilla smiled sadly, the harsh words from earlier echoing in her mind.

"I know. They always do."

When he had left, she dropped to her knees. She felt weak; disturbed by the conflict. Even if they repaired their rift, Edwin would one day leave; she knew that. He'd left before and she had borne it.

Men came and they left; it was the way of it. She flourished in their company then ebbed in their absence while she waited for the next one. It was the way she had always been.

By nature she was solitary but there were others of her kind. She had not always been alone. She remembered the times when there had been others beside her. Other trees, other memories. Other spirits, older than she was.

But as humans arrived and took possession of the land, the trees were hacked from the earth and their spirits faded. Their stories ended when the axes struck. Now there were no others like her within easy reach. If she reached her thoughts down into the roots and up to the tips of the frailest twigs she could sense a great system of life, like the beacons that had once flamed across the land; a pulsing sent within the earth, whispered on the gusts of the wind. It took effort though. To really manage that would require great skill and energy.

Perhaps she had been too hasty in dismissing the Sapling. She was reasonably sure he would return and she would allow and accept his apologies.

Chapter Ten

The hunt was as horrendous as Edwin had predicted. For what felt like hours the pack and riders covered miles across fields, cantered through villages and even the outskirts of the town itself. On an unfamiliar black mare with four-or-five-years' experience, he hung back in a trot when he was able. The horns were less jarring and the crush less stifling back there. He ignored Robert's urges to go faster until his friend gave him a disdainful glance and spurred his mount on. As such, Edwin missed the eventual grounding and kill. They were in open fields when, a short way in the distance, the excited howling of the dogs changed into snarling as they fought for a lick of the unfortunate vixen's blood.

Edwin tasted vomit and forced himself not to retch. He slowed to a walking pace beside a woman of late middle age who was riding side-saddle dressed in the fashions of the previous century.

"No point rushing now. The fun's over," the woman sniffed in annoyance. "Lucky for the Master that the quarry didn't head over that way. For some reason the hounds dislike those fields. Must be something in the soil."

She flicked her riding crop in the direction of the mill. Edwin sat higher in the saddle. The houses and church of the village behind his fields were in sight. He raised his brows in surprise. He'd lost most of his sense of direction in what was already unfamiliar countryside and had not realised they were nearing the road that led back towards Greete Mill. He sat back again thoughtfully. Drusilla had said she would never let a hunt take place near her tree. He wondered whether the hounds knew enough to stay away.

"Stupid idea," he muttered to himself. Sometimes he caught himself imagining she really was what she said and had the ability to turn back a pack of dogs at the boundary.

"Did you speak?" his companion asked sharply. "Are you one of those white-livered chaps who weeps at the sight of a butcher's shop?"

"No," Edwin said hastily. "Just thinking aloud."

"No shame if you were. My uncle was." She harrumphed and her previously stern face crinkled into something warmer. "Personally, I can't stand the damned carnage but family obligations and all that..."

"Yes," Edwin agreed.

She leaned across confidentially. "My husband knows I'm really only here for the riding and the food. Speaking of which, come along, young man. We'll miss the toasts. Convenient that the kill took place on the right side of old Stuffy's estate. Not too far to go back."

~

The hunt breakfast took place on old Stuffy's estate (or as he was formally known, Gerald, Viscount Stanley) which was to the west of the town. A marquee had been set up on the edge of the lawn that was at least double the size of the one at Greete Mill House. Waiters were walking through the clusters of guests, serving Champagne to the scarlet-clad men and women. Edwin's new friend was hailed with cries of "Bitsy, over here!" by two leathery-faced old women. Edwin bade her farewell and walked inside.

A table bore a large crystal bowl of fruit punch with strawberries in bowls of ice. A longer table was laid with dishes of bacon and kidneys, boiled tongue, ham, spiced beef, cold mutton, and black pudding. Riders were eating with gusto, hungry after hours in the saddle. Edwin eyed it all, feeling nauseous. There didn't seem to be an animal not represented on the table, barring the fox itself.

"Edwin, there you are."

His grandfather hailed him. Edwin fixed a smile and turned. Stephen was wearing his best suit but looked dreadfully out of place amongst the men in their coats and jodhpurs. His brow was slightly furrowed. Edwin felt a stab of pity and uncharacteristic affection. He could almost forgive Stephen for forcing him into this situation. Stephen walked over in the company of a younger man with an impressive set of whiskers who was dressed in riding clothes. Edwin didn't know the man and almost hadn't recognised his grandfather, owing to the pleasant smile with which he greeted Edwin.

"I'd like you to meet Alderman Crossle," Stephen said.

The whiskered man held out a hand. Edwin shook it, heartily, noticing grime and the unmistakeable residue of dried blood ingrained in the folds of the alderman's fingers. He resisted the urge to wipe his down his riding breeches.

"Excellent ride," Alderman Crossle said. "I didn't see you at the end. Were you one of the chaps with the shovels? We harried the vixen right back to her den. Dug out a litter of five cubs."

A cold sweat of queasiness flooded up Edwin's neck. "No, I wasn't. I'm afraid I'm a bit out of practice in the saddle."

"But you were there for the kill of course?" Stephen said, as he helped himself to a large plate of bacon, kidneys, and eggs.

It was less of a question and more a confirmation. Edwin didn't bother to contradict him.

"Would you excuse me for a moment, I need to go pay a call."

Alderman Crossle waved a hand and guffawed. "Of course, say no more. I think I've drunk one too many glasses of that fruit concoction myself. Must have another."

He shook hands with Stephen and ambled off towards the punchbowl again. Edwin put down his empty plate. The marquee felt stifling and he didn't want to be one of the men to whom the old woman had referred who fainted. He walked towards the exit.

Stephen came alongside and caught his arm. "Where are you going?"

"I said I need to pay a call of nature," Edwin said, shaking Stephen's hand free and walking out of the marquee into the bright sunlight.

"And that couldn't have waited for ten minutes? Are you still a child of five?" Stephen lowered his voice as he followed. "I expect you back soon. Alderman Crossle is on the town planning board. He mentioned the possibility of expanding a branch line across the country. I intend to invite him and his wife to dinner soon. He has three daughters."

Edwin scowled. "Is this your attempt to arrange a marriage for me?"

Stephen bared his teeth, leaning towards Edwin. The sickly scent of the fruit cup wafted between them. "It would be a start for you to at least speak to someone female."

"If you want an heiress so much, why don't you marry one yourself?" Edwin snapped. "I'm sure plenty of widows would like a second chance at married life."

Stephen's eyes narrowed and his mouth became a rigid line. "I had the only wife I wanted," he growled.

Edwin stepped back, shaken by the tone of Stephen's voice. It wasn't grief but anger that blazed out of his eyes, Edwin was certain.

A couple of people nearby had stopped talking and were openly watching the two men.

"I'm sorry," Edwin faltered. "I didn't mean to offend you."

At that point, Bitsy walked past, her arm through that of an elderly gentleman. Both were holding empty Champagne glasses. She noticed Edwin and smiled widely. "Ah, my young friend. Have you taken advantage of the collation?"

She turned to her companion. "This young man joined me at the rear, well away from the bloodshed. We trotted back together."

The elderly gentleman inclined his head. "Bit of a waste to miss the fun but much obliged. She gets terribly frustrated with all the young men leaving her behind. She was quite a belle in her day. Still is in my eyes, of course."

"Oh you!" Bitsy said, swatting him playfully on the cheek and they strolled off. Edwin watched them enviously. How lovely it must be to grow old and happy together. He looked back to his grandfather and the cheerfulness ebbed. Stephen looked far from happy.

"So you didn't keep up with the hunt? You ambled behind in the company of a woman closer to my age," he said coldly. He shook his head. "Why did I even bother to wrangle you an invitation if you weren't going to take advantage of it."

His voice was laden with disappointment and it was more than Edwin could endure. He glared at Stephen.

"I rode and chased that poor animal across the countryside. My legs ache, I stink of horse and sweat and I've just shaken hands with a man who had blood beneath his fingernails. What more do you want from me? I'll turn up to your dinner and make eyes at his daughters but I'm sure I'll still do something to disappoint you."

Stephen stared at him with a look if incredulity, as if Edwin had stripped to his underwear and climbed into the punchbowl. Far from feeling cowed at the response, Edwin felt a rush of pride at having spoken. He spotted Robert leaning against a stable door, deep in conversation with one of the grooms. He waved an arm in the air to attract Robert's attention.

"Excuse me, sir. I'm going to go speak with Robert Carfax – strengthen the connection, you know." He pushed his hair back from his forehead and smiled widely. "I believe his sisters are still eligible too."

He stalked off, leaving Stephen standing alone. Robert watched him approaching and grinned.

"Cross words with the old man?"

"Just a frank exchange of views," Edwin answered. He took a breath. Now he had moved away and his pulse was starting to slow, he was filled with a sense of dismay at having been so outspoken. "Let's go to the courtyard and pretend to admire what's left of the carcass. I want to slip away as soon as I can."

They ambled over to the courtyard.

"What was Lady Stanley saying to you?" Robert asked.

"Who?"

Robert peered at him and spoke slowly. "Lady Stanley. Elizabeth Stanley. The viscountess. Wife of Viscount Stanley whose house we're in. Just outside the marquee before you began ranting at your grandfather."

"Bitsy?" Edwin coughed.

That odd, outspoken woman had been the wife of the viscount. He began to grin again. Stephen had presumably been unaware too, otherwise he would have never criticised Edwin for spending time with her. He'd make a point of dropping it into the conversation at some convenient time. Better still, he hoped Stephen would realise himself at some point over the afternoon.

The courtyard was full of people milling about though most were staff rather than members of the hunt party. The hounds were eating from bowls and a young boy was sweeping the last evidence of the horses from the cobbled ground. The pathetic remains of the fox were on display. Not much was left – a single forefoot, the brush, and the head – though all of it was matted with blood. Excited flies buzzed around the glassy eyes and stumps, warded off by a young groom with a bamboo flywhisk.

Edwin's stomach twisted. Blood and death. The baying of the hounds and the whooping of glee echoed in his mind. It was an abysmal state of affairs.

"This isn't for me," he said. "I have to speak to someone. There's a friend whom I offended and I need to go and make things right. Cover for me if you see my grandfather. Tell him you saw me speaking to someone or other. We'll go for a drink in the next week or so."

He left. The quickest route home would have been back along the London road, into the town centre then out again, but he decided to walk through the countryside instead. The afternoon was warm and the air was fresh. It was an idyllic day and he would have loved to have spent it walking or sketching. After half a mile he was too hot in his red jacket so balled it under his arm and continued in his shirtsleeves. He traced some of the route the hunt had taken, which was easy to see because there were places where the crush of horses had flattened or uprooted bushes, and horse dung littered the narrow lanes. He wrinkled his nose in distaste at the destruction. No wonder Drusilla hated it. He quickened his pace, anxious to find her.

He approached the village from the rear and paused in the churchyard to tidy a few straggling dandelions from his father's gravestone.

"I know Grandfather wishes to secure me a good future but there must be other ways of doing it," he sighed. He picked a couple of daisies and put them by his mother's headstone. "He loves you dearly. I miss you both."

He waited, but there was no answer from beyond the veil. He was becoming quite fanciful. He left and walked up to the sycamore from the other side of the field. Approaching from this direction he was impressed by how magnificent it looked; the branches spreading wide as if they were loving arms enveloping the fields. He remembered what Bitsy Stanley (that woman was the viscountess – really?) had said about no hounds chasing prey onto those fields and he could see why.

He hoped Drusilla would be there but she was nowhere in sight.

"You were right, Drusilla," he shouted. "Are you there? You were right about the hunt. I should never have gone. I'm sorry for what I said."

He stood for a full five minutes, hoping she would appear from behind the tree. Or from up in the branches. He realised that despite what he had said to her, he did half believe that she was some unearthly creature. A low humming sound made him shiver with dread. It was bees droning in the wildflowers, no doubt, but they sounded strangely loud. His imagination was running away with him.

Of course Drusilla wasn't up in the tree; she was no doubt sitting at home, probably paying Edwin no mind whatsoever, sewing or reading a book or doing whatever it was young women did in the evenings. He stuffed his hands in his pockets and began to walk back along the path towards the road, then decided to lie on the grass and enjoy the sunshine. He stretched out, using the red coat as a pillow, and closed his eyes. His eyes felt heavy and his thoughts thick, as if pressure was gathering. It felt like there was going to be a storm but the sky was clear. He felt his aching thighs begin to unknot and decided a doze would be pleasant, when something sharp struck him on the forehead.

"Ow!"

He jumped in surprise and lifted his hand to the sore spot. He sat up and looked down at the ground. There was a small pebble that must have been the object which struck him. He turned and looked back towards the tree. Drusilla was standing at the edge of the clearing.

"What are you doing just lying there?" she asked. She looked agitated. "You can't do that, not now."

Edwin clambered to his feet and walked back towards her. She came out to meet him, walking swiftly. They reached the spot midway between road and tree at the same time. Edwin extended his hand and Drusilla took it. As their fingers touched, the air was punctuated by a loud blast on a hunting horn. They both jumped in surprise, letting go of each other's hands.

"The hunt!" Edwin exclaimed. "It can't be again."

Drusilla said nothing. Edwin turned to her and was shocked to see she had gone deathly pale.

"It's the other hunt," she whispered. Her voice sounded harsh and cracked, almost unrecognisable. She looked and sounded terrified.

"The Wild Hunt. That's why you can't just lie there. You must come with me." She grabbed him by the hand and began walking away. "There's no time. We need to get into the grove."

When he didn't move, her hand twisted into a claw in his palm.

"I said there's no time. Come now."

152

Chapter Eleven

E dwin followed Drusilla towards the tree. The back of his neck prickled with trepidation and he had to resist looking over his shoulder. Whatever was scaring her was really scaring her. He glanced towards the house. Surely it would be safer there if there was danger approaching? He spotted a figure in the bottom lawn, standing by the stable. Sykes. It was too far away to see his features, but Edwin got the impression that the old man was looking directly at them. It wasn't a nice feeling. He realised he had left his red coat where he had folded it, but he hurried on at Drusilla's side.

As soon as he walked under the leaves and into the grove it felt like someone was releasing his rib cage from a crushing embrace. He hadn't even realised how tight his chest had been feeling. He heard the horns again, this time discordant and loud; much closer now. He looked up through the budding leaves to see dark clouds gathering in the distance, coming in from the direction of the edge.

Drusilla was leaning with her back against the tree trunk,

pressing her arms and body back against it, as if she wanted to disappear inside it.

"Tell me what's wrong," Edwin urged.

"Do you think you could climb the tree?" she asked.

"Of course." Edwin hadn't tried since that one time back in childhood but now he had more than doubled in height. He touched her shoulder. "Do you need me to help you?"

For the first time since hearing the initial blast of the horn, Drusilla looked less apprehensive. "The day I can't climb this tree is the day you can put me in the ground."

She took a couple of steps away from it, turned round, and with two steps forwards, jumped up. Because of her long skirt drifting about her, it seemed that she was floating, suspended in the air. She grabbed hold of the lowest branch and swung herself over it, then up to the next. With significantly less elegance, Edwin jumped up and clambered onto the branch beside Drusilla. She urged him higher, until they were almost two-thirds of the way to the top and the branches bowed slightly under their weight.

"This will do," Drusilla said.

"Now will you tell me what's happening?" Edwin asked.

She frowned. "Something is coming but I don't know what. They only ride out when there is danger or transformation."

"Who rides out?" he asked.

She held a finger to his lips and he listened carefully. There was nothing at first, but gradually, from the edge of his consciousness, came the sound of hoofbeats. They reverberated inside his skull, bouncing from hill to hill. Edwin pushed aside the smaller branches and peered through. The view over the village and back towards the town was excellent from that height, but he couldn't tell from which direction the riders were coming.

"Not there," Drusilla said, pointing a hand upwards, "there." Edwin craned his head.

The sky above them was filled with streaming tapers. Over the edge, black clouds were gathering, congealing as he watched them. White and wispy on top, black and solid underneath, they seemed too heavy to stay in the sky.

"We will be safe here," Drusilla murmured. "It's always best not to touch the ground when they ride, but here we are between earth and sky."

"Do you think there will be lightning? Edwin asked. "I know you're not supposed to stand beneath trees in case the bolt goes through you too. I think I saw Sykes in the field."

He twisted to look but they were too far around the other side of the tree for him to see the stables.

"Yes, he would be there, but I don't think anything is going to harm him and he'll know to keep away," Drusilla said.

The sound of hooves got closer and faster. Edwin looked out but could see no horses; the roads in all directions were empty. He looked up again and let out a cry of surprise. Almost above them the clouds had changed, coming together in a way that should be impossible. When he stared at them for too long, to Edwin's heightened imagination they took on the form of horses.

The pressure in his head was growing, and there was an aching in his temples. He pressed his fingers into the hollows above each ear.

"Can you feel that?" he groaned.

Drusilla nodded. She looked slightly less uncomfortable

than he felt, but her pupils had grown large. "Lean against the trunk," she said, and Edwin did as she commanded.

The sound of galloping grew closer. The horses were almost upon them. He raised his eyes, expecting to see actual horses, but there were only the clouds. It made his eyes swim to look, but if he let the focus blur, he imagined he could see loosely formed cloud horses with cirrus manes and cumulus flanks.

The sky had darkened. The clouds were tinted sulphurous yellow but beyond the edges the sunset had turned them an arterial red that hurt his eyes. His mouth tasted sour and old. He licked furiously at his teeth with the tip of his tongue but it was too dry to help. Drusilla lent forward and put her hands to his head. Her fingers were cold and he felt the tension in his jaw relax.

"Close your eyes; that will help."

Again, he obeyed and felt the gentle pressure of her fingers massaging his skull. It began to ease the pressure a little. He wanted to open his eyes but the thought of that awful yellow made him feel almost physically sick.

"Don't stop," he croaked.

The horn blasted again, this time joined by a second and third. Edwin's chest tightened, his pulse racing. Fear drummed in his ears. The tree swayed, rocked by a gust of warm wind that brought with it the taste of grit and gunpowder. Edwin moaned through bared teeth. Was this how the fox had felt?

"They're upon us. Be strong," Drusilla urged. "It will be over soon."

Rain began to plummet, a deluge of ice-cold bullets that crashed through the covering boughs and hammered against

Edwin's skin. His shirt was soaked in seconds, clinging to him uncomfortably.

Drusilla leaned against him, moving her hands from his temples to around his waist. Eyes still closed, Edwin felt the softness of her breasts pushing against his chest, closely followed by the pressure of her lips on his. He reached out a hand and cupped her face, holding her gently. If she broke away, he would not survive the storm, he knew.

She pushed her mouth more firmly against his, parting her lips a little more. He drew her bottom lip between his, revelling in the soft plumpness, and ran the tip of his tongue along the smooth inner.

The storm still surrounded them but he cared nothing for the cacophony.

Then it was done.

The air grew still and the heaviness in Edwin's head lifted though the scent of rain lingered on.

He opened his eyes a fraction. It was light again, a normal, bright evening. He risked glancing up and the sky above them was pale blue. No blood-red horizon. No sulphur.

He looked back at Drusilla, confused but relieved. She was smiling, her eyes glinting. Her skin was dewy and she looked somehow more real than the tree.

"Oh, Sapling," she breathed. "You are so sweet. Was that your first proper kiss?"

"No," he answered quickly. He met her eyes. "But I do believe it might be the first one that really matters."

She gave a rippling laugh. "I've endured many Wild Hunts but never with company, and never in that manner. I don't believe my head even hurts at all."

She briefly linked her fingers through his then turned and swung her legs over the branches. She clambered down, Edwin followed, and they emerged together from beneath the branches. The grass and earth that covered the grove was drenched from the rainstorm and the delicious brown scent of warm earth filled Edwin's nostrils. He had the urge to press his hand into it but thought it would look foolish. Then he remembered who he was with and did it anyway. When he rose again Drusilla was smiling at him.

"I heard what you said. Before you lay in the grass."

Edwin smiled cautiously. "Does this mean you accept my apology?"

"I haven't forgiven you for joining the hunt," she said, glaring at him. Her eyes softened. "Yet. I can see you're troubled and after what has just happened it seems silly to hold grudges."

The release of weight on Edwin's chest took him by surprise. He hadn't been aware of how heavy the load was.

"What did happen?" he asked. He suppressed a shiver. "I've never seen a storm like it."

Drusilla bowed her head. Her hair fell thickly, a curtain hiding her expression from view. She looked smaller, frailer. She knelt at the foot of the sycamore, reached a trembling hand to the trunk, and pressed her palm against it. Edwin curbed his frustration, waiting for her to answer. After a minute or more she lifted her head.

"Something bad is coming. A person or an event to change the world. The Wild Hunt only rides when there is danger. I've never seen them with these eyes, but the older memories recognised them."

"What is it?" he asked. He squirreled away the odd comment about memories for another time. "What are they warning of?"

She blinked. "As if I would be party to the precognition of the Wild Hunt! I'm nowhere near important enough!"

She turned and gripped his hand tightly. Her fingernails were short and rounded but nevertheless they bit into his palm. He jumped, not expecting such ferocity from her.

"Promise me you will be safe, Edwin. Whatever it is, do your best not to play a part," she pleaded.

"If I knew what you thought was going to happen, I would find that easier," he replied. He stroked her hand, disconcerted by the sight of the usually self-assured woman reduced to a bundle of nerves and practically begging on bended knee. "No, I can't promise something when I don't know what I'm promising."

He looked up at the sky again. Drusilla was still holding his hand. Edwin knelt and drew her to his side, putting his arm about her shoulders. He leaned his head on top of hers and closed his eyes. She felt stiff and wooden at first but gradually relaxed against him. Selfishly, comforting her felt good. Protecting someone he cared about. It was a new experience for him.

"Don't be scared. Perhaps you're wrong," he murmured. "Or the hunters might be wrong. Just because they're old, it doesn't mean they're right."

He bit his thumbnail thoughtfully and glanced up at the sky for reassurance that it was the usual blue.

Her eyes were watching him when he looked back. "You're starting to believe, aren't you."

"I don't know. It is too fantastic. How can what you say you are even exist?"

"I don't know why, or how, anything exists." Drusilla gestured to the stump of the old sycamore which peeked out from beneath the drift of snow. "I see memories or echoes of how I came to be. A woman was chased. Hounded. She ran and fell and her life and the life within her passed out. But I didn't die. Somehow the essence or soul – call it what you will – passed into the new tree. A sapling, barely more than a shoot from the old tree, waiting to be filled. Then the old spirit's tree died and she faded with it, and I was alone here."

Edwin put both arms around her and held her tightly. Robert's childhood tales of hanged witches came back to him – haunting the place she died. Was there truth in it after all?

"Look, I need to go and face my grandfather. I'm sure he will have all sorts of things to say to me after I left the hunt party without his permission. He had a whole host of dignitaries lined up for me to meet."

He suppressed a tremor of anxiety. He'd made his choice and would have to face the repercussions.

"Perhaps the Wild Hunt was foretelling the row we're going to have."

Drusilla cocked her head on one side. The colour had returned to her cheeks and to her eyes. Edwin inhaled, drawing in the sweet smell of blossom.

"You are special but don't imagine you are that important, Sapling! Never mind your local dignitaries. You have witnessed the Wild Hunt. Few of your kind can say that they have done this. It will be something to tell your children and your grandchildren."

"I suppose so," Edwin said. "Not that I have any yet, nor intend to for a long time."

Drusilla wriggled out of his embrace and straightened her hair. "One day you will, I'm sure of it. And then what will become of me?"

"I'll always be your friend," Edwin said. "Besides, don't you want another acolyte?"

"I've had so many before. I wonder if I'll ever get tired of the change." She smiled but it was a ghost of her usual expression, more like someone had overlaid one photographic plate on top of another so they didn't quite line up, but the original expression was visible beneath.

"Perhaps you could marry one day," he said.

She pulled away and walked swiftly to the edge of the grove. She stood with her back to him, her arms lost in the folds of the flowing gown she wore. The cloth was something silken and was already dry. His own shirt still clung to him uncomfortably and he didn't relish the thought of walking home in sodden trousers.

"What? What did I say? Did I offend you?" he asked.

"My kind don't marry," she said without looking at him. "You should go."

"Yes, I should," he agreed, trying not to be stung by her dismissal, especially as he had already said he was leaving. He walked to her side. She caught his fingers as he passed. He turned, his breath catching in his throat.

"Take care, my Edwin. You're still a young thing in the eyes of the old world. Make sure you get the chance to grow firm foundations. Do you still have the leaf I gave you? Keep it with you."

"It's in my notebook. I will."

He lowered his hand and walked out from beneath the branches. He squared his shoulders but couldn't shake the feeling of unease that filled his limbs and belly as he glanced warily at the sky, half expecting to see the ghostly forms he had glimpsed before. The clouds looked perfectly normal now, even parting slightly to allow for a little of the dusk sky to peek through. The horizon was edged with red, but it was the ordinary colour of a late spring sunset.

Edwin gave a small gasp of surprise. The time had gone much more quickly than seemed possible and he would be late returning to the hunt ball. The air was cooling but Edwin's clothes had dried by the time he reached his red coat and picked it up. The grass he had lain on showed no evidence of the rainstorm; the coat was dry too. Both should be sodden after the relentless downpour. He put the coat back on thoughtfully.

He wasn't sure when he had started to accept that the sky had been filled with invisible riders and that he had borne witness to something unearthly, but he realised that he did. It could have been the unearthly echoing of hooves, or the colour of the clouds. It was more likely the expression of terror on Drusilla's face. It was difficult not to believe what she was saying in the face of such unflinching belief.

And if that was true, then what did it mean for Drusilla's tales of what she was?

He walked back to the house on slightly shaky legs.

Sykes was leading Stanley out of his stable and into the field when Edwin arrived at the bottom. The old man tipped the edge of his cap.

"Bad storm, wasn't it," Edwin said, stopping to run his hands over the horse's flanks.

"What storm?" Sykes sucked his teeth and gave Edwin a look that seemed to pass straight through his flesh and made his bones feel cold. "It's been fine all afternoon."

Edwin was about to correct him but closed his mouth. The dry grass and coat, the rapid passing of time, and now a denial. It was just another piece of evidence to suggest there had been some supernatural elements at work.

"Must have imagined it. The heat of the day confusing you," Sykes said. He gestured to Edwin's coat which Edwin noticed had grass stuck to it in places. "Fell asleep up in the field, did you?"

"Perhaps," Edwin agreed slowly. "I must have dreamed it."

He hadn't imagined it. No hallucination could have been so real. The rain soaking through his shirt; the thunderous hoofbeats.

The kiss.

He swallowed, as the memory of that shot sparked through him.

They had been real, not a dream.

His certainty of the world he had always known began to waver. He looked back up to the tree, not knowing what he expected to see. There was no wind but the boughs waved, seeming to reach towards him. He had to find out for certain, but after the overwhelming day he was reluctant to return to the sycamore now.

"Sykes, can I ask you something? Did a woman ever die by the old tree stump? Or near the mound."

Sykes's eyes narrowed. "Why are you asking such a question? Who's been gossiping?"

Edwin gave an offhand shrug, surprised at the fierceness in Sykes's voice. "No one. I remember Robert Carfax telling us about a witch being hanged there and her ghost haunting it. I wondered if there was any truth in it. An accident rather than a hanging though."

Sykes unbent slightly. "There could be. Long before this land belonged to the Greete family it was common land. There were bound to be deaths. No witches or ghosts though. You'd have to be soft-headed to believe that sort of nonsense. You aren't that foolish, are you?"

Edwin dropped his gaze.

"No, I'm not. Thank you, Mr Sykes."

He walked back to the house, feeling Sykes's eyes on him. His certainty about Drusilla's tales was crumbling. He wished he could speak with Harold whose belief in something greater than their understanding now seemed appealing. His cousin would not mock him, surely? He recalled that he had promised Harold and the girls to invite them but had neglected to do so and determined he would write the following day.

In his room he stripped off the soiled riding clothes and ran a bath, submerging himself beneath the cool water and scrubbing his skin until the odour of horses was gone. Lying on his bed, wrapped in his dressing gown, he found his notebook and scribbled down everything he could remember of the afternoon. The leaf lay beside him on the bed but he was reluctant to touch it.

The Hunt Ball passed without event. He returned late, slept late the next morning and occupied himself with correspondence all day. He didn't encounter Stephen so that evening he went down for dinner, prepared for the expected argument. Whatever may or may not exist beyond human comprehending, his grandfather's disapproval was something most definitely real.

Surprisingly, Stephen was in a genial mood. He poured Edwin a glass of wine before filling his own, whereas usually he poured his own then pushed the decanter in Edwin's direction. Edwin thanked him then ate silently. Waiting for his grandfather to speak was wiser than trying to pre-empt the conversation.

"Why didn't you tell me who you were riding with yesterday?" Stephen asked once the fish plates had been brought in. "Lady Stanley seemed quite taken with you. It's not often I admit I was wrong." There he gave a humorous laugh that Edwin tried to join in.

"I suppose that's because it's so rare. In this case it seems you did more to distinguish yourself by chaperoning the old dame than racing at the front. I could almost forgive you for leaving. Carfax told me you had a friend to see."

Ah, here was where the argument would start, Edwin thought. He chewed the mouthful of skate wing he had just taken to buy him time, though it was beautifully soft.

"Yes, I did. I thought you would rather I left than embarrass myself in some way."

Stephen's humour vanished and the angry glint in his eye replaced it.

"I'd rather you had stayed and not embarrassed yourself. Still, I spoke again with Alderman Crossle. He has accepted an invitation to dine here. He isn't free for a month unfortunately, but that will give us ample time to set this place to rights."

He laid down his fork and glared around the room, as if the air of neglect was the fault of the dining room itself.

"I'll have to hire more staff of course, but he and his wife and their eldest daughter, Myrtle, will be pleased to meet you."

"Myrtle Crossle," Edwin murmured. "Poor thing."

Stephen glared at him. "Don't be such an impudent rat. What does the name matter? Besides, Myrtle Hope has a better ring to it in any case. Now tell me about this friend you were so keen to visit."

Edwin toyed with his fish knife and fork, taking a few moments to slide the skate wing from the bone. "Just an acquaintance," he said.

"An acquaintance who is more important than the guests at Viscount Stanley's party? One I would approve of?" Stephen asked.

"I doubt it," Edwin said. His throat tightened. The effects of the previous afternoon's oddness hadn't quite worn off and he wasn't sure right now whether he approved of Drusilla either.

"A woman?" Stephen steepled his fingers and gave Edwin a stern look over them. Edwin nodded.

"I suppose it's too much to ask for you to choose better friends?" Stephen said. "This new friendship with the Crossles could be exactly what the factory needs: an influential man who is progressive enough to see that expanding the town is the way for us all to prosper. For the next month or two can you at least stop flirting with whichever barmaid or waitress you have your loins set on?"

Edwin put his knife and fork down. Once he might have

refused on principle but with the unsettling memory of rain that only he had felt still fresh in his mind, he was happy to oblige.

"I think I'm happy with that. For now."

Susan, the maid, took the plates and brought the main course. As usual, conversation ceased while the servants were in the room. Edwin was glad of the chance to collect his thoughts. When Susan left, he speared a few broad beans and ate them before asking,

"Grandfather, did you see a storm yesterday afternoon?"

Stephen shook his head. "Nothing. There was a slight chill when the sun set but apart from that it was a perfectly pleasant day."

Edwin chewed thoughtfully. He'd half wondered whether Sykes had been toying with him by denying the truth but it appeared not.

"Can you think of any reason … anything that…" He tailed off, not sure how to put into words the odd premonition of trouble. "Do you think anything bad is likely to happen?" he asked.

Stephen refilled his glass. "Only if you make an ass of yourself in front of the Crossles next month."

A month of changing moons had passed since the Wild Hunt had ridden out. A month since Edwin had visited. She had not even glimpsed him. It tore at her to imagine him shying away.

Drusilla had not ventured far past the edge of the grove without Edwin. The night she had tried it she had felt the tugging of the tree holding her back. It had been unnerving but after the Wild Hunt had passed overhead, she felt compelled to try. If wickedness was coming, she would not cower.

She would not leave the sanctity of her home unprotected though. She climbed into the boughs and stretched out full length, closed her eyes, and ran her hand over the branches. When her hand tremored, she plucked the most vibrant leaf she sensed. She held it lightly in her curled fist and walked out from beneath the branches. The tug of safety was strong but she drew in a breath and released it slowly as she walked across the meadow towards Edwin's house. She planted her feet carefully, spreading her weight and feeling the earth and grass on her heel, instep, and each toe. In her mind she formed a thread of green that connected the roots and branches to the leaf in her hand and to whatever beat inside her body.

Did she have a heart? She must, because something had tightened and tried to break free from her chest when Edwin held her.

Cautiously she approached the house. Most of it was in darkness but the window of one room was lit up and she could see Edwin and a man who must be the grandfather of whom Edwin spoke, because he shared Edwin's jaw and stature. The eyes were different though. The older man's were hard and deeply set, unlike Edwin's wide, friendly gaze. Edwin was formally dressed in dark trousers, a white shirt, and a grey waistcoat that drew his waist in and gave him a trim outline.

There were five people dining altogether, as Edwin and his grandfather were accompanied by an older couple and a young woman with glossy chestnut hair piled high about her face.

Drusilla drew a sharp breath of envy. The woman was about the age that Drusilla appeared to Edwin. She was delicately beautiful with high cheekbones and large blue eyes. She was holding the room, talking in an animated way that made her curls dance.

Drusilla stepped closer and eyed the woman curiously.

Shoulders were visible at the edges of her gown and there was a suggestion of an impressive bosom concealed beneath drapes of soft pink. Drusilla clenched her hands. The woman brought to mind roses in summer. Already tense from leaving the sanctity of her grove, the sight of the young woman made her shiver unpleasantly.

Whatever she was saying must have been fascinating because Edwin somehow managed to keep his eyes from straying to her breasts.

Drusilla stepped into the shadows. She glanced down at her own clothes and altered them subtly, drawing the flowing skirts in and forming a subtle folding over her breasts, widening the neckline so her own shoulders were partially noticeable. It took more effort than it should have. It weakened her.

It was the answer to why Edwin had abandoned her. Her breath came with difficulty and she felt the leaf in her palm flutter.

Time to leave.

She turned, but then turned again, drawn to the window and the scene within. She watched as they ate and drank, talked and laughed. Her Sapling in his own world. He was not completely at ease but he was oh so charming.

The dishes were cleared. The diners rose and left. Drusilla

urged herself to follow to another window. Which room would they light now? After eating women often played pianos and sang for their men. She remembered that from a previous acolyte and had no reason to assume that times had changed. How long before the sound of nimble fingers on ivory reached her ears?

Instead, she heard voices from the other side of the house; the closing of a door. They were leaving. Had Edwin kissed the girl's hand? Her cheek?

She put her fingers to her lips, recalling the touch and taste of their kiss.

Another door slammed. Closer. She jumped back and saw Edwin and his grandfather had returned to the dining room.

They stood at either side of the circular oak table and were clearly arguing because as Drusilla watched, the older man thumped the table with his fist. Edwin stood straighter and lifted his chin, his cheeks flaming scarlet. He glared and opened his mouth. Drusilla pressed her hand against the window frame, wishing she could send him strength, and maybe she did because he closed his mouth again and ran his hands through his hair. The colour ebbed from his cheeks and he began speaking slowly. She felt a rush of pride that he had controlled himself.

Whatever he said was met with anger, however, because the grandfather stormed out of the room. Edwin leaned against the table and buried his face in his hands. Drusilla put both hands on the glass, wishing she could go and comfort him. She willed him to look up, but he didn't.

"Is someone there? Show yourself!"

She jumped at the voice from close by. She had been so

engrossed in watching Edwin that she hadn't been aware of the presence of someone else. Swiftly she pressed herself against the window frame, concealing herself in the shadows and wood. Edwin's grandfather strode along the terrace, long limbs and heavy frame seeming to fill more space than he was entitled to. He stopped and looked almost at where Drusilla was standing but she allowed herself to slip away from his gaze. No one saw her unless she wanted them to and she very much did not want this man, who had caused such pain to her dear Sapling, to see her.

He shook his head and carried on walking. Just past the second window he stopped and looked into the room Edwin occupied.

"My only heir," he said bitterly.

He shook his head, sighed, then took a pipe from his pocket and lit it. The tobacco smoke drifted to Drusilla, heavy with the scent of chocolate and tar – delicious and indulgent. It was an outrage that he should be outside enjoying the starlit sky while his grandson sat alone in misery.

He strolled towards the steps between the ponds. Drusilla opened her hand containing the leaf and blew on it. The leaf floated on a breeze that had not been there previously and landed on the edge of the top step in front of his foot. As soon as he stepped on it, his foot shot out from beneath him. He cried sharply, flailing his arms, but succeeded in maintaining his balance. His pipe, however, fell from his hand and plunged into the pond where it sank with a small sizzle of extinguished flame.

Drusilla laughed aloud and the grandfather turned his head sharply. He still didn't see her, but his gaze lingered longer than Drusilla was comfortable with. The trick had used up a lot of her energy. Her skin shivered as if unseen woodlice were crawling the length of her body.

Stupid!

It was a petty retaliation that had achieved nothing and which had endangered her concealment. She was tired by the effort and if the grandfather came closer and studied the place where she was standing carefully, she was not sure she would be able to keep hidden.

Fortune was on her side, though, because he shook his head and turned away, walking back up the steps and along into the formal garden behind the brick wall. Drusilla allowed her frame to relax. A few moments to rest and she would be able to return to her tree.

"Drusilla."

A second voice, but this one she loved.

"Edwin," she answered, turning away from his grandfather's retreating form.

He strolled towards her, hands in his pockets.

"What just happened to my grandfather?" he asked.

"I sent him a leaf," Drusilla answered triumphantly. "He slipped on it and lost his pipe. I didn't know if I was capable!"

She giggled, heady with exhilaration and it took a moment for her to realise Edwin wasn't smiling.

Doubt edged towards her.

"He could have broken his neck or cracked open his head," Edwin snarled.

"He would do no such thing, and even if he did that's no more than he deserves for upsetting you," she said.

"He doesn't deserve to be injured for that!" Edwin

snapped. He peered at her. "What sort of woman are you that you could say something so callous?"

Drusilla recoiled at his ferocity. She felt as if the ground had tumbled away from her and she was floating an inch above it. She flexed her feet in an attempt to keep her balance, but of course she was standing on flagstones. No welcoming earth, only the hardness of rock.

"You know what I am," she said. "You are my acolyte and I will let no one transgress against you."

Edwin winced. "Stop it! I don't know what you are. Reason tells me you can't be, but the Wild Hunt... If you did influence his fall..."

Anger. Disbelief. Confusion.

Each emotion was an axe blow to Drusilla.

Edwin spun away, heading towards the steps between the ponds where his grandfather had stood. She ran after him but felt herself weakening. Slowing. She'd done too much. The feeling of age grew on her. A winter feeling, not the start of summer.

This time it was she who fell...

Chapter Twelve

Drusilla's cry of alarm was weak, a kitten's forlorn meow or a breath of wind through the branches of a dying tree that barely registered in Edwin's mind. He turned back, curiously wondering what the sound was in time to see her falling.

Her body collapsed as if her bones had softened and were no longer able to hold her up. A whole body going limp. He dashed back and caught her in his arms before she hit the bottom step. She was heavier than he had expected for her size and build. He grunted slightly, shifting her into an easier position.

She opened her eyes and gazed up at him, pupils large and black. Edwin let out the anxious breath he had been holding.

"You don't need to carry me. I can walk. It's fine."

Her voice was clipped but weak, and she gave a half-hearted wriggle, stirring against his chest. The muscles in his arms clenched and a ripple of desire ran through him. He'd

175

spent the evening in the company of a very beautiful woman who had affected him not in the least, but the moment he had touched Drusilla he felt as if his blood had been heated.

All unease he had felt over the odd night of the hunt vanished. He cringed inwardly, thinking of the cruel words he had flung at her. He couldn't take her as far as the tree so he carried her over the lawn in the direction of the summer house.

"You fainted. Of course I'm not going to make you walk," he said soothingly. "Don't argue, Drusilla."

She settled against him but as soon as they were on the grass she tried to stretch again.

"Put me down. I'll feel better if I walk."

"Are you sure?"

Edwin's arms tensed at the thought of letting her go. The dread he'd felt when his grandfather had fallen had been nothing in comparison to when he'd seen Drusilla drop. His heartbeat was only now returning to something approaching normal.

"Yes. I want to feel the grass. I need to." She pointed her toes, trying to reach to the lawn. Edwin gently lowered her and she gave a sigh of contentment. "That's better."

Edwin opened the door to the summer house. "Would you like to go inside and rest on a chair? Shall I bring you some water? Something stronger?"

She wrinkled her toes in the neatly trimmed grass and gave him a slight smile then sat down, feet tucked under her. She spread her hands, palms down, beside her, almost caressing the lawn as she ran her hands over it.

"I'll feel better soon. You don't have to wait with me." She dropped her head. "Don't you want to go and speak to your grandfather? To confirm I did him no harm?"

"Absolutely not," Edwin said. There was a momentary stab of alarm in his chest as he recalled the sight of the old man rocking precariously on the step but he banished it. Stephen was proud and wouldn't relish the thought of anyone witnessing his vulnerability. He'd have most likely put it down to his age causing him to slip.

"I don't need to do that. I don't think he would welcome my company." He sat beside Drusilla. The grass was damp with late night dew. He wasn't sure what time it was but guessed it must be after eleven. The evening had dragged interminably.

"Would you welcome my company?" he asked cautiously. He winced as he thought how rude he'd been.

"Will you tell me what you were doing tonight?" Drusilla asked. "You know I'm always happy to listen." She spread her hand palm down on the grass again, closer to Edwin's, and tilted her head slightly to one side. She looked at him through her eyelashes and the effect sent Edwin's pulse racing again.

"Who was the woman you were with?"

"Myrtle Crossle," Edwin answered.

Drusilla snorted. "Goodness, what a name to be afflicted with. Now I feel sorry for the poor thing."

Now? Was she jealous? Edwin looked at her surreptitiously out of the corner of his eye. There was something different about her and he realised it was her dress. Usually she wore a gown that was loose and floaty but now it looked similar to the one Myrtle had worn with the gathered bodice and narrow skirt. The neck was wide and only grazed her lightly tanned shoulders. Myrtle was beautiful but she paled in comparison to the woman at his side.

"Don't feel sorry for Myrtle," he said firmly. "She's the most tedious woman I've ever spent time with. All she could talk about was the scripture cross stitches she has done and what she plans to call dogs if she ever owns any. It quite made my head hurt trying to keep up with her so I could ask intelligent questions."

"I suppose you would have preferred her to just listen while you talked," Drusilla said, scowling. "Most men do."

"That's not fair. You know I'm perfectly happy to converse and listen. I listen to you all the time." Edwin scratched his head. His opinion of Myrtle had been the reason for the argument with his grandfather. "Oh, I'm sure it's not Myrtle's fault. Her mother seems to be the domineering kind. Grandfather didn't like it when I told him I have no intention of squiring her about town – and what an old-fashioned way of describing it, for goodness' sake! Of course I was bound to do something he didn't like. I always do."

"What happened to make your grandfather dislike you?" Drusilla asked quietly. "I could feel the anger rising off him like steam."

"I don't know," Edwin said. He felt his fist clenching unintentionally. "When I was a child I thought he was angry when I broke my arm and then defied him by coming back to the tree. Now I feel there must be something else."

He stretched his legs out and leaned back. Above them, innumerable stars filled the sky. The weather had warmed up in the last week, as if summer had realised it was lagging behind and redoubled its effort to appear. Even though it was late, the air was warm and fragrant with night-scented stock and recently mown grass.

"I do what he asks. I diligently work away in a role that holds no intertest for me. I write letters, catalogue whatever he wants me to, account for wages and materials, but still I seem to displease him. Just the look of me seems to displease him, if I'm perfectly honest."

"Have you asked him?" Drusilla gave him a concerned look that made Edwin's guts twist.

"No. I don't know if that's something I should do."

"Well, can you make his animosity any worse?" she asked.

Edwin grinned. "I suppose not. I don't know. Maybe it would. Mostly I just wish I could leave here."

"I hope you don't. At least not for the time being," Drusilla said quietly. "I have missed you."

Edwin bit his lip. He'd remained resolute about not seeking Drusilla out until he could devote the time to untangling his thoughts and he had tried not to think about her, but she had sprung to his mind too easily.

"I've been busy," he said. It sounded as weak an excuse as it was. He sat a little straighter. He owed her the truth.

"What's wrong?" she asked, taking him by the hands. He looked down at them, at her perfectly normal hands. Nothing mystical or magical about them. He might be about to make a complete fool of himself.

"I need answers. I think I'm going insane. What happened before, when I thought I saw horsemen in the clouds, was unnerving. It didn't make sense and I've tried to explain it to myself." He gave a weak grin to pre-empt possible offence.

"You don't make sense to me."

"You don't believe me, do you, when I say what I am. I can tell." Drusilla squeezed his hands gently and cupped them together inside hers. "Let me hear it from your lips though."

"Honestly? I don't." Edwin freed his hands and raked them through his hair. He tried a game smile. "You must admit it's very far-fetched. It was fun to indulge in when we were younger but now…"

"But now?" She pursed her lips.

He shrugged. "I like that you're eccentric. I like that you have this imagination. Until today that's all I thought it was. But that afternoon I saw things that I'm unable to explain."

"What if I could prove it to you?" Drusilla asked. She sighed, stared up at the sky, and huffed. "Oh, this is difficult. No man before you has ever needed convincing. What is it about this awful modern age that everyone doubts everything? You go along to your church every Sunday, I'm sure. Do you genuinely believe what you are praying?"

"It's difficult to answer." Edwin thought. It was a ritual. It was what he did. Of course he believed. But if he had to say he believed to the same extent that Harold believed? No, he didn't have that faith.

"Honestly, I'm not sure what I believe. I'm not sure I believe anything with my heart."

He ran his hands through his hair once again, ruffling it. He'd drunk more wine than usual and his head was feeling slightly fuggy. He should probably go to bed but his senses were alert and he felt like he was on the cusp of something.

"I want to have you prove it one way or the other. I'm a little scared of what I might discover. How I might feel afterwards."

Drusilla gave him a wide smile. "Admitting your fear is bravery in itself. I want to prove it to you, so I will. It matters to me that you are happy. I've told you before that your attention feeds me. That's true, but the attention of a believer is even more powerful. I'm going to prove it to you."

She took his hands again, only this time she pressed them to Edwin's heart. She stared deeply into his eyes and he swallowed as desire for her swelled.

"Trust me. Whatever happens tonight will you trust me? Will you believe I mean you no harm?"

He looked into the open face that he knew so well and saw no trickery, only concern. He felt the warmth of her hands substantial and heavy just like a woman's. She wasn't a ghost and her flesh was as real as his. Whether or not she was a tree nymph or goddess was an entirely different matter.

"I believe you, Drusilla," he said.

She knelt on the ground and pulled him down so he was opposite her. She smiled and raised her eyes.

"In that case, kiss me."

Edwin didn't need commanding twice. He leaned forward hesitantly and kissed her. Her lips were waiting for his and as he felt the warmth, he understood that she wanted him as much as he wanted her. He put his hands to either side of her face and slipped his fingers into her thick locks of hair, at the same time opening his mouth slightly and letting the tip of his tongue brush over the fullness of her bottom lip. Her tongue met his and fireworks burst in his head. Drusilla slipped a hand down to his waist and the other around his back. Her touch was like a current of electricity racing up the length of his spine.

Edwin made a noise that was half-growl, half-moan as he felt the rising pulse and rushing blood that signalled the beginnings of an erection. He pulled away.

She looked at him with gleaming eyes.

"Your sap is rising, my Sapling. So is mine."

Edwin swallowed. Women shouldn't be so frank, he suspected, but that was part of Drusilla's charm. It was quite invigorating and intensified the stirring in his trousers. He looked at her again. Her skin had almost a glow to it in the twilight.

"Kiss me again."

She tilted her head back, leaning forwards until her lips were close. He heard her sigh and felt her breath warm on his neck. As he bent towards her, she ducked past him and clambered to her feet with a laugh.

"What are you doing?" he asked.

She spun around in a circle, arms outstretched and head tilted back. Her hair danced and her skirts spun, a whirl of green. The colour of summer leaves.

"Kiss me again but catch me first."

She darted away. Edwin leapt to his feet and chased after her, guessing that she was heading back to the tree. She was faster than he expected and he actually had to exert himself to keep up with her. They reached the grove at about the same time. He caught her by the hand, laughing.

"I've caught you. Now give me my prize."

She laced her fingers in his and stepped backwards under

the canopy of the tree. She pushed her lips up to his and caught his arms, spinning them both around. They were still kissing as he backed her against the tree. Drusilla opened her mouth and he pushed his tongue inside it, so desperate and hungry for her. He was properly hard now and when she reached down and unbuttoned his trousers to stroke him with her hand he almost swooned. He closed his eyes and kissed her harder, pushing his body up against hers.

He groaned as fire ignited in his groin and spread through the rest of his body. He was a virgin – nothing to be ashamed of, whatever the boys at school had said. All thoughts of waiting for the wife he might one day have slipped from his mind. He wanted Drusilla. Now. Here.

"My Sapling," she breathed.

Her breath smelled like grass after summer rain. Her voice sounded odd, with an echo to it as if two women were speaking at once.

He felt her arms come around him, one at his neck, the other encircling his waist. She pulled him towards her and slipped her hands beneath his open collar. He must have lost a moment because now his waistcoat was gone and his shirt was unbuttoned and hanging loose. He shrugged it off and let it fall to the ground. He burned where her fingers touched the bare skin over his collarbone and traced downwards to his chest.

"Do you want me?" she murmured.

"More than anything," he gasped. He was struggling to speak, a huge weight pounding in his chest. He opened his eyes and stared deep into hers then put his hands on her shoulders, hooking his thumbs under the gathered cloth at the wide neck of her gown. He raised his eyebrows questioningly and she nodded, smiling.

"So polite," she murmured. "My gentle Sapling."

Gently he eased the dress down over her arms until the loose silk fell to the ground and she stood before him naked. He heard a strangled gulping growl of desire and blushed, knowing it had come from him.

She wore no corset or slip, none of the fussy, restrictive garments that he'd spent more hours than was healthy poring over in advertisements or the photographs that had been covertly passed around his dormitory at school.

He couldn't bear to tear his eyes from her body, but with difficulty he raised them to her eyes. She was still smiling as he reached a trembling hand to her bare shoulder.

"Do you love me?"

He nodded and nuzzled against her neck. "More than anything," he murmured again, knowing it was the truth.

She bit the corner of her lip and looked up at him with a mischievous glint in her eye.

"Do you want to see something very special?"

Edwin nodded, unable to think of anything more special than what she was already displaying.

"Come with me, Sapling. Worship me. Love me."

He pressed his body against her again and closed his eyes. His head spun and he felt as if he were falling, then his limbs grew heavy, tensed, then eased.

He started to open his eyes but Drusilla reached her fingers up and brushed them over his eyelids and he closed them again.

"Not yet."

He caught the scent of soil in the back of his nose and throat, distilled summer grass and autumn leaves all in one. He felt her lips kissing him lightly on each eyelid. Stars burst beneath his closed lids. It was the most arousing touch imaginable.

"Open your eyes and see me as I am."

Chapter Thirteen

"Truly see me."

Drusilla whispered the words, but it was nevertheless a command. Edwin opened his eyes with slight difficulty, lids feeling heavy, and looked at her. His blood ran hot at what he saw and he felt lightheaded. The feeling came over him that he had lapsed into a dream or worse, madness.

Her skin was smooth and the shade of freshly cut wood. Her body was still shapely and full. As alluring as the brief glimpse he'd allowed himself, her limbs firm and slender, dusky shadows at the fork of her legs and between the full curves of her breasts but she had changed. Her naked body glowed inhumanly as if lit from candles that Edwin could not see.

She was still herself but now she was something other. Her hair wafted out around her in twisting tendrils, rising upwards and defying gravity. Splitting, fanning, spreading out as branches grew from the trunk. Her pupils were large, almost filling her eyes, which were iridescent, the irises brighter green and with deeper flecks of hazel than seemed natural. She was captivating.

"What happened to you?" Edwin croaked.

Drusilla smiled sweetly. "Nothing, other than that here, I am every aspect of me."

"Every..." Edwin trailed off, too confused to finish the question.

"You said you wanted to know the truth. This is who I am. This is what I am. The spirit of the tree. Its child and its guardian."

As if the altered Drusilla was not enough to send Edwin's senses reeling, they were no longer against the tree. Somehow now they were standing in a hexagonal room. Six pointed arches rose upwards from a dozen vertically grooved columns, all seemingly carved from pale wood. Edwin's impression was of a cathedral combined with the oldest of forests. There was a bed of some sort. Yes, he'd been about to make love to Drusilla. He glanced at it and his stomach lurched. It was wrong somehow, seemed to be part of the panelling that covered the walls, with no suggestion that it was separate; as if the whole room had been hollowed out rather than built.

"I'm dreaming," Edwin murmured, staring around. "I must be."

"No you're awake." Drusilla spoke, and again her voice had an echo to it that was not possible.

Whatever light was allowing him to see was from a source he could not identify. He was overwhelmed by the scent of sap. If the colour green could be distilled, this is what he imagined it would smell of.

"Where are we?" He forced the words through trembling

188

lips, fighting to remain sane. "What have you done to me? Am I drunk?"

Drusilla's hands came up to his face, her fingers spreading over his cheeks and jaw. Still soft, but at the same time hard and wooden. Two Drusillas overlaid on top of each other, like a double exposed photographic plate – the woman he knew and a carved wooden figure.

"I've brought you into my sanctuary."

Edwin looked around again at their surroundings, tilting his head back to stare above him. The soaring columns seemed unending but as his eyes grew accustomed to the dimness, he saw passageways branching off – branches. A great pressure settled on his chest. He couldn't feel his feet but at the same time he felt planted to the spot. Rising up from beneath him, he could feel a slow, regular pulsing and realised it resembled a heartbeat. The burls and grain in the wood seemed to shift when he caught them out of the corner of his eye.

She meant the tree. They were inside the tree.

Panic gripped Edwin's throat. He swallowed and tried to focus. This room was much larger than the tree. Why, he could encircle that with his arms, but this place was double his arm span.

"No, I don't believe it. Where are we really?"

Drusilla took a step away and reached her hand to the wall, running it down the grain of the wood. A sigh filled Edwin's ears, as if something were responding to her caress. He tried not to think that moments before she had been touching him. Her skin was the same colour as the wood. She looked back over her shoulder and smiled, and her familiar beauty in such abnormal surroundings was terrifying to see.

"We're in my tree, Sapling. We *are* the tree."

"Oh God, that's not possible!" Edwin was gripped with fear. Paralysed. Claustrophobia overwhelmed him and the residual desire expired.

The great sycamore was encasing him. Entombing him. A coffin not a temple.

"Don't be scared. I love you. I will keep you safe. I told you nothing would harm you. Look how beautiful it is here. Your devotion has helped it become so."

"No! It's impossible," Edwin croaked. His legs began to tremble. He reached out a hand towards her but at the last minute whipped it back. She was still naked and the curves of her breasts and belly now suggested the contours of the tree.

"For God's sake put some clothes on!"

Drusilla's mouth drooped and the iridescent eyes dulled a little; became pained. She tilted her head to one side, the human Drusilla and the slightly off-focus copy moving in perfect synchronisation. She shuddered and at once was clothed in a loose shift of fabric so fine and flimsy it was almost translucent. It did little to conceal her shape and nothing to rid Edwin of the memory of her naked body.

"You wanted to believe. Now you can believe," she urged.

She walked back towards him, hips swaying gracefully and his cheeks flamed. Even despite knowing what she was, he was still madly attracted to her. Edwin clenched his fists, ashamed of his depravity, and stepped away. It struck him with horror that there were no doors or windows.

He backed away again. "Stop this! You have to let me go."

"I'm not keeping you here." Her step faltered and her

shoulders drooped. Some of the glow left her skin. When she looked at him next her expression was undiluted misery.

"I thought you wanted to see," she whispered.

The distress in her voice twisted his heart, even while he was almost sick with fear and disorientation.

She tried to stroke his face but he ducked to the side again and found himself pressed against a column. He pushed hard, his fingers scraping against wood. He pushed with all his might and felt himself falling forwards.

He landed face down heavily, the breath forced painfully from his body. He twisted over and his head reeled. He blacked out and when he opened his eyes he was lying on the grass staring up at the branches of the sycamore tree. It was daylight and Drusilla was standing beside him. It was the Drusilla he knew. No rising hair, spreading like branches, no glowing skin, no shadow woman behind her. She was dressed in a loose gown the same colour as the wooden columns with a pattern of whorls running through it. It had been near midnight when he had kissed Drusilla, backing her against the tree. Now dawn was upon them. He had lost hours.

"Edwin, I'm sorry."

She stepped towards him, hand outstretched, and pure terror gripped his heart. For one moment he was completely unable to move and his brain scrambled for meaning, seizing on Medusa who petrified men with a single glance. Then the adrenaline flooded him and he scrambled away.

"Monster," he spat. He retched and covered his mouth.

Drusilla flinched. "Sapling! Edwin, my Sapling. I never meant to scare you."

"Don't call me that!" He pushed himself over onto his

hands and knees then stood. The change made him wobble. He reached out a hand to the tree trunk to steady himself, realised as he touched it what he was doing, and snatched his hand away as if it were on fire.

"You wanted to see what I am," Drusilla whispered.

Now the despair had gone from her voice and was replaced with indignation. It inflamed him. Her eyes were their usual mixture of green and hazel again and she looked fully human, her hair hanging loose over her shoulders and cascading down her back. Even now, knowing what he did about her, he couldn't tear his eyes away. She was beautiful and tragic. Her eyes glinted. As he watched, tears formed and fell down her cheeks.

Saltwater or sap?

He didn't know, but either way, the effect was to fill him with guilt at the sight of her distress and that was insufferable. She had brought this on herself with her deception.

"You didn't warn me what you were going to do!" he said accusingly.

"You told me you were brave. I've never shown anyone what's inside the tree before. You were the first." She took a step towards him, hands out in front of her, imploringly, then stopped and frowned. "You look pale. It's worrying me. I'm not sure I did the right thing."

He did feel slightly ill, as if he had a heavy cold coming. He glanced down and noticed his arms were covered in goose-pimples. Drusilla reached a hand to his face. Instinctively Edward raised his hands in protection. She flinched. He dropped his hands and gave a cry of despair and frustration.

"Stay away from me," he growled.

She stepped backwards against the trunk of the tree. Her tree.

Was she about to disappear into whatever the odd place had been? Once again, the feeling of claustrophobia rolled over him. He couldn't really believe he had been inside the tree but there was no other explanation that made sense. He was utterly convinced now that Drusilla was what she claimed to be and it terrified him. His world had tilted beyond comprehension. Edwin's knees shook and it was all he could do not to vomit. Shame coursed through him at his cowardice.

"Don't come near the house again," he said. "Don't try to hurt my family. Stay away or I'll have the tree cut down."

He turned on his heel and walked away, staggering as though he were drunk. As he left the grove his skin prickled with cold. He turned to look back and briefly thought he saw Drusilla's silhouette but there was only the tree there now. Whether she had gone inside it or was behind it he couldn't tell. Wherever it was, she had vanished.

Sykes was wheeling a barrow away from Stanley's stable towards the compost mound behind the walled garden. He glanced up, saw Edwin, and slowly lowered the handles of the barrow. Edwin stopped walking and stared back. Snatches of conversations reverberated inside his head and something inside his mind clicked; a cog turning and the teeth slotting into place. He stalked across the field towards the old gardener.

"You're up early, young Mister Hope. Or is it back late?"

"You knew what she is," Edwin blurted.

Sykes stared evenly at Edwin from beneath half-lowered eyelids. He didn't need to ask what Edwin was talking about, for which Edwin was grateful. It was a relief to know he was not going insane after all.

Sykes sucked his teeth. "Aye, I do. Didn't you?"

"Of course not! I mean..." Edwin brushed his hair from his eyes. It felt gritty. "She said she was a goddess but I thought it was a game she was playing."

"Goddess? Ha! That's a bit rich. A sprite of some sort at best but you've given her delusions above her station."

Edwin felt cold. His head ached and his throat felt dry. He couldn't remember the last time he had drunk anything since the wine at dinner. "You're talking as if it all makes sense! It doesn't."

"I tried to warn you to keep away, but you wouldn't listen. You knew best. I thought you must have known. You look pale. What did she do to you?"

"She showed me the truth. What she is. The tree is special." Edwin bit the inside of his cheek. He stopped talking. He was reluctant to tell Sykes where Drusilla had taken him.

Sykes shook his head and reached for the wheelbarrow handles. "You told me years ago not to grow the hedge back. Begged me. If you've changed your mind, I'll be glad to replant it. Even happier to set a fence. Iron is what you need. The hawthorn worked effectively enough but you broke through. It isn't permanent."

"What will iron do?" Edwin asked. Something in Sykes's tone set his teeth on edge. He seemed too eager to do it.

"Keeps them in. By all accounts, their kind can't cross it. Fence in the tree and she'll stay there."

"It seems very drastic," Edwin said. "Is that really what it will take?"

"Do you want her roaming free?" Sykes asked. His eyes were fixed on Edwin. "You'll know to stay away now, but who will be next?"

"I don't know."

Edwin dropped his head. The motion made it throb. He needed to sleep. He glanced at his wristwatch, but it had stopped, though he was scrupulous about winding it each morning. The hands were stuck at one minute past midnight – about the time he would have been pulled into Drusilla's world. He had no idea if time had been different inside the confines of the sycamore or if he had been insensible on the bare earth for hours, but either way he felt exhausted and ill.

"Drusilla hasn't done anything wrong. It is her nature, isn't it?"

"It's a snake's nature to strike but it'll still leave a corpse. Let me know what you decide," Sykes said. He sauntered off with his barrow, whistling.

Edwin made his way home and crept into the house. The smell of frying bacon wafted from the kitchen but instead of whetting his appetite, it turned his stomach. It was Sunday morning so he should be preparing for church but he could not face it. He staggered upstairs and barely made it to his bedroom before his strength gave out. He kicked off his shoes and crawled into bed, fully clothed, dragging the counterpane high. His teeth began to chatter and his feet felt as heavy as lead.

When his grandfather knocked on his door, demanding to know where he was, he muttered an apology. Who cared if his grandfather disapproved? There was precious little of which he did approve. He found his notebook and began to scribble down everything that had happened. The previous entry was from the afternoon of the hunt and he read that back. His vision blurred and he had to blink once or twice to clear it. He'd seen things no man should see and been somewhere no man had been. He should be rejoicing at what had been revealed, but all he felt was alarm and bewilderment. He dropped the book back on the table and lay down.

By lunchtime he was soundly asleep, and by six he woke in a tangle of damp sheets, his forehead and the back of his neck burning hot. He stripped off his trousers and shirt and dragged on his nightshirt then returned to bed.

He dreamed of branches encircling him and pinning him to the ground.

When Edwin awoke it was to semi-darkness. He groaned.

"Edwin, you're finally awake."

The female voice was familiar. Instantly, an image of Drusilla flashed across his mind and his limbs stiffened; then he remembered who the voice belonged to. A woman was sitting in the corner of his nursery. The same place she always had.

"Annie?"

His nursemaid. Disorientation rocked him. Was he a child still, the victim of the most incredibly realistic dream?

"I think I had a nightmare. It was terrible."

"I imagine you did. You've been asleep for over two days."

"Two days?"

Edwin sat bolt upright. His clothing felt stiff and reeked of perspiration. His belly ached from hunger. Annie crossed the room and pulled open the curtains. Sunlight filled the room. She turned back to him. She was the right age. He glanced surreptitiously at himself. An adult body.

"Yes. It's Tuesday now. You were ill so your grandfather requested my help. He said there was no one else who could tend to you. Mr Sykes said he had met you coming back from an early walk on Sunday morning and thinks you caught a chill. I'm glad I came because you were muttering about trees and coffins and if it had been left to that silly housemaid I'm sure you'd have scared her."

She passed him a glass of water. It was lukewarm but Edwin drank it thirstily then lay back on the pillows. He grimaced. The clock in the hallway chimed five. "I'm sorry you were troubled. Your family will have needed you."

"I haven't been here all the time. Just popped in occasionally to check on you. I'll go now I know you're well. I'll mention you are awake to your grandfather." Annie wrinkled her nose. "And ask the maid to draw you a bath."

She picked up a canvas bag with knitting needles poking out of the top and left. Edwin ran his hand over his face. It was rough with stubble and needed shaving. He pulled back the covers and swung his legs to the floor and, as he turned, his eye fell on the notebook. He opened it and looked at the writing that started neatly but descended into a barely legible scrawl. He closed it again and put the book back in the drawer. Anyone reading it would assume he was insane. He wouldn't blame them. He rubbed his hands across his face and through his hair. What he'd witnessed defied explanation. He needed to think about the implications, not least that the land owned by his grandfather was home to a supernatural being. Should the town become another Lourdes with pilgrims coming to pay their respects? He had no doubt Drusilla would like nothing more but he didn't feel particularly inclined to give it to her. He couldn't think here, when she was so close.

Once bathed and dressed, he made his way to Stephen's office. His grandfather gave him the merest hint of a smile and Edwin belatedly recalled that the last time they had spoken had been the clashing of opinions over Myrtle Crossle's desirability as a bride.

"I'm feeling better," he announced.

"Glad to hear it. Fortunately the factory has survived your absence."

"Good. Then it can survive a little longer without me," Edwin said. "I'm going to pay a visit to Yorkshire. A change of scene will do me the world of good, I think."

Drusilla fled into the safety of her sanctuary, passing through the barriers as easily as a finger bursting a bubble. It had taken more effort bringing the Sapling with her and she should have realised then that it was a mistake – a stupid, incautious urge to share everything with him.

An impulse.

Tears flowed freely, a torrent that stung her cheeks. She cared nothing for the discomfort. Rejection was a sharper knife. She dropped to the floor, wishing she could wipe the sight of Edwin's horrified expression from her mind; the harsh, guttural fear in his voice as he had turned from her.

Monster!

She had gone too far. She needn't have done what she did. Needn't have shown him the preternatural aspect of herself. She could have remained as human-seeming as him, but she'd wanted to show off and it had cost her dearly. She cringed, dropping to the floor in a huddle, and groaned. The tree pulsed with a throb of sympathy.

Mingling with her despair was disappointment. She had expected more from him. She had credited him with courage he did not in fact possess. She should never have brought him here. Ignorance would have been better.

She stood and stumbled over to the bed, sliding onto it and letting the firm, smooth frame support her. It wasn't very comfortable. She'd have gladly made love on the ground but she'd had an inkling that humans liked beds. Perhaps if she had created a whole room, Edwin would have been less unnerved.

She bit her lip. No, he would still have been terrified.

She closed her eyes. She was exhausted from the conflict, yet at the same time pulsating with energy that the level of his belief had given her. She took a deep breath, filling her lungs with sweet wood-scented air and closed her eyes. The hammering of the blood running through her veins slowed and the tree's heartbeat became more even.

She would think about the problem later.

Drusilla dreamed.

Dreamed of caressing Edwin, of making love to him as she had so wanted to, but as she did, her limbs changed. They became the wood, froze and seized up, her flesh turning to bark, encasing him in the confines of her arms however much she struggled to free him until they were both trapped, lifeless and immobile in a sarcophagus of her making.

She screamed and woke to the sound of it echoing all around, reverberating off the walls. It took her a moment to realise hers was not the only voice.

"Come out, if you're there! Face me, if you're brave enough."

The Old One.

She stood and ran her fingers through her hair, calming it, and gave herself a plain, narrow gown. She took herself up and out onto the thick branch and let her legs dangle.

"I'm here. What do you call me for in such a manner?"

He was standing there, leaning on a thick walking stick, and when he looked up and saw her, his face cracked into an unpleasant grin.

"Well you've done it now. He came to me this morning, wild-eyed and trembling. Demanded to know what sort of monster you were and why I let you out."

"Did he?" Drusilla's heart cracked. It was all so easy to imagine Edwin's frenzied state after the way they parted. Not for the first time since the sun had risen, she cursed herself. Cursed her stupidity and hubris.

"I got carried away in the pleasure of the moment," she admitted. "We both did. But I never meant for what happened to happen."

The old man's expression remained supercilious. "I'm sure of that. All the fun, none of the repercussions. You're older than me. I don't know how old, but for all that you're as naive and blind as a newborn lamb."

He chuckled unpleasantly. "Your kind are coming to an end. The world is changing. No one truly believes."

The Wild Hunt. Was the end of her kind what it heralded?

"He does now," Drusilla replied. She felt a warm glow in her belly. It was almost immediately extinguished by the frost in her heart, true, but Edwin's belief had been real.

"And what did it get you? You expected anything other than revulsion? I could have him begging me to enclose your tree in iron before the day is out."

She sat straighter, outraged at his insolence. The threat was the most severe she could imagine, short of destroying the tree. She'd be bound within it more surely than the hawthorn hedge had kept her weak. Her flesh pricked with fury. She threw her legs around and leapt out of the tree, landing slightly in front of the old man. He took a step back.

Good.

"How dare you come to my grove and taunt me! How dare you make threats!"

She flexed her feet, feeling the earth beneath them and took a step towards him. He backed away. His eyes bore the same glint of fear she had seen in Edwin's but she didn't care. She relished it.

"I am what I am. I can't change that and I wouldn't if I could. I make no apologies for it. In this place, if no other, you would be wise to show me some respect."

"Respect?" The old man's lip curled. "What do you deserve that for? A harlot spirit whose only purpose is to tempt men."

Drusilla reached her mind out and the bough closest to the gardener flexed, sweeping down as if a great gust of wind had caught it. The slender twigs at the end brushed against his cheek. Not enough to hurt, but enough to make sure he felt it. Alarm filled his eyes and she felt a rush of exhilaration.

"Speak to me like that again and the next one will take your eyes out," she snarled. "I could do it. I'm strong enough now. I'm strong enough."

"No doubt," he said. "But stupid enough? Do it and prove to me – prove to young Edwin – that you're the monster he thinks you are. I'll go back, blood on my face, straight to him and he'll have the saws and the tar pot here before you can snap your fingers."

"He wouldn't. Not to me." Drusilla curled her fingers in the folds of her dress. Her Edwin doing something so barbaric was beyond imagining.

"Wouldn't he?" The old man smirked. He narrowed his eyes and looked at her with a nasty expression. "Do you think he'd choose you over a fellow man? I don't."

She dropped her head, unsure. Until today she would have answered with certainty but after their parting she could not say with confidence.

"Good. You remember your place." The old man gave a satisfied laugh.

"Why have you come here?" she asked. "Just to taunt me?"

"No." The old man sucked his teeth. "I bring a message from him."

"From Edwin?"

She stepped forward eagerly then stopped as she saw the twisted enjoyment her eagerness gave.

"What does he want? Why didn't he come himself?"

"He won't be coming again. That's the message. He's gone to his family in Yorkshire for a time. When he comes back – if he comes back – he wants nothing to do with you. If he sees you before the day he dies it will be a day to soon, he says. You're not to go near him or his home."

Devastating.

The words cut deeply. Such pain in her chest and belly that she'd never before experienced. She wanted to fall to the ground and weep. She swallowed and tried to keep her voice steady. She would never let him see the effect of these words on her.

"I suppose this makes you happy?"

"It gives me satisfaction," the Old One admitted.

"Well you've told me the message. Now you can go."

"Gladly. But first, for your trick with the branch...."

He strode forward swiftly, lifting the cane, and pulled something from the handle. Metal glinted and she recognised it as a swordstick. He thrust it past her, the blade slicing across the bark of the trunk.

She felt the cut.

She staggered, a cry escaping her lips as she slumped back against the wounded trunk.

Agony in her side...

She slid to her knees, her limbs giving way from shock and pain. It was searingly acute. She pressed her hands to her waist but the pain didn't decrease.

The old man looked at her and, even through her shock, Drusilla saw the astonishment in his eyes.

"I didn't know that would happen. Do you need help?"

"Just get away from me!" she growled.

He replaced the blade in the stick and left.

Drusilla gasped, tongue and lips dry as the air entered her, colder than was natural on a warm day like today. Her hands trembled as she lifted them away from the throbbing wound, bracing herself for what she might see. To her relief there was no blood, only a long, livid weal, red in colour, surrounded by whiteness where it was raised up. She had no way of knowing whether a firmer stroke or an iron blade might have resulted in a different outcome.

She would heal but it would take time. All the reserves of energy she had gathered from Edwin's company would be used up.

It was her own fault.

She stared upwards. The sky was vivid blue, sunlight dappling her face through the criss-cross of branches; small pale-green samaras, already growing in clusters, waiting for autumn winds to break them free and spiral them away. They should have months of summer to grow full and yellow but as she lay there, she saw them begin to fall, fluttering over her as she lay.

She reached her hand to the tree, feeling the gouge in the trunk, and her eyes filled with tears.

"I'm sorry," she murmured, though she wasn't sure if she was speaking to the tree, to the Old One, or to the Sapling.

She was tired. More so than she could remember. There was no reason to remain awake so she closed her eyes, one hand still raised against the wound in the bark, the other crossed over her waist in an attempt to lessen the burning pain, but it didn't help.

Drusilla slept.

Chapter Fourteen

The Yorkshire house was unchanged but empty of the friends he had hoped to find. Demetria had received the proposal she had hoped for, so she and Eleni were spending most of their time in London, arranging wedding gowns. Joanna was in school, and Harold at the seminary. Edwin rattled around the too-large house. The silence was comforting, but every time he walked through the grounds he couldn't help glancing at the trees with suspicion. How many of them housed dryads like the sycamore at home?

Every day he scoured the newspapers, looking for signs of the trouble that the Wild Hunt had foretold. There were plenty of possibilities. Europe was increasingly ill at ease – lately there seemed to be petty conflicts breaking out everywhere, however nothing that was significant.

In later years Edwin considered it ironic that he, who had been watching so carefully for signs of impending disaster, paid barely any notice to the assassination of the Austrian archduke. It was only when war was definitively declared that he realised what that event had sparked off in Europe.

"I need to return home, I think," he told Aunt Madeline and Panos over afternoon tea in early September. "Kitchener wants men to enlist and I should do it from there rather than here. Grandfather would no doubt be happier if I was taking the opportunity to make connections with men from the town. I can't say he'd be wrong."

"Do you have to go at all?" Aunt Madeline asked, wrinkling her brow. "They say it will be over before too long. It won't last long enough to need boys of your age to train, I'm sure."

"It will last a shorter time if they go," Panos said. He gave Edwin a wide smile. "Good for you, young man."

Aunt Madeline still looked unconvinced. "Harold won't be going. Do you think he should abandon his studies and join one of these battalions?"

"Harold should stay where he is. He will be doing the Lord's work and helping in other ways," Panos said, crossing himself, before pouring a small cup of thick Greek coffee. "My country has decided on a course of neutrality at this point, though Eleni wrote to me begging me to let her go to France as a nurse. I refused of course. War is no place for women and she's far too young. She'll be wanting the vote next!"

Edwin kept his thoughts to himself. Eleni would no doubt have plenty to say on that matter.

Panos drove him to the station in his prized six-cylinder Belsize and on arrival presented him with a silver cigarette case.

"I know you don't smoke, but if you're going off to war, you'll make more friends by offering one."

Edwin took it, more touched than he would have expected by the gesture.

Stephen Brice had plenty to say on Edwin's decision, when he announced his intentions of attending the drill hall on Copse Lane.

"I see no reason why you should join these men," he thundered. "The 'Pals' they talk of are workers in factories, not their owners – the lower classes, in the main."

"London stockbrokers are hardly lower class and they formed the first battalion," Edwin pointed out, then quietly enjoyed the expression of indignation on his grandfather's face. "I'm going to enlist. It's the right thing to do. I'd have joined my old school but I thought I should fight with men from home. I hoped you'd be proud of me for answering the call."

Stephen clenched his jaw. "And if you don't return? What about your safety?"

Edwin's heart stirred, only to be dashed by his grandfather's next words.

"To whom shall I leave the factory if I have no heir?"

Edwin swallowed down bitterness. "To William, if you like. Or you could adopt a protégé. Excuse me, I don't want to be late and create a bad impression from the start."

He began to rise from his armchair.

"Wait." Stephen thrust out a hand. "Go and represent your family. For King and country and for Greete Mill."

Edwin took the extended hand and shook it. For the first time in his life he felt his grandfather's genuine warmth.

He walked out of the house and made his way to the drill hall, but as he neared it his resolve began to waver.

For all he'd said, he didn't want to die.

A voice boomed loud as Edwin approached the drill hall.

"It's a shame I never went to university. I could have gone straight in as an officer then."

Edwin stopped halfway up the path, his shoulders sagging as he recognised the voice of the man standing beside the door. It was even worse than he expected. Robert Carfax was already there, speaking to a pale blonde man Edwin vaguely recognised. Robert turned, saw Edwin, and pointed to the chevron on his arm. Lance corporal. He grinned.

"Looks like I'm your superior officer, Private Hope. Don't worry, I'll see you come back safely."

"How did you manage that?" Edwin asked. His heart sunk a little at the idea of Robert lording over him, with legitimate authority to do it.

"Words in the right ears." Robert tapped his nose. "Come inside and sign away your life."

Edwin obliged, and that was that.

Two days later he would be required to join the two-thirty train, bound for a park on the outskirts of Manchester that had been hastily turned into a training camp. He was provided with no uniform, only a kitbag to fill, and spent a long evening looking around his room and wondering what to take. His notebook was by the bed and he read the scrawled account of his aborted lovemaking with Drusilla. He was on the verge of tearing the pages out to twist into fire spills but hesitated. For the first time since that night he felt a pang of longing for her. He closed the book and put it beneath piles of detritus in his bedside drawer. If he didn't return and someone found it, they would assume it was made-up ravings. In that eventuality he would be dead and beyond caring what impression he left on the world. He supposed his grandfather would regret his death, even if only for the inconvenience it would cause. The Yorkshire family would be sad, of course, though not acutely.

He looked at the leaf, smoothing it with his fingers before placing it inside the cigarette case. The one friend he'd made had betrayed him in such a devastating way, but with a few months of distance he felt the bud of shame at his reaction.

If she'd shown him the truth in a less dramatic way, wouldn't he have revelled in the chance to learn about her?

He couldn't bear to leave without trying to see her. He doubted she would try what she had done before, but even so, he'd be cautious.

The day he was due to leave, he walked up to the sycamore tree at noon and stood outside the boundary to the grove. He called Drusilla's name softly, slightly troubled that it took three attempts before she appeared. She walked halfway between the trunk and the edge of the grove. Her face was in shadows that rippled over her hair. Her dress was pale, barely green, and shapeless, and hung from her frame. The cape she wore matched the leaves which looked yellowed before their time. Edwin understood now that her attire was in keeping with the seasons – more evidence he should have spotted that she had been telling the truth all along. It was mid-September and had been slightly drizzly for days, but he was not expecting to see her at her most fragile. She shouldn't be like this now.

He walked towards her, forgetting his resolve not to step into the grove but she held a hand up and he stopped.

"Are you unwell?" he asked in concern.

He gestured at the tree, seeing now he was closer that it looked unkempt. "Is this because I left?"

"Not your doing."

She closed her eyes, shaking her head. She swayed slightly. Above them the wind blew a gust through the branches that sounded like disappointment.

"I thought you didn't want to see me," she said. "After what happened I don't blame you."

Edwin winced inwardly. "I should have come sooner. I was in Yorkshire for a while."

"Yes. The Old One told me when he brought your message."

"What message?" Edwin frowned in confusion. "When?"

Drusilla took a step forward. She was moving slowly, awkwardly, Edwin realised. Something was badly wrong with her. A wash of protectiveness took him by surprise, greater than when she had fainted on the steps on that devastating night.

"The evening after … after what happened between us. Then I didn't see you again. He told me you wanted nothing to do with me. Told me to keep away." She smiled sadly. "And I've done it."

Edwin looked at her in horror, fury rising in his breast at Sykes's deception. "I never said that to him. I never sent him at all. Why, for a few days I was ill and incapable of speaking to anyone."

"Ill? That was my fault." Her face twisted and she put her hands to her head, digging her fingers into her hair. "I shouldn't have taken you where I took you. I can come into your world but you obviously can't come into mine. I didn't realise what would happen."

Once again, Edwin felt the tightening of branches round him, squeezing the breath from his lungs. Claustrophobia reared up. He shook it off as best he could.

"Tell me about the message," he insisted.

"He came to me. The Old One. We spoke angrily. He told me you said that if you saw me before you died it would be a day too soon. Didn't he come at your behest?"

"No he did not!" Edwin exclaimed. The vein at the side of his temple pulsed. He glanced over his shoulder towards the house. Sykes was nowhere in sight, otherwise Edwin might have stormed through the meadow and demanded an explanation.

"You must believe me, I never said such a thing."

He'd thought it though. Had been determined to stay away from her forever. Had called her a monster. Self-recrimination bubbled up inside him.

"Look, I have to go soon. Oh, this is dreadful. I can't talk to you now. I have so many questions. What you are shouldn't be possible. I don't even remember half of what you told me before I believed. I want to learn everything about you. You are a marvel. A miracle. Just imagine what science could do for our understanding of you! Why, there are machines now that can photograph the bones inside you and look at your organs."

Drusilla frowned. "And what if I don't have them? What if I enter this machine and discover I have branches for arms and twigs for fingers?"

"Why then it would be wonderful," Edwin said with a laugh. "You would be the first example of a new species. The first understanding of a literal miracle."

Her fingers paused against his jaw.

"What then? What happens to me? The doctors would let me go and I would return here to live my life in peace? Of course not. I would be paraded across Europe – across the world – as a monstrosity. I'd be put on display for all to see."

She held her hand up in front of her, flexing and bending her fingers. "Why everyone knows new shoots can grow where old ones have been cut. Shall I let them chop off one of these to see if another grows in its place? An arm and a leg?"

"Good God no!" Edwin said. He wanted to wrap his arms around her, hold her close and feel her bare skin against his. It would be impossible, then, to tell that she wasn't human but she spoke the truth. "I would never let them do that."

She gave him a sad smile.

"Do you think you would be given a choice?"

"No." Edwin reached for her, overcome with emotion and a surge of protectiveness. "I swear to you that I will never let you come to harm."

Drusilla stepped closer. Edwin should have met her halfway but he was still reluctant, feet made heavier by what he had experienced before.

"Come tomorrow," she said, reaching out a hand to him. "I'll explain what I can."

He shook his head. "I can't."

Her lips twisted. She dropped her hand. "Don't worry, I know not to try to take you inside again."

Edwin blinked. She didn't know about the train, of course. Did she know about the war? If she'd spoken to no one besides Sykes since that fateful night it was entirely possible that she didn't.

"I can't. Really. There's a train I have to be on. Drusilla, we're at war. Not just Great Britain, but the whole of Europe. I think it's what the Wild Hunt was warning of. I'm joining up. A whole battalion of the men from the town are going. We leave on the two-thirty train."

He watched as her face fell, eyes growing wide. She shook her head. "I knew something had happened but I was barely paying attention to the world. You can't go. It will be dangerous."

"Oh, it won't last long," Edwin said brightly, using the same tone everyone seemed to use when making that prediction. "I imagine it will be a great adventure. I probably won't even fire a shot. Which will be just as well because I don't know how to fire a rifle," he finished with a chuckle.

Drusilla didn't laugh.

"Then you can't go," she said. She came to his side, reached for his hand, and clutched it tightly. It was the first time they had touched since that night, but he felt no fear now, only the sensation of comfort that someone cared enough about him to want him to be safe.

"Wars always lead to death. I remember the militia going off to the war in their red uniforms. The women cheered as they marched away but were crying afterwards. I counted them as they went but I don't know

213

how many returned." She drew her hand back and hugged her waist.

"I remember the glint of their sabres in the sunlight. Young men going off to be slaughtered. Don't be one of them."

"I have to do this. What right do I have to refuse and send others in my place? What sort of man would I be?"

"A living one," Drusilla snapped. She turned away then back again and her eyes glinted with tears that were caught by thin beams of sunlight. "Oh, I know I can't stop you. You will be in my mind and in my heart every day."

"Drusilla, I…" He didn't know how to finish the sentence; wished he hadn't started it. The tears in her eyes were speaking to something inside him, daring him not to release his own. He walked to her, took her face between his hands and placed a gentle kiss on her forehead. He half tasted, half smelled a lingering sensation of leaf mould and bonfires and a dull leaden feeling in his belly worried him. Something was wrong but he was out of time to discover it.

"Do you forgive me?" she asked.

"I do."

He cringed.

"Do *you* forgive *me*?"

"Yes."

She lifted her head and brushed a finger over his lips. "Wait here!"

She walked back to the tree. Edwin watched as she pressed her palms against it. Her body seemed to ripple and take on the form of the tree. Looking at her made his eyes water. He blinked rapidly and when his vision cleared, she had vanished. He swallowed audibly, wondering whether that was what he had looked like when she drew him inside it. He stared at the place she had last been. The trunk had an odd blemish running down it where the wood was a slightly lighter colour and looked like fresh growth. He stared at it, wondering if it had always been there and he'd just never noticed it. He planned to ask Drusilla, then she reappeared, the trunk bulging and forming the vague sense of womanish curves that grew more solid, at first the colour of the bark then taking on the honey-brown hue of Drusilla's skin. She stepped towards him with her hand outstretched.

"I have something for you." She pressed something into his hand and closed his fingers over it. She stepped back and smiled. "A charm of sorts."

Edwin opened his fingers. On his palm lay a small wooden figure, arms at its sides, legs straight but lacking in detail. It was about the size of Edwin's little finger and carved (or formed) from smooth sycamore wood, but anyone who would not know what they were looking at might mistake it for a twig. The figure wore a thin stole or scarf of tightly braided hair.

"Thank you," he murmured.

Drusilla shrugged. "The Welsh use sycamore wood for lovers' spoons and the hair is mine."

"And the wood is yours as well?" Edwin asked, already knowing the answer.

She must have blushed, because a little colour appeared in her previously wan cheeks. "Yes. I don't know if you will encounter anyone like me. I don't know how many of us there are left."

Her eyes dropped and Edwin shivered at the loneliness

emanating from her. To be the last of one's kind must be a terrible thing.

"If you do encounter anyone then they will know that you are protected by me. It might help you. I don't know."

"Am I?" he asked. "Protected?"

"And loved," she whispered, biting her bottom lip. It was almost impossible to believe she wasn't a flesh and blood woman. She met his gaze. "It's all right. You don't have to say anything but I wanted you to know. And that I'm sorry for scaring you before."

Her lips twitched. Edwin flushed, his neck becoming warm. He felt boorish now for his reaction towards her. He should have been braver.

"It's all forgotten," he said. It was a lie. The alarm would last for much longer, but this might be the last time they met and she didn't need to bear that burden.

"Please come back safely, Edwin. Perhaps we might be friends again."

"I'll try," he said, grinning wider than he felt inside. "And what of you? You're looking far too wintery for my liking. I wish there were something I could do."

"I shall survive, as I always do. I'm brave and I'm happy to have seen you again."

"The war will be over soon. By Christmas, I've heard some say. I'll be back before too long."

"When I shall no doubt be sleeping and will miss the news," Drusilla commented.

Edwin took her hands. "When I get back I shall hang a garland on your tree so that when you wake in spring you will know."

"That would be nice. Yes, do that please," she said, raising her head to look into his eyes. She tilted her head slightly on one side and his throat tightened as he felt the familiar stirrings of desire, but accompanying it, a swelling of affection of which he'd previously barely been aware.

"I need to go," he said. "My grandfather is waiting to walk me down to the station."

She nodded, but he didn't move, feeling something was unfinished. He reached out and tucked a loose strand of hair behind her ear, wishing it had the lustre it once had, and it came to him then.

"I don't know if you'll find another acolyte while I'm gone, but in case you don't, I hope this will sustain you a little. Consider it payment for your charm."

He put his hands to her face and kissed her fully on the lips. There was the briefest moment when her mouth remained inflexible but then she softened, her arms came around his neck, and she was kissing him back, as passionately as he was kissing her. He closed his eyes, giving himself up to the kiss. She tasted sweet. The scent of warm grass came to mind; summer dew on early morning lawns. Tearing his lips from hers was a torment but when he looked at her he would swear in a court of law that her eyes were brighter and her cheeks smoother.

"I believe in you, my goddess," he murmured.

He stepped backwards out of the grove, the sighing of the breeze through the boughs echoing in his ears.

Chapter Fifteen

The war was not over by Christmas. For Edwin and Robert, it did not strictly start until the July of 1915 when their battalion finally embarked for Le Havre.

The interim period was spent training.

Marching. More marching. Swedish Drill. Learning to shoot. Learning to dig trenches (and assault them). More marching.

"We could have marched to Paris if we'd gone in a straight line," was the grumble most frequently heard, as every man demonstrated his keenness to go and fight.

Edwin, like most of the lads, chafed at the bit, frustrated, and was ecstatic to finally set foot in France. Years later, like many others, he preferred not to talk about what he had encountered there. Many of the months were monotonously alike. New trenches, new company, new commanders; none particularly remarkable. Edwin kept no diary and committed little to memory beyond the names of friends he made and later lost.

Some events were seared on his mind.

He spent his twenty-first birthday in a bar-cum-brothel in a backstreet of Amiens. Robert had slipped the eventful date into conversation as the men huddled in their trench drinking tea.

"We need to make a man of him, chaps," he'd said, nudging Edwin in the ribs.

The rest of the men hooted and cheered enthusiastically. Edwin grimaced, a sinking feeling growing in his belly that had nothing to do with the mealy, hard biscuits he was eating. He resigned himself to his fate and later that evening, when the shift changed, he duly strolled into the town with Robert and the two men he now counted as his closest friends.

Amiens was a thriving city, frequently visited by the Allied troops and the battalion considered themselves lucky to have been stationed close by.

"One day perhaps you'll get in there too," Edwin joked, as they passed the Hotel Carlton which the British officers frequented and wound further into the narrow streets of the Quartier St-Leu. The other lads sniggered. It was common knowledge that Robert's lack of promotion from lance corporal irked him. Robert grinned grudgingly and they carried on.

"Somewhere to make us all feel at home," he said as they made their way past factories and tanneries huddled together on the banks of the river Somme. A couple of bars and late-night cafés were already full, and women lounged against walls in what they presumably thought were enticing poses, cheap skirts hitched above their knees and breasts half-visible.

"Don't you think it's odd that we've come all this way and we've found ourselves surrounded by textile mills," Edwin commented, looking around.

"You're more interested in the industry than the women." Robert rolled his eyes and made a rude gesture.

"It's a good omen that we'll get back home," said Davy Lucas, a lanky cardmaker from the mill at the other end of town.

"I hope so," Edwin agreed. He shoved his hands into his pockets to find a handkerchief and felt the small figure that Drusilla had given him. It had always been there but usually it nestled in the corner so it felt odd that it had come so readily to hand. He drew it out and twisted it between his fingers and thumb.

"What have you got there?" Robert asked.

"Just a good luck charm." Edward closed his hand over it protectively then uncurled his fingers, reasoning that Robert would sense his defensiveness. Most of the men had something they kept in their pockets along with tobacco, mints, and general clutter – coils of a wife's or lover's hair (in one case, both); others had a rabbit's foot or pressed flowers.

"What! Do you have a sweetheart back home? I didn't know that," Robert said, raising his brows in an exaggerated leer. "Are we too late to make a man of you tonight?"

"Just a friend." Edwin rubbed his fingers over the smooth wooden figure before slipping it back into his pocket. He felt a flash of guilt at what he was about to do, though Drusilla would never know or probably even care.

"Let's get this over with."

The collective bravado began to ebb slightly as they turned down a lonely unlit alleyway and found themselves outside a seedy-looking establishment where a heavy-set man sat on a stool guarding the entrance. Whether he was there to stop people entering or prevent them from leaving later was something on which Edwin decided not to dwell.

"Are we really doing this?" he muttered.

He exchanged a glance with Davy, who looked even more nervous than Edwin felt. Robert slung his arm around Edwin's shoulder and his other around that of John, who by the look of his stance had already been waiting longer than he wanted to be.

"Of course we are!"

"It works like this," John explained. "We go in, paying the gentleman on the door, of course, and then we have a glass of wine at the bar. Then, if you want to negotiate anything else with the fair ladies, that's up to you. Personally, I plan to skip the drinks and get cock-deep into a big-titted French whore as soon as possible."

"Don't you have a wife at home?" Edwin asked.

John winked. "At home. Not here. Look here, Hope, for all I know I'll be dead within a week so what she doesn't know won't hurt her."

"Unless you give her the clap," Davy said nervously.

"That's why we're here," Robert said, jerking his thumb towards the door. "The girls are clean. Come on, we need to be back in two hours and I'm not wasting any more time while you decide what you're capable of. Sit and play with yourself in the corner while the rest of us have fun, for all I care."

Edwin glared. "Maybe just a drink. To start off with."

The bar was stifling, with an overwhelming smell of competing perfumes and large vases of drooping flowers. The walls were papered in red and gold, with furnishings consisting of shabby tables with half a dozen stools not particularly arranged at them. A couple of middle-aged men were sprawling on stools at the bar, women on their laps. True to his word, John disappeared with a woman almost as soon as they stepped through the door. She was black-haired and did indeed have the largest pair of breasts – barely contained in a red blouse – that Edwin had ever seen. Despite his nervousness, he couldn't ignore the flutterings of excitement at being so close to women.

Robert ordered a carafe of red wine and they sat at a table in the corner. The wine, when it arrived, tasted sour so it was probably a blessing that it had been watered down as well.

"This isn't for me," Davy whispered to Edwin. "I'm going home."

"I'll come with you, I think," Edwin replied. He put his almost full glass on the table.

"No you don't," Robert said. He grabbed Edwin's hand and raised it aloft. "It is his birthday today. He is a man," he cried.

He repeated it in halting French, which received a couple of cheers from the other patrons, and Edwin hoped he was saying the same thing. None of them had got particularly proficient at the language yet. The woman who had been serving drinks spoke rapidly in French and three youngish women walked from behind a heavy curtain beside the bar. The madam waved her hands, proudly displaying what was on offer. There were two blondes and a brunette. The brunette was scrawny and looked tired, with very red lipstick. The blondes looked slightly healthier. The one on the left was younger, maybe only a few years older than Edwin. She had bare arms which were covered in curious smudges which Edwin realised in horror were bruises caused by fingertips.

"That one," he said on impulse. The sight tugged sympathy from him through his nerves. He would be kind to her and, selfishly, he hoped she would be gentle with him if she realised he had no intention of hurting her. She led him down the corridor behind the bar in the same direction John had gone. The July temperature was already hot but in the windowless corridor the air felt almost tangibly thick, smelling unappealingly of sweat and bodily functions. The room the woman led him to had a small window which thankfully let a little air in. She left the door unlocked and gestured to a bed. They stood opposite each other. She was quite pretty with big eyes and a sweet smile. Her breasts were quite full and she had invitingly large hips.

"What should I do?" Edwin asked.

She spoke in French, frowning.

Edwin cringed. It was dreadful.

"You want hand, mouth, or *foufoune*?"

"Oh God, I don't know." Edwin's cheeks flamed. They all sounded terrifying. They all sounded enticing.

"You first time are we, yes?" The woman pouted then narrowed her eyes at him. She put her hands to his chest and began to unbutton his shirt. Edwin tried to stop himself from trembling, ashamed of the way his body responded. Every speck of morality in him told him this was wrong.

"What's your name?" he asked in faltering French.

She pouted again and stopped unbuttoning his shirt. "What you want it to be?"

The blood drained from Edwin's face; drained from his cock, leaving him limp.

Drusilla's face filled his mind, asking him the same question. With horror he thought of what he was about to do. This woman meant nothing to him. He meant nothing to her so what on earth was the point of this uncomfortable, embarrassing coupling?

He stepped back. "I've changed my mind."

She looked puzzled, either not knowing those words or unused to what he was doing. He wished he knew them in French.

"No. *Non, merci.*"

She took a step towards him and began to unbutton her dress. She slipped it off when it was unbuttoned to the waist and stood in a thin slip that was so transparent he could see her deep pink nipples through the fabric.

"*Non,*" he said again, but she kissed him. She tasted of wine and garlic and unbrushed teeth. He didn't want to kiss this woman. He wanted lips that tasted of grass and sugared almonds. Cherry syrup and warm sunlight.

He wanted Drusilla.

"I'll pay you anyway," he said twisting out of her grip. "It's not your fault."

He pulled out his wallet. How much should it cost? It wasn't fair that she should lose out because he changed his mind. He shoved some notes into her hand and left.

He walked warily down the corridor back towards the bar, planning to have a drink and wait for the others to come back. It occurred to him belatedly that he could have just asked the woman if he could stay in the room until a decent time had passed. After all he had paid for it, but it was too late to go back now.

His heart sank when he saw Robert appear at the end of the corridor and turn the door handle on the first room. He had clearly finished the carafe of wine before choosing and had a fresh one in his hand.

"Are you finished already?" Robert leered. "Good going, Hope."

Edwin forced his mouth into a smile. Robert's smile dropped. "You didn't do it, did you!"

"Excuse me," Edwin said backing against one side of the cramped corridor to edge past. "I'll see you back at barracks."

"Wait a minute," Robert said catching his arm. Edwin shrugged him off.

"I'm going back to the barracks. You go on in," Edwin snapped, cocking his head to the room. "You're wasting your time."

"I know I am," Robert said. "What are you playing at, Edwin? Have some fun."

"That isn't fun," Edwin said waving his arm towards the corridor.

"You won't know if you don't try it," Robert said. "Don't be such an old maid. It's nothing to be ashamed of. The natural needs, and all that."

"I'm not ashamed!" Edwin swallowed. He looked at the carpet and took a deep breath.

"Hopeless Hope," Robert sneered.

Edwin couldn't say where the urge came from but he lunged forward and pushed Robert hard in the chest.

"Don't ever call me that again, Carfax! Never again."

Robert staggered back, fortunately too surprised to respond physically.

"I could have you on a charge. Assaulting a superior officer."

"Then do it," Edwin yelled. "I don't care."

He squared his shoulders and planted his feet firmly. He met Robert's mocking gaze, seeing in the man's eyes the boy who had tormented him as a child.

Robert scowled then sighed wearily. "Oh for goodness' sake, Hope, don't be such a prude. Look, I'm busy. Go sit in the bar and wait."

The door Robert had stopped at opened from the inside. A tall, lean young man stood there, white shirt unbuttoned, revealing a smooth chest, and a roll-up hanging from the corner of his mouth.

"Bobby? Are you coming in? You 'ave the wine?"

Edwin looked at Robert, who was standing frozen, his face a mask.

"Bobby?"

The gigolo looked at Edwin and his eyes widened. "You have brought another?"

Edwin blanched as realisation of what Robert had planned struck him. "*Non, merci,*" he said, addressing the man. He stumbled into the bar. Robert followed him.

"You weren't meant to see that!" Robert muttered, catching his arm. "Didier and I—"

"I don't care what you do." Edwin shrugged him off. "Your sins are your own."

He pushed his way through the curtain and back into the bar. There were two new patrons sitting at tables, presumably

227

waiting until a girl – or man – was free. He ignored them and walked out into the street. He took a deep breath of night air. It was muggy but a hundred times clearer than inside the brothel. His head spun and his tongue tasted sour from the cheap wine.

Robert rushed into the street, saw Edwin, and hurried over.

"Are you going to blackmail me now?"

He sounded desperately worried for the first time that Edwin could remember. It should have given Edwin a rush of power, but he felt empty.

"Don't insult me," Edwin snapped. "Do what you like, with whomever you like. I'm done with you. Yes, I am a virgin but so what? Let me tell you something: the girl who gave me that charm is a girl worth waiting for. If you think it's fun, fucking some poor man you have to pay, then go back and enjoy yourself."

Edwin dropped his eyes and shoved his hand into his pocket and felt for the charm. The familiar shape of the wooded figure and the smooth lock of hair was calming and slowly he felt a trace of serenity settling on him – the first he had felt all evening. By God, he wanted Drusilla. Not just to make love to her (though he really did want that too) but to talk to, laugh with, argue with even.

"I'm willing to wait for something good," he said a little calmer. "I don't expect you to understand but really I don't care if you don't. Have a good evening."

He turned and walked away, exhilarated. It felt like putting childhood scores to bed. It felt wonderful. Half a dozen paces later Robert caught up with him.

"Wait, Hope. Edwin. Please."

Edwin stopped, crossed his arms, and stared in suspicion.

"I don't pay Didier! It isn't like that. He isn't one of *them*. We pay for the room, that's all." Robert muttered. He dropped his head. "It would kill my father if he found out. I've tried to ignore the feelings but I can't. I don't want to quarrel with you, Hope. You're the only real friend I've got here. Can we forget this happened? All of it. We're supposed to be fighting the Hun, not each other."

Edwin ground his teeth. There was real despair in Robert's voice and Edwin felt pity for him. "Then don't be such an ass. I don't care what your tastes are. I care that you are a bully and a boor." He sighed, seeing Robert's face twist into mortification. "If you can try to be tolerable for five minutes at a time I might endure you until this is all over"

Robert gave Edwin a lopsided grin of relief. "Just don't make me grow a damned conscience, will you. Let's go find a bar and have a drink. Just a drink, I promise. John's going to be a while and hopefully we'll find Davy lost just down the road."

Edwin felt something had shifted. The Robert who strolled at his side could, in time, become someone he could like.

"All right," he muttered.

They walked away from the brothel. Edwin gave the charm one last rub for luck and tucked it safely away.

She'd tried to keep track of the days but it was hard. Easier to count the months. Easier still to count the seasons. There had been eleven since Edwin had left, including the autumn when they had spoken. Three and a half years.

Two springs where she had woken to find no garlands on the tree, and now a third. Drusilla hadn't idled away her time in the summers but had kept watch and listened for any trace of conversation she might hear from people who passed by the field. Nothing good came to her ears.

Now it was early spring. Blossoms were beginning to bud and the air was losing its icy bite. It was from her vantage point high in the branches that she spotted the Old One walking up the meadow with an axe over his shoulder.

Fear paralysed Drusilla. While Edwin was away the Old One intended to rid himself of her, finishing what he had started with the sword stick. Try as she might, Drusilla couldn't prevent her fingers straying to the scar at her waist. They trembled as they brushed over it. Like the bark of the tree, she had healed, but the memory of the pain and the shock remained.

She clambered down and stepped forwards, cladding herself in a dress of pale green, taking her inspiration from the women who occasionally walked or cycled past. Fashions had changed and hems now came to mid-calf. The breeze around her lower legs felt delightful; the grass beneath her bare feet already deep and springy. She had no time to appreciate it, however, as the Old One had arrived.

She stood at the edge of the grove to await her enemy. While she was under the canopy of leaves she felt safer and doubted he would push past her to enter her domain. The branches reached further than they once had, she noticed absent-mindedly. She had grown. The old man swung the axe over his shoulder and rested it on the ground, leaving his crossed arms over the top. He lifted his eyes to meet hers then made a show of looking up at the tree, assessing it.

"He'll know you did it," Drusilla said. She stepped forwards, doing her best to hide the fear that simmered inside her. "We spoke before he left. He knows you lied to me about him not wanting to see me."

She sensed slight uncertainty emanating from him.

"When he returns from war, how much do you think he'll care?"

"He'll care," Drusilla said with certainty that ebbed as soon as the words left her mouth. A horrifying thought struck her: the Old One wouldn't risk Edwin's rage.

"Why today? The Sapling... Is he...? Has something happened to him?"

"No, he's alive and as well as anyone could be, from what I gather. At least he was a month ago when his grandfather last heard from him." The old man's eyes narrowed and he sucked his teeth. "You genuinely care, don't you."

"You sound surprised." Drusilla felt her jaw clench.

"I am."

Drusilla licked her lips, feeling them forming into a soft smile. "So am I if it comes to that," she admitted. "Yes, I care for him a great deal, my gentle Sapling."

"Ha."

He steepled his hands on the upturned axe handle. He frowned. Not angry exactly, but uncertain. Drusilla took a cautious step closer, sensing his resolve was starting to crumble slightly.

"What have you come here for today? What supposed injury have I caused you now?"

"Facts are, we need wood. Fuel's becoming scarce. Food too. This war has gone on for longer than anyone suspected it could and if it carries on into another winter we will need all the fuel we can get."

The old man removed his hat and rubbed a rough hand across his forehead. He had the grace to look slightly abashed. He looked tired too. A well-directed branch thrust at him could probably put him out of action long enough for Drusilla to reach the axe. What then, though? He'd just return with another, possibly with help, and she'd have to hide.

"The wood needs time to season so we can't leave it too late to cut it."

"So you'd hurt me or kill me for that?" Drusilla asked. "If the tree dies, I die with it."

"Sure about that, are you?"

He was perceptive indeed, this Old One. Her eyes flickered towards the stump of the old sycamore. It had existed for as long as she was conscious. Had an aspect of herself once lived there, or was that another dryad altogether? She reached out towards it and saw flashes of someone else. Pain and comfort. Death and life. The thought of surrendering herself to discover it made her limbs feel hollow and leaden.

"You're not prepared to sacrifice yourself for the war effort? Edwin is. There are mothers who work in the factory whose sons are. Some already have. What makes you special?" Sykes glanced around and curled his lip. "That said, if you care to suggest another victim to save yourself…"

"There are no other victims to offer," Drusilla said bitterly. "The old oak by the church gate once housed a spirit back when I was barely formed, but she's long gone. None of these trees hereabouts are what I am. I'm the last of my kind that I know of within distance of reaching."

A great sob welled up inside her, pushing from her suddenly tight chest into her throat. Her bottom lip trembled and she bit it, doing her best not to show her sadness to her enemy.

The old man pursed his lips. "You're not going to start sobbing now are you, lass?"

Drusilla shook her head, then raised it and looked him in the eye. "Not in front of you. I wouldn't give you the satisfaction."

He blinked first, but seemed unmoved, because he hefted the axe. "What's it to be? Will I get to hack off a few branches? They'll grow back. Or shall I take the whole tree?"

Drusilla closed her eyes. She took a deep breath, filling her lungs with sweet spring air. Another year – another winter – alone and what would she be in any case? If Edwin didn't return would she care that she survived the axe?

The old man coughed and she opened her eyes. He was looking at her almost kindly.

"Fact is, I have no intention of harming your tree. I remember what happened to you before. I don't like you but I'm not a murderer."

She sagged. He'd been toying with her.

She looked around at the fields – wild grasses starting to make their mark on the post-winter soil. In a moment of clarity she saw another option.

"You need food as well as fuel, don't you? I can help you, you know. Not with fuel but I can influence the land. Anything you want to grow I can help with and it will prosper. Wouldn't that be more use?"

"You can make the crops grow?" He sounded sceptical. He wouldn't be the first.

Drusilla gestured around them. "Look at my tree. Look at the grass in the grove and just beyond the edge. Better already than that surrounding it. That's my doing. There's a reason my kind was courted and worshipped."

The old man stood silently but she could see his eyes moving side to side.

"And what do you want in return? I know your kind work on bargains," he said.

She thought. Now it was her turn to make him wait. That was the least he should give her for the effort it would take. He wouldn't worship her; there was too much bad blood between them. She most certainly didn't want to take him to bed, but the old man's grandfather had been her lover once and it felt incestuous for it even to be a passing consideration. More than that was the knowledge that somewhere out there was a man whom she valued.

And that was what he could give her of course.

"I want news of Edwin. If he writes to his grandfather and you hear anything, please let me know. If he feels well or ill. If he's scared or lonely."

The old man barked a laugh of genuine amusement. "Do you know him at all if you think he'd write that to Mr Brice? They aren't close."

"I know. What causes a grandfather to hate his only grandchild?" Drusilla asked. "Do you know? You've been here for long enough."

"Well..." The Old One stopped. He narrowed his eyes then grinned. "That's how you do it, isn't it? Draw a man into a conversation. Next you'll be telling me how clever I am and then you'll be beguiling me."

Now Drusilla laughed. "Don't worry about that! I don't want you for a lover. Just as an occasional messenger."

"Aye, that I can do. Is that it?"

He seemed friendlier than ever. They'd never be friends but he might not always be an enemy. "I'd like newspapers or periodicals. I want to know what is happening in the world. Perhaps the occasional book too? Edwin used to read Wilkie Collins to me," she said hopefully.

This brought a smile to the old man's lips. "You don't ask for much, do you?"

"The happier I am the better I'll be able to help you," she pointed out. "There's a world out there and I live on the edges of it. I'd go further if I could but I don't know if that's possible."

"Probably best you don't. Yes, I think I can bring you those. I'll do the planting, you do … whatever it is you do, and if the crops grow well I'll bring you a book or two. Agreed?"

"We have an understanding." Drusilla extended a hand. It took a lot of effort to ensure it didn't shake. As it turned out there was no need.

"My word is my bond," Sykes said. "That's as much as you or I need to agree. No shaking or anything like that, thank you very much."

He lifted the axe over his shoulder. "Of course, if you don't keep your part of the bargain there's always this."

He walked away, whistling an old tune.

As an alliance it was successful. Sykes and another man turned over the gardens and the gentler slope of the meadow to vegetables. He planted apple tree saplings along the ridge. At dusk, when the light cast long shadows, Drusilla walked between them, feeling the life sprouting and spreading beneath her feet. She watched each tree carefully, hoping for signs of ownership or occupation by one like her, but there were none.

Sykes was as good as his word and once a month brought a pile of Saturday newspapers and a periodical. News of Edwin was less frequent and, as he had warned her, very sparse – trenches dug in foreign fields; marching; food eaten; tiredness; nothing intimate or demonstrative – but he was alive.

The harvest was abundant. The year had been a good one. By the arrival of winter, she was ready to rest. The December clouds had been growing grey by the day and she was unsurprised when she felt the first soft flakes of snow brushing the uppermost branches.

She'd wait another day or two. Sykes was due to bring the newspapers the following morning. She would read them and stare longingly at the advertisements for clothing, imagining herself wearing the silk and lace garments to seduce Edwin into her bed.

Such a shame that he had never made love to her. She walked down through the meadow which now bore few signs of the lustrous vegetation. Never mind. The rock-hard ground would thaw again come spring. She spent some time talking to the old horse. His eyes were losing their lustre and his coat felt rough. She doubted that he would be there when she woke in spring.

When Sykes arrived, she greeted him halfway down the meadow.

"I'm going to sleep soon. Winter's a time for rest. I'll see you in the spring." She folded her hands into the sleeves of her coat which was long and heavy with a soft, high collar. He still made her wary but she was determined not to show it. "My tree will be safe, won't it?"

"Aye. It will. Maybe by the time you wake the war will be over and the men will be back."

She felt her eyes moisten. "He said he'd put a garland in my branches if he returned and I was asleep."

Sykes rolled his eyes, but there was no malice in them. "Silly romantic notions! Well, maybe next year will be the one. It'll be 1918. This can't go on forever."

She woke when the blossoms began to bud and the air lost its bite.

No garland.

Dejected, she slipped out from beneath the boughs and a little way into the meadow, keen to see if the ground was rejuvenated, and took a deep breath. She expected the familiar freshness of spring dew but there was a pungency to the air that stifled her.

She sniffed again, trying to catch the meaning. The sickly, iron aftertaste of blood filled her nostrils. Something had happened or was about to happen.

Edwin?

Her fingers flexed and for a moment she felt paralysed.

A crow shrieked from the church spire, breaking her

transfixion.

She raced back to her tree and under the shelter of the branches.

Something was coming.

She didn't know what, but some evil was about to befall her Sapling and she could do nothing to prevent it.

The Old One was leading the horse into the meadow and she felt a brief pulsation of joy that the animal had survived the winter before the crushing panic claimed her again.

She ran through the mud, remembering at the last minute to clothe herself. The Old One heard her approach and turned.

"The Sapling," she cried as she grew close. "What has happened?"

Sykes straightened. "Nothing, as far as I know. What makes you ask?"

She pressed a hand to her temple, head pounding.

"Something is coming for him. I don't know what or where and I can't do anything to prevent it." She glanced back at her tree. The branches reached out to her like an embrace.

"But I'll do what I can."

She walked away from the old man and back to the grove. It was too early in the year for her to be at full strength but she pressed her hands to the bark of the trunk, feeling the ridges that she knew as well as the loops on her fingertips. She closed her eyes and bent her head in supplication as she passed her thoughts through the wood, up into the air, down through the ground.

If there was any way of preventing harm coming to Edwin, anyone who might help, she would do her best to reach out to them.

Chapter Sixteen

SPRING 1918

The wind began to scream and rain spattered down – not enough to drench, but cold and persistent enough to annoy. The fact it was only rain, not shards of ice or hail, was something Edwin never thought he'd have considered a blessing.

"What's the time? How long before the end of the watch?" he muttered. He adjusted his rifle and pulled the collar of his greatcoat as high as it would go.

Robert looked at his pocket watch. "It's almost five. Another hour to go. What I wouldn't give for a pint of beer waiting for me."

"Bit chilly for a March night. I'd settle for cocoa with a good glug of brandy in it," Edwin replied.

They both looked at Harry, their fellow sentry. He grinned. "You know I'm a Methodist. Nothing for me in that line of things."

"How long before you're on leave?" the fourth man asked – Owen, a Welshman who was on his last shift before returning to the reserve trenches that Edwin's detachment had recently vacated. They were back in Amiens, their first posting, after almost two years being moved from place to place.

"Another two months for us," Robert groaned. "At least by then the weather should be better so we won't be in this sludge."

"That will be wonderful." Edwin kicked his heels against the bottom step, scraping off some of the thick clay that stuck to them. "I can't even imagine a time when we won't be living up to our knees in mud."

"Knees! Ha! It was waist deep when I was at the front in December," Owen muttered.

Robert, Harry, and Edwin exchanged glances. It was probably true, but they'd all encountered soldiers who liked to have had it worse than anyone else in the conversation.

"What will you be going home to, when we're back in England?" Harry asked.

"Wales for me, not England. I'll be back in the copperworks in Swansea," Owen said.

"What about you, Edwin, back to the factory?" Robert asked. He held out Edwin's cigarette in cupped hands. "Here, take this back, thanks for the drag."

Edwin took his cigarette, shielding it from view while he considered the answer. In the pitch black of night no one would dream of lighting up and drawing attention to where they were, but there was a velvety mauve tinge to the horizon and the glowing tip was small.

"I don't know. I'm an adult now, though it's hard to believe somehow. My grandfather was my guardian but now I've reached my majority he doesn't have that claim on me."

He paused, remembering the night of his twenty-first birthday and the fight that had ultimately brought him and Robert closer. He wondered if the poor whore with the big eyes and the bruises was still alive, though he had no desire to go looking for the brothel. He took a drag on the cigarette, hating the taste but relishing the way his senses prickled as the smoke wound down his throat.

"I always said that when I reached twenty-one I'd make my own way but now I don't know. Do we even know what we'll be returning to?"

Harry cleared his throat. "I got a letter from Mother. She said the village is doing as well as possible. She's turned the garden into a vegetable patch and planted apple trees. Apparently, all the parks have been turned into allotments."

"Really?" Edwin leaned forward, his damp neck momentarily forgotten. He wondered what Drusilla would say if he returned home and announced he was planning to fill the field with trees. It was something to think about.

From a trench in the distance across no man's land came the crackle of gunfire. Ten or twelve miles away were men like themselves, but their enemies. Edwin huddled down against the wall of the trench.

"I'd rather be here than at the front right now. Do you remember when we said it would be over by that first Christmas?"

Robert laughed bitterly. No one laughed any other way when they were in the darkness and mud. "What idiots we all were."

Above them, clouds rolled over the sky, snuffing out the early light. It was obviously going to be darker before the dawn. Edwin took another quick puff on the roll-up. He wrinkled his nose and coughed. There was a bitter aftertaste that he hadn't tasted the first time. Who knew what was mixed in with tobacco though. Probably dried horse manure. Out of habit, he pinched out the end of his cigarette. He'd got into the habit of keeping half each time to reserve them but didn't think he'd want this one again. He glanced at the sky. More clouds, with a sickly ochre-coloured tinge to the edges. Globs of spilled ink across the vast expanse. He shivered. For no reason he could think of, he dug his hands into his pockets and felt for Drusilla's charm.

"I think I'll do a quick round. Go for a piss while I'm at it," he said.

"I'll come," Robert announced, stretching. "Harry, Owen, you keep watch here."

"I'll give you ten minutes then I'm going for a smoke in the dugout," Harry said, winking.

They began the slow trudge of tired men in wet boots along the narrow trench, heading for the ladder up.

"When we get home I'm going to burn my socks," Robert growled, offering a hand to Edwin to pull him up.

"They'll be too damn wet," Edwin answered.

They laughed as they crouched and made their way out towards the barbed-wire fences. The sound of their humour was punctuated by rapid cracks of rifles. In the distance, the horizon was lit with fire-flashes. Edwin raised his eyes. There was a whistling sound that was far too close, the screaming of speeding metal. Shells were being dropped. The stench of smoke filled the air, momentarily obliterating the stink of bodies and excrement.

"Shit, that's close!" Edwin said, looking in alarm at the burst of light off to the left and forward. Another explosion made him jump. This one closer still. Then another. They threw themselves to the ground, hands protectively over their heads.

"We can't stay here. We'll be sitting ducks," Robert whispered. His voice sounded choked. In the dim yellowing light, his eyes were wide with fear.

Edwin tightened his fist and realised he was still holding Drusilla's charm. It felt reassuringly heavy in his hand and his palm felt warm. His head began to pound. He rolled onto his back and stared upwards. The clouds were curling in on themselves in the wind, forming fluffy turrets that solidified as they collided. He tasted sourness. A screech erupted from him, thick tongued as he was.

He rolled back onto his front and pointed to their destination: a lone oak close to the edge of a small copse. It was a popular destination for a piss out of the cold and it always amazed Edwin that it had survived the war so far.

"Let's get to the shelter of the tree."

"What about the others? We should tell them what's happening." Robert said. "We can't leave Harry."

Edwin swallowed his terror.

"I think they'll have realised something's happening by now. They're better in the dugout and we can't get back to the trench now. That's our best choice."

They were in the middle of a full-scale onslaught before they knew it. The wind began to scream, dragging across them. The ground a little to their left exploded.

"On three," Edwin muttered.

Robert nodded. They counted then ran.

They reached the tree and hurled themselves under the protective branches.

"Shit on this for a morning," Robert said. His voice trembled. "Do you believe in God? Better start praying."

Knowing what Drusilla was should have confirmed the existence of the divine, but it hadn't. If anything, the years of conflict had strengthened his conviction that the world was godless. It was hard to believe Drusilla was real and not some fevered fantasy brought on by poor rations and sleep deprivation. He gripped the charm between his hands and held them together as if he were indeed praying.

The shells ceased and there came the silence that was almost louder in Edwin's ringing ears.

"We should get back," Robert whispered.

Edwin nodded. Gingerly they took a couple of steps out from beneath the branches. The sky exploded into light. The branches creaked and tipped. Edwin heard a whisper like an ancient voice. He looked up and even though his eyes saw the great branch falling towards him, his mind was not quick enough to comprehend the meaning. Fortunately, his body acted of its own accord and he pushed Robert forward, flinging himself after.

A sharp pain speared his back and his leg and something heavy flung him forward. He screamed. Another voice joined his and he realised as he fell that it belonged to Robert. He managed to half roll over but before he could fully move, something heavy crushed his torso. He felt softness beneath him and movement above then he was pinned immobile where he lay, branches to his left and right, and above him.

The dreadful night inside Drusilla's tree sprang into his

mind. He screamed again, not caring what Robert thought, but the weight of something heavy on his chest caused such pain that he had to stop. The falling branch had cleared a patch of sky and as he lay on his back, he realised that was what had pinned him down. A cage of branches was entrapping him. There was a gentle whimpering close by and he understood the softness beneath him was Robert's legs.

The sky, now visible where the branch had once stood, was alive with fire. The clouds rolled on. The Wild Hunt? Or a French equivalent? Edwin delved into his memories and tried to pull out the words, long forgotten, from a French lesson but all he could remember was aunts and chairs.

The squirming beneath him ceased.

"Robert, get up. Look at the horses."

The words came back to him. *Chasse sauvage.*

"Drusilla, look! They're here too," he murmured.

Somewhere close by came a deafening shrieking and more explosions, followed by the panicked shouting of multiple voices. He picked out his CO's and knew he should be preparing to fight but he couldn't move.

He tried to rise but the branch was too heavy, imprisoning him, and the searing pain in his left side was enough to snatch away the power of speech. He thought he was probably bleeding but wasn't sure. He was going to die alone in the middle of a battle, crushed beneath a tree.

His vision began to cloud and he must have been delirious, because he was certain that he saw Drusilla's face floating above him.

"You came."

He reached out a shaking arm; tried to give her the charm,

to show her he still had it, but as he opened his hand it slipped from his palm. He clawed at the dirt with his fingers but he couldn't find it. He began to weep, the tears hot tracks down his face.

Faire taire. Calme-toi. Je te vois.

A woman had appeared at his side, a woman with a soft voice, speaking in French. Not Drusilla, as Edwin had first thought, but with similar delicate features. This woman was much older with hair a mixture of soot and ash in the curls that fell almost to her waist. Her lined face was the colour of old oak bark. Her eyes were fixed on him, though she smiled benignly. She reached down and held something up to the light, turning it back and forth. The charm.

Tu es protégé.

She pressed it into Edwin's hand and nodded at him. Before his eyes, she became luminous and translucent. The pressure of her hand decreased and she faded until she had vanished.

Edwin felt his breath sucked out of him. He was too tired to feel terror. Almost too tired to notice the pain any longer. All around him became dark and then the horizon lightened as dawn broke. The wind softened; became a lullaby in susurrus through the leaves.

Powerless to do anything else, Edwin closed his eyes and surrendered himself to whatever would happen next.

Edwin awoke to a multitude of voices, some whispering, others crying. One or two screams sent jolts through him. He'd last been conscious in the dark but now he was lying in warm daylight. More confusingly, he was surrounded by softness and a smell of carbolic soap that made him sneeze and think of school. The sneeze resulted in explosions of pain throughout his ribs and he shrieked.

"Oh good, you're back with us." The voice sounded familiar. Edwin put a name to it.

"Robert? Where am I?"

"The CCS. Out on the Amiens–Villers road. Now you're awake they'll move you to the base hospital. You've got a broken ankle and broken ribs."

Edwin turned his head to see Robert sitting on a chair beside him. The right side of his face was covered in small cuts and bruises and he had his right arm in a sling. The moustache he'd grown so proudly had gone and his top lip was puffed up. Past Robert he could see a row of beds, all occupied by men. Another row was opposite them.

"You look dreadful," Edwin said – wheezed, really, given that the words were painful to get out.

"I'm not the one in a bed who looks like an elephant sat on him."

"The tree. I remember a tree that fell on us. There was an old woman too. Or at least I thought there was."

He swallowed down the feeling of betrayal. She'd been a nymph like Drusilla, he was certain, and yet she had left him pinioned there in pain and fear.

Robert grunted. He leaned in a little closer. "You saw her too? I thought I was hallucinating. After all, why would my grandmother have been on the battlefield?"

Edward tried to sit up but let out a yelp as a sharp, intense pain stabbed him low in the ribs. It was a change from the pain

247

in the back of his leg which was like a constant dullness he couldn't ignore and more pain in his ankle. He lay back against the pillow. An actual pillow, with a clean cover. He wasn't entirely sure this was real.

"So I didn't dream her then? What about horses?" He reached a hand up and felt his chest. It felt tender along the left side of his ribs. "Ow!"

"Stop doing that." A stern-looking young woman in a grey dress and starched white cap walked over and stood at the end of the bed. "Prodding at your ribs won't aid your recovery at all. Are you in much pain?"

Edwin considered her words, unsure what counted as 'much'. She smiled. "I'll be along in a few minutes to give you your next shot of morphine."

She walked off along the rows of beds, stopping at the foot of a bed three down from Edwin and began speaking to the occupant.

"Lucky you. She's quite a pippin!" Robert whispered. "Better than that old, starched matron over there. See if she'll give you a bed bath!"

"Where's your bed?" Edwin asked, ignoring Robert. She was quite attractive though.

"I don't have one. I'm not severe enough. Just a broken wrist and a few bruises. A hint of concussion so I'll get a couple of days of rest. I think you caused most of them when you landed on me." Robert gave a small laugh that sounded strained.

"Someone was looking out for you last night. An inch or two more and the branch that fell on us would've crushed your neck. Another one sliced a good five or six inches along the back of your thigh, I hear. I haven't looked to confirm it myself; I don't need to have the memory of your lilywhite arse in my brain." Robert laughed again, though it sounded more forced, then lowered his head. His eyes became glossy.

"I think someone was watching over both of us. I have bad news, Ed. The trench suffered a direct hit from a shell. They're all gone."

It took Edwin a moment to make sense of his friend's words. When he did, his stomach plummeted.

"No," he groaned aloud, this time from the pain in his heart that crushed his chest more than the ribs had. "Are you sure?"

"Positive." Robert passed a hand over his eyes. "If we hadn't gone for a piss we'd have been hit too."

Edwin's eyes swam with tears. Crying wasn't manly but how could he not? The lads he had slept alongside, and with whom he had played cards, argued, and laughed.

"They can't be dead. We aren't the only two who made it, surely? What about Harry? He was going to go for a smoke when we got back."

"I said all of them, didn't I! Everyone else is dead!" Robert swallowed. His lip trembled and he clamped down on it hard with his teeth until Edwin feared he was about to draw blood. "Harry lost both legs, I heard. He lasted until lunchtime. And I wasn't there. I should have been with him."

He dropped his head, shoulders shaking as he sobbed.

"I'm so sorry. I didn't realise," Edwin murmured. The words were inadequate for the enormous swelling of grief in his chest. He began to shiver, though the room they were in was hot. He'd feel more later, he suspected, but for now he could only shake his head in bewilderment.

"Of all the odd luck. If the tree hadn't fallen on us!"

"That's what I meant. Someone is looking out for us," Robert said darkly, wiping his eyes on his sleeve.

Edwin closed his eyes. The dryad must have done it. Drusilla had said the charm would signal that he was under her protection. The old woman had given it back to him. It must have been her tree. He wondered where she was now it had fallen. Did she move onto another or did she die when it did? For the first time, he felt anxious about Drusilla. He'd assumed she was permanent, but perhaps he had been wrong. He ached for home. For Drusilla.

He rubbed his hands over his face, wanting to block out the world. "How much longer can this go on?"

"I don't know. As long as it takes to beat those bastards."

The nurse returned, casting a disapproving look at Robert for his language. She was carrying a metal dish in which Edwin could see a glass syringe with an ominous looking needle. The pain was bad but the heartache was worse. Morphine would dull both temporarily. He barely registered the scratch as the thick needle penetrated his arm.

"I'll find you at the base hospital, if I can," Robert said. "We'll be back on the front line before we know it."

He held out his good hand to Edwin who grasped it as firmly as he could manage. Already he could feel the effects of the injection working through him.

"Where are my clothes?" he asked, yawning.

The nurse patted his hand. "You won't need those now. You'll be spending a fortnight in the base hospital, possibly longer with cracked ribs, I imagine."

"My charm," he slurred.

She leaned over Edwin and adjusted the pillow. "I don't know about that, dearie."

"I need it, you see. My friend is a tree and I think I love her. I love..."

He felt his eyes growing heavier; fought against sleep, but to no avail.

He sighed.

"I love her."

Chapter Seventeen

WINTER 1918

T he injuries Edwin and Robert suffered at the hands of the toppling tree had saved their lives. Not only in the shelling of their trench, but by ensuring they were on light duties when the intense fighting began. They returned to England after the armistice, along with the thousands that had survived. Of the ninety-seven men who had left the town to fight, those two alone returned.

They shook hands at the station and went their separate ways home. One day they'd meet and talk, cry and mourn, but for now the wounds were too raw to acknowledge.

Greete Mill House was faded and dilapidated on the inside as well as the outside. The furniture was oppressive, the walls dark and overly patterned, the ornaments cluttered. It looked funereal. It felt unbearable.

"We need to redecorate," Edwin suggested to Stephen the afternoon after his homecoming. He threw open the heavy velvet curtains in the sitting room to let in the thin winter light. "We could even get electric lighting installed. Robert was telling me yesterday that his father is planning on it. Apparently, it's perfectly safe."

"And perfectly expensive," Stephen grunted. He was dressed in his usual black, and the war seemed to have shrivelled him. His back was slightly hunched and he walked with a cane. He sat now with a blanket over his lap by the coal fire.

"Surely we could draw some profits out of the mill," Edwin suggested. He poured a cup of tea from the blue and white pot. Drinking from a china cup was a novelty he suspected wouldn't wear off for a while. He handed Stephen a cup and sat on the brown Chesterfield sofa. Through the window he could see snow beginning to fall in feathery flakes.

"Grandfather, I yearn for bright colours. I've seen my fill of browns and khaki and such like. It's nearly Christmas and this year I wish to decorate the house. We're at peace now and we should be celebrating."

He paused to sip the tea and took a furtive look at his grandfather. Stephen was staring into the flames.

"I might even invite Aunt Madeline and her crowd. What do you say?" he continued.

"I say we would have to spend far too much money if that were the case," Stephen answered gravely. "The war has been hard on everyone's pockets."

"Don't I have money? My father left me some, I know, plus whatever I inherited from my mother. I'm over my majority now, after all."

"I suggest we continue this conversation later. I'm tired. Help me up." Stephen's hands tightened on the cane in his hand.

"Of course," he said pleasantly.

He helped Stephen out of his chair, startled at how light the old man felt.

He wasn't too downhearted at the refusal. He hadn't really expected to receive effusive permission straight away. He would set about decorating the house bit by bit, and of course there was something else he had to decorate too. Something he had promised four long years ago.

It was one of the rare, beautiful winter days with strong sunlight. The meadow was a blanket of white where the indentations of his footprints cast violet and indigo shadows across the ground. There was a fresh scent in the air and it was cold enough to make his throat ache as he breathed in. The sycamore tree was leafless and the upper branches heavy with snow, though the ground beneath it was bare scrub where the snow had not reached.

"I don't know if you can hear me, Drusilla, or if you're sleeping, but I've come back. It's been four years since I left. I had a bad time of it out there. I don't suppose that makes me too different from any other chaps though. Perhaps one day I'll talk to you about it properly."

He swallowed. He wasn't ready yet and his throat tightened at the thought of what he could say about what he had seen. Some of the men had kept diaries. Edwin hadn't. He pulled the collar of his coat higher and set his shoulders against the cold. The scar on the back of his thigh from where the branch had pierced him itched occasionally and his ribs ached in the cold. Sometimes he felt like he would never be warm again. He waited for any reply but, as he anticipated, none came. The last time he'd been gone for longer than expected she hadn't realised the passing of time and had been indignant but he hoped she wouldn't hold it against him. It occurred to him belatedly that she might have forgotten him and found another man to keep her company. His stomach tied in knots.

"I nearly died." He shoved his hands in his pockets and looked at the ground. "A tree fell on me but that wasn't what did it. The whole trench was wiped out. All of my friends."

He choked and closed his eyes, faces of the dead passing behind the lids in the blackness. "There was a tree and an old woman. One like you. I didn't realise at the time but between them they saved my life. I don't know if you had anything to do with that but thank you."

He looked up again, hoping in vain that she would be standing before him but there was still no response, not even the answering wind whistling through the leaves. He reached out a hand to stroke the bark but then pulled it back, remembering that the last time he had touched it he'd been drawn inside it – or through it, or whatever had happened to transport him into Drusilla's realm. As much as he wanted to see her, he was too afraid of that.

"I brought you something," he whispered, almost embarrassed at his sentimentality. "It's almost Christmas and I know that doesn't mean anything to you but I thought you'd like to look bright and I promised I'd do it."

He pulled out the garlands of red and gold that he had found in the attic. He looped them around the lowest hanging boughs then wound the final one around the trunk. He added a couple of green glass baubles. The sunlight made them sparkle and the snow flickered green where it caught their reflection..

"There. You look beautiful now. You always look beautiful."

He pictured her smiling when she awoke to see the decorations, wishing he could be there to see it. His nightmares of being encased in the branches had come true, but in a way he'd never anticipated, and his fear was no longer as strong as it had been. Summoning his courage, he reached out and patted the trunk quickly.

He turned and slowly made his way back to the house, taking his time to enjoy the clean air. Up in the hills he could see children and hear their gleeful shrieks as they tobogganed down the slopes. This incline was too shallow, he suspected. Halfway down he felt a whisper of wind that ruffled his hair.

"You saw another like me?"

Edwin turned back slowly, holding his breath. The sun was bright and he had to shield his eyes from the glare but beneath the silhouetted tree he spotted her: an outline against the trunk that hadn't been there before. A jolt of electricity galvanised his limbs. He ran, clumsily and slipping on the snow, and arrived back at the tree out of breath which left him embarrassed. War had made him fitter than he had been before he left and he'd have to be careful not to lapse back into idleness.

"Did I wake you? I'm sorry."

"Don't be. Yes, you woke me. I heard you and felt you."

Drusilla was dressed in white with patterns of branches picked out in grey and black, like the outline of the tree against the snow. Her hair fell to her waist and there were fine strands of silver amongst the deep brown. Her eyes were moss green in a face that was thin and angular. She smiled sweetly then covered her mouth to yawn. "Did you really see another?"

"Yes. But she was much older. Her tree was shelled and fell and she faded. I think she died." He frowned. "Is that possible?"

"It's possible. It happened here. The old stump was once home to one such as I."

"So you'll get old when the tree gets old? You'll die?" A cold hand gripped him by the throat.

Drusilla smiled gently.

"We all die one day, Sapling."

She looked around her, eyes wide and wondering. "You decorated my tree, didn't you."

Edwin felt a blush creeping round his neck at his foolishness. "I hope you don't mind. It just looked so bare and I promised I'd let you know when I was back."

"It's bare every year, Sapling. It's winter. That's why I sleep."

She smiled again and the skin beside her eyes creased. "Thank you for doing it. No one has ever done it for me."

She reached out her hand and ran the palm over the place on the trunk Edwin had touched. Her arm was slight and her skin was paler than he remembered. It stood out against the bark like a bolt of undyed silk on a table. Perhaps by summer that would change again. He thought he was beginning to understand how the seasons influenced her.

"What if you didn't sleep? Could you stay awake all year round if you needed to?" He lowered his eyes. "Or wanted to."

"I imagine I could, though I would be very tired. It would take an awful lot to keep me awake through winter."

"I suppose a few garlands won't do that, will they," Edwin said gloomily.

"Perhaps not, but it's a start. The kiss you gave me sustained me for a long time but I haven't spoken to anyone for months and I've been lonely. Come see me again in the spring and I'll be young again."

Relief that he hadn't been replaced swelled Edwin's heart. His eyes strayed to her lips. He wondered whether another kiss would have a similar effect. Drusilla's eyes gleamed. She reached out and stroked his cheek with the same softness with which she had caressed the tree.

"Oh Sapling, I've missed you. I know what you're thinking but there's no need now." Her lips curved upwards, teasingly. "Unless you'd like to, of course."

"I would."

He put an arm around her waist and drew her close. Holding her felt wonderful, even though he was acutely aware that she was slimmer than he remembered and missing the curves he liked. He tilted her chin up with a fingertip and held her gaze for a moment before kissing her. Drusilla gave a deep sigh that sounded contented rather than weary as their lips parted. She reached up and tugged at the lock of hair that had fallen over his forehead.

"I think you've been doing more than fighting," she breathed. "I'm surprised you came back to me."

"I told you I would." Edwin smiled, though a little worm of guilt burrowed in his belly. Though he'd never ventured inside another brothel, he'd had a brief romance with the French nurse who had tended his recuperation and considered himself slightly more expert at kissing than when he had left.

"I think this year the meadow will look particularly beautiful. I'll make it so. Goodnight, Sapling. I'll see you again soon."

March 1919

Edwin supposed he should thank his grandfather for the garden party but he was finding it hard to celebrate. The occasion had been prompted by Aunt Madeline and family inviting themselves to Cheshire. The timing could have been better because the first snowdrops had appeared and it was a full moon. Drusilla would be waking up and he wanted to see her rather than play host to a crowd of people he barely knew.

There was dancing and music but Edwin noticed he wasn't the only fellow to flinch at the crackling of the drumbeats. Too much like gunfire for his liking.

"God above, I feel ungrateful," he mentioned to Robert when they bumped into each other at the punchbowl. He'd been invited, naturally.

"Don't be." Robert tipped back his cup and refilled it, sloshing the ladle inaccurately. "It's rotten that we're the only ones who made it back. When I think about the men we lost. The friends I loved…"

His eyes glazed then hardened. "But I don't feel guilty for surviving. Have a drink and toast their memories. That's what I'm doing. Lots of people to remember. Empty desks in the banks. New faces in the courts. I've got my own desk now at work. Got a plaque with my name on it too."

"Not your first glass?" Edwin asked, smartly relieving Robert of the ladle. Robert focused slightly blurrily on him.

"You are not my keeper, Hope."

"I am your friend though," Edwin said patiently. "And I'm not going to let you make a fool of yourself here. Come on, let's get some fresh air."

He took Robert's arm and led him out to the croquet lawn where a late-night game was in progress.

"Do you remember the mud? And the tree? Bloody old woman laughing at us. Then... frrrkkk! Chaos. The dugout!"

"Yes, I remember. I remember them too," Edwin said.

He took the punch glass from Robert's unwilling fingers and gave him a gentle prod between the shoulder blades.

"Go and take a seat by the pond, old thing, and try not to fall in."

Robert staggered off obediently and sat by the edge of the pond. Very soon he began to offer a loud commentary on the performance of the octet of croquet players. Edwin sighed. He shared Robert's despair at the loss of their friends, but the thought of getting blind drunk scared him more than it appealed.

"He always was an ass even as a child, if I remember correctly."

Edwin turned to see Harold strolling towards him. He wore a dog collar and had his arm linked through a young woman's.

"Hello Harold," Edwin said. "That's not very Christian. He was though, wasn't he. I like him better since..." Since their shared experience. He couldn't say it aloud yet. "Well, you know what I mean. Nice to see you. Have you settled into the hotel all right?"

The family were wisely staying in the Station Hotel. To spare Stephen the cost, Aunt Madeline had explained in her letter, while Harold had explained it was so they could laugh without feeling they needed to ask permission from the old man.

"Yes. Ma and Panos have gone to find your grandfather to pay homage. They're hoping he will introduce me to your vicar."

"You're kinder than I would've been to your friend," the woman remarked, raising a brow. "I'd have dunked him headfirst in the pond." She had wavy shingled hair in which she wore a band adorned with peacock feathers. She looked familiar. Edwin smiled faintly.

"You don't remember me? I'm heartbroken." She grinned. "I'm Eleni."

Edwin's jaw dropped. She'd changed in the last five years. She was willowy and almost as tall as he was, with excellent cheekbones and dark eyes ringed with lustrous lashes. She must be almost twenty now, or perhaps just over.

"Yes, I'm no longer a child, my darling." She laughed, seeing his surprise. Her laughter was infectious. Harold and Edwin both joined in.

Robert roused himself. "She's too good for you. Give up, Hope. Give up hope. Ahaha! You won't like Hope; he's obsessed with snails and beetles and that sort of thing."

"I happen to like snails," Eleni replied. She linked her arm through Edwin's.

"Come on, let's leave him to sleep it off. Harold will make

sure he's all right. I've never been here before but Harold told me all about the gardens."

Edwin allowed himself to be led around the edge of the terrace towards the formal gardens. He saw his grandfather walking in the company of a couple of men he vaguely recognised from church. Old as he was, Stephen was hoping to inveigle his way onto the parish council and still held out hopes of becoming an alderman or similar. Stephen caught his eye and nodded slightly. Edwin returned the gesture.

"Do you really like snails?" he asked Eleni.

"Not particularly, unless they've been cooked and dipped in garlic butter. Do you?"

"Not to eat!" Edwin exclaimed. The idea turned his stomach in truth. "I suppose I do. Not just snails. I'm quite keen on all natural things. I used to want to be an explorer as a child and discover new species."

"And now you don't?"

Edwin glanced back at the house. The number of people crammed onto the terrace was quite disquieting. "I think I've seen enough of the world. I'm quite content here."

"Was it really dreadful?" Eleni asked. She stopped walking and clicked her teeth. "I'm sorry. That was a stupid question. Of course it was. How could it not have been? Did you know our house was given over to convalescing soldiers? I got to nurse after all. Some of their injuries and tales from the front line were awful."

"I didn't know that. Tell me about it."

He listened to Eleni's tales of nursing as they walked along the edge of the wall that bordered the formal garden. She made it sound amusing, but there was a brittle edge to her voice that she couldn't hide. As Edwin glanced up, he spotted a figure under the sycamore tree, silhouetted by the full moon against the black, star-speckled sky.

Drusilla.

Tonight was the first full moon. His whole body tingled, then as quickly as it had risen, the excitement subsided. His throat dried.

If he hadn't been with Eleni he would have rushed from the party to greet Drusilla, but Eleni had slipped her hand through his arm and he could hardly run off to go chasing after another woman.

"What are you looking at?" Eleni asked.

"The sycamore."

He looked up at the tree again and saw the figure of Drusilla. She had moved out from underneath the branches and was staring down the hill. As he looked, she raised a hand, waving to him. Edwin came to a decision. He would take Eleni back to the house, leave her with Robert and a glass of punch and then come back to see Drusilla. At least that was his plan, except Eleni raised an arm and pointed.

"Look, there's a woman under the tree. Who do you think she is?"

Until that point it hadn't occurred to Edwin whether or not Drusilla was visible to everyone. No, of course she must be. Robert had seen the old dryad on the battlefield after all. He'd just never been in company when he saw her.

"Of course I can see her. I wonder why she's snuck away from the party? Let's go and say hello," Eleni said.

A feeling of trepidation filled Edwin. Not so much because of what Drusilla might say, but the thought of introducing his old friends to her could be awkward. Even aside from her mystical aspect, Drusilla was unconventional. Besides, he wanted to keep her to himself. He wasn't sure how she would react to another woman. It was too late now though because Eleni had already begun walking across the field.

Chapter Eighteen

"Oh my goodness," she called back to him, "this is ridiculous. We should have gone by the path. My heels are sticking into the mud."

"Why don't you go back," Edwin suggested hopefully.

She merely lifted her hem a little higher. "Never mind, we've started now."

As if she were gliding over the grass, Drusilla came down the gentle slope to meet them. For all Edwin knew, she *was* able to float.

"Edwin, how lovely to see you after all this time. You have a new friend." The tone was pleasant but her eyes glinted.

"You know each other?" Eleni asked in surprise. She gave Edwin a stern look. "Edwin, you didn't tell me that."

"I didn't have time before you began marching up here," he pointed out. Eleni laughed.

"Well that's true. Hello, I'm Eleni. Pleased to meet you."

She stuck out a hand. Drusilla hesitated momentarily and her eyes twitched slightly. Edwin held his breath, tensing in anticipation at what she might do. Thankfully, she took Eleni's hand but instead of shaking it, she lifted it to her lips and kissed the back.

"Oh my," Eleni breathed. "You are too perfect. And your dress! It's simply wonderful. You must share the name of your designer with me."

She took a step back, better to examine the gown Drusilla was wearing. Edwin gave his attention to Drusilla's outfit. She was wearing pea green, mottled with a slightly darker green in a pattern that seemed random but that to Edwin's mind resembled the veins on leaves. The neck was wide and square with soft folds across the front, and the waist was dropped like the one Eleni wore. She looked almost like a modern woman. Her hair was caught back behind her head and for the first time Edwin could remember it wasn't loose or plaited low but was coiled at the nape of her neck and secured in place with a silver ribbon. With delight, he recognised it from the box of sweets he had given her at Christmas way back before the war. Drusilla smiled at him, the corner of her lips turning up beguilingly and her steady eyes meeting his. He swallowed, feeling as though a bolt of lightning had speared him, welding him to the spot. It was spring of course and she was at her youngest and most alluring.

"You look very beautiful," Edwin agreed, feeling the sentiment was inadequate. She was ethereal. If he had come across her in a Greek temple he would have believed what she was in an instant.

"I feel refreshed. Did Sykes tell you what we accomplished?"

"The vegetable garden?" Edwin asked. He slid a glance at

Eleni, wondering if it was safe to talk about the subject of Drusilla's part in nurturing the land but they weren't saying anything incriminating. "Yes, he did. I was surprised, given that you apparently dislike each other. Pleased, though, that you've become friends."

"I wouldn't say we are friends," Drusilla said briskly. She jutted her bottom lip out, looking thoughtful. "In fact, I would certainly say we aren't, but it was a useful alliance and what we both needed."

Edwin took her hand. He rubbed his thumb into the palm, circling it slowly. He had to swallow to contain the feeling of desire that touching her evoked. "I'm glad of it all the same. I wish I'd known while I was away. I worried about you being alone."

"Have I uncovered a secret romance? Are you two lovers?" Eleni stepped forward, coming into Edwin's view. He'd forgotten she was there.

"No," Edwin said, dropping Drusilla's hand.

"Yes," Drusilla replied at the same time as he spoke.

They looked at each other and smiled, slightly amused, slightly embarrassed. They'd never finished what they had started, but maybe in Drusilla's eyes that was enough to deserve the label.

"Almost, once," Edwin admitted.

"It was not a success," Drusilla added.

Eleni beamed. "Oh, that's so often the case. I remember my first time. One of my father's friends. Old Smoky. You know him from Yorkshire, Edwin. Alderman Dale."

"But he's at least forty-five," Edwin exclaimed. He wasn't

sure if he was more aghast at the lover's age or the fact Eleni had had one at all.

"Yes, he is," Eleni answered with a shrug. "I shan't be making that mistake again until I'm at least twice that age. Now, should I leave you two alone or will you both come back to the party? Or shall we all stay here and become friends? This tree is beautiful, and someone has decorated it ... how lovely. Was it you, Edwin?"

He nodded, noticing now that the garlands and glass baubles he had strung had survived the harsh winter weather. He looked back to Drusilla and found her watching him.

"I've looked after them."

He felt the sudden urge to kiss her, but with Eleni there it was out of the question. He drew Drusilla to one side, leaving Eleni staring at the tree.

"It's good to see you. I'm sorry for bringing Eleni," he whispered. "I saw you but so did she. I would have come alone but I couldn't send her away without being rude."

"Who is she?" Drusilla asked.

There was a hint of suspicion in her voice. Possibly even jealousy. He should probably feel flattered but he didn't particularly relish the idea of animosity between the two women he liked.

"She's an old friend. My cousin's stepsister. I'll take her away and come again as soon as I can."

"Let her stay. She's interesting." Drusilla peered past him to where Eleni stood now, admiring the tree. She laid a hand on his forearm. "I heard the music and saw the lights. I didn't think you'd come tonight so thank you."

Eleni wandered over to them. She began fishing in her

reticule. "I have a hip flask of gin and some cigarettes. We could have our own party here, the three of us. What do you both say?"

Edwin glanced at Drusilla who nodded and smiled at Eleni.

"You are welcome in my grove, though I would rather you didn't smoke by the tree," Drusilla said.

Eleni had been about to light a cigarette in an ivory holder but paused with the lighter halfway there. She tilted her head slightly and gave Drusilla a quizzical look.

"I have an aversion to fire," Drusilla explained.

"Oh of course. If you would prefer me not to, I don't have to." Eleni lowered it and flicked the lighter closed. "To tell the truth, I don't even like the damn things but it's expected, isn't it?"

"Is it?" Edwin asked.

"Oh yes," Eleni replied tossing her head and causing the seed pearls of her silver earrings to dance. "Not for you perhaps, but if a woman is going to be interesting then she must have a quirk. You don't need to, of course, with those melting eyes of yours."

He thought she'd been talking to Drusilla but realised she was talking to him and felt himself blush.

"And as for you..." Now she did address Drusilla, taking her by the hands. "You are the most captivating creature I've ever seen and I can't imagine any man who would not be transfixed by you."

"I've never found one yet," Drusilla said with a modest smile.

She slid her eyes to Edwin who gave her a nervous smile.

He wasn't quite sure what was happening but he was content to be swept along in the spontaneity.

"Edwin, dear, please go and steal us a bottle of Champagne. We could try mixing it with the gin and seeing what happens."

"Yes please," Drusilla said. "It's going to be a warm night and I've never tried Champagne or gin."

The two women stood side by side, joint queens commanding their subject. They were almost the same height, though Edwin could have sworn Drusilla hadn't been that tall when they had arrived. Knowing he was beaten, but not particularly objecting, he made his way back down to the party on his quest.

He encountered his grandfather sitting at a table on the lawn with Panos, Henry Carfax, and the headmaster of the school. They had a bottle of whiskey between them. Edwin spent a few minutes making small-talk and noticed during that time that Stephen refilled and emptied his tumbler twice. He left them, feeling slightly ill at ease. Stephen had been drinking increasingly more and more since the war had ended. Now his lips almost disappeared inside his puffy face. The war had taken its toll on the men who had stayed, as well as those who had left.

"The old guard," Harold commented, as he beckoned Edwin over to the table where he and Robert were waiting for their bridge partners. "Probably wishing they'd had a war of their own."

"They're idiots if they are," Robert growled, casting an angry look at Harold who had spent the years ministering to the sick in a Yorkshire hospital.

"Actually, I'm worried about Grandfather," Edwin confided

to Harold and Robert. "He's drinking to excess and barely speaks to me over dinner. Last night I reached for the wine after I drank my first glass only to find the bottle was completely empty. He drank the lot without me even noticing."

"Drink faster then," Robert laughed with a shrug.

"Lots of people drink," Harold said. "Besides, what do you care? He's never liked you and you've never liked him."

Edwin leaned back against the table, slightly bemused at Harold's lack of Christian concern. A vicar should be more caring, shouldn't he?

"That's not the point. He's family and naturally I am concerned about him. The war demanded a heavy toll from lots of people."

"He didn't fight though and he didn't lose his son or grandson. He should look around the town and see the grieving families and then he'll see his good fortune," Robert said. His eyes tightened. He'd lost two sisters to the Spanish Flu; a cruel blow to a family who had believed Robert's return had made their children safe.

"I'm not sure he sees it as good fortune that I came home," Edwin muttered, his guts tightening. He glanced back over. The men had been deep in what appeared to be a serious discussion. "He's being very secretive about the accounts too. I wonder if that is the reason. When I go there next I'll see if I can get William to distract him long enough for me to have a glimpse and try and get to the bottom of a mystery."

"What are you up to now?" Robert asked.

"Just getting a drink. I might go for a walk by the stream to clear my head. Come, if you like," Edwin answered, knowing Robert wouldn't leave his game. As expected, his offer was declined. He threaded through the couples dancing on the terrace beneath the bunting of red, white, and blue flags, and helped himself to a bottle of Champagne. He eyed the glasses then decided against it. He suspected neither woman would mind drinking straight from the bottle. With that plan in mind, he slipped away, feeling daringly bohemian.

The Sapling left to do their bidding. Drusilla watched him walk away. He held himself differently. A stiffness in his torso and slight weight on his leg.

Wartime injuries?

Drusilla chilled inside when she considered how much worse it could have been. Her gentle Sapling, what scars did he carry on his heart that were invisible to the human eye? She would do what she could to ease them.

She turned her attention to the young woman standing beside her, marvelling at how effortlessly she had commanded Edwin.

Eleni. Glossy hair. Smooth skin with an attractive olive tone. A Greek name for a Greek woman.

Tall.

Beautiful.

The branches above them swayed.

Eleni turned to her and folded her arms across her impressive bosom.

"What are you?"

A spear pierced Drusilla's chest.

The shock of recognition. She tensed, ready for flight, but Eleni gave a gentle smile.

"Don't be scared of me. You're something special, I can tell. Does Edwin know?"

"Yes, he does." Drusilla smiled.

Eleni laughed, her wide mouth revealing good teeth. "How wonderful. I've always wanted to meet someone mythological. You see, I was born in Greece and lived there until I was nine. My *giagia* told me old stories all the time. Are you a dryad?"

Drusilla remembered Edwin asking; remembered her haughty retort concerning oak trees. She felt a slight budding of shame at how prickly she'd been. How important it had been to impress.

"Close enough. How can you tell I'm different?" she asked curiously.

"I'm not sure. Perhaps one of my ancestors was raped by a god or demigod and left me with some hint of the unearthly." A frown crossed Eleni's high forehead. "Is that what happened to make you? Like poor Daphne?"

Drusilla walked under the boughs. She stroked the trunk, fingers briefly straying to the sword-scar.

"No. No one raped me. I think there was a death though." She leaned against the tree and closed her eyes. Vague memories of a woman screaming as she fell; the flooding of blood and birth onto a struggling seedling; animation passing from one form to another.

"But then it happened again," she murmured. She closed her eyes, remembering a day when she'd been high in the branches – a woman who looked familiar but not one she knew.

"What did?" Eleni leaned her back against the tree.

She opened her eyes and shook her head to clear it. "A woman falling. It doesn't matter."

Eleni gave her an appraising stare then pushed herself away from the trunk and strolled to the edge of the grove.

"Where is Edwin? I hope he hasn't forgotten and gone off with Harold or that awful Robert. Perhaps his grandfather has made him go and talk to someone."

Uncertainty flickered within Drusilla. She followed Eleni and stood looking at the house and garden, lit and celebratory. She suspected there was more to tempt him back here. If not her, then the woman beside her. Sadness bobbed at the edge of her consciousness.

"No, he'll be back. He always returns eventually."

Eleni's face creased. "Oh, you poor thing. Do you just sit and wait for him here? That's no life at all!"

Her indignation was beautiful to see.

"It's what I do. It's what I am."

"Does it have to be?" Eleni asked. She sat on the grass and gestured for Drusilla to join her.

"That's what I do. What I've always done." Drusilla lowered herself beside Eleni. She pursed her lips. "My kind need adoration as much as our trees need the rain and sunlight. Once we could grant or dismiss favours at whim because there were enough men who believed in us and wanted us."

"But do you have to be?" Eleni asked.

"I'm bound by laws, I suppose you could call them, that I can't change."

Eleni sighed. "I'm bound in different ways but I know what

you mean. Father will expect me to marry. I'll settle down with some doughy old fellow. A barrister or a lawyer of some sort, I'm sure. Or a partner in a bank. I'll be a dutiful wife and have English babies."

"You don't want that?" Drusilla asked.

"Let's just say the thought does not make my heart rush." She pulled a stem of grass and blew it up into the air. "Oh look, Edwin is coming back."

Her eyes sparkled with glee.

With love?

Cold hands seized Drusilla's heart. She watched Edwin returning, bottle in hand. She could have leapt to her feet like Eleni did and greeted him before he reached the tree. Instead she waited where she sat on the dewy ground and made space for him to sit beside her.

To sit between them.

She smiled as he popped the cork – enjoying the eruption of foam despite the growing sense of bleakness within her – and accepted the tall glass.

Tartness and fruit, making her senses muddle, spinning her head.

He showed no preference for either woman and she watched carefully to spot any indication. He chatted idly about the trouble he was having trying to keep enough workers in the factory; told them anecdotes from his time in France. Did Eleni see the pain in his eyes and suspect there were tales he would not tell, as Drusilla did? She longed for time alone with him but she would have to wait.

Perhaps she understood. She told her own of nursing wounded men. Of being obeyed by men.

"I can't wait to be thirty and be allowed to vote," she declared, raising her glass. "If I stay in this country at all, that is."

She was perceptive and intelligent; lively and witty.

Drusilla hid a rueful smile.

She was human. A perfect match for Edwin.

At the house the lights began to be extinguished. Edwin groaned and clambered to his feet.

"We'd better go back, Eleni. The others will be waiting to take you home. I'm sure they'll all be wondering where we've been."

Eleni smirked. "I'm sure they'll have their own dreadful ideas."

He held his hands out and pulled her up, then did the same for Drusilla.

Eleni kissed her cheek, swaying slightly and steadying herself with a hand on Drusilla's waist. Soft, female lips were a new sensation; the scent of lemon and rosemary on her hair and skin; sunshine and vitality.

"It was lovely to meet you. I do hope I can see you again. I might see if Baba will let me stay when they all leave. I want to watch you change as the summer comes."

Edwin stiffened. The women turned to him, united. It felt good. A friend. For the first time she wondered what a female acolyte would be like.

"I know what Drusilla is, Edwin," Eleni said.

Edwin's eyes widened and he looked to Drusilla for confirmation.

"It's true. It's not a problem. Eleni, I would be honoured if you would return."

Eleni sauntered off, swinging her bag and whistling.

"Did you tell her?" Edwin asked.

"She guessed."

Drusilla wrapped her arms around herself and looked at Edwin.

"So this is the woman you're going to leave me for," she said sadly.

"No, she isn't!" Edwin stepped closer to her, lowered his voice. "Why on earth do you say that?"

"You like her, I can tell. Is she the one who improved your kissing?"

"No!"

He flushed, still the mild, sensitive young man she adored. "I've never kissed Eleni. I like her, yes, but that's all. I promise you. Look, I'll come back alone tomorrow and we can talk."

"I'd like that," she replied.

She watched them walk away. They looked well together.

Perhaps it was time to say goodbye.

Unless…

Eleni had recognised her, but she was remarkable. The Old One had known her, but he'd been aware already. Edwin hadn't, even though she had told him outright.

Who else would know, if she walked amongst them?

She walked back to the tree and climbed into the branches. Down below, she could see the last remaining guests leaving and the servants clearing the tables. She reclined along the sturdy bough and thought.

Chapter Nineteen

He tried not to let it show at the time but Drusilla's prediction had unnerved Edwin. Why did she think he would leave her for Eleni? Of course he liked Eleni, but he had no deep feelings for her.

To his surprise, Stephen had been pleased she was going to stay in the area, even going as far as inviting her to join them at Greete Mill House, advising that a young lady could not stay unchaperoned in a hotel. And so it was, three days later, that she moved her luggage from the hotel into the house and took up residence in a small bedroom opposite Edwin's.

It was quite sickening to see the way the old man fawned over the young woman as he walked her around the house, to the extent that Edwin wondered if he was considering a proposal himself.

He took a slice of ginger cake from the spread that Stephen had put out for Eleni, excused himself, and went to find Drusilla. He hadn't had the opportunity to speak to her privately since she had awoken.

The tree was in blossom earlier this year than Edwin could ever remember, heavy clusters of sticky pale-green buds with insects buzzing back and forth. He stood back, admiring the sight, until Drusilla joined him.

"How are you?" he asked, offering her the cake.

"Wonderful!" She bit into the cake enthusiastically. "I feel so alive. So refreshed. It's the best I've felt for longer than I can remember. Thank you for bringing your friend to meet me. I think her admiration has invigorated me more than I suspected it could."

"Oh. Well, I'm pleased she has done you some good," Edwin said. He had to slightly force his smile as jealousy took root in him. He'd been used to being Drusilla's only source of adulation.

She wiped a crumb from the corner of her lips and threw her arms around him, causing him to stagger back. "Oh, Sapling. You're jealous. I can taste it in the air around you. Don't be. Your love means more to me than anything else."

"Does it?" He drew her head onto his shoulder, setting his feet in case she decided to knock him off balance again. She sighed deeply, sending a cool breeze over his neck.

"Yes. Do you think I could have bloomed so beautifully without knowing you were back. I almost feel that I shall have to wake each winter to see you. But I did like meeting Eleni. She's fascinating and she's given me some ideas."

"I'm intrigued." Edwin took her hand and they sat side by side. Drusilla began to pick blades of grass and twist them into a wreath. Either she had a technique he didn't know or she was using some sort of magic to bind them together. She spoke as she crafted.

"Eleni is fascinating. Drinking, smoking cigarettes (though I don't like that and I would never do it), wearing what she wears. Voting, whatever that is."

"Not until she's thirty. Women below that age aren't permitted – at least not yet," Edwin pointed out. Though he suspected that if women like Eleni had their way, suffrage would be granted to all women before the century was out.

"A finger-snap in the life of the world," Drusilla said. She leaned against Edwin, her legs curled beneath her body. The sun was warm, with no breeze. A sense of peace descended on Edwin that he'd long forgotten. Not since before his time in France could he remember feeling so contented. It was short lived, however, because Drusilla's next words were astounding.

"I want to become a modern woman like Eleni. I want you both to help me."

"How? Why? You're perfect as you are," he spluttered.

"I know I'm perfect," she said, without coyness or false modesty. "I think I was always content with my lot, but since meeting you and seeing Eleni, my eyes have been opened to the possibilities of the world out there."

Drusilla stood and walked to the edge of the field.

"I have been reading the magazines and newspapers. Women worked during the war. Oh, I know they always have in many roles but women have flown aeroplanes and driven ambulances. They have become people in themselves. I want to be one of those."

"But what about your tree? What about being a muse?" Edwin asked.

Drusilla folded her arms and gave him a determined look.

"I have been a muse for as long as I have existed. I want to be your equal. I deserve that."

The idea of a mythical being wanting to drive an ambulance or voting was amusing. Edwin laughed, then made himself stop. Drusilla's enthusiasm and wishes were sincere and he didn't want her to feel like he was mocking her. He walked to her side and took her hands, looking into her eyes.

"Aren't you happy? What can I do to make you happy?"

She stroked his cheek. "You do make me happy. Perhaps I want more than that. There has to be more to existence. There's a whole world. My kind are disappearing."

"What do you mean?"

"The trees are being cut down. They always were, of course, but now it is faster. I think I remember – or part of my memories remember – when all this was woodland. I have memories of not being alone."

She walked along the top of the field to the gate that led down into the village.

"How long before all this is gone?"

Edwin looked at what had once been a small cluster of houses. It had grown recently and he knew there were plans to expand it further: a larger school than the one-roomed building that stood beside the church; more houses; a pub, even. Before too long it would link seamlessly with the town itself and then Greete Mill House and the grounds would be surrounded. How long before someone came knocking on the door offering to buy up Stephen's land? How long before he sold it?

Edwin's skin crawled. He remembered the old nymph in France, vanishing before his eyes when her tree fell. He wrapped his arms around Drusilla, holding her tightly as if that could prevent the same thing happening to her.

"I won't let that happen to you; I swear it. Whatever it takes, I'll keep you and your tree safe."

"Thank you."

Drusilla rested her head on his chest and he felt the overwhelming desire to protect her. His grandfather had spoken in passing of changes he wanted to – or perhaps needed to – make to the business. Meetings that sounded dull to Edwin but that he probably should attend if possible.

"I still want to make some changes," Drusilla murmured in his ear.

"Then I'll do anything I can to help you," Edwin said. "I'm sure Eleni will too. Do you mind if I mention this conversation to her?"

"Not at all. I was going to ask her myself but I'm sure if you do then she'll agree. Maybe one day soon you will come and find the pair of us taking afternoon tea dressed in the finest gowns. Real ones, not ones that I have created myself."

She ran her fingers over the bodice of her dress, tracing the patterns of overlapping leaves that were picked out in a brighter green on the pale background. Edwin's eyes widened as he followed the path of her hands. She probably had no idea that he was less concerned with the clothes as his mind had strayed to what lay beneath them.

"I'd like to see you in them," he murmured. "It's a shame you aren't Eleni's size. I'm sure she'd let you borrow a dress and … whatever else you need."

"I could be her size if I wanted to be," Drusilla said, giving a laugh that suggested she knew what he was thinking.

"Then I'll look forward to seeing your transformation," he said. "I'd better go and see whether Grandfather has proposed to Eleni yet. I wouldn't put it past him. She's very rich, or at least she will be when her father dies."

Drusilla's smile grew less wide. "Then you should probably marry her yourself sooner rather than later."

Edwin felt a tightening in his jaw. It appeared that Drusilla had already decided that was to be his fate but he wasn't prepared to discuss it now. He bade her farewell and returned home.

Eleni had unpacked and was dancing to gramophone recordings of American music while Stephen was sitting in the armchair by the window, watching with an indulgent smile on his face.

"Come and dance with me!" Eleni shrieked when she spotted Edwin. She pulled him by the hand onto the carpet and, knowing there was no point in refusing, he took her in his arms and led her around the room.

"Have you been with the delightful Drusilla?" she whispered. "Yes, I can see you have because your eyes are dreamy and you look hot under the collar. You really should take her to bed soon before she decides you're frigid and finds a better acolyte. Do you think there is any chance she might love women as much as she likes men?"

"Eleni, you are completely shocking!" Edwin spluttered. Eleni had hinted before that her tastes were slightly unconventional, but he'd never really considered her being serious. "I don't think I should let you anywhere near her if that's how you're going to speak."

"You do want to make love to her, though, don't you?"

He nodded. His heart was beating fast from dancing, pushing against the ever-present ache in his ribs, and now it felt like it was about to burst free and fly away. And as for what was happening in his trousers... Well, he'd better not dance too closely to Eleni or he'd never be able to look her in the eye again.

"I can't promise her marriage or a future. I don't want to take advantage of her."

Eleni gave him a sympathetic look. "Why not? The future, not the taking advantage, I mean. That's very honourable of you, my dear, but really, I know plenty of men and women who make love to each other without being married and don't see it as being taken advantage of at all. It's much more romantic without being chained in matrimony, don't you think?"

Edwin gave a sigh, wishing he had a tenth of Eleni's progressive views.

"Let's see," he said. He raised his voice. "Grandfather, would you object to me marrying a penniless woman with no family and no home?"

Stephen scowled. "Don't be ridiculous. Is she one of those displaced persons that lingered here after the war ended? You had better not be intending to do that if you want to inherit this house and business."

He got up from his chair and left the room, his walking stick tapping angrily on the parquet as he went down the corridor.

"There you go," Edwin said with a shrug. "It isn't as though Drusilla and I could go and live somewhere else. She needs to be near her tree."

ELISABETH J. HOBBES

"Yes, I see your problem," Eleni said sympathetically. She glanced in the direction of the door. "He's always been rather direct and humourless, hasn't he."

"Yes, with me, at least. I want to know why my grandfather dislikes me so much. It feels as though my very existence is a burden to him, even though I'm no longer financially beholden to him."

The song came to an end. Eleni kissed Edwin's cheek and excused herself. Edwin walked to the window and looked out. He *was* financially dependent on his grandfather, that was the problem. He drew a small salary for his work at the factory but his food and lodgings were dependent on Stephen's goodwill. He'd redouble his efforts to make the factory prosper and then...

Then what?

He'd demand a larger salary in recompense. Get the means to buy a house in the village where he could see Drusilla's tree and visit her daily. He wouldn't care what Stephen would think because Stephen would be an irrelevance. And Stephen was growing older and surely must want to retire from the decision-making at some point in the next few years.

How wonderful it would be to spend his life with Drusilla, if only he could find a way of doing it.

The thought of a future with Drusilla galvanised Edwin. He offered to go to meetings in place of Stephen and began trying to charm customers. Late one afternoon, he arrived home from a meeting with the borough council to hear voices and strolled out onto the terrace to investigate.

The sight he encountered made him stop in his tracks. Eleni was serving afternoon tea. Stephen was sitting with her and was chatting to a third person.

Drusilla.

Edwin knew he hadn't spoken her name out loud but she looked up and their eyes met. She gave him the most subtle of winks.

"Why Edwin, you're back already. Just in time for a slice of cake. May I present our guest. This is Miss Drusilla Moore."

"Miss Moore." Edwin smiled at the pun. He walked across the terrace to stand by her chair. She extended a hand and he took it politely. His fingers tingled; pulsated with excitement at her touch.

"How lovely to meet you, Mr Hope. May we offer you a cup of tea?" She turned her eyes to Stephen, wide but demure. "Mr Brice, would you care for a drop more?"

"That would be delightful," Stephen replied with a dreamy smile. "Edwin, do stop gawping and pull up a chair. Miss Moore can't be holding the teapot all afternoon!"

Edwin sat down between Eleni and Drusilla, opposite his grandfather.

"Miss Moore is an artist," Eleni said. "A woman after my own heart. We met whilst looking around a gallery."

"I just sketch, really," Drusilla said, giving a modest smile. "Botanical observations mainly."

Stephen coughed. "I'm trying to persuade Miss Moore to show me some of her work. I have an eye for artistry and after the horrors of the last few years I believe our customers might have a hankering for fresh designs too. What do you say?"

Stephen raised his eyes and looked at Edwin as he spoke.

"You are asking me?"

Stephen frowned. "No one else, boy."

Clearly, whatever charm Drusilla had placed on him did not extend to being overly civil with his grandson, Edwin thought wryly.

"I think that's an excellent idea. I've had a few of my own too," he said, drawing his chair closer to Drusilla. "The dyes themselves fascinate me. The plants and creatures that hold such vibrancy within them. Murex, for example."

The women tilted their heads questioningly.

"Little sea creatures. When crushed up, their shells produce a vivid purple that was so prized that only the Roman emperors were allowed to wear it. Could you imagine if chemists were able to produce the same colours within their laboratories? It would be available to the poorest labourer. Or a turquoise that never fades, for example. I find it fascinating."

"Man made woad." Drusilla gave him a wide smile. "A small plant used by the ancient Britons to dye their skin. We could all wear it."

"Exactly," Edwin said. He smiled at her enthusiastically, then caught his grandfather's eye. Stephen wore an expression he had never seen before. He couldn't tell whether it was disapproval at his ideas or at him talking with a supposed stranger so enthusiastically.

"Perhaps I'm looking in the wrong direction. I should be looking to the natural world, not the chemical," he finished thoughtfully.

He coughed. "So, Miss Moore, how did you come to be here?"

Eleni smiled at him. "Poor Drusilla is an orphan from the

war. A refugee to our shores. She's from an old family but sadly she lost everything. I intend to introduce her into society while I am staying here." She leaned close to Edwin and whispered in a stage whisper, "Perhaps I shall find her a wife."

Stephen put his teacup down and reached for Drusilla's hand. "If you will excuse me, I have matters of business to attend to. Dull things that unfortunately tear me away from your company."

"Oh, what a shame," Drusilla said. She slid her eyes from Stephen to Edwin. "I'm sure your grandson must be a great help, however."

Stephen's smile became a rictus that Edwin suspected the women didn't spot but that he recognised from years of familiarity with the old man.

"Miss Moore, please feel free to call whenever you like. I shall leave you to your tea."

He walked off stiffly, his progress along the terrace maddeningly slow.

Chapter Twenty

Edwin waited a minute until his grandfather was safely around the corner then put his teacup in the saucer with a clatter.

"What the devil is going on?"

Drusilla took his hand. Her nails were painted a pale pink that looked artificial, he noticed. She giggled. "I told you that one day you would come home to find us both taking afternoon tea. Eleni and I hatched a plan."

Edwin swept his hand over his hair. "Yes, but I thought you were joking."

"We thought how wonderful it would be to see if Drusilla can pass as human. It was successful, wouldn't you say?" Eleni dropped a lump of sugar into her cup then twirled the silver tongs around her little finger. "Great Uncle Stephen didn't suspect there was anything odd about Drusilla. If anything, he was completely charmed, I thought."

"Yes, he was, wasn't he," Edwin growled, withdrawing his

hand from Drusilla's and picking up a biscuit as an excuse. "He looked like he wanted to swallow you up whole."

He gave Drusilla a quick glance. There was nothing at all to suggest she wasn't entirely human. Her clothes looked perfectly in fashion, with a light skirt and blouse in matching green with a fashionable kimono-style coat patterned with sycamore leaves. Even her hair was neatly coiled into a chignon at the nape of her neck like Eleni's was. She was even wearing shoes!

"Well whatever charm you put on Grandfather seemed to work."

Drusilla's eyes flashed with amusement. "I didn't put any charm on him, not intentionally. He did seem very fond of me, I think."

"He's fond of lots of people. Sadly I'm not one of them," Edwin mused. He finished his biscuit. "Miss Moore, if you are ready to return home, shall I escort you?"

"Thank you, Mr Hope. I would like that." Her cheek dimpled. "Thank you, Eleni. I had a lovely time."

"You're welcome." Eleni blew her a kiss then rang the little silver bell to summon the maid.

Edwin held an arm out to Drusilla. She slid hers through and leaned close to him. He could sense the knots in his stomach unwinding as he felt the warmth of her body. He hadn't seen her for what felt like a long time and was reluctant to take her straight back to the tree.

"Shall we walk into the formal garden before we go back?" he suggested.

"Yes, I want to see how the plants are doing," she replied.

They strolled along the terrace and through the brick archway into the walled garden that he now thought of as another part of Drusilla's domain. After his initial surprise at seeing the garden changed from ornamental to functional, Edwin had grown used to the change from rose knots and sunflowers to vegetables. They strolled down the central path, and as they passed a slightly limp bed of cauliflower plants Drusilla trailed her hand over the top, fingers caressing the leaves. By the time they passed them again the leaves were looking healthier and crisper. Edwin shook his head in wonder.

"Drusilla, you are a marvel. Is there nothing that is beyond you?"

Her smile faltered. "I don't know. Some things."

She opened her mouth as if she were going to say something then stopped and carried on along the path, twisting off some leaves, blowing away insects, encouraging stems up the canes.

"Have you ever been beyond the grounds of the house?" Edwin asked.

She turned to him, wide-eyed. "Never. You know that. I don't know what would happen if I tried."

He tucked her arm under his. "Let's find out. If you feel at all odd let me know and we'll come straight back here. Will you trust me?"

She glanced up at the tree then back at Edwin. "I will."

They walked round the side of the house, pausing as they stepped over what Edwin thought of as the threshold to the grounds and onto the street. He felt Drusilla tensing against him and squeezed her arm reassuringly. She stood on the pavement and let out a breath. Her eyes gleamed with triumph.

"I did it."

"Yes! Come on. Let's go further."

They walked steadily arm in arm, through the streets with which Edwin was familiar and down roads he had never bothered to investigate. Stately garden squares surrounded by large homes from the time of the old queen gave way to rows and rows of tightly packed houses, many with three storeys and long upper windows to give as much light as possible to the weavers who had once worked in their homes. Drusilla said nothing, but her eyes grew solemn as the green of trees and lawns gave way to grey as they reached newer, crammed-in terraces with shared yards and privies.

A group of children were kicking a football against the end wall of a row of terraces. They stopped and watched.

The ball came towards Edwin and he felt a mild panic. He'd never been able to kick a ball straight. He kicked it back, slightly off target, resulting in good-natured laughter from the children.

A stout little girl with tightly curled hair ribbons ran for it and slipped. She began to wail as her bare knees scuffed in the grit. Mortified at being the cause of her injury, Edwin picked her up and dusted down her knees. Blood spots welled and she wailed louder.

"Do you have a handkerchief?" Drusilla asked.

Edwin handed it over. Drusilla licked it then wiped it across the girl's knees and the crying stopped.

"Wouldn't you rather play in the nice grassy square a few

streets over?" Drusilla asked. "The grass is much nicer than the road."

The girl wrinkled her nose. "We'd get a slipper on the arse if we went there! Those aren't our squares. You got any pennies, miss?"

Drusilla's mouth fell open. Edwin hurriedly fished out a shilling and handed it over. "Go and buy yourselves some ice cream from Angelli's."

The children ran off, squealing with delight, towards the factory shop.

Edwin watched them vanish then took Drusilla's arm and they walked on.

"You weren't like that as a child," she remarked.

"Poor kids, with only the road or a washing-filled yard to play in," he said.

Drusilla looked around sorrowfully. "Places like this destroy the soul. Take me home, please Edwin."

They walked home, Edwin keeping a close eye on Drusilla for signs of anything untoward. She was quiet, looking around at the densely packed streets as if they were the gates of Hell. He couldn't blame her. He'd hate to live there himself.

As soon as they arrived back at Greete Mill House, Drusilla let go of Edwin's arm and ran down the terrace steps onto the croquet lawn and lifted up one foot then the other to take off her shoes.

"Ah, that's better." She sighed in contentment as she placed her feet back on the bare ground. She dangled the shoes by their thin straps. They were more like dancing slippers, soft brown suede or moleskin, with low heels.

"You should take your shoes off too. Even for humans,

feeling the ground beneath your feet is important. It connects you to the world."

"You're right, I should. I've spent too long this afternoon in tedious meetings," Edwin said.

He sat down and took off his shoes and socks. He stood again and wiggled his toes into the springy lawn. It did feel wonderful, even more so because of the impulsive aspect to it.

"Those poor children, having no grass or trees. Not even a flowerbed," Drusilla said sorrowfully. She brightened. "They didn't see anything different in me, though. I passed, didn't I. And I don't even feel too weak. I've never been so far."

"You passed," Edwin agreed.

The knots in his stomach tightened a little more. He'd gone as the factory's representative to the meeting of the town council, the purpose of which had been to discuss the expansion of public buildings and housing. He stared in contemplation at the fields beyond the sycamore tree. His grandfather had hinted strongly that he would be willing to sell the grounds beyond the croquet garden and summer house. It horrified Edwin to think that Drusilla's meadow might very soon be covered with more rows of the cramped grey houses. What would become of her then?

"You look troubled. Do you want to tell me what's wrong?" Drusilla still had her hand on his shoulder. He looked down into her eyes, on the verge of telling her, then changed his mind. She didn't need to know the plans that could affect her. Yet.

"No, nothing much," he said. "Let's walk by the stream. It's been a long time since I dipped my toes in. I feel like being a child again."

They held hands and strolled together. Edwin rolled his trousers up to mid-calf then they stepped into the water together. It was still chilly, though the warmth of the summer sunshine had lessened the bite.

"Oh, that's wonderful," Drusilla said. "Don't you think so, Edwin? There's nothing like the feel of raw elements on your skin."

She lifted her skirts and waded a little bit deeper into the water.

"You'll get your dress wet," he cautioned, seeing how the hems trailed in the wake of small waves caused by her movement.

She tossed her head back and gave him a broad grin. "And it will dry, won't it. Nothing stays the same forever. Nothing is ever too cold or too hot or too wet or too dry permanently. The seasons change just as I do."

She smiled at him then dropped her head slightly and looked at him alluringly through her lashes. He waded towards her, only belatedly realising that he had soaked his trousers to the knees. She put her arms around him and raised her face.

"Of course if you wish me to take them off I could. Would you like me to?"

"Good God, here? Now?" Edwin blinked in shock.

"That wasn't a no," Drusilla said, drawing her lips into a seductive pout.

"No it wasn't," Edwin agreed, quietly.

She parted her lips, clearly expecting his to meet them. Though it frustrated him to do it, he turned his head slightly away. Edwin's pulse began to thump, drumming swiftly in his neck. He was desperate to see through what he had brought to a halt before the war. Europe was at peace and he had no intention of going away. He suspected most of his friends had surrendered their virginity long before now and the only woman he could imagine making love to was standing beside him.

"If I kiss you, I won't want to stop," he cautioned.

"You don't have to," she murmured, flicking a lock of his hair behind his ear.

His pulse throbbed even faster.

"No, I mean I won't want to stop at kissing."

She trailed her finger down his neck. Her smile deepened, her eyes full of promise.

"You don't have to."

Edwin glanced towards the house. It was late afternoon. The house was occupied but Stephen would be in his office or at the factory. Eleni would be either sketching in the drawing room or dancing alone to gramophone records. He could probably sneak Drusilla up to his room unseen but he didn't want it to be a furtive act that they rushed so nobody discovered them. That would remind him too much of the poor woman in the brothel at Amiens and the last thing he wanted was that shameful memory to be associated with Drusilla.

They could go to the sycamore and lie down together beneath the branches, but the memory of the first time still made him sweat occasionally.

Her world or his. Neither seemed right, and he felt to his core that it had to be right.

"When is the next full moon?" he asked.

Drusilla's lips curled beguilingly. "You're getting the idea of significance. Nine nights hence."

Edwin put his hands to her cheeks and turned her face upwards. He kissed her gently on the lips, controlling his urge to carry on and contenting himself with the merest touch.

"Then I'll come for you on the night of the full moon."

They parted and Edwin went into the house.

"Is that you?" Eleni called as soon as he closed the front door. He would never have been able to smuggle Drusilla past her. He followed the sound of her voice into the drawing room where she was lying across a sofa with a book open across her belly. It was in Greek, an alphabet he had never managed to master.

"Oh, my heart is weary," she said. "Be a dear and make me a drink of some sort. I don't care what, I just need something. I suppose you and Drusilla have been enjoying yourselves. Didn't she do well with your grandfather. He was quite enchanted. She has such a gift for charming people into loving her, doesn't she. I'm completely infatuated with her."

He wasn't entirely sure how far Eleni's devotion to Drusilla went, but he was surprised to feel a prickling of envy.

"That makes both of us," Edwin said. He walked to the drinks cabinet and fixed a gin sling for Eleni and a whiskey and soda for himself. He settled on the sofa beside her.

"Eleni, what do women like?"

"Gin slings," Eleni giggled, waving her glass at him. She stopped laughing. "I'm teasing. I know what you meant. We all like different things so there's no point you asking me because she might not. Clean teeth though, that's pretty universal. Are you finally going to make your move?"

"I think so." He could feel himself blushing. "I'd like you to help me."

Eleni clapped her hands together, almost spilling her drink. "Edwin, you daring darling!"

"With the preparations," he said hastily, his cheeks flaming. "I have an idea but if I make arrangements myself it might raise some questions."

Eleni leaned forward and listened as Edwin explained what he wanted of her.

"You romantic creature," she sighed. "I wouldn't know you had it in you to look at you."

Edwin glanced at himself in the mirror. He wasn't bad looking. His suit was clean and smart, his waistcoat buttoned, and his tie knotted fashionably. He was the epitome of respectability. And dullness. He gave his reflection a stern look and was immediately reminded of his grandfather. He stiffened.

Eleni might be right. He'd have to dress more carefully on the night of the full moon. Drusilla wanted to be a modern woman so she was unlikely to want a stuffy old man.

Later in the week he went to visit Annie McAvoy at the school. Edwin presented Morag and Mairibeth with two ounces each of sherbet pips which they accepted with delighted thanks before running out onto the lawn in front of the boarding house.

"Thank you, Edwin. The girls don't get many treats and they work so hard around the house. It's very good of the school to allow them to play on the grounds."

Annie poured out the tea and sat down with a groan. Her husband had lost an arm in the war. He was still a valued teacher but Annie was the one who now spent evenings marking the pupils' work, ticking and crossing in red ink where he directed. The twins had taken on housework and looking after their young brother who had been born in the first months of the war.

"I was wondering, Annie, do you have any spare old clothes?" Edwin asked. "I know a young woman who is down on her luck and who is trying to look respectable."

"Really? And why are you asking me?" Annie tipped her head on one side and gave him a quizzical look.

He'd planned his answer beforehand. "You are the only woman I know really. I mean, I know other women such as my cousin, Eleni, but the woman I know would probably rather have clothes the owners wouldn't recognise."

Annie set down a plate of biscuits. "Well I do have some clothes from my slimmer days, but if she's planning to appear with the company you keep she won't want to be seen in any of my clothes either. If she's young then my styles will seem far too matronly for her and if she's hoping to appear well-to-do then they'll be too plain."

"Oh, well, thank you anyway." Edwin dipped a ginger biscuit in his tea, ignoring the way Annie winced.

"Do that and you'll leave crumbs in the bottom."

Edwin took a bite and swallowed. "I don't mind. I'll drink them up anyway."

"You used to do that as a child." Annie smiled and pushed the plate of biscuits towards him. "Not with tea of course, but with rusks and your milk. I remember one time warning you not to but you did it anyway and then half the rusk fell in and you cried until you were brought fresh."

Edwin put his cup back in the saucer. "What was my mother like, Annie? It's as if she never existed at all. Grandfather still refuses to talk to me about her. Her room is still shut up. I suggested to him that Eleni might use it while she's staying with us and I thought he was going to strike me."

"I didn't know her except by sight. I'm sorry I can't help you." She patted his hand. "You need to talk to your grandfather really. You're a grown man now, Edwin. You're not beholden to him anymore and you should confront him."

Edwin sucked his teeth. "Confront. That's a very drastic word."

Apt though, he suspected.

"Ask him, then." Annie squeezed his hand. "You are a wonderful young man, Edwin, and your parents would have been proud to see you, I'm sure."

The conversation kept repeating in Edwin's head over the next week. Moreover, coupled with the reason for his visit to Annie, he had a fresh idea. Were any of his mother's clothes still in the house? They would be even more out of style than anything Annie could've given him but surely someone would be able to alter them, and things like blouses and shifts would do. If not for Drusilla, then for the poor women in the town.

Annie's words had lit a fire inside him and he was determined to discover the circumstances of his mother's death. Even the idea of confronting Stephen sent a chill through his bones that he was not ready yet to face head-on. Instead, he embarked on what might be a riskier plan.

"I'm going to go into her room. Grandfather is going out on

Thursday evening for a meeting in the town hall. He's invited me but I am going to decline and say I've got a headache," he explained to Drusilla.

Drusilla put her pencil down and gave him a look filled with uncertainty. They were sitting by the stream, sketching the wildflowers. It must have been Drusilla's influence because Edwin's pictures were much improved. Eleni was sunbathing in an oversized hat close by.

"Are you sure that is wise? It's very devious. Why not just ask him directly?"

"I've asked him directly. He's refused directly. No, I want to go in there and get a sense of who she was. Then I will ask him."

"What if you find out something that you don't want to?" Eleni called.

"I can't imagine finding anything that I'd regret too much," Edwin said.

Drusilla laid her hand over his. She frowned.

"Don't do it. Some mysteries are better left unsolved."

"Are they? Perhaps so for some people, but I have to know why her death led to him hating me."

He turned his palm and linked his fingers through hers. All the nerves in his body twitched. He smiled at her, hiding his concern.

"Besides, Thursday is the full moon. I'll come and see you afterwards."

She lowered her head and gazed at him through her lashes.

"I'll be waiting."

· · ·

When Thursday evening came and Stephen had left the house, Edwin made his way to the room. He paused outside the door, hand hovering over the doorknob.

"What are you doing?"

He jumped at the voice from behind him. He lowered his hand and turned around. Stephen Brice stood at the turn in the corridor, dressed in his outdoor coat.

"Grandfather. I thought you had gone out to a meeting."

"Yes, I gather that. I reached the corner and realised I had forgotten my pocket watch. Why are you doing this now?"

"Because meeting Miss Moore made me realise that there are women who have lost everything and there must be useful clothes in here."

It was only half a lie, but why lie at all? Edwin forced himself to breathe calmly then continued.

"Because I want to know why her death has caused you to despise me."

"Do you?" Stephen said quietly. "Do you really?"

Edwin nodded. "I'm a grown man. Whatever the reason, I can face it. Will you tell me once and for all what happened to my mother?"

Stephen ground his teeth "You're right. You're not a child and you are no longer dependent on me. I should have told you this long before now."

Edwin felt a shiver go down his back. Stephen opened the door and waved a hand.

"In you go."

Chapter Twenty-One

E dwin hesitated, half anticipating that he was about to
discover a mad woman in her lair. He felt sweat on his
palms as his fingers balled into a fist.

The room was in darkness but it was empty. It smelled
dusty and old but underlying that there was a hint of
something floral. He inhaled.

"Lily-of-the-valley," he said.

Stephen nodded. "Your mother's favourite scent."

Stephen walked to the curtains and opened them. Evening
light flooded into the room, caressing the furnishings.
Everything was thickly covered with dust.

"You have kept it as a mausoleum," Edwin gasped. "Why?"

Stephen winced and Edwin wished he could eat back the
words. He'd been tactless but, even so, the state of the room
struck Edwin as deathly wrong.

The bedroom was as Edwin remembered it, even though it
was over twenty years since he had last stood there. The heavy
floral counterpane was turned down on the bed. His father's

pipe stood on a stand on one side of the bed. On the other was a leatherbound Bible and a posy of dried lavender. A pair of black button boots stood beside a wardrobe on top of which were two hat boxes. Beside the bed was a baby bassinet on a frame, hung about with lacy drapes and lemon-yellow ribbons. Edwin walked across the floor towards the dressing room. He must have stepped on a loose floorboard because the bassinet began to rock slightly. It was very eerie to see, as if a ghost hand had nudged it.

"Was this mine?"

"Look at the picture," Stephen commanded, gesturing towards the dressing table in the window-bay. His voice was hard.

On the dressing table, beside a long-unused mother-of-pearl handled hairbrush was a frame. It contained a very old photograph. It must have been one of the early examples. The photograph was of a family grouping. A younger Stephen stood beside his son-in-law, Archibald Hope, who had his arm about his wife's waist. Edwin as a young boy stood in front of his father, his outline slightly blurry as he must have wriggled. Adelaide Hope smiled at the camera with one hand on her son's shoulder and the other cradling her belly. The fashions of the day were impossibly old-fashioned to Edwin's modern eyes but even he could not fail to see the vast swelling of a pregnancy. His stomach plummeted.

"My mother was with child?"

"Yes. This was taken in her sixth month. At Christmas."

Edwin moved to pick up the photograph but Stephen seized him by the wrist.

"Nobody touches that. Nobody but me has touched anything in this room since your parents died."

Nausea began to rise inside Edwin. His legs felt shaky and his stomach acidic. If she had been pregnant at Christmas...

"She died in childbirth?"

Stephen's lip twisted then shook.

"You don't remember at all, do you? The casual disobedience that led to her death?"

Edwin shook his head, wordlessly. He swallowed. His mouth felt parched but that did nothing to alleviate it. He looked back again at the photograph, noticing now that the figures were standing at the top step beside the fishpond. In the background, alone on the hill, stood the sycamore, bare of leaves and cutting a lonely figure. Twenty years younger and twenty years smaller.

"That damned tree," Stephen said harshly. "You were obsessed with it as soon as you could walk. You'd try to crawl there each time you were in the gardens or the field and gabble on about the fairies. Adelaide humoured you. She used to take you up there in summer to play and in the autumn to throw the seeds. But you weren't content with being taken. You had to go yourself."

Stephen walked to the window and stared out. The branches were swaying gently in the wind and Edwin wondered if Drusilla was there or still in the summer house. He'd spoken of fairies. That must have been her.

"Your mother lost sight of you one day in winter. We were all frantic, thinking you might have fallen in the pond or the stream. Too late, Adelaide realised where you'd gone and she followed. You didn't come back when she called you,

309

disobedient little child that you were, so she chased you."
Stephen closed his eyes. She chased you and she fell. Caught
her foot on something. Went over. Landed on her belly."

He closed his eyes and made a sound that was a bit like a
sob. Edwin stood fixed to the spot, unable to move or speak.

"The baby came early. Dr Graves tried to stop it but it was
too late. Adelaide lost too much blood and the baby died a day
later. Too small to survive. Your sister."

Stephen turned on him with blank eyes.

"Your sister and your mother in the space of a day, all
because you could not obey a simple command. Damn you!"

His face was grey. He pressed his lips together and turned
away.

"You killed your mother and your sister."

Edwin looked at Stephen in disbelief. The tragedy of the
story was immense, but his hatred made Edwin's blood run
cold.

"You blame me?"

He felt weak. "I was a child, for goodness' sake. How could
I have known the consequences?"

He sank onto the bed. Stephen's eyes filled with loathing
and Edwin stood again, smoothing down the cold sheets.

"Of course you couldn't know the consequences," Stephen
muttered. "But you were the instrument of the loss of my
daughter. All my dreams for the future died on that day. A
month after we buried Adelaide, your father died. His
drinking became excessive. Your nursemaid found him at the
bottom of the stairs one morning, his neck broken."

Edwin felt the colour drain from his face. His throat
tightened, sorrow piling upon unbearable sorrow.

"I didn't know that."

"You were a child; we made sure to keep it from you. From everyone, in fact. The nursemaid was found a position in Essex and Annie replaced her. She knew nothing of the matter. I could not let the world know that my daughter's widower was a drunkard who killed himself."

Edwin swung around. The callousness with which his grandfather spoke brought flames to his cheeks and hot tears to his eyes.

"You had a grandchild. An orphan. You could've had a future with me if you had not closed your heart to me, but you didn't want that, did you?"

"When should I have told you? When I sent you to live with your aunt? When you returned, resentful at being called back? Before you left for war? There was never a right time, so all times became wrong."

Stephen hung his head and bowed his shoulders. They began to shake and to Edwin's horror he realised his grandfather was weeping. He had seen men break down and sob in the trenches, had done it himself even, but never his grandfather, and this sight was unbearable to him. The grief and resentment Stephen had carried must have been immense.

"It's not too late. How can I help you?"

He rested a hand on Stephen's shoulder but Stephen jerked him off roughly. He raised his head.

"You can't. You know now. Use what you will from this room. I pass that on to you, with the knowledge of your part in it."

Edwin sagged onto the bed, not caring that the sheets became rumpled, and dropped his head into his hands. He barely noticed Stephen leave the toom, and, to his grandfather's credit, he had not insisted Edwin leave too. He felt sick. Numb. Unable to absorb everything he had learned. The mystery of his parents' deaths was nothing like his childhood speculations. The circumstances were mundane and tragic, but though he tried, he could not see Stephen's view as anything other than cruel and crazed.

The texture of the light had changed, thin evening sunlight giving way to moonlight. The pale globe of the full moon was framed by the window. Drusilla would be waiting for him and Edwin's heart tightened. She'd played an unknowing part in the tragedy of his mother's death. He needed to be with her, needed to pour out his grief and take comfort in her arms.

He made his way out of the bedroom, but not before dragging the sash up and purposefully leaving the door open to allow fresh air in. The musty scent sickened him and he wanted rid of it. Everything he had prepared was waiting for them; he only needed to lead her to the summer house. He stopped in the dining room and poured himself a glass of whiskey, drinking it in one go.

It was drizzling as he walked across the meadow to the tree, his belly full of flutters that the glass of whiskey he'd drunk as Dutch courage did nothing to calm.

"Drusilla! I need you," he called, hearing the edge of tears in his voice.

Drusilla was waiting at the edge of the grove, dressed in a floor-length gown made from some sort of diaphanous cloth that moved in the soft breeze. It had cap sleeves with a high waist and low neckline that reminded Edwin of a painting from the Regency period. Around her shoulders she wore an equally delicate shawl. Her hair was loose and tumbled in soft waves to her waist.

She was beautiful.

He stopped at arm's length from her.

"I know what happened," he said. His voice cracked and tears filled his eyes.

She stepped into his arms, pulling his head onto her shoulder.

"Oh my Sapling. Tell me your tale."

He tightened his arms around her. Eyes closed, he poured out his story, leaving out no part. He jerked as he made a connection with something she'd once said. He stared around at the tree and blanched.

"The woman you told me about once – the woman who fell and died and caused you to become. Was that my mother? Are you my sister? Are you my mother?"

His skin prickled and a cold sweat broke out over his back. It was unbearable to think of that connection between them.

"Oh Lord above when I think what I had planned! What we almost did together."

"Edwin, Edwin, no. I'm not either of them." She caught his face between her hands, forcing him to look at her. Soft fingers brushed his cheeks and temple. "That's the echo. The memory gets jumbled, but no. I saw that happen but you were there. I was already there long before. My tree was already older than your mother lived to be."

She stepped back and looked up at him with wide, sad eyes.

"Do you hate me for my part?" she asked.

"No." He shook his head gently. Speaking had felt

313

cleansing. A confession to which her presence gave absolution. His heart would remain heavy but there was space in it for other emotions.

"What happened was an accident. I've seen what blame and resentment has done to my grandfather."

He extended a hand to her, remembering the original purpose of their meeting this night of the full moon.

"Will you come with me, my nymph?"

She took his hand and he clasped it tightly, slightly afraid that she would fade into mist or simply run from him.

"I have something to show you," he said.

"What is it?"

"You'll see."

He had thought about blindfolding her to make the surprise even greater but had dismissed the idea, knowing how much he would hate that himself, even with somebody he trusted. He led her by the hand down through the meadow towards the summer house. His belly flopped with every step he took as excitement grew. It was anticipation at seeing Drusilla's reaction but also at the prospect of what was finally going to happen. He could feel himself becoming aroused and had to take a couple of deep breaths in the hope of slowing the beating of his heart.

"The summer house?" Drusilla asked.

He nodded. "Close your eyes."

She looked uncertain but did as he asked. He opened the door then stepped behind her and put a hand over her eyes.

She stiffened then giggled.

"Just making sure you're not peeking," he whispered. Standing so close to her was electrifying. He felt ready to burst into flames. He put his free hand around her waist and guided her inside the summer house. He gave everything a quick once over and then took his hand away from her eyes.

"Welcome to your temple, my goddess."

He took a step back and watched as she opened her eyes. She gave a small breathy gasp of surprise, turning slowly around in a circle. Edwin's heart swelled. He'd worked hard on this, arranging the cushions and pillows that Eleni had gathered at his behest, and had draped the walls with all manner of silks (mainly samples of designs waiting to be turned into swatches for the books) to create Aladdin's cave of wonders for her.

In the centre was a rug covered with a sheet and his own counterpane and eiderdown – a makeshift bed. He'd agonised over whether it was too presumptuous but he saw the moment her eyes fell on it because her lashes fluttered and the corners of her mouth curved into a smile.

"This is your sanctuary. A grove for you of my making."

She reached out and stroked the nearest silk, a rich wine-coloured brocade, then looked up at him. With a flash of anxiety Edwin saw her eyes were large and solemn.

"What's wrong?" he asked.

"Edwin, are you leaving me?"

"No! No, not at all! Far from it."

He took her in his arms and held her close. "We didn't have much success when you took me into your sanctuary before so please let me try again," he said. "This is for us. Something between your world and my world for us both to share. I hadn't planned for the evening to start the way it did but it feels right that a night that started with grief and revelations should end in love. Come and sit with me."

He led her to the cushions and sat down, then took a cloth off a tray, revealing a dish of sugared almonds, a bottle of Champagne, and a plate of strawberries. Her eyes lit up. He took a sugared almond and held it out to her. She took it into her mouth, gently tugging at his fingers with her lips.

"A goddess needs somewhere to be worshipped," he murmured, reaching for her hand and drawing her to the eiderdown.

He knelt and tugged gently on her hands until she did the same and they faced each other. Edwin swallowed, his heart hammering in his chest violently enough to burst through his ribcage and soar free. He slipped his hands beneath the scarf she wore and eased it from her shoulders, letting it slide to the floor. She unbuttoned his collar and brushed his neck with her fingernails. His cheeks flushed; his blood raced faster.

"I've never done this before," he admitted. "Will you show me how to begin?"

She leaned forward and kissed him, leaving a taste of sugar.

"Gladly."

Chapter Twenty-Two

Afterwards, they lay wrapped around each other. Edwin had never felt an exhaustion like it, not even in the wearying hours of marching and keeping watch in the trenches. The actual deed had been quick – was it too quick? He'd have to ask Drusilla that if he could pluck up the courage – but the kisses and embraces, touches and murmured words that had led up to it were alive in his memory as clearly as if he had a photographic plate to look at.

"Do you have to go?" Drusilla murmured.

Her eyes were heavy-lidded and she looked as spent as Edwin felt. He hoped he had satisfied her. He shuffled onto his side and wrapped his arms around her. Her body fitted into the shape of his perfectly. She was warm and smelled of fresh grass and sweetness. Returning to the house and Stephen's company held no appeal. He'd much rather stay in the warmth and love of Drusilla's company.

"Not just yet," he replied. He blew upwards to clear the hair that had fallen across his forehead, held in place by the perspiration on his brow. "I don't think I can move anyway. I think this must be what fruit feels like when it ripens. Too heavy but joyous with it."

"You've turned into a poet." Drusilla's gentle laughter echoed in Edwin's ears as he closed his eyes and promptly fell asleep.

When he woke up it was morning and the mauve light of daybreak was growing more golden as the sun rose higher. Edwin jerked upright. He had only intended to rest for a few minutes but he'd slept the night with Drusilla in his arms. He was lying in a tangle of the silks and Drusilla was lying on her back, her arms extended above her head, fingers spread wide. He smiled, seeing the limbs forming the shape of tree branches.

His goddess.

He kissed her lips and she stirred, smiling up at him as she opened her eyes.

"Good morning, Sapling. I'm glad you're still here."

"Of course I am! Aside from the fact that I just woke up, it would be the height of rudeness to leave without saying goodbye."

"Not everyone would agree. Even with a true woman, many men would leave once they'd had their pleasure." She laughed in a voice like the sound of autumn leaves rustling then stretched her arms up elegantly and ran her fingernail down his belly, causing him to yelp. "You did have pleasure, didn't you?"

"Oh yes." Edwin exhaled loudly, feeling the rushing of excitement once again. He settled back down beside Drusilla, rolling onto his belly and burying his hands in the thick tresses of her hair that spread out on the pillow.

"I am your willing acolyte and it would be my greatest joy to worship you in every way you need for the rest of my life. I adore you."

"Do you?" she asked. Her eyes grew momentarily serious.

"I do."

"Even though I'm not a true woman?"

"You felt convincingly womanly last night. I don't care what you are. I care how you make me feel."

He began twiddling her hair, looping it over and around his fingers. She stroked his cheek.

"Whatever it takes, I will keep you safe and happy."

Drusilla slipped her hands around his back and tugged at him. "You can make me happy now, my Sapling. There are lots of things I want to teach you."

"I'm ready to learn," he whispered, dropping his lips onto hers. He slid himself on top of her, feeling the swelling of desire. He stroked his hand lightly over the mound of her belly and round to her hip. As he did so, his fingertips felt a change in her flesh that he hadn't spotted the previous night. He shuffled over and peered down, running his fingers over the skin of her waist. A long scar ran diagonally from a spot just below her ribs and ended at her hip bone.

"What's that?"

She moved his hand away and covered the silver line with her own.

"It's nothing."

"Yes it is." He leaned up on his elbow and stared at her

anxiously. "I don't remember that from before. What happened?"

She dropped her eyes.

"The Old One. He came to me when he … when he told me you had gone to Yorkshire. He struck my tree. It left its mark on us both."

"Sykes?"

Edwin drew in a sharp breath then swore. Rage heated his blood, sending anger coursing through his limbs. He clenched his fists, swinging to his feet and forgetting he was naked, as his hatred of the old gardener lit a fire inside him.

"I'll beat him from here to Yorkshire for it!"

Drusilla stood and put her hand to his arms, smoothing her palms over the tensed muscles.

"Don't. He didn't know it would happen and we've made our peace since. I want nothing to rile him again."

He lowered his hands, though the anger didn't immediately ebb. The idea of Drusilla being harmed was appalling, even if it had been unintentional.

"If the tree is harmed it harms you too? I came to steal your leaf. You broke one off for me. Did that hurt?"

"No more than clipping your fingernails hurts you," she assured him.

"Why does Sykes hate you so much?"

She smoothed her hair down. "He says I destroyed his grandmother's happiness. His grandfather was my acolyte until he grew the hedgerow that encased me to stop himself being tempted any longer."

"Did you tempt him?" Jealousy flared inside Edwin. He'd known about them already but now they'd made love, he couldn't bear the thought of another man with her. Not before, certainly not afterwards. He had no idea how long dryads lived but while he lived, he wanted to be with her and only her. They belonged together.

Drusilla gave him a crooked smile. "I didn't need to. I've never turned away an admirer. Why would I?"

He had a flash of memory, the look in the whore's eye as she'd been preparing to let him bed her. Resignation and indifference. Drusilla spoke in a matter-of-fact way about her previous lovers. "Did you care for any of them?"

"I cared for all of them. Without the love they felt for me I'd be nothing."

"And me?" he asked. His heart pounded, fearful that the night before had meant less to her than to him.

"I care for you, Edwin. I care a great deal."

She reached her hand over and stroked Edwin on the side of his neck, causing the hairs at the nape to prickle.

"Will you make love to me again, my gentle Sapling?"

He shivered at her touch and almost resolved to stay with her for the day but the sun had fully risen and he was growing conscious of voices coming over the wall from the factory courtyard. He'd be missed before long. Already his grandfather would be eating breakfast and noting his lateness with annoyance.

"I can't. I have to go," he said with regret. "But I will come back and see you later."

He dressed, throwing his clothes on quickly. Drusilla was still naked and the gown that Edwin had removed from her lay discarded on the rug. It was interesting that it did not simply cease to exist when she took it off.

He kissed her once again before hastily making his way across the lawn. He stopped at the steps up and turned back. Drusilla was standing in the doorway, her naked body partially hidden by a swathe of silk which she wore like a toga. The sight made Edwin smile. He crept stealthily along the terrace and round into the house. Little bursts of desire kept firing within him, dizzying and exhilarating him. A cold wash would put him in the right frame of mind for the day and give him an outside chance at being able to concentrate.

He glanced longingly at his bed with the untouched covers. Making love to Drusilla outside was intoxicating but he missed the comfort of a proper bed. Maybe he would try to slip her inside after all. He couldn't spend the rest of his life sleeping on the floor of the summer house.

He washed, changed his clothes, and went out of his room. He almost collided with the maid who was about to open the door to begin cleaning. They exchanged laughing exclamations of surprise and apologies. The maid bobbed a curtsey.

"Please, Mr Hope, I have a message from Mr Brice. He says not to worry about going into the factory this morning, but to please be at the lunch table at twelve."

"Thank you, Libby. No need to make my bed, by the by. I had a go myself this morning."

Libby bobbed another curtsey and went into the room. Edwin went downstairs to the kitchen to ask for toast. He couldn't deny the relief the message had brought him. He'd have to speak to Stephen about the previous night's revelations and confrontation, but Edwin was in no hurry. With the advantage of a free morning, he walked into the town centre to the library and occupied his time in reading the local newspaper.

He returned to the house precisely as the clock in the hallway was striking twelve and went straight to lunch, only to be greeted by a sight for which he had not prepared. As well as his grandfather and Eleni, his aunt and uncle were sitting at the dining table which was strewn with coffee cups and used plates. Edwin stopped in the doorway and smiled, genuinely pleased to see them.

"Aunt Madeline. Panos. How lovely to see you. I didn't know you were returning yet. Good morning, Eleni. I'm sorry I'm late down. Must have overslept."

"Late night?" Eleni asked, giving him an innocent-looking smile. She'd known his plans after all.

He returned her smile with a grin and moved towards the sideboard to help himself to a plate of ham and boiled potatoes from the cold spread. His appetite had come on him suddenly.

"We will get down to business straight away, Edwin," said Stephen, giving him a disapproving look. "Take a seat."

"Business?" Edwin put his plate down in his setting, unease growing in his stomach. What further revelations was he about to learn? It struck him that Aunt Madeline might not have known the circumstances of her brother's death. "Is something wrong?"

"Not at all," Panos said. He reached across the table and took hold of his daughter's hand. "Eleni, I know you are very fond of Edwin. So you will be delighted to know that Mr Brice has given his permission for Edwin to court you formally. We think a spring wedding will be best, unless you'd prefer autumn?"

"What!" Edwin exclaimed.

Eleni burst out laughing.

"But I never asked for that!"

"Aunt Madeline, did you know about this?" Edwin asked. His throat felt tight, blocked by astonishment.

"I did indeed," Aunt Madeline said. "Edwin, Eleni, I am so pleased for you both. I've always secretly nursed hopes for you. When you asked to stay here for a bit longer, we knew some deeper feeling was growing between you."

She rose from her seat and embraced her stepdaughter. Eleni looked at Edwin over her shoulder and pulled a face. Edwin turned to Stephen. He couldn't believe this was actually happening. After he had spent the night with Drusilla and was planning a lifetime with her, the timing seemed like a cruel joke. The timing. Would Stephen have done this if Edwin had not pushed him for answers the previous day?

"What on earth do you think you're doing?" he asked in an undertone that he hoped the others would not be able to hear. "Eleni and I don't want to marry each other. You know that, don't you?"

Stephen's eyes narrowed, glinting unpleasantly. "Panos, Madeline, if you have no objections, I will leave you to congratulate your daughter for a moment while I have a quiet word with my grandson. Shall we speak in the office, Edwin?"

He eased his way out of his chair and walked out of the room. Edwin gave Eleni a quick glance. She furrowed her brow slightly then turned back to her father who was speaking in rapid Greek. Edwin joined Stephen.

"What the hell do you think you're playing at, Grandfather?"

Stephen glared. "Do not speak to me in that impudent tone! I am playing at finding you a wife who finds you tolerable and who will bring us the money we need to get the factory back on its feet."

Edwin frowned. Despite his anger, Stephen's words caught his attention. "I didn't realise it was off its feet."

"You know we've been struggling but it's worse than I have told you." Stephen moved his desk and began to pull the chair out. Edwin instinctively moved to help the old man sit comfortably. Stephen grunted acknowledgement.

"The war was hard on us. We've lost men, and business and supply was disrupted for more reasons than I care to bore you with and we are in very grave danger of losing what little profit we have been scraping together while being able to meet our responsibilities." Stephen pulled a ledger towards him and put on his spectacles. He peered at Edwin over the top.

"I know we've not been doing as well as before the war, but why now?" Edwin asked. He sucked his teeth. "I can't help feeling this is not coincidental with yesterday's revelations."

"Then you are a completely self-centred imbecile. It has come about because after last night's meeting with the town aldermen I have two options that I am prepared to consider. The first is that you marry somebody with a decent dowry and a family that is interested enough to potentially invest further."

"And what if I have met someone else? What if I am in love?" Edwin asked.

"Are you? Is the girl rich?"

Edwin shook his head.

"Then that is irrelevant. Your uncle is wealthy and it

325

appears his Greek investments did well during the war. The dowry Eleni will bring could be invested."

"I'm sure Eleni would have something to say about that," Edwin said firmly.

"It is more palatable than the second choice, which is that I sell off the remaining land we have. There are developers who would pay me well for those fields. The town is growing and the working classes are demanding better housing now that this new Ministry of Health appears to be permanent and the Ministry of Reconstruction subsidies are starting to be granted. I don't like it but with clever design I dare say there could be five streets of houses there. It would link the village seamlessly with the town. It would mean Greete Mill House would become surrounded by people of the lower orders but we can stipulate the boundary walls are built high so we don't have to encounter them too frequently. Greete Road. Brice Street. They have a nice sound to them, don't you think?"

"But the fields and the stream. The old tree," Edwin said.

Stephen gave Edwin a look of distaste. "God above knows I'm tempted enough as it is for that reason alone. That damned tree has fixated you since you were born. I should have listened to Sykes and had it cut down after your mother died. He said it would cause more trouble."

"Sykes should keep his opinions to himself," Edwin snarled. Already incensed by Drusilla's revelation of the harm the old gardener had done to the tree, his throat filled with bile. All the time his grandfather had been speaking, Edwin had been listening quietly. He'd been appalled at the revelation about the factory's finances, incensed by the fact his grandfather had kept it secret, horrified at the way he was to be used as a tool for bartering, but now his senses grew alert.

"There is a buyer interested in the land, and selling it would clear our debts. If I don't decide soon he will find another seller."

His lip twisted and Edwin felt the full force of his dislike. It was bewildering that a grandfather could hate his only flesh and blood so deeply.

"I will leave the decision to you – the first of your life as a future owner of this factory and land."

Edwin felt sick, but nevertheless he lifted his head. The weight of responsibility settled on his shoulders like chains around a prisoner. "I shall consider everything you've told me and make my decision before too long."

The choice he faced was impossible. Stephen's plans posed a real threat to Drusilla's existence and he had no doubt Stephen would go ahead with them. Houses needed to be built – that was clear enough from the tangle of slum streets in the town that were over-crammed with families – but not at her expense.

The memory of the sight and feel of her scar made him flinch as if he'd been struck. An attack on the tree meant physical harm to her. Cutting it down would kill her. He couldn't let that happen, even if it meant marriage and renouncing her forever.

Chapter Twenty-Three

Eleni was sitting on the terrace, accompanied by Aunt Madeline. Despite lunch barely being over they had a plate of sandwiches. Then again, Edwin hadn't eaten and perhaps the women hadn't either.

Eleni greeted him with a warm smile. Edwin had no idea how her discussion with her father had gone, but she seemed outwardly calm and happy. Perhaps inside she was as shocked as Edwin.

Feeling numb, Edwin kissed his aunt's cheek and sat down. He half listened to a detailed description of her tour around the grand houses of Cheshire and Shropshire. Apparently, without exception they were struggling to replace staff who had been lost during the war. The world was changing and, according to Aunt Madeline, it was not for the better.

"The lower orders are demanding a quality of life above their station," she remarked, biting into a triangle of meat paste sandwich.

"I fought with plenty of excellent men from working class

backgrounds," Edwin argued. "Many of them were braver and more able soldiers than I was. Don't you think they deserve a decent life? Egg and cress sandwiches, not bread and scrape, for example."

Aunt Madeline wrinkled her brow. "Of course everyone deserves sandwiches! What are you talking about? Why can't they have sandwiches and still be content in service? You'll see that when you have charge of your own household, and a wife nagging you for an extra scullery maid because the silver is never clean." She gave Eleni a pointed look then turned. "Mr Sykes!"

The old gardener was standing nearby, deadheading flowers. He stood up straight and tipped his hat. "Mr Sykes, you are content in your role, aren't you?"

"Aye, Mrs Hatzis, I am."

"Now, may I borrow your excellent horticultural brain? I'm having a problem with my roses and they'd be perfect for a wedding bouquet. Eleni, you'd like roses, wouldn't you?"

She left with a smile at Edwin and Eleni and joined Sykes, who gave Eleni and Edwin an appraising look that Edwin didn't much care for.

"At this rate Aunt Madeline will have a date announced in *The Times* before the day is out! Did you know they were coming up with this plan?" Edwin asked with a sigh.

"No. I'll try not to be offended that you sound so unenthusiastic, however. I know you're in love with Drusilla. If it's any consolation, I have no interest in marrying you either." She toyed with a teaspoon then flicked it onto the table. "We'll just tell them all there's nothing doing. I imagine my father will be disappointed but not for too long. Assuming

Stepmother hasn't picked out a dress and flowers by dinnertime."

She gave him a grin and Edwin was struck by how much he liked her. He couldn't smile back though, not with a weight in his stomach so heavy.

"What?" Eleni asked. "Did your grandfather give you a beastly time over it? His face was a complete gargoyle when he led you out."

Edwin dropped his head onto his hands. "Yes. But not just about marriage. Oh hell, Eleni, there's so much I haven't told you. Grandfather caught me going into Mother's room. He told me what happened to my mother and father. It's worse than I could have ever imagined. I caused her death, and, by extension, led to my father's."

Eleni listened in silence as he poured out his tale. His voice cracked as he spoke and by the time he had finished his eyes were glossy with tears.

"That's so sad, but how can he have treated you like that?" Eleni asked indignantly. "Do you really blame yourself?"

Edwin sat back. "Not when I think sensibly. How could a child have anticipated a tragedy like that? *He* does though."

"Forcing you into marriage almost out of spite is ridiculous, even if he does need the money, though I'd gladly spend any dowry I have in your factory so Drusilla's tree is safe."

Edwin glanced around. Sykes had finished listening to Aunt Madeline and was once again tending to the flowerbeds surrounding the lawn. He may have heard Edwin's words. He'd known how Adelaide had died, even if the truth of Archibald's death had been covered over. Rage bubbled inside Edwin at that thought, combined with knowing the harm that the old man had inflicted on Drusilla. Before he could stand up and inevitably make the day even worse, Eleni poured him a cup of tea. It was lukewarm but welcome. He sipped it but stopped when he saw Eleni gazing at him, a thoughtful look on her face.

"Maybe we should do it," Eleni said.

"What? Get married?" Edwin almost dropped his teacup.

"Yes. We could have a civilised agreement."

Sykes ambled closer with his trug and trowel. Edwin put a hand on Eleni's to make her pause. Her eyes flickered in understanding. When the old man left, she continued.

"I don't want a husband. I mean, I have no interest in a husband at all. We could marry in name only. It's been done before. My friend, Agnes, married a man twelve years her senior, who... Well, that's not important. The point is, you could keep seeing Drusilla and I can indulge my own tastes as I wish. It's quite perfect really."

"Your tastes?"

Eleni gave him a sweet smile. "You're so innocent, aren't you. I can see why Drusilla adores you. Did you have an exquisite night together? What I mean is, I don't like men the way women are supposed to and I like women the way we aren't."

She sat back and chewed the peel on her slice of lemon while Edwin untangled her words.

"Oh," he said thoughtfully. "I see."

Eleni lit a cigarette, took a quick drag, and waved it around.

"I can be a good wife and be completely discreet if I have any love affairs myself. Probably more so than if I wanted male lovers because most people can't even imagine such behaviour.

And I really wouldn't mind if you made love to Drusilla as often as you like."

Edwin finished his cup of tea. The past two days had been rather too much for him to take in. There was almost sense in Eleni's suggestion, even if the idea was unconventional.

"What of Drusilla? She might have her own opinions about this," he said.

Eleni laughed. "She had another woman's husband as her lover. Sykes's grandfather, remember?" Eleni said, raising her brows. "If she knew I was happy with the situation, why would she care?"

"I don't know. I don't feel like I know anything anymore." He stood. "I'm going for a walk."

"Are you going see Drusilla? Shall I come?" Eleni asked.

He looked up the hill, catching a fleeting glimpse of Drusilla dressed in a green dress beneath the tree. The world ground to a halt as feelings of love, lust, and despair assailed him. The memory of what they had done was intensely sharp, like a bee sting but altogether more pleasant. Thinking of everything that had happened since diminished it and that was unbearable.

"No. Thank you. I don't want to see Drusilla until my head is clearer." He raked his hands through his hair and wiped them over his face. The mustiness from the room clung to him and he felt grimy. "I don't know what I'll say to her yet. I need time to think. I'm going to walk into town and pay a visit to Robert. I haven't seen him for days."

He gave Drusilla one last look and turned away.

. . .

Robert was sitting at his desk when Edwin entered the solicitor's office. Edwin wasn't sure exactly what position he held, but he had a nameplate proudly displayed at the edge, right where a client would see it.

"Marvellous, you've come to save me from drudgery. Shall I ring for coffee or will we go to the pub and have an early pint?"

"A pint, I think," Edwin answered.

Robert grinned. "The correct answer, Hope. You can tell me your troubles as we drink. I can tell you've got some because your face is as gloomy as a bishop at an empty table."

They strolled to the Old Coach Inn that stood in the town square. As its name suggested, it had once been the destination for travellers in the days of horse-drawn transport. Once they were settled with pints of stout, Edwin began.

"Apparently, the factory is doing worse than I knew and last night's meeting with the Municipal Borough Council has galvanised Grandfather. He has given me two choices: marry Eleni Hatzis and use her dowry to prop up the business, or he'll sell the land for housing."

"He'd better do it quickly," Robert said, wiping the froth from his moustache. "It isn't long until your birthday. You are twenty-four this year, aren't you?"

"Yes. In August," Edwin said. "But why is that significant?"

Robert looked shifty. "I shouldn't have said anything. Really. Father will grill me if he finds out."

"Finds out what?" Edwin leaned forward eagerly. His scalp prickled with the sense that something significant was about to happen. "Come on, tell me. You can't half say something then leave it. And you know I can keep a secret. I've kept plenty, haven't I, Bobby."

Using the nickname that Robert's lover Didier had used was a low blow and Edwin regretted it almost as soon as it had left his lips.

The skin around Robert's eyes tightened.

"Blackmail, is it?"

Edwin shook his head. "I'm just reminding you that I know how to keep my mouth shut. Calling in a favour, perhaps. Please, if you know something that could get me out of this scrape, tell me."

Robert let out a long sigh and drew a squiggle in the moisture that had pooled on the tabletop.

"In the old days, back before the war, Father used me as a clerk – copying out documents, filing them and so on. Tedious work that really was beneath me. Naturally, I had to read them as well as copy them."

"Do you know what's in my grandfather's will?" Edwin asked in excitement.

Robert coughed and lowered his voice.

"Goodness, no! That's sealed safely away until it needs to be opened. Not *his* will. My father has handled your family's affairs ever since he joined the firm as a junior solicitor. His grandfather had done it until then, but that's by the by. The point is, I spent a very dull week sorting through old documents. I don't mean your grandfather's affairs. That's all I can say."

He finished his pint and stood. "It's good to see you again, Edwin. I'm sorry I can't be of any more help."

"You've been a great help," Edwin assured him. "I'm not sure exactly how, but I intend to find out."

He sat alone and worked his way through another pint, wondering what he might discover and how it could be of use.

Dinner was an awkward affair and Edwin was glad when it was over. He thought about creeping away to see Drusilla, but with Aunt Madeline and Panos there it would be impossible. At least Eleni appeared in high spirits, keeping conversation going, and when it lulled, suggesting a dance. Edwin wound the gramophone then took her in his arms for a foxtrot around the room.

"Did you clear your head?" Eleni asked.

"I don't think so," Edwin murmured. "I have a few answers I need from Grandfather. I don't know how it will help me, but Robert seemed to think there was something significant about my twenty-fourth birthday. I'll speak to him tonight."

Eleni put her arms around his neck and kissed his cheek.

"I'm sure you will think of something."

Over her shoulder, Edwin could see the sycamore through the open curtains. He turned away, not wanting to dwell on his fears. Thank goodness Drusilla had no idea of the turmoil that was taking place inside him.

Aunt Madeline kept early hours and summoned Panos to turn in with her. Edwin winked at Eleni when they left and she made her excuses, leaving him alone with Stephen. He poured out two glasses of whiskey and added soda to his. He took them over to Stephen who was playing a game of clock patience. He held out the glass and when Stephen reached for it, he put his down beside it. He cleared his throat.

"Tell me what happens when I'm twenty-four."

Stephen reached for his cane.

"I should be going to bed. I am speaking with my doctor in the morning. I expect it will be tedious and I should like to be rested."

Edwin moved quickly, taking hold of the cane and moving it out of Stephen's reach.

"You can spare me five minutes, I'm sure. Otherwise I might be forced to ask questions in town to see who can help me discover the answers I crave. Or who might reminisce with me about my parents and their untimely ends."

There was a moment where he saw anger in his grandfather's eyes. The lids twitched and Stephen sat back.

"Well played, Grandson," he said. "I assume someone has been loose-lipped." There was a definite hint of grudging admiration in his voice. "When you are twenty-four your mother's fortune, which she inherited from my late wife, passes to you entirely. That includes the shares in the factory my dear Cornelia inherited from her father. She was determined to ensure her only daughter had the autonomy that she had enjoyed."

"Why twenty-four?" Edwin asked.

"I don't know. That was your mother. She was as headstrong as *her* mother. I've spent years contesting it but to no avail. It was Adelaide's inheritance; hers to do with as she wished." Stephen gave a twisted smile. "Damned Married Women's Property Act."

Edwin looked out of the window. The factory and the

house would always have passed to him on his grandfather's death, but he would receive shares and financial independence beforehand.

"How many shares?"

"Fifty-one percent," Stephen muttered, as if the sound of the words burned his tongue.

Edwin's heart soared. It was in his power to permanently keep the fields as they were.

"Of course, until then I make the decisions," Stephen said. "And you have a short time to reach yours."

Stephen reached for the cane and Edwin passed it to him. He sat alone in the sitting room.

Among the revelations of the day, that one shone like a beacon to a lost man. If only he knew how to use the information to his advantage. All he needed was some way of delaying the engagement until after his birthday. First thing in the morning he would visit the factory and see what else he could discover.

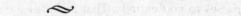

Drusilla lay on the highest branches. Too thin to hold her weight, they nevertheless supported her, so light did she feel.

The elation of being worshipped so thoroughly…

Her limbs flexed, remembering the touch of Edwin's hands and lips; his strength and gentleness; his eagerness and uncertainty. It had been an intoxicating potion.

She felt loved.

She loved Edwin. Her Sapling.

It made the nerves in her fingertips shudder, sent waves of

pleasure through her core, and warmed her from the inside. The tree swayed gently, responding in its own way, and she stared upwards, dreamily. The sky was cloudy tonight, small puffs tinged with pink and grey closing in. The stars would be visible for an hour or two more. Perhaps he would come before then and they could lie together in the branches.

She laughed aloud, anticipating glorious years of life with her Sapling ahead of her.

"Are you there?"

The Old One. Surprise rippled through her, followed by a note of caution. It was months since she'd spoken with him and now he came at night. She dropped to the ground and walked out from under the branches.

"What's wrong?" she asked.

"Nothing's wrong. Far from it. I've come to tell you the happy news," Sykes said. His eyes gleamed and he smiled widely.

"About the marriage between Edwin and Miss Hatzis."

A hard beat resounded through her. The leaves stirred as the tree echoed her shock.

"Edwin and Eleni? That's not possible."

He lifted his chin. "I heard them talking about it this afternoon. Mr and Mrs Hatzis are at the house now. Mrs Hatzis asked me about roses for bouquets. Look, if you don't believe me."

She walked towards the house. The lights were brightly lit in the living room, clearly illuminating the dancing figures of Edwin and Eleni. As she watched, Eleni reached up and kissed Edwin's cheek. He stared past her at the window. Drusilla stepped towards him, never losing sight of him, hoping their eyes could meet. She yearned for a silent connection. She thought he must have seen her because his frame stiffened. Then he turned away, spinning Eleni with him back into the dance.

Her heart plummeted, almost dragging her to the ground. She remained standing through strength of will alone.

"You must have expected something like this," Sykes said in her ear.

She looked back at him. Nodded. Expectation didn't make reality any less painful to bear.

"Why are you telling me this?" she whispered.

"Thought you should know." Sykes dipped his head. "I went into the summer house earlier. Saw something that could only have meant one thing. Was that him and you, or him and her?"

"Me."

Her voice was small. Edwin had spent the night in her arms, left her this morning, and within half a day had offered himself to Eleni. Drusilla wrinkled her lip and dug her toes into the earth. All his talk of devotion had been just that.

Talk.

Sweet lies to seduce her.

It hadn't felt like it at the time, and she'd been so often told words of love but this had sounded different. The words had tasted genuine on his lips.

"This makes you happy, I suppose," she said.

He shook his head. His expression had dropped from triumph to pity. "I'm sorry, miss. Genuinely. Once I'd have laughed in your face; now I pity you."

Drusilla stared back towards the house.

If she walked down there now, he'd come to her. She felt it inside her as surely as she felt the roots beneath the earth. As she watched, Edwin appeared again in the window. He spoke to Eleni, their heads close together, then he went to kiss the older woman on her cheek and began to dance with her.

Family. Belonging together.

All the books she might read, all the drawings and hair ribbons, the teacups and sweets ... she wasn't human and never would be.

His world was different.

The Old One touched her shoulder. She jerked at his touch but saw solace in his face.

"Don't be downhearted. You've had lovers before and you'll have them again. That's what you do, after all, isn't it? Find one acolyte then move on when you're bored."

"Or they move on," Drusilla agreed. "Perhaps not any longer."

She turned and walked away back under the branches. The grove was far bigger now than it had ever been. There was a subtle difference in the ground where her domain ended that only she could tell; an invisible texture to the grass and earth. Traces of it stretched down as far as the summer house and to the edge of the lawn. Almost the whole meadow was under her protection now, a legacy of the nourishment she had given the ground during the years of war, and the strengthening influence of Edwin. She had more freedom that she'd ever had, but what use was that freedom now she had no one to share it with. If he stopped coming, how long would it take for her to diminish?

She rested her hand on the bark and closed her eyes,

remembering her creation through the eyes of the fragile young tree that had already been waiting for her. She only had vague memories of it but the weight of years felt heavy on her.

She turned to Sykes.

"Will you do something for me? A task?"

"Why should I?" Sykes folded his arms. "What will you give me in return? An exchange?"

Drusilla raised her eyes to meet his. "Because it will be to your advantage and it will be the only thing I ever ask of you."

He clicked his teeth. "Go on."

"I want you to build a fence around my tree." Drusilla swallowed and squeezed her hands into fists to stop them shaking. "I want you to use iron."

"Why's that?"

"Because I'm not sure I am strong enough to resist Edwin's call. It's what I am; how I was created. I live for adoration. If I'm gone he will turn his heart to Eleni. Once he marries her, I know he will love her and intend to be faithful, but he and I are bonded in ways he won't understand and he'll come back to me if I beckon. And I'd do it if he so much as thinks of me."

The Old One's expression was unreadable. "You've changed since you tempted my grandfather. All my grandmother's pleas could do nothing to unfreeze your heart. What changed?"

Drusilla looked to the house.

"I learned to love," she whispered. "I genuinely love Edwin with whatever passes for my heart and soul."

"You don't think he loves you back?"

She closed her eyes. "I think he does, but I don't think that will make him happy, and I want his happiness."

"Will you be inside or outside the fence?"

A chill went through her.

"If I'm inside then without Edwin's adoration to sustain me, I'll grow dormant as I did before. At least until someone else comes to adore me. If I'm outside then without being able to access the tree I'll die."

She glanced towards the stump of the previous sycamore. The woman dying. Life from the unborn child passing from the mother to the sapling. The old spirit whose life was ending waiting to receive her. That guardian had faded when Drusilla's sapling had swelled with life. There was no sapling waiting to replace Drusilla, and no life to spark it.

"The tree will become just a tree." She pressed her lips together and closed her eyes. "I haven't decided which is more frightening."

Sykes's mouth twisted and he dropped his eyes.

"Stay within the binding. You never know what might happen in the future. That's the only condition I'll impose."

He held a hand out.

He was right. There might be another, far in the future, when Edwin had faded from her memory. She took his hand and held tight.

"I accept your terms."

He sucked his teeth, looking, if not happy then at least … satisfied. "Then I'll do it. First thing tomorrow, I'll begin."

Chapter Twenty-Four

"Good morning, William. Can you tell me the precise amount of debt the company is in?"

William Wills looked taken aback by Edwin's request. Or possibly his appearance in the office before nine.

"Please, I mean. If you are able," Edwin added, amending his tone and curbing his briskness. He'd spent a night thinking and planning, but without figures he wasn't sure his plan would work and he had woken early.

He looked at his watch then sat and fiddled with the pen on the desk, anxious to get the information he needed before Stephen arrived at noon. He looked up to see William standing pensively.

"I am not sure if Mr Brice will permit me to show you everything," William said.

"That's why I am here early. I know he has an appointment with his doctor this morning. Just a glance will do." The factory bell rang eight. He stood and walked to the window, beckoning for William to join him.

The workers who had been standing in groups in the walled yard began making their way to the large double door which opened as they approached.

"I want to do right by them," Edwin said. "I need to know how bad our debt is. I believe there must be savings we can make, or a way of increasing our profits without increasing our overheads. I would be more daring in our designs, for example."

"Your grandfather would take a lot of persuading," William said. "I agree though. We are not adventurous. When you eventually take control, I hope I will still be working here to assist you."

"As do I," Edwin said, smiling. "Without wishing my grandfather's demise, I am eager for that day."

William smiled. "I'll find you the ledger."

Edwin spent the morning reading back over accounts for a decade. The purposeful atmosphere was broken by the arrival of Eleni who barged breathlessly into the office.

"Edwin, you have to come now."

"I'm a little busy," Edwin said politely. "William has gone to a lot of trouble to help me."

Eleni smiled at William but it was brittle and her mouth wobbled slightly. "Pardon me, but I need him to come with me. Right now. Edwin, Sykes is doing something dreadful. Please come. I've tried to speak to him but he ignored me."

She twisted her hands together, looking on the verge of tears.

Edwin's pulse began to race. He fixed the lid on his pen. "I'll come. William, thank you for your help. I can catch up with my correspondence this evening."

He left with Eleni. There were tears smarting in her eyes by the time they reached the factory gates.

"Now, take a breath and tell me what's wrong," Edwin urged.

"I saw him a few moments ago. I haven't been outside all morning because it's been a little chilly but I wanted to pick some roses." She spoke at double her normal speed, waving her hands around for emphasis.

"Eleni, breathe for a minute and tell me, or show me," he said again, more sternly this time.

She flung her hand out. "Iron railings! Sykes is taking them to the sycamore. I fear he plans to do something dreadful to Drusilla."

"Iron?" Edwin's blood drained. He broke into a run. Sure enough, as they rounded the corner into the park, Edwin saw the old man walking upright and dragging a small cart behind him. His heart seized and he spat out an expletive. Together, he and Eleni raced through the fields. Sykes had reached the grove by the time they were halfway there. Edwin paused for breath and saw Sykes lifting a bundle of thin railings, perhaps six foot in length.

"Stop!" Edwin shouted. Distress ripped through him.

Sykes either ignored or did not hear Edwin, because he picked up a mallet and walked to beneath the branches. Edwin continued to run. If Sykes was going beneath the tree, he was not intending to surround the grove but the trunk itself. He would imprison Drusilla inside its confines.

Edwin didn't know what malice had spurred the old man to act and the reason could wait. All that mattered was preventing him. Even the first iron spike driven into the ground might be enough to finish Drusilla off. He ran on but caught his foot in a hole of some sort – rabbit or badger perhaps; it didn't really matter. He fell, sprawling out and sending pain through his hand when he landed on it. He righted himself and carried on.

"Sykes! Stop! What you are doing!" Edwin yelled. He had never felt rage like it. He reached the grove and staggered beneath the covering of the branches. "Stop, I tell you!"

Sykes turned. He had one railing from the bundle at his feet in his right hand, and a mallet in his left. There was a coiled roll of thick wire beside the pile on the ground. When he saw Edwin, he held both out in front of him like some ghastly representation of a gladiator. Ignoring the potential weapons, Edwin advanced on Sykes, fists raised.

"What in Hell's name do you think you're doing, you monster? Iron will trap her. Maybe even kill her."

"I'm only doing what she told me," Sykes said. He licked his lips and held his hands up in surrender.

Edwin looked back over his shoulder. Eleni was standing at the edge of the grove, just outside the reach of the branches.

"You?" Edwin asked. He swung around to face her, tasting bile in his throat that surged up at the betrayal.

"No. Me."

The quiet voice made him halt in his rage. He turned to see Drusilla standing beside the trunk of the tree. She looked up at Sykes. He nodded at her.

"I asked him to. *Told* him to."

Devastated, Edwin took a faltering step towards her.

"But why? You know what it will do to you. I don't understand."

Drusilla tilted her head on one side. "Come along, Edwin. You're not stupid."

"I think I know why," Eleni murmured. "It's to do with us, isn't it?"

She walked into the grove and stood beside Edwin. He tensed, starting to see the light and not wanting to give any indication that he felt more for Eleni than friendship.

Drusilla nodded.

"But Drusilla, you're making a mistake," Edwin said urgently.

"Am I?"

"Drusilla, you were going to kill yourself!"

She looked at him, eyes dull. "I couldn't bear the thought of life without you. You deserve to be happy and I'm standing in your way."

"But we don't love each other," Edwin said, looking at Eleni who nodded enthusiastically. "We talked about marrying, but that's not the reason."

Drusilla shrugged. "Does the rain care if a tree loves it? The effect is the same."

"I love *you*," Edwin said. "You know that. After the night before last, how could you doubt I want to be with anyone else?"

"You didn't come. You turned away."

Her voice was small. Waves of self-recrimination flooded Edwin. He reached for her hands but she drew back.

"I know. I had to. I've been tangled in ideas and decisions and I knew I wouldn't be able to think clearly if I saw you. The moment I get close to you, I become your devoted acolyte."

"I know. That's why I've made this choice. With me gone,

that won't be a consideration anymore. You will grow to love each other and you'll be happy. It's happened before, hasn't it, Mr Sykes? When your grandfather sealed me in."

"But that was with hawthorn not iron," Edwin gasped. "You were alive."

She raised her eyes to his. "Maybe I've lived long enough."

"No." His heart twisted. He flung himself towards her and held her tightly, the thought of what she was intending to do causing his lungs to fill with acid, dragging the breath from his chest.

"You are the only woman I want. The only woman I've ever wanted and I'm not going to let you do this."

He buried his head in her hair and inhaled the sweet summer scent. If green had an aroma, this would be it.

"I'm not going to marry Eleni. I don't care what that means for the land or the factory. Hang it all! We don't have to stay here. We could just leave."

Drusilla lifted her face to his. "How can I leave? I can't go further than the town. My tree is here."

"Then we'll uproot it and take it with us."

Drusilla gave a quiet laugh and kissed his cheek. "Oh my darling Sapling. How? It's a lovely idea, but it's a dream."

"Then I'll find a solution somehow. Give me a day. A week." He turned to Sykes, still holding Drusilla close, unable to trust that if he let her go, she would stay. "Mr Sykes, I'd like to think you are doing this because Drusilla asked you to and not because of a vendetta. If I ever find out otherwise, I will see to it you are gone within the day."

"He did," Drusilla said firmly. "I had to persuade him."

Edwin nodded. Drusilla's good nature allowed her to

believe that, but Sykes had clearly wasted no time before informing her of the marriage plans.

"You can go now. Take all those things with you and don't bring them back," he said.

Sykes gathered the railings and the wire. "It was a kind thing you were doing, miss," he murmured to Drusilla. "I've been wrong about you, I think. I hope you find a way through this."

Edwin waited until the old man had gathered everything. As soon as the iron spikes had left the grove, Drusilla's manner changed. The pinched look left her cheeks and her eyes looked brighter. It was chilling to see the difference in her.

He took her face between his hands, gently cradling it. "From the moment I first laid eyes on you, you fascinated me. I not only adore you, but I love you. More than that"—he put a hand to her cheek and tilted her head back a little so she was looking up into his eyes— "I am in love with you. I am not whole when you are not with me."

She turned her head away, pulling her cheek from the palm of his hand.

"You don't mean it. How can you when I'm not even human?"

Edwin felt an urgency rising in his belly; a shuddering in his breast that heralded a great misgiving. "I don't care what you are. You are what I need. The woman who makes me laugh. The woman who fascinates me and provokes me and opened my eyes to the beauty of the world. With you gone my life will be empty."

He turned his head to Eleni. "I'm sorry but you know what I'm saying."

"Oh yes," she replied. She pushed her hair behind her ear. "This situation is intolerable and fencing yourself in is not the answer. You two should be together. Edwin, we can't marry each other."

"No," Edwin agreed fervently. He frowned. "But your chance of making a marriage you could be happy in…"

"Oh, that was just idle daydreaming," Eleni said brightly. "I've half a mind to bury myself away on an island in the Aegean where I can have affairs and never return to England. Perhaps I'll find my own nymph."

Edwin grinned, barely able to summon the humour her generosity warranted. "I will find a solution. I swear it. I've spent this morning looking at the accounts. I know money isn't the only thing driving Grandfather."

He kissed Drusilla, knowing as soon as her lips touched his that spending his life without her was not optional.

"Give me a day. Promise me you won't do anything rash until I've tried something."

"Are you going to speak to your grandfather?" Eleni asked.

"I don't know what I'll say to him yet," Edwin admitted. "But something has been playing on my mind, trying to get my attention. I'm going to walk and clear my head. It was what I did yesterday and something almost came to me."

He touched Drusilla's cheek again, unwilling to leave her. As if understanding his reluctance, Eleni put her arm around Drusilla's shoulder.

"Why don't you invite Miss Moore to lunch. I'm sure Aunt Madeline would love to meet her," he suggested to Eleni.

"Wonderful idea," Eleni said brightly. "I have some new

fashion magazines I'd love to show you, and Stepmother always orders cream cakes for lunch."

Edwin watched the two women walk down the hill together, arm in arm. Drusilla would be safe with Eleni and no harm would come to her at Sykes's hand.

He walked out of the gate at the top of the field and along the road between the old village and the town, forcing himself to try and think of a solution to their problem. Without paying particular attention to where he was going, he found himself wandering back through the outskirts of the town in the direction that he had walked with Drusilla.

A late morning milk delivery was happening and women and children bearing jugs formed a line at the horse-drawn cart laden with churns. He spotted the girl who had scuffed her knees playing with the football. She was standing in the queue with a serious expression on her face, holding an earthenware jug. He waved at her and she wiggled her fingers back at him. The other children weren't there.

He bought a pie from a corner bakery and leaned against a wall, trying not to let the gravy dribble onto his jacket as he ate it. It was hot and peppery with chunks of steak and kidney. Delicious.

A few families sat on doorsteps catching a bit of the sunshine that made its way along the narrow roads; mothers holding babies talked to each other, men sat on dining chairs in shirt sleeves and waistcoats, enjoying lunchtime mugs of tea; a couple of girls played hopscotch on a board drawn with chalk. Edwin knew he could not endure living there with not a tree or flower in sight. What of the pale-faced babies and the families who had lived through war and survived the terrible flu only to live these cramped lives? He'd grown up with the freedom to run and roam. They deserved better than grey streets too.

Drusilla deserved safety.

The idea that had evaded him fluttered into his mind, like a brightly coloured bird landing on a branch. There was a way of reconciling the two. By the time he had reached the centre of the town, he had a plan forming in his mind. It was ingenious and he'd have to think carefully how to go about it, but if he could see it through and sway his grandfather, he might save Drusilla and give his grandfather something he craved too.

He walked purposefully to Carfax & Carfax and asked to see Robert again.

"Back for another pint?" Robert asked. "You know I can't give you any more information. I shouldn't have opened my mouth in the first place."

Edwin pulled up a chair. "Not that, Robert. Thank you for the tip-off. I questioned grandfather and once he knew I knew, he didn't bother to conceal it from me any further. Your father is on the town planning board, isn't he? I know he was at the meeting the other night which grandfather went to."

"That's right." Robert looked intrigued.

Edwin leaned forwards, speaking confidentially, even though he knew there was no one else listening.

"I have a proposal for him. An alternative that might give me what I need while still satisfying my grandfather."

"Do tell me," Robert asked, steepling his fingers and leaning in, as if hoping Edwin would whisper in his ear.

Edwin shook his head. "I don't want to tell you yet in case it doesn't come off but I have some thoughts that've been nagging at the back of my mind for a while now. Try and get me an appointment to speak to your father and if it comes off I'll tell you." He smiled. "If it comes off you will hear about it anyway."

"All right." Robert smiled, standing. "I'm intrigued. I'll see if he's free this afternoon."

"Thanks, Robert." Edwin shook his hand out, and another thought occurred to him. "By the way, you don't really know my sort-of cousin, Eleni. You'd like her, I think. You might find you and she have a lot in common. Come to dinner when this is all over and I'll introduce you."

Robert was as good as his word and within the hour Edwin had spoken with Carfax Senior. The plan had been suggested and approved. Now, the only remaining obstacle was getting Stephen to agree. Edwin returned home and spoke briefly to Eleni.

"I think it's going to work. I'm going to go speak to Grandfather now. Do you think you can find Drusilla again? Bring her for afternoon tea. If all goes to plan, I want her to be here."

Chapter Twenty-Five

S tephen had returned from his visit to the doctor and Edwin found him in the office at the factory. William had cleared away all the evidence that Edwin had been there before. He gave Edwin a subtle wink.

Edwin went to the shelf and pulled down the ledger and a sample book. Before his grandfather could ask what Edwin was doing, Edwin spoke.

"Grandfather, you said the factory was in dire straits. It isn't as bad as you led me to believe. Our output is lower than before the war but we are employing fewer staff. Of course our productivity will have dropped."

"I see."

"If we employ more staff we can produce more output," Edwin said. He pressed his lips together before continuing. "But I think there's another way."

He dragged over a sample book and opened it.

"Some of these designs have not changed for as long as I can remember and they need to. Grandfather, with the greatest

357

of respect, I think our biggest problem is appealing to the younger purchaser."

"Do you?" Stephen's eyebrows clashed together. "Impudence!"

William gave a discreet cough. "I'm sorry, Mr Brice. You know I've been loyal to you all these years I worked here and I still am, but I think young Mr Hope talks good sense."

"Does he?" Stephen stared at William, then at Edwin, then back to his trusted employee. He harrumphed. "There so! You may be right, and I would trust your opinion, William, however my grandson is inexperienced."

"I am inexperienced because I never get experience. With time and commitment I'll grow more experience," Edwin said sharply. He took a breath before continuing. "Perhaps by the time I am twenty-four, for example. Shall we discuss that?"

"Interesting," Stephen said. His eyes lingered on Edwin and the air grew hot between them.

"I used to fear you. Hate you at times. Now I merely pity you. For years you let your grief and resentment keep you from me when we could have shared our grief. Do you want to go to your grave with that between us? Believe me, I will walk away from you and this factory if I need to."

Edwin lifted his chin and looked his grandfather in the eyes. "Or we could put the past behind us and work together. Build a relationship that your daughter – my mother – would have wished us to have."

Stephen looked away first. "Go on."

"I have some proposals for you. I think we need to be going further with our designs. Being braver. The war is over and Europe is at peace. It should be a joyful time. People need brightness and new ideas. The sketches Miss Moore has made, for example."

"Miss Moore? Ah yes, the charming young friend of Eleni's." Stephen's eyes sparkled and Edwin had the suspicion that part of his plan would be a lot easier than he worried.

"Yes, I think Miss Moore has a talent that we should exploit before anyone else in town discovers her. I think we can make some changes and our situation might not be so desperate. And that leads me on to my other suggestion. One that will benefit us. Benefit you, I mean, and the people of the town."

"I've told you your options. Have you made your choice?" Stephen drew the ledger towards him but there was a hint of interest in his voice.

"I've made my choice."

Edwin squared his shoulders, hiding the apprehension he felt. He was not entirely certain he could carry this through, but he had to. Stephen was more receptive than he had expected him to be.

"I've been walking around the town, watching the working men and their families. Yes, houses are needed, but so are places for leisure. Places that will be good for the soul as well as the body."

He drummed his fingers on the table then stopped. Showing nervousness wouldn't do him any favours.

"I propose a public park. A legacy of which you can be proud."

Stephen's eyes flickered with interest, though he didn't smile. "Go on."

Edwin smiled. He walked to the window and turned back. "You want to make a mark in the town. You deserve to, after the years you have given and the number of men and women you have employed. What better way than a legacy which will last and will benefit all? Donate the land to the town council. Or, if you can't afford to donate it, sell it at a fair price that gives us close to what we need."

He smiled at his grandfather and William. Both men looked interested.

"Queen's Park at the other side of town is small. Imagine all these fields as lawns lined with trees; ornamental flowerbeds, and a fountain; Mr Angelli selling his ice creams from a cart on Saturday afternoons; a bandstand. Why, you could even be the first factory in town to start a brass band! I met fellows in the war who played for their mills up in Yorkshire and Lancashire."

He felt the swelling of excitement at speaking his idea out loud and played his trump card.

"A stone proclaiming the land was gifted to the town by Stephen Brice. What do you say to that?"

Stephen joined him at the window. The old man stood silently, hands behind his back. His face had remained immobile as they had spoken.

"A park," he mused.

Edwin tensed his shoulders anxiously. "Do you remember the day of the coronation when you opened the grounds to the families? I can remember that day vividly."

"You broke your arm so I imagine you do!" Stephen remarked coldly.

"I remember it," William said from across the room. "My girls paddled in the stream. They had such fun. There's nowhere else so beautiful to spend a warm afternoon."

Edwin could have hugged the foreman for his enthusiasm.

"Somewhere for families to walk, children to play, lovers to meet, friends to gather together," Edwin said softly.

He was nearly there and he had a sense that he had carried his grandfather along with him. There was one final incentive he had.

"I've spoken to Mr Carfax already and he is willing to put the proposal to the planning board. The choice of name would be yours, naturally. Brice Park. Greete Park. Whichever you choose."

"No, I think not," Stephen said finally after licking his lips.

Edwin's heart sank. He could fight it, hold out and delay until he was twenty-four, but it might not be soon enough.

Stephen coughed and turned to him. His eyes were slightly moist.

"Adelaide Hope Park," he said. He gave a creaky smile. "After the last few years I think there needs to be more hope in the world, don't you?"

Edwin's eyes misted. He'd done it.

"Yes. I do."

He extended his hand, and after a moment, Stephen shook it.

"Will you walk back to the house with me, Grandfather?" Edwin asked. "I believe Eleni and her parents will be taking afternoon tea."

Stephen grunted but allowed Edwin to take his arm and escort him back to the house. Loud laughter hailed them as they walked out to the terrace. Edwin could not say whether he or Stephen was more surprised at the sight that confronted them. Edwin had suggested afternoon tea but there was a jug with a small quantity of lemonade at the bottom and Eleni and Drusilla, Aunt Madeline and Panos were playing a game of croquet. The quartet cheered as Drusilla's ball rolled steadily through the hoop, then seemed to twist and hit the centre peg. It appeared Drusilla had made herself popular.

"Grandfather and I have something to announce," Edwin said, once the congratulations were ended. He stepped back and gave Stephen the floor.

"I am pleased to announce that I will be entering into negotiations with the town planning board to transform the fields you see beyond this garden into a public park."

Eleni clapped her hands together. "Wonderful!"

"Oh how lovely," Aunt Madeline breathed.

Edwin looked at Drusilla. Her eyes sparkled and her smile was radiant.

"Somewhere for the trees to grow and nature to flourish," he murmured.

"There's one more thing I need to tell you," Edwin said to Stephen. "I am afraid Eleni and I will not be getting married."

"Is that right?" Stephen frowned. "You come to me and tell me that you have arranged matters concerning my land behind my back, without my consent. Now you tell me that the wife I prefer for you is thrown over?"

"I'm afraid so, Grandfather. Eleni and I have spoken and we both agree the marriage is not for us," Edwin said. He crossed the lawn and stood beside Drusilla. She looked up at him, raising her brows in a question. He smiled. "I intend to marry Miss Moore, if she will have me."

"You want to marry me?"

She sounded shocked. He hoped it was disbelief rather than dislike.

"I do." He held out his hands to her. She took them and they stood at arm's length, regarding each other closely. "And I want you to help me plan out the park, and design new lines for the factory; to be my companion in life and in work."

"But you barely know Miss Moore," Stephen protested.

"Oh, but I know her well," Edwin smiled at his grandfather. "Well enough to know that she's the only woman for me."

"Mr Brice, I love your grandson." Drusilla smiled at Stephen and whether it was her charm or glamour, or whether it was just that Stephen was susceptible to a beautiful woman, he mumbled his congratulations.

"Obviously there will be practicalities to work out, but I have a friend who is a solicitor," Edwin said. He paused, wondering exactly what a wedding to a dryad would take. Not a church, he suspected. She might have ideas herself of what was necessary. He tugged her closer, so their joined hands were held securely between their bodies and lowered his voice.

"I promise that whatever form our union takes, our marriage will be wonderful. I will love you for the length of my life. Worship you day and night, throughout the seasons. In winter I'll decorate your tree and in summer we'll picnic beneath the branches."

In the far distance Edwin heard the sound, very faintly, of a hunting horn, triumphant and euphoric. He and Drusilla glanced upwards at the same time. The clouds to the west were fluffy and light. To Edwin's eyes they looked just like horses, riding in triumph.

He knew then that everything would be all right.

~

When does a story end? Is it when the lovers take their first kiss in the knowledge that their lives will be as one from that day forward? Or is it the day when they discover their legacy will continue after they are gone?

~

1921

Drusilla woke early, as soon as the edge of the curtains grew bright. Even after two years of sleeping inside, she still felt attuned to the changing elements. This morning was no different, but there was an added texture to the light, and an added feeling within her. She slipped from the bed and walked to the window, ducking behind the curtains to stare at the tree. After their wedding, Edwin had insisted that they took the suite that had belonged to his parents, with the view of the gardens and the new park. And the tree, which stood proudly on the mound.

A secret thrill bubbled up, something small wiggling deep inside her. She didn't need to see with her eyes to know what she would find there.

When she heard Edwin stirring she opened the curtains wide and walked back to the bed. He yawned.

"What time is it?"

"A little after dawn. Come with me, Edwin darling," Drusilla said.

He climbed out of bed. "Is something the matter? Let me get dressed."

"Nothing is the matter but I want to show you something before the park gates are unlocked. Don't bother to dress. Just put on your dressing gown and slippers."

His expression radiating intrigue, he did as she told him. She slept naked but slipped on a silk dressing gown herself. Light green with patterns of yellow blossoms printed on it – one of Edwin's favourite designs in the newest range. She was barefoot, of course. Shoes were something she only wore when absolutely necessary. Hand in hand, they crept through the house. No need to be quiet; Stephen slept heavily these days.

The croquet lawn was dewy as they walked to the private wooden gate in the new wall. The air smelt of fresh rain and the hems of Edwin's pyjamas were sodden within moments of beginning the walk. He still hated the sensation.

The lake was settling well and small insects buzzed over the surface. Edwin tugged her hand and she stopped, letting him pull her into a kiss.

"I never fail to be struck by how beautiful you are in spring. You are stunning at all times of the year, but even more so when the world is springing to life after the long winter."

She kissed him back, letting her happiness course through her and out through her lips and hands until he shivered and opened his eyes.

The sycamore now stood resplendent in the grove. From the bottom of the hill it towered majestically over the roof of the bandstand Edwin had designed – a Greek temple the significance of which only the couple, Eleni, and Sykes knew. They walked up the steps through the temple and down the other side. She slipped her hand tighter into his; led him to the tree and then left past it.

"Look," she whispered.

"What am I looking for?" he asked.

She squeezed his hand, resisting the urge to run her fingers over her belly. "You'll know when you see it."

Slightly along the ridge from the tree was a small plant. It didn't look like much, yet – a slender stem with two twigs starting to branch off.

"What is it?" Edwin asked.

Drusilla put her hands around his neck.

"Don't you know? You with a great love of all things natural? There's another one a little further along, and a third down by the stream."

She stood on her tiptoes and put her mouth close to his ears.

"They're saplings, Edwin, my darling."

"Saplings?"

He turned his head and looked at her and back to the plant, then to her eyes again. "Sycamore saplings?"

She nodded. "It's wonderful, isn't it!"

"Your tree has reproduced."

"Yes. There's another one a little further and a third down by the stream. But not just my tree, Edwin. Each tree will need someone to attend it."

She put her hand on top of his and pressed it against her belly. His eyes widened.

"Are you telling me what I think you're telling me?"

"Three saplings and three babies," she murmured. "You are going to be a father. I'm going to be a mother."

"And what will they be?" Edwin asked, his hand still on her belly. His hand began to shake. "Children? But will they die? You told me how you came to be."

She shook her head rapidly. "No. This is different. You planted these children in me. They're half of what I am, and half of you. I can feel it. They will be what they will be. Who knows? But whatever they will be they will be loved and cared for."

She walked to the sapling, already reaching towards the light and brushed her fingertips over a new bud on the fragile shoot.

"All my children will be loved. We will make sure of that."

When does a story end? Is it when lovers part for the final time after a lifetime well lived and well loved?

1987

Edwin Clarence Hope died a month after his ninety-second birthday. Drusilla sat on the reclining chair beside his bed. Both chair and bed faced out onto the park where they could watch the sun setting. Two of their three children, Ellen and Archie, sat on slightly less comfortable chairs at Edwin's other side. Adelaide, the youngest born, was in Australia visiting her daughter and son-in-law, and had been unable to change her flight when the doctor announced Edwin had only days to live.

"We've had a good life, haven't we," he murmured, his voice breathy.

Drusilla held his hand. "The best."

"The family will be well," Edwin sighed.

Drusilla stroked his hand. "The children are well; the trees are strong. The grandchildren too."

"We'll look after them," promised Ellen, the oldest born.

Edwin turned his head and looked at his wife. "I don't suppose you know what happens next?"

She smiled through the tears that were filling her eyes. "No, that is something we will both have to discover for ourselves, I'm afraid."

"Oh." Edwin licked his lips. "I thought I'd feel afraid but now I think I'm ready. It feels like the right time."

"Yes, it is." Drusilla squeezed his fingers.

Ellen and Archie kissed their parents and left the room, holding each other for comfort.

Alone, Edwin and Drusilla looked at each other, holding hands.

"Can I see you how you were when we met?" Edwin asked.

Drusilla patted her hair, steel grey and piled into a high bun. Her face was lined, the skin as thin as a new leaf. She'd been careful to age.

"You don't think I'm beautiful enough now?"

"Of course I do, but I'd like to see you when you were beautiful then."

Drusilla glanced towards the closed door. The MacMillan

nurse had left, saying she would come back shortly. Drusilla and Edwin both knew when she meant.

Drusilla concentrated, breathing in and remembering. Aging had been a conscious decision and now she found the old form wanted to return. The grey hair darkened, the lines lifted from her cheeks and forehead, and the skin around her neck snapped back into place.

"My goddess," Edwin murmured. Drusilla leaned over and kissed him. He closed his eyes and, with a smile on his lips, he died.

Drusilla wept and grieved as all widows do. Three weeks after the funeral she walked around the bungalow. Greete Mill House had been sold, when the children had grown and left home, and the bungalow the couple had built alongside the entrance to the park had suited them both. Greete Mill itself was now apartments. Who knew what they might become in ten years or fifty. She could of course wait and find out, but she didn't want to.

A life well lived. She couldn't have asked for more. She didn't want more.

The weather was changing. She sniffed the air, smelling the edge of a storm. It would not be long in coming.

When dusk fell on a mild October evening, Drusilla wrote letters to her daughters and left them on the dining table beside the teapot. She pulled on her coat but walked barefoot to the door, locked it, and put the key under the flowerpot painted with white roses. She looked to the sky. Clouds were gathering, despite the weatherman predicting a calm evening. There was a yellow tinge on the edge of the sky, and the scent of rain.

She walked up the hill to the mound where her tree stood, pausing at each of the younger sycamores as she passed them and kissing her lips against the bark.

They were tall and straight. They would do well and she had no fear of leaving them.

She walked to her own tree and looked at it. Overhead the clouds were rolling in. She heard hoofbeats.

The Wild Hunt.

Her lips curved into a smile.

Was she to be so honoured?

If she'd been wavering – and there was a part of her like Edwin that was filled with fear at the thought of her long life ending – this was the final indication that her choice was right.

Overhead a storm broke out, the first swell in the wind that gusted around her, whistling her name through the branches.

Drusilla walked to her tree and pressed her palms and lips against it.

"I'm ready to come home," she murmured.

She heard a rumble of thunder, the crack of lightning, and she smiled.

2022

It looked like a nice area to bring up a child. There was a school on one edge of the park close to the children's playground and sandpit. Even though it was November, the sun was bright and the park was bustling and families were picnicking and playing. There were even a few black faces amongst them which was good. Martine didn't want Caleb to be the only black kid in his class.

"Tree dressing today. Greete Mill & Adelaide Hope Park Friends Association" a brightly coloured sign proclaimed. There was a large basket of ribbons and baubles standing on the steps of the bandstand. A young woman with very bleached blonde hair in a high bun was distributing them to kids.

"Mummy, can we?" Caleb asked, tugging at her hand.

"Sure, why not? Let's go and see what's going on."

Martine let Caleb lead her over to the basket. The woman was about thirty, with pale skin covered in freckles. When they arrived, she pushed her sunglasses up onto the top of her head and Martine was greeted by a pair of warm greenish-hazel eyes.

"What's happening?" Caleb asked, with the confidence of an almost four-year-old.

The woman smiled. "Tree dressing. It's an old tradition. Every year we come and decorate the trees for winter. Hi," she said squatting down to talk to Caleb. "I'm Adelaide. Like the park. Addy for short."

Caleb stuck his lip out. "Why are you called after the park?"

"Caleb!" Martine said, but Addy grinned.

"My family used to own this land back a hundred years or so ago. After the First World War they gifted it to the town to become a park. I run the town museum in the old mill. What colour ribbon would you like, Caleb?"

"Yellow," he said immediately.

"Yellow *please*," Martine reminded him.

Addy pulled one from the basket. "Here you go. Go find a tree to leave your ribbon around. Someone will help you."

He ran off, leaving the two women behind.

"It's perfectly safe," Addy said to Martine. "This park is great for kids. Will his dad be along soon?"

Martine adjusted her shoulder bag. She didn't usually explain about the complicated situation, but she noticed Addy had a variety of rainbow flags as pins. Her smile was warm and it made Martine glow. Some things were better clarified sooner rather than later.

"His dad lives in Manchester. I co-parent Caleb with Jabez and his boyfriend. It's unorthodox but it works for us. I'm Martine, by the way."

"Hello Martine By-the-way."

They both laughed.

"So what brings you here?" Addy asked. She tilted her head on one side, giving Martine another warm smile.

"House hunting. I've just got a job in a school on the other side of town. I was looking for something more convenient but being close to the park would be lovely."

Addy smiled. "It is. Why don't I get someone else to take over giving out the ribbons and I can show you around it? We can follow your son. Mr Sykes!"

She hollered to an old man who was leaning against a wall. He ambled over, tipping his hat to the women with a smile.

"Mr Sykes volunteers with the gardening club. He's got green fingers like no one else I know. Will you do the honours with the ribbons?"

"Of course, Ms Carfax."

Martine walked beside Addy, a sense of contentment

settling over her. This side of town was definitely looking more attractive. Caleb was standing beneath the branches of a sycamore, watching a group of children who were throwing the helicopter seeds up into the air and laughing as they fell into the stream.

"What a gorgeous tree."

Addy smiled. "Isn't it. There are two more up on the ridge, near the old split trunk. That one was struck by lightning back in the 80s when there were the big storms. Such a shame."

Caleb saw them and skipped over. He looked thoughtful. "Mummy, what's a sapling?"

"It's a baby tree. Why?"

"The girl said I'm one."

Martine wrinkled her nose, turning to Addy. "It's crap. Even at his age he's been called all sorts of names and it makes him wary."

She knelt in front of Caleb and took his hand. He had a leaf scrunched tightly inside it. "It's a strange thing to be called, but it isn't bad. Which girl was it, Pud? One of those ones?"

"No, the one sitting in the tree. I gave her my ribbon. She has eyes like you," he said, pointing to Addy. "Only her hair is the same colour as a conker."

Martine peered into the tree.

"I can't see anyone there," she said.

"She's there," Caleb said insistently, pointing to where the ribbon was tied in a bow around a branch. "She said I can come back whenever I want to. I want to."

Addy was staring up at the branches, a thoughtful look on her face. Conscious that Caleb might be about to have a tantrum, Martine took his hand. So what if he wanted an imaginary friend.

"Well, if you want to come back and see her, then I think we should. Let's go and see what else we can find."

She held out her hand to Caleb. He paused before taking it and waved with his free hand back at the tree.

"Bye-bye!"

The park was full of people, so it could have been anyone speaking, but Martine could have sworn she heard a laughing voice blowing on the wind as they walked away.

"Bye-bye, Sapling. Come back soon."

When does a story begin?

Acknowledgments

I've always loved myths, fantasy, folk tales and suchlike. I've often wondered whether certain mythological or folk tale creatures are specifically geographical. Are there centaurs who are part human and part Shetland pony? Are the only trees inhabited by spirits found in Greek olive groves or might they inhabit the British countryside, and if they do, which would be their choice of trees?

From that pondering, and a lot of dog walking in my local park, this story emerged. My adopted town is a mill town (silk in our case). The story is not set here, but it is set in a town whose map could almost rest on top without too much trouble.

Thank you as always to my wonderful editor Charlotte for great advice and encouragement.

Thank you to my colleagues in the Day Job who are a bunch of wonderful people. We laugh together, cry together and bemoan the number of glue sticks without lids together. Without them, I wouldn't get through the week in one piece to be able to sit down and write, so I feel truly lucky to work with them all.

Lastly (but by no means least), thank you to all my readers who gave such positive feedback for *Daughter of the Sea* and encouraged me to have a crack at another romantasy.

YOUR NUMBER ONE STOP

ONE MORE CHAPTER

FOR PAGETURNING BOOKS

One More Chapter is an
award-winning global
division of HarperCollins.

Sign up to our newsletter to get our
latest eBook deals and stay up to date
with our weekly Book Club!
<u>Subscribe here.</u>

Meet the team at
<u>www.onemorechapter.com</u>

Follow us!
 <u>@OneMoreChapter_</u>
 <u>@OneMoreChapter</u>
 <u>@onemorechapterhc</u>

Do you write unputdownable fiction?
We love to hear from new voices.
Find out how to submit your novel at
<u>www.onemorechapter.com/submissions</u>